Greetings from the author
Michael Davenport

Dear Michael

Best Wishes in the
Years to come

Norman and Saulye Tauber

BEHOLD *the* FIRE

Also by MICHAEL BLANKFORT

NOVELS
I Met a Man
The Brave and the Blind
A Time to Live
The Widow Makers
The Juggler
The Strong Hand
Goodbye, I Guess

BIOGRAPHY
The Big Yankee, the Life of General Evans F. Carlson, U.S.M.C.

PLAYS
The Sailors of Cattaro (adapted from Friedrich Wolf)
Battle Hymn (with Michael Gold)
Monique (with Dorothy Stiles Blankfort, adapted from the novel by Boileau-Narcejac)

SCREENPLAYS
The Juggler
Broken Arrow
Halls of Montezuma
My Six Convicts
Tribute to a Bad Man
The Vintage

(In collaboration)
Adam Had Four Sons
The Caine Mutiny
Lydia Bailey
An Act of Murder
Texas
Blind Alley

MICHAEL BLANKFORT

BEHOLD *the* FIRE

A novel based on events that took place between 1914 and 1918 in London, Cairo, Constantinople, Jerusalem, and some of the villages of Palestine.

AN NAL-WORLD BOOK
PUBLISHED BY THE NEW AMERICAN LIBRARY

To Yehoshua Brandstatter, my friend,
who for over fifty years has helped build Israel,
and to my grandchildren born in that land,
Yardena, Dan, and Naftali Camiel,
who will be the defenders of its future.

And Isaac spoke unto Abraham his father, and said,
My father: and he said, Here am I, my son.
And he said, Behold the fire and the wood: but
where is the lamb for a burnt offering?

Genesis xxii, 7

Donnez!
Pardonnez beaucoup pour qu'on vous aime un peu,
Aimez sans fin pour qu'on vous pardonne parfois.
Dans le regard de l'ami voyez un voeu,
Que celles du coeur soient vos seules lois!

Ici bas, lorsque, malheureux, il faut penser
Que le plus grand malheur n'est pas encore né
Et quand on aurait toute sa vie des plaies à penser,
Nul ne saurait dire: J'ai assez aimé!

——Absalom Feinberg
(An excerpt from a poem written circa 1911.)

CHARACTERS

MEMBERS OF NILI

Naftali Brandt — *poet and farmer*
Judah Singer — *agronomist*
Rachel Singer — *sister of Judah*
Avram Liebermann — *farmer*
Dmitri Liebermann — *farmer and cousin of Avram*
Saul Wilner — *horse trader and peddler*
Nissim Vidali — *farmer*
Yoshua Camiel
Manfred Gersh
Reuven Schechter
Miriam Bloch — *friend of Rachel*

MEMBERS OF HASHOMER

Remenov
Lorchanovsky
Mara Schalet
Levine
Dr. Bloch
Dov Berg

OTHERS OF IMPORTANCE

Papa Singer — *father of Judah and Rachel*
Mrs. Brandt — *mother of Naftali*
Nahum Cohn — *husband of Rachel*

Mustafa ibn Musa — *sergeant of the gendarmes*
Colonel Hamid Bek — *commandant of the gendarmes*
Gimmel Cohn — muhktar of *Har Nehemia*
Reb Mottel — *butcher of Har Nehemia*
Chana Haimowitz — *farmer's wife of Har Nehemia*
Mordecai Anuskevitz — *friend of Naftali Brandt*
Said Ali Pasha — *retired Turkish government official*
Colonel Ali Fuad — *commandant of Beersheba, later of Jerusalem*
Riaz Bey — *last civilian governor of Jerusalem*
General Edmund H. H. Allenby
Colonel T. E. Lawrence
Colonel John West — *intelligence officer on Allenby's staff*
Lieutenant John Miles — *intelligence officer at Port Said*
Captain Clothier, of HMS *Loch Ness*
Lieutenant Terunian — *Armenian supply officer of Turkish Army*
Sir Basil Thomson, of Scotland Yard
Captain von Fricke — *German intelligence staff officer*
Father Gregory — *Greek Orthodox priest*
Captain Ali — *Syrian aide to Colonel Hamid Bek*
Captain Sayek — *aide to Jemal Pasha*
Jemal Jasha — *commander of the Turkish Army*
Captain MacDonald — *engineer*
 and
Chaim Weizmann

BEHOLD *the* FIRE

The Beginning and the End

For what the day was to mean, the sky was too clear, too blameless. It should have been dark, uneasy, with rumors of thunder. To the
east the Carmel range should not have been so serene clefting the Sharon
plain.

In the crystal October morning light, Judah Singer saw the gray-
green leaves of the vineyards as if through a magnifier. Taint had
weakened the grape stems and blotched their skins. They had been
badly tended. War has a way of loosening the conscience even of good
farmers.

How long had he been away? Three years? In the geometric re-
gression of time there was no counting.

He slowed his pace to keep in time with the old man, his father,
walking alongside, still limping from the bastinado. They had time
enough to get to the cemetery at the north end of the village. The
street was empty. He supposed that the villagers were getting dressed
for the ceremony at Rachel's grave.

The neighing of a horse from the pastureland above the village recalled his sister riding swiftly, waving her hat, calling to him to wait,
dancing her great brown mare into the dusty street.

It angered him that he had not yet absorbed her death ten months
after the dark day he had first heard of it. How long would it take be-

fore he could enclose it finally, knowing its truth in the soft gray in-
dent of his brain? There was only numbness. In the place of grief, a
paralysis of regret. If only he could weep.

The white square concrete houses along the street were drab and
peeling from the poverty the war had spawned. Old trees he had known
well were gone, cut down no doubt to cook Turkish Army lamb.
Without them the familiar sky had lost some underpinnings, the horizon seemed inappropriate.

Papa limped along in silence. They had talked enough. But it was
he who wanted to get to the cemetery early.

Judah thought that if he were not too old he would like to marry
someday and have a daughter to name after his sister. A yearning, still
fragile, to be less alone stirred him. He was, after all, in his forty-
third year.

The day was warm; his British major's uniform was heavy and he
loosened the collar. Now that Damascus had fallen to Allenby, soon he
would be discharged. A civilian again. The idea left him unmoved.
He was in a passive intermission. Since his return to the village he
had not even ridden out to Atlit to see what had been done to his
wheat fields, his tree nursery, his experimental station. Once he would
have thought it impossible to wait so long.

The road, an immobile fall of rocks, descended abruptly from the
broad main street. The villagers had been digging out rocks for thirty
years, but there were always more.

Gulls rose in a fan from the blue sea to the west. He remembered
the locusts bitterly. How long ago, with Rachel alive, and the noble
flame, Naftali?

The son and the father entered the broken gate of the cemetery.
The stone walls had been breached like a fort during an assault.
Slowly they followed the winding path past the other graves, each with
a name they knew well. They entered the family plot in the oldest
part. Four small time-pitted blocks of granite lay over the infant brothers and sister who had died three decades before from malaria. And
there, higher than the rest, was the gray block over the mother. The
cedars that had once protected it from the sun and wind had been cut
down.

Deborah Singer, 1856-1910. Judah was a grown man when she
died, but her death even now was more real to him than Rachel's.
His heart had ruptured then, some important part of him nullified.
He had recognized her death as an end. But with Rachel it was dif-

2

ferent; it was as if she still flowed around him, encompassing more than himself.

A large blue-and-white banner masked Rachel's headstone. Judah had been given it by some friends at Helmieh, in Egypt, where the Jewish battalions of Allenby's army were quartered.

A bird crossed his vision and circled above the cemetery, swerving now and then toward the battered tree trunks, moved by an inherited memory of an old nest.

He stood on one side of the banner, his father on the other side. They remained without talking for the hour before the first villagers arrived.

Judah heard the steps on the hard earth and turned to face them. The whole village, over a hundred, those who were his friends and those who were his enemies, their children and wives. The men wore hats and white prayer shawls over their worn dark clothes. He saw little Ebria Bloch clutching a bouquet of dying wildflowers.

The sound of an automobile came to him from the long, curving road rising from the coast. He followed it in his mind; every curve, every foot, every rock was known to him even in the darkness; this hill to Har Nehemia that his father and mother had helped to clear many years ago had been the cradle of his youth.

The car stopped at the cemetery gate. Colonel West emerged, thin as a blade unfolding itself. Captain MacDonald, last seen when they dug for water before Khalassa. And, like a gift from heaven, the tall Avram Liebermann and his cousin Dmitri, both in the uniforms of the Thirty-eighth Royal Fusiliers, the Jewish regiment.

The greeting was a warm clasp of hands, then good news about other friends found alive in the Damascus prison.

Colonel West asked if he could say a few words on behalf of the commander in chief. Judah gave his gratified assent. The villagers opened the way for the guests.

Judah waited for a sign from his father, whose eyes were closed behind his metal-framed glasses, his pale farmer's face intent on some thought or memory. He was immobile except for a slight shifting of his legs.

Judah motioned to the hazan to begin the service.

In a strong voice the bearded old man slowly chanted, "Lord, what is man that Thou art mindful of him?"

And when he came to the end he wailed the great "Father of Mercy" hymn. His voice trembled with petition for the repose of the

3

souls in eternal rest and for those of the living who delight in God's goodness.

The crowd stirred, a few sobs rose.

"Amen and amen," the hazan cried.

"Amen and amen!" the villagers cried in confirmation.

Judah murmured the prayer numbly.

When it was over he introduced Colonel West. The tall, thin officer moved erectly to the flag-shrouded stone, saluted, then stepped to one side in order to face Judah and his father and the assembly. Papa Singer seemed to become aware of him for the first time.

West spoke in a low voice at first, scarcely audible to the last rows. People crowded nearer.

"I have the honor on this occasion to bear the condolences of General Sir Edmund H. H. Allenby, commander in chief of his Majesty's Egyptian expeditionary forces, to Mr. Moses Singer and to his son, Major Judah Singer, the eminent agriculturist, on the loss of that extraordinary and heroic woman Rachel, daughter and sister. We have come here today to pay our profoundest respect to her memory. General Allenby wished me to say that he is keenly aware that the lives of thousands of his men were saved by the dauntless labors of this noble lady and her stalwart comrades, living and dead. In the general's own words, 'They were mainly responsible for my field-intelligence organization behind the Turkish lines.' In due course he intends to make known these deeds and his gratitude to his Majesty's government."

Colonel West paused, gazed for a moment at the blue-and-white banner, then turned back to the villagers.

"May I add my personal respects to those of General Allenby's. As a Christian"—his voice deepened with unaccustomed emotion—"and as an Englishman, I vow to my friend Judah Singer that I will do all I can to help his people attain for themselves their ancient dream of Zion redeemed."

West ended abruptly, saluted the banner over the grave, and stepped back. A slight movement of uncertainty stirred in the crowd of farmers, as if a long-deposited sediment of faith in the goodwill of any Christian was rising through a murky millennial sea of suspicion and despair.

Judah moved slowly to the stone and put his hand on top of it. The simple gesture, tender and loving, brought sobs from the women.

In a stricken voice that he did not recognize as his, he cried, "Rachel . . ."

BOOK *One*

1 ◇◇◇◇◇◇◇◇◇

On August 3, 1914, the day before the German Army invaded Belgium and turned the wheel of the future, Turkey's first minister, Enver Bey, who had long before overcome his Muslim scruples against alcohol, drank several toasts to the Haji Wilhelm, and reassured the nervous German Ambassador Wagenheim that the Osmanli people would stand firmly at the side of the Teuton folk. And toward that end he signed a secret protocol of alliance. As swiftly and as diplomatically as he could, Wagenheim left the ornate office of the first minister and forwarded the message of reassurance to Berlin.

But as August passed, and September, the Turkish government remained passive, putting off Wagenheim's plea for action with excuses that mobilization was being sabotaged by the Christians, Jews, Armenians, and dissident Arab tribes.

But the truth was that Enver Bey was having great difficulties persuading his fellow triumvirs, the elegant black-bearded Jemal Pasha and the obese Talaat Bey, to agree to the secret treaty. Talaat was generally pro-French, and Jemal, minister of the navy, argued that Germany was across the seas, which England commanded, while Russia, the greatest enemy of the Ottoman Empire, lay waiting in the shadow of the Bosporus. Turkey's best interest was to remain neutral, or at least to wait to see which side would offer her the greatest advantages. If England and France would guarantee them against the czarist bear, what was there to gain by going to war? He coined the phrase "Switzerland of the Levant." Turkey could grow rich on a clever neutrality.

Behind his political argument was his dislike of being a subordinate to the arrogant German officers who were flooding his government's offices and straining for the moment to act upon orders given them by Field Marshal von der Goltz, the old Goltz Pasha, who for thirteen years had supervised the training of the Turkish Army. Jemal had once been badly treated by the tight-mouthed East Prussian and had grown to hate the sight of the kaiser's uniform.

The Germans grew more and more anxious for Turkey to move, and Turkey did not move.

In the Turkish province of Palestine, the few Jews of European descent living there watched with uneasiness the courses of great battles thousands of miles away. News came late and distorted by propaganda at its sources. No one could tell in the haze of deceit whether the reports of victories and retreats, marching and countermarching (the cossacks in East Prussia, the uhlans deep in the Ukraine, the French across the Rhine, the Germans approaching Paris), were "good for the Jews."

The sultan ordered mobilization, but still no one believed that war would come. His ministers, who had the real power, continued to affirm their country's neutrality.

At the end of October Germany decided to take Turkey's fate into her own hands, and using the device of hoisting the Turkish flag on two of her own ships, the *Goeben* and *Breslau,* she attacked without warning the Russian Black Sea ports of Feodosiya and Sevastopol. The sultan and his disputing ministers had no choice but to respond to Russia's indignant declaration of war with an indignant declaration of their own.

Jemal Pasha was appointed co-commander of the Fourth Army with Count von Kressenstein. His mission was to attack the English at the Suez Canal and invade Egypt. Palestine was to be his base from which to win the Middle East for sultan and kaiser.

2 ◇◇◇◇◇◇◇◇◇

The land was a worn land, desirable only in a dream. It was a land memory kept alive; its heroes were corrupted by death and the usages of man. It was a land where trees were taxed and the poor tore them up to avoid paying. In this land they killed gods, destroyed temples, stoned prophets, and murdered brothers. And yet there were people who were willing to bleed out their lives in hard work and disease under threats by neighbors and a corrupt government in order to live there because God had promised their ancestors that it would be theirs one day.

Although Mustafa ibn Musa, a Turkish sergeant of gendarmes, had been told of the attack on the Russian ports—the word had scarcely reached even Jaffa or Jerusalem—he didn't listen, for he had more important problems. There was the *hamsin,* which bore into his skin like hot fleas, there was the matter of the search for arms in the Jewish villages, but crowning all the problems was the fact that there was a new commandant in Jaffa.

Any change in authority was a mystery and a distress. When one doesn't know who has the power, there are too many chances of making mistakes. Orders become unclear, punishment a certainty.

Leading his armed three-man mounted patrol toward the Jewish Agricultural Station in Atlit, he sullenly pondered the meaning of it. Once before he had suffered from a change of command. Back in 1906, during the war with the Armenians, he had been given orders to burn a village. The sight of the children and old people had weakened him. He evacuated the village before setting it on fire. How was he supposed to know that he was to kill the villagers? Who can read what goes on in the great salamlik of Constantinople or in the mind of the new pasha who had passed on the order? The old one would not have cared if he killed or not. Poor Mustafa was punished. They took his rifle away and whipped him with fifteen lashes. They would have sent him into exile to some mountain in Anatolia to freeze his life away if it hadn't been for a mullah to whom he gave all he owned in baksheesh. The mullah was the cousin of the cousin of the pasha.

Now again there was a change of command. The new colonel, Hamid Bek, was a mystery. Where he came from, what his dislikes were, no one at the gendarmerie in Caesarea knew.

His orders were not clear. Search Atlit for arms. Did it mean to take them or to list them? Did it mean really to search or to accept the word of the Jew whether he had arms or not? And if he did any of these things, what were his chances of baksheesh?

He was thirty-three years old and his life was a burden. He cursed all the great ones from Hamid Bek to those who lorded the world in Constantinople and Damascus. They were all the same, sucking the marrow of the poor. But either way, there had to be baksheesh. He had a wife and three children; how else could they live?

With a thin finger he razored the sweat from his dark cheeks and around the edges of his black clump of moustache and wiped it on his saddle. Ah, if he could only find a Jew to blackmail. Then he could buy himself out of the gendarmes and even have enough left over for a cow and chickens. But where do you find a man with enough money yet without the influence that goes with money? An influence that could cut Mustafa, poor man, in half.

From his mount he could see the agricultural experimental station on the flanks of a hill above the old Crusader ruins of Atlit. It was owned by Judah Singer, of Har Nehemia. It had two stories, a windmill, and barns. On all sides were huge plantations of wheat and corn, apple trees, walnut and citrus, peanut bushes, and even a patch of cotton. The Jews seemed to be able to grow anything where nothing had ever grown before, he thought bitterly. But the part of the station he detested most was the two double rows of palm trees that made a broad avenue from the station almost down to the Caesarea-Haifa road a quarter mile away. If he hated pashas who built such grand approaches to their villas, why should he not hate the Jews even more? Their hard work, their planning, their wealth, were an affront to him. If Allah had wanted such rows of palm trees, He would have caused His own to grow them there.

Naftali Brandt lay in a sea-bottom sleep on a cot on the second story of the station. The night before, he had tried to numb himself with arak and it had given him dreams in which he wrote words on a blank parchment that someone erased before he could read them. Although he was only twenty-four, his thin, handsome face was marked by permanent lines of tension that at times made it seem stronger than it was, and at other times gave the odd impression that beneath the skin and skull was someone else trying to get out.

He groaned a little, the sweat of the *hamsin* dripping down his forehead onto the straw pallet. One hand was flung toward the floor. A half-empty bottle of arak awaited his wakening.

The room was huge and smelled of grain. Books ranged the high whitewashed walls like a many-colored rampart. Samples of wheat and other cereals were in glass cases surrounded by potsherds, clay lamps, rocks—the debris of ten thousand years. Charts of Palestine's rainfall and the stars, of surface elevations and the world's wheat-growing areas hung everywhere. Bunkers of pamphlets and reports from the universities of the world, work tables, chairs, a microscope, a telescope, and cacti and dwarf oak lay about like disordered parts of a great maze. Crowning everything was an enlarged five-foot drawing of the *Triticum hermonis,* the uncultivated wild wheat that Naftali's mentor and friend, the director of the station, Judah Singer, had discovered some years before.

The workroom had the apparent chaos of combat in which men worked with single-minded intensity to master small tasks of large meaning. It was Judah Singer's fortress and Naftali Brandt's refuge.

A barking dog awoke him. He opened his eyes, saw the hot slash of sun on the ceiling, and closed them again.

What had been written? Who had erased it?

Again he heard the sound of the barking dog and he remembered a dog caught in a sudden rush of carriages and buses on the Boulevard Montparnasse. He had left his friends at La Coupole to save the animal and was knocked over by a horse. They teased him afterwards. Pablo, an artist, asked him why he thought his life was worth less than a stray dog's.

They were all there. Warm May night. Chagall, Apollinaire, André Salmon, exiles from everywhere. There were marvelous men at the table.

In Paris he had been burdened by homesickness for Palestine, his native land. As a result he became conscious of himself as a Jew (he had never felt that defensive at home) and smelled out anti-Semites in the streets in order to fight them, went to Yiddish plays to yell curses

9

at scenes of Russian pogroms and submissive Jews, lived in the Bibliothèque to read the old Hebrew manuscripts. Paris, to which he had come the year before, a poet hungering for poets, had transformed him, as he said, into an uncoffined corpse.

"I'm going home!" he shouted suddenly, as if Pablo's question had settled everything. "I'm dying in this alien world."

His friends were silent for a moment. Glasses on other tables tinkled out of key; walkers on the street sounded like cards being shuffled.

André said, "You are a poet. You belong here. What is Zion to you and you to Zion?"

A thousand answers, not one to win an argument. He felt ashamed. But he could kiss the rotted dust of Jerusalem.

"Another stray dog," Pablo said, "your Zion. Why do you risk your life? Why Palestine?"

"Why Paris?" Naftali had replied in a burst of clarity. "Explain why you all have come to Paris to work, to live, to create? Left your Spain, your Russia, your Italy? If you can explain Paris, I can explain Palestine."

In the heated room of the station the aftertaste of arak filled his mouth. The dog whined outside. It wasn't Ahab, Judah's dog. Perhaps one of the Arab workers'. Not likely. What fellah could afford to feed a dog?

He heard the clatter of horses on the bridge across the wadi. He sat up slowly and groaned with the heat and the constriction in his throat. His thick black hair was wet. He felt feverish. The arak? Malaria again? He rubbed his eyes angrily as if their simple flesh was, in some stupid sense, responsible for the waste that filled his heart.

At the window he saw the station's Arab workers cultivating a patch of corn. The shadows told him it was close to noon. It suddenly occurred to him that it was late. Why wasn't Judah Singer at the station? His co-workers, Mordecai and Nissim? Then he remembered and slapped his hand against his cheek with annoyance. It was the ninth day of Ab, the anniversary of the fall of the temple. His mother had asked him to go to the synagogue with her to read Lamentations. Instead he had bought the arak and gone to the station to forge an ecstasy.

It was just as well. He hated the lamenting in the candle-smeared darkness of the old synagogue, the men weeping and the women wailing as if Titus had taken them captives from Jerusalem only yesterday. Lamenting was a disease of the Jews; it sickened him.

10

On the other side of the wadi the sea shone like cracked glass. The shore ruins of the Crusader Fort pointed bluntly to the open sky. From its dead gray stones gulls flurried up and followed the gendarme patrol inland toward the station as if it were a fishing boat from which there would be refuse. Why was it coming here?

Naftali recognized Mustafa, friend of baksheesh, his sword momentarily flashing in the sun. Not the vilest of the vile. A fair-weather *flic* with whom you could drink coffee and play checkers at Omar's in Caesarea. For a Turkish policeman he was a passable human being.

The short noon-hour shadows of the patrol fringed the golden wheat fields with scallops of blue. Uneasily the Arab workers stopped and watched them pass.

"*Yallah!*" Naftali yelled, stepping out on the balcony. He continued in Arabic, "Feed your beast somewhere else!" One of the men had permitted his horse to nibble the high grain.

Mustafa gave an order and the man pulled away.

"What do you want here?"

The sergeant dismounted without answering and walked carefully in his new boots to the front door directly below the balcony. "Open!"

Naftali knew he was going to be sick; the hollow pain in his joints and muscles was beginning. (Perhaps if he had been a good son and gone lamenting with his mother, "How solitary doth the city . . .") Well, the arak hadn't helped either. He held onto the low balcony rail. Below him Mustafa's figure wavered in the heated air like a coin beneath water.

"Open!"

"Whom are you frightening—the gulls?"

"It is an order. Open!"

"Brother fool, it is open."

Mustafa said something to his three men, who took up positions with their rifles at the ready. Then he mounted the inside stairway. Naftali turned to face the door, supporting himself against a case of books, and shivered from the onset of malarial fever.

Mustafa clumped up the stairs and entered sullenly.

"Eh, Mustafa, what ails you?"

The sergeant wiped the wetness from the lobes of his ears; he worked his mouth under the black moustache. "I have orders." He took out a document from the inside of his jacket and waved it in front of him as if it were an amulet to protect him from the books and papers that crowded the large room. What danger lay in them he did not know but could easily suspect. "I have orders to make a counting of arms."

Naftali knew that there were two Winchester rifles and an American shotgun in a cupboard. They were useful against thieves. It would be very costly, if not impossible, to replace them.

"Why, suddenly?" he asked.

"Orders, effendi."

"Whose?"

"Colonel Hamid Bek, the new commandant of Jaffa."

Naftali was anxious. The malicious whims of the Turkish gendarmerie were well known to him.

He spoke sharply, as one speaks to a thief. "You have no right even to be here without permission. Have you forgotten the law that protects foreigners?"

"You and Singer Effendi are subjects of the sultan."

"But this house is owned by Americans."

Naftali tried to breathe slowly to clear his head; he was swaying between blackness and sun. If he could only get back to the cot.

Mustafa touched a pile of books as if he were beginning and gazed hard into the large room. "I will search."

"If the American consul or his Excellency Mr. Morgenthau, the American ambassador to the Sublime Porte, knew of this trespass, you would no longer be Sergeant Mustafa of the Turkish Police but an unknown Mustafa in a prison where you would be mocked by other breakers of the law."

Mustafa lowered his eyes momentarily, feeling fear. "These are my orders, effendi."

"I do not recognize your orders. Not even if they were signed by Enver Bey or Jemal Pasha."

Mustafa fanned himself with the paper. He knew about the Law of the Foreigners, the devil take it, which the sultan had been forced to sign years ago. But Hamid Bek must have known that too. He sighed, tasting the seeds he had been chewing. The poor are always ground between the nobility and the foreigner. Would there ever be a day when the poor would do the grinding?

"I do not wish to become your enemy, Brandt Effendi."

"Then we will remain friends."

The sergeant shifted from foot to foot. His boots hurt. "But if I do not make a counting of your arms, I will be an enemy to myself."

"This property is on file in Damascus."

"But the rifles and the amount of ammunition. Is that also on file?"

"There was never a request for that information. Besides, Singer Effendi is the director. Only he can answer your questions, and he is away. There is to be a celebration in the family."

"Ah, yes." Mustafa smiled placatingly. Like an old whore, Naftali thought. "Why should I disturb Singer Effendi on the eve of his sister's wedding? You are his friend. Tell me what there is—write it on this paper, and it will be sufficient. Singer Effendi is a noble and famous man. Everyone knows that his friend will tell the truth."

"Say that at Atlit they have neither rifles nor ammunition."

"Hah! Who would believe that?"

Naftali knew he had made a mistake.

"Then I will tell you nothing and you will leave immediately!"

Mustafa saw that he also had made a mistake, but he had no choice. He touched the hilt of his sword as if by accident and said, "I will have to search, effendi."

He saw the Jew stiffen. He had never liked this one, for he dressed like an Arab and acted like a pasha. Jews knew too much, pretended too much, wanted too much. Most were cowards, but not this one.

"You do not like it, effendi. But what will come of it? You or your master, Singer Effendi, will go to Jaffa to protest to Hamid Bek, who will tell you that his orders came from Damascus. You will then go to Damascus. There it will take two months to find the proper official, and he will deny that he had anything to do with the order and tell you to go to Constantinople. So you will go to Constantinople and wait another fifteen days away from your honorable and important labor. And what then? You know our saying about the cucumber. No matter how long it is, it can always be cut up into smaller pieces."

With the tip of his boot he touched a pile of books on the floor. "And how shall I protect these valuable books from the ignorant peasants who are my soldiers and who await my orders?"

Naftali wiped his eyes, blurred with the malaria. Baksheesh is what he wants. The vomit of the Ottoman Empire.

"Mustafa, you are a scoundrel. The American ambassador goes directly to the ear of Enver Pasha."

The smile did not leave the face.

"You are wise, Brandt Effendi. I have known that since you and I had our first coffee together at Omar's in Caesarea. Surely you know that Enver Pasha would say to the American Excellency, 'Sir, you are right. I will find the transgressor and punish him.' But would he hasten to find the transgressor? A year, two years. In your wisdom, you

13

know that it would take a long time. Now, effendi, I am not as wise as you but I am not a camel. . . ." Mustafa felt a great surge of pride. He was speaking well; Allah himself was placing these very words in his mouth. "I do not want to be punished, even after years. How then can we avoid all trouble?"

"You are also wise, Mustafa. What is your answer?"

"I will suppose that you and I have met in Caesarea. We are having a coffee in the shade. I am there to collect a tax from Old Omar, who never pays anything until he is threatened with the bastinado. You and I talk. And what will we talk about, effendi?"

"About your wife and children, whom you do not care for enough."

"I care much about them, but do I ever have enough money to feed them?"

The whore beginning to bargain.

"That is not all we will talk about. We will mention this noble station where your Singer Effendi discovers new things to grow where nothing has ever grown before. We will say that it is filled with papers and books that must not be touched by anyone who doesn't know exactly where each thing belongs." Again he permitted the sword to edge a pile of books, but his eyes were on Naftali's. "And then, before we finish our coffee, you say, 'Ha, Mustafa, did you know that there are only two rifles and ten shells at the station to keep away Abu Bekr and his thieves if they should come and try to steal our fruit and animals?' And I listen and nod."

His dizziness was getting worse. Mustafa was doubled and singled; Naftali frowned hard to keep his eyes focused.

"Afterwards, I sigh and think of how poor my life is and how hungry my children are."

"Yes . . ."

"Only yesterday I had to borrow from a moneylender. The interest alone eats me alive."

The room circled slowly; the malaria was covering his skin with another skin of sweat.

"With your permission, effendi, I will see how my men are."

Gravely Mustafa stepped onto the balcony, took off his cap to wipe the top of his head with a broad hand, and waited with his back to Naftali.

Naftali knew this was the ritual. He would have to pay baksheesh to protect the papers and specimens; the glass cases could so easily be broken during a search, the papers torn, the books thrown about into

14

a confusion that would take months to clarify. No amount of protest would compensate for the damages or loss of time. But in his fever the act of bribery had become monumental, demeaning, impossible. Yet he moved dreamlike to a large wooden box where the money was kept, took out six liras, put them behind a pile of magazines on a table near the window. He scratched the words "two and ten" on a notebook page, placed it over the money to hide it, and called Mustafa.

He was a victim, and he squirmed with his helplessness against his obsession not to be a victim. Baksheesh. The open leprous sore of the Ottoman Empire.

Mustafa returned to the room and saw the notepaper.

"Ah, yes."

He moved so that Naftali could not see him taking the money. Invisibility was another ritual of baksheesh; it had to appear accidental, like the fall of a leaf. One did not receive money for payment of an act of omission or commission, but one pretended that the money was found and acted from a feeling of thanksgiving to a generous destiny.

The six liras were less than Mustafa had hoped for. His men, who would never believe him if he said he'd received nothing, would take three, and one again for his Syrian lieutenant. Two left for himself. These rich Jews! With their stations and fine horses, with that automobile of Singer's. But even baksheesh had a lock on the door.

"What are you chattering about?" Naftali demanded, deafened by fever and anger.

"Effendi, I thanked you for the note."

"Go now."

In his humiliation, Naftali saw himself joined to Mustafa. In the discontent on the Turk's face he saw they were brothers in corruption, Levantine bribe givers and takers. They were products of each other —the same.

"Brother thief," he whispered, and walked unsteadily to the balcony door to see the clean sky.

He lost the sense of light. He thought twilight had fallen.

"It's late."

He heard the gulls crying. He thought of an important question.

"Come closer, Mustafa."

"I am close to you now, effendi."

"Why are there orders to search for arms?"

"I do not know."

"Only here?"

"Other places. But I was ordered here."

"Why the search?"

It pleased Mustafa to be humble, and he said plaintively, "If I asked, who would tell me?"

Naftali felt Mustafa's hand on his shoulder. "If the effendi is ill—"

"I am only tired. Go."

"It will please me if you bear to Singer Effendi my good wishes."

"For what?"

"The marriage of his sister. It is not a good time to get married, although all is in the hands of Allah."

He sensed a slight stir in the room. Was it the *hamsin* breaking or Mustafa leaving? He raised his arm to the open window. Let the winds blow at last. Perhaps they would blow him out like a candle. He had no worthier destiny than to be blown out like a candle in a foolish storm. Bribe giver, bribe taker. There was no difference.

Ah, Pablo, you were right, he thought. I was wrong and you were right. Paris is where an artist can make himself. But how does one make a nation?

He had run away from Paris back to Palestine, brimming with hope, filled with the murmurs of the revolution that he heard everywhere he went—Greece, the Balkans, Poland, Russia. Young men like himself were gathering their strength to overthrow the baksheesh lords of the old world. It was time for the Jews, time for Zion, to be redeemed, not by the antlike labor of lawyers turned farmers, like his own father, but by the might of arms.

The Ottoman Empire was the most corrupt of its time. Its hold on Palestine could be broken by a handful of brave men.

His friends at home thought he was crazy to speak of a revolution of Jews. When he charged them to remember Bar Kochba, who had downed the Roman Empire and rewon Jerusalem, they yelled back at him to remember that when Bar Kochba's revolt was defeated its death had burned out the seed of Jewish dignity for two thousand years.

He had flung himself into rousing his people. No one listened. The Jewish workers had no other thought than to find work, for the Arabs had undercut their wages and there was great unemployment. The Zionist leaders had no other thought than to teach intellectuals how to plant vines and corn, build roads, live from day to day, and die from malaria. Like his own father. Gaunt and good man, a lawyer from Minsk, come to redeem the land, looking out of the window from his deathbed in a cold stone room, seeing the nothing of his labor, hearing the nothing-echo of his energy and love, saying calmly, "It is not enough we have done. But it is better in Eretz Ysrael to die a pauper than to live an emperor in Schönbrunn."

It wasn't better if a Jew lived without power to make his own nation.

Naftali's friends accused him of being a Byron, a romantic, of endangering the few tender threads of colonies and villages that had been woven to bind Jews to Zion.

Baksheesh, all baksheesh. The bribery of the soul; Levantines all.

He had come back from Paris on fire and had plunged his fire into a cold muck of indifference.

How does one die meaningfully? By trying to save a stray dog from a bus on the Boulevard Montparnasse?

Recalling his despair in his fever, he stood in the huge workroom of the station and howled Jeremiah, "The carcasses of men shall fall as dung upon the open field . . . and none shall harvest them!"

Stumbling against the edge of a table, he felt nothing. The cot and the arak waited. He thought of Judah Singer. Judah, his North Star, isolated too from the Palestine community of Jews, the remnant of Israel, the Yishuv, as they called it. Judah, who had had his own failures and despairs and had hidden himself behind the mask of his great labors. Had the mask become the face? Would Judah ever rouse himself from his science and take the banner? (How many days had they argued, Naftali pleading for some action, any action; Judah reasonable, peaceable, aloof?)

The burning arak dribbled into his throat and down his chin. "Again I will build thee, and thou shalt be built, O virgin of Israel. . . . Thou shalt yet plant vines upon the mountains of Samaria. And there shall be a day . . ."

But the vines were already planted, the frail vines, and by a whim they could be torn up by Mustafa! Or the villages ruined, the virgins deflowered as even now in Jaffa and Rishon the girls dared not walk the open fields or across the sand. Prisoners in our own Zion!

He fell on the pallet and murmured.

"Papa, don't be so proud. Don't be so dead."

He saw in the haze of malaria his mother shoveling the first earth on his father's grave. Without a tear!

"Mama, don't be so strong."

Death is more valuable than this. But how to die?

He forced the regret out of his mind and babbled in his delirium some verses of Hölderlin he had translated into Hebrew. "When I was a boy a God would ofttimes come and rescue me from the noise and punishment of men. Then I played confidently with the flowers in the woods. . . ."

Should he leave and warn Judah at Har Nehemia? Go to Alona, his mother's village, and warn her?

What was there to warn about? Who could fight Mustafa and Hamid Bek and the pashas who strode Damascus, Jerusalem, and Constantinople like clay gods gilded to look like iron?

Mustafa had given him a message: "Bear to Singer Effendi my good wishes on the marriage."

He had forgotten she was to be married. Ah, Rachel. Rachel Singer. He had read to her first his translation of the Hölderlin.

Rachel Singer was also the product of his failure. He had rejected himself in her. How could love be permitted when there was a mission that possessed all of him, and later when there was despair stronger than love? He had done all he could to deaden what she felt for him, mocked her and himself, played fool and blind man, and he had finally succeeded; she was getting married and going away.

How could he have forgotten? Rachel. . . .

"I will not be a victim!"

The breeze stirring through the open window brought him the scent of the grain.

It was good but not enough. That grain was bought with sweat and daring, but also with baksheesh.

Bialik's phrase rang through his mind. "To me the whole earth is one gallows."

"I will not be a victim!" he murmured and closed his eyes. Darkness fell like blocks of masonry across the exits of his mind.

3 ✧✧✧✧✧✧✧✧✧

The road from the station at Atlit southeast to Har Nehemia, where the Singer family lived, follows the broad beaches of the Mediterranean for a few miles, then rises in long winding loops toward the green prow of the Carmel range slicing into the plains. In the spring the road is lovely, passing great islands of wildflowers, anemones, mallow, narcissus and iris, roses of the Sharon, and lilies. On all sides lie the glazed ponds of the late rains, holding blue fragments of the sky between the green reeds and rushes. The air is sweet and fertile with bee and butterfly intent on life. As the road grows steeper, flinty rocks fill it and the going is hard. Finally the road twists past the cemetery and reaches the broad main dirt street of the settlement, with its row of one- and two-story whitewashed stone and plastered houses, gardens, and vineyards. The biggest house, surrounded by the greenest garden, belongs to the Singer family.

Har Nehemia had been founded in 1882 by a small band of earnest, impoverished young Romanians who loved Zion, wanted to rebuild it, and like other returning Jews of that time, arrived ignorant of how to work. All they had were their books and their devotion to the grand Davidic illusion of a free society of the soil in an independent Jewish state. The hilltop in Samaria had been bought in their name by a small group of passionate lovers of Zion from an absentee Turkish bey, and when they ascended to it the first time, the way was so steep and rocky that they had to take apart the ox-drawn wagon that carried their few possessions and carry it piece by piece up to the plateau that was to be their home.

They called the place Har Nehemia, after the hard-minded Persian Jew who some twenty-three hundred years before had led another group of exiled Jews back to Zion.

For five years these European romantics with their biblical stubbornness lived in earth huts and dug out rocks. The neighboring Arabs called them "Children of Death" because so many of them died of overwork, malnutrition, and malaria from the mosquitoes of the lovely springtime ponds. Each year the women, in a druglike dream of being fruitful for this promised land, bore children. Each year they buried them, until the cemetery dead were more numerous than the settlers. The mother of the Singer family, Deborah, buried four infants and had no doubts of the future. She was made, as they said, of salt and iron and had a crazy notion that her family was fated for greatness. She kept one son, Judah, alive, and with her husband learned how not to weep.

On the high slopes behind Har Nehemia, the silver olive orchards of the aloof and waiting Arab neighbors were a reminder of heaven's ironic promise.

In those years there were other pioneering settlements in the Galilee and Samaria that suffered, died, and yet somehow lived. But the sounds of the future grew more and more inaudible. The zealots were becoming weaker.

They would have died out altogether had it not been for the elegant zealot of Paris, Baron Édouard de Rothschild, who gave them money, seed, plows, work animals, and managers. The first grain and poultry and medicines were brought in. But with these benefactions, as certain as rain with winter, came the inevitable rigidity of a managerial bureaucracy. The baron's men ran the settlements like fiefs; the hopeful pioneers became their serfs. Bread was more plentiful but it stuck in the throat.

The pioneers, however, who had managed to survive everything else also survived benevolent despotism. By 1914, using their now seasoned skills and cheap Arab labor, and despite the constant demands for baksheesh by Turkish officials, they had cleared the fields, if not the road, of stones, planted hundreds of eucalyptus trees whose spongelike roots absorbed the malarial swamps and ponds, built their vineyards and wineries, seeded and harvested grain fields and olive orchards, raised their houses, bought books and pianos, given their children music lessons, sent some of them to Europe for a year of study, and achieved the mild prosperity of independent landowners. The broad central street of Har Nehemia had become shaded and pleasant. There was time even to cultivate flower gardens and arbors.

Judah Singer had became a famous agronomist, as his mother had predicted. Another child, Rachel, born much later, survived malaria and had been sent for a year to a school abroad. Papa Mosheh Singer, a lover of his vineyards, had his advice sought by the young and knew the joy of respect. But Deborah, the salt and iron wasted by hard years, died in 1910 and was buried alongside the four infants in the cemetery, where trees had been planted to bring shade to the mourners as well as the dead.

All that August day Rachel Singer, now twenty-four, tried in vain to avoid thinking of her forthcoming marriage. She kept putting off the fitting of her mother's wedding dress. Her young friend Miriam Bloch told her that alterations were necessary and today was the day to start. Late in the afternoon, when she could find no further excuses, Rachel mounted a chair in her bedroom and permitted Miriam to dress her in the white brocaded satin gown that her mother had worn in Bucharest forty years before. In the tall mirror where she had studied herself with admiration so often in the past, she saw her woman's figure floating grotesquely in another world. Her blond hair, fair Slavic face, and full bosom seemed to belong to someone else; only the unhappiness in the blue eyes was her own.

"Beautiful," Miriam murmured, her mouth filled with pins.

"It is too short."

"Wait."

The *hamsin* made breathing difficult, and she felt the moisture rise to her skin. What books should she take with her to Constantinople? Certainly the Bialik, the Rimbaud, the Rilke, and the Lermontov, which she loved but found silly sometimes. She must also take the steel engravings of Bach and Mozart that Judah had brought to her from his first visit to Berlin, Naftali's broken flute—why hadn't she thrown the flute away? Once she planned to have it repaired, but he never played anymore. Did he stop before or after he had come back from Paris?

"Even if you put a hem on it, I can't wear this dress!"

Miriam shook her head, pointing to the pins in her mouth.

"It's forty years old. People will laugh at it."

Nahum Cohn, although he was the eldest, had not been the least of her suitors—handsome, considerate, protective. Besides, they would be living in Constantinople, far away from her village. To be far away was a blessing.

She dared to look at herself again in the mirror, her face whiter than the dress. Suddenly she raised her arms from her side and pressed them yearningly against her breasts.

Miriam spat out the pins and said sharply, "Don't move your arms.

21

How can I get the hem straight? You're not going to be married holding your arms over your chest. That'll come later, and it won't be *your* arms either."

"Be quiet!"

No man had touched her there, even though she was twenty-four. But she mustn't think of that. Be difficult, pout, give in to her bride's anxiety, anything, but not permit doubt to engulf her. And if poor Mama's dress was the scapegoat, then Mama would forgive her.

"It's absolutely impossible. I won't wear it!"

"But your mother's dress——"

"She's not getting married."

"That's heartless!"

"Then call me heartless. I will not wear it. Look at it, Miri. Be honest. Look how yellow it is."

"It's the sun on it."

"It's yellow with age. I should have my own dress. It's my wedding."

"You look beautiful in it. I wouldn't say so if I didn't mean it. I'm no hypocrite."

"Nor am I!"

"It would please your father."

"Whose wedding is this? His or mine? My God, Miri, don't argue with me and help me take it off. I don't want to get married—in this dress!"

"You are either too spoiled to know your own mind, Rachel, or you're crazy. What is it? I'm your best friend. You can talk to me."

Miriam waited. She was good at waiting. Less temperamental than Rachel, she was brought up by her socialist doctor-father to think of personal eccentricity as harmful to the cause.

"Of course, I can talk to you." Rachel was ashamed and switched from Hebrew to French, as if it helped. "But what is there to talk about?"

"Your marriage."

"Don't you like Nahum?"

Miriam laughed. "Personally or socially?"

"You don't like businessmen. But *les affaires* are not our concern."

"Personally, I like him. But he's a little too sure of himself. And stop talking French." Miriam was a fanatic of Hebrew.

"Don't we all admire Judah for being sure of himself? That's what makes him strong. Shouldn't a woman marry someone who is strong? If you don't like him, you can say so. Do you think he is too old? I won't be offended. After all, you're not marrying him either. Or perhaps because he is an importer of goods, a businessman?"

"I said I liked him."

"Then what do you want to talk about?"

"You."

"Do you think I don't know my own mind?" Sudden tears fell on her cheeks. "Oh, Miri!"

"What is it?"

Rachel raised her hands to cover her face.

"Rachel. . . . Tell me."

This she could confess; for a Singer of Har Nehemia, Judah's sister, it was not too great a weakness. "I know so little. . . ."

"Nahum will teach you what you have to know."

"But he too is innocent."

"What? A bourgeois, innocent? For generations they have exploited women sexually. The poor women of——"

"That's crude and ugly! Nahum is an honorable man. A believing Jew, a religious——"

"They can be just as bad. Beasts. Some of them. Think of our own village. Oh, I can tell you stories. That is, if I were permitted. You should know what a doctor's daughter hears. You'd think that Har Nehemia was different. A paradise. Aristocratic pioneers of 1880. So conservative. Our noses we hold up to heaven as if the rest of the Yishuv smelled like burning chicken feathers." She tossed her head from side to side like an old grandmother. "You should hear what the women say to my father. My ears burn."

"Don't listen."

"Who can help it? Have you ever tried *not* to listen to Chana Haimowitz? Such a husband. An Austrian who thinks he's better than the Romanians. And you know how you Romanians think you can go to the bathroom without——"

"That's enough." Rachel thought she was not a prude, but that was too much.

"Such a pious man, this Haimowitz, with his mumbling prayers and swaying back and forth like a frightened goat. He made her cut her hair off and wear a wig when they got married. And do you know what he does to her at night?"

"Nahum is not like that!"

"He covers her face and——"

"Be quiet, Miri!"

23

Miriam dropped a pin and bent to look for it.

"Nahum is pure. He told me that himself."

"Ha!"

Rachel found a target to exercise her doubts. "You socialists who love humanity—you have no love for man."

"In man, we do. In men, that's another question. So you're frightened because—how shall I say it for your delicate ears?—you are both virgins. But, Rachel, you've seen the animals——"

"It's not that!"

"Then it's what?"

"I don't want to have children right away."

Miriam was annoyed that she had not understood her friend from the beginning. And Rachel, now that she had spoken, marveled at the intricate tricks of the mind, for until that moment she hadn't thought of not having children. She had wanted to be a good wife, a full woman, a mother. But there was another voice that spoke a truth from a place she didn't know existed.

"Why don't you talk to my father?" Miriam said.

"Hasn't he told you about such things?"

Miriam shook her head and picked up the satin hem for the dress. "It's getting late."

"But I thought you knew."

"Why should I know? Am I going to be married?"

Rachel couldn't help laughing, but it was more a cry of confusion, and she looked at her face in the mirror. Her blond hair had been loosened; the golden sun swept the gilt top of the mirror in a ring of flame, enclosing her sad face.

"I thought— Miri, I thought . . . socialist girls . . ."

"Oh, Rachel! Free love? But there has to be a lover even for free love, no? We have known each other for five years. Best friends, we are. Yet——"

"Don't say that because I am middle class and you——"

"Human beings never really know each other."

"Not even lovers? A husband and wife?"

Miriam thought; loneliness had a way of crossing class lines.

"You'll be married soon, then you tell me," she said.

"You were thinking of Yosef."

"I was thinking of the malaria that buried him in Degania." Miriam held the satin band against her dark sunburned cheek. "The enemy of love . . ."

"Please, darling, forget what I said."

Miriam knelt to pin the white band of satin to the hem. Rachel's blue eyes scanned the bedroom, the disarray of clothes, the dark wood of the bureau, the red of the sofa, the checkered inlaid mosaic of the Turkish table, the lamps, the mirror with the gilt edges darkening as the sun left, Naftali's broken flute on the bureau. She thought of her brother, Judah. She adored him, but he was difficult to talk to, so much older, so remote. She looked down at Miriam. The pins were going gently into the hem.

My friend, Rachel thought, is putting stitches in my shroud.

4 ◇◇◇◇◇◇◇◇◇

Judah Singer, the world famous agronomist, adored of his sister and North Star to Naftali Brandt's passion, left his home early one morning for a secret meeting in Haifa with representatives of Hashomer, a small underground group of Jews that some years before had assumed the task of armed defense of the settlements against unfriendly Arabs and bedouin bands. He had arranged the meeting through Dr. Bloch.

He rode his horse with the assurance of a centurion, his stocky, muscular body erect and commanding. Beneath his Arab kaffiyeh, his blue eyes studied the distant Carmel range like a ship's captain about to assault an enemy fleet. Between Hashomer and himself lay years of ideological conflict. The shomrim whom he was to meet were not his friends. They were mostly socialist Zionists with dogmatic notions of Jewish labor and he was an independent landowner who was convinced that to use untrained labor, even Jewish, was impractical and cruel. He had the certainty and arrogance of a native; they were newcomers, refugees of the failure of the 1905 Russian revolution, with the arrogance of youth. Yet now that war had come to Turkish Palestine, he had decided to see them, for the future of the Yishuv was uncertain, and an effort had to be made to organize all the groups to take concerted action. Hashomer was only a fragment of the community, but its physical and moral courage gave it an influence beyond its numbers.

Dr. Bloch, the one socialist of Har Nehemia and a man he was on friendly terms with, told him that Hashomer welcomed the meeting because of Judah's importance. "They'll listen to you, Judah. But I beg you to listen to them too."

"Since the war began and the census of arms, I've listened to everyone," Judah replied.

Indeed, he had conferred with the farmers' organizations of the Galilee, Samaria, and Judea, the town committees of Jaffa and Jerusalem and the chief rabbis of those cities, and most of all with the statesmen of the Palestine Office of the Zionist World Congress. They all saw the dangers but had no plans to meet them. Some were for the victory of the Allies, some were for the Germans and wanted the Jews to go into the Turkish Army. The rabbis, speaking for the thousands of their followers who lived on foreign charity, said they would support the sultan as long as he didn't interfere with their religious rites. Weakness and indecision were all he heard. No one was interested in combining under one leadership.

Now, as Judah rode north toward Haifa, he thought again of an important decision he had made a week before. The American consul had offered passage on an American ship for him, his family, library, and laboratory. "You can have your pick of any of our universities to continue your studies," Mr. Hardwick had said. "If you stay here the war will isolate you. Come to my country. We would welcome you and be honored by your presence."

Although the decision was a grave one, it had been arrived at quickly. Palestine was home; he could not think of deserting it. More than that—and this he did not tell Mr. Hardwick—he had larger dreams than a professorship at an American university.

Judah Singer was a victim of too many early failures and a success that came too late. His mother, a strong-willed woman whom he loved above all women, told him when he was old enough to understand that she had felt greatness in him even while carrying him in her womb. Later, Baron Édouard de Rothschild, always eager to help the more promising of his Palestinian wards, was impressed by this lad of seventeen who had a taste for growing things and sent him to France to study at a school for agronomists. But then, in the manner of suspicious benefactors, he withdrew his support a few months before Judah was to graduate on the theory that his protégé might succumb to the seductions of Europe and not return to Palestine. This was a terrible blow to Judah. He had nothing to show for his years of study, and it appeared that the baron had lost confidence in him. He raged against Rothschild and his advisers who had compounded this dislocation in his life. On his return he suffered the vindictive gossip in Har Nehemia of families not as successful as the Singers.

As with men who feel their destiny strongly, Judah's sudden change of fortune made him doubt others, not himself. He withdrew from parties and organizations. For a decade, during which he was supported by his father, he seemed unable to finish any task, and went from job to job. Finally he gave up altogether and masked his unappeasable chagrin by wandering alone through the land, mastering its secrets— the meaning of the fall of a wadi, the rise of a tel, the texture of the earth that might hide a long-forgotten well. He filled thousands of notebook pages with his observations and took on the task of finding Hebrew names for plants and trees known before only by their Arabic nomenclature. He published a number of articles abroad and had the beginning of a reputation. And he waited patiently for his day.

One spring morning in 1907, when he was 33, while climbing the eastern flank of Mount Hermon he saw among the rocks a plant that he recognized as a variant of emmer wheat. He knew that agronomists all over the world had been searching in vain for the wild-growing parent plant of wheat to use in strengthening the overcultivated strains. With cold excitement Judah knelt to study the plant's flattened heads and narrow, pointed kernels. Could this be the wild wheat? Carefully he took a cutting, marked the place on his map, found a few similar plants nearby, and returned as swiftly as he could to his little laboratory in a small shed back of his home in Har Nehemia. There with great skill he completed a series of ingenious experiments and determined that he had indeed found the wild wheat, the *Triticum dicoccoides*. He wrote of his discovery to scientists in Germany and the United States, published his reports, successfully cultivated hybrids of the old and the new plants, and within three years of that spring day on Mount Hermon received an invitation from the United States to lecture to learned societies on his findings. He was a guest of President Theodore Roosevelt and was offered a chair at the University of California. All this was less important to him than the action of a group of well-known American Jews who volunteered to underwrite the building and continuing support of an agricultural research center in Palestine of which he would be the director.

When he returned to build the station in Atlit, he was confronted with a crisis in a liaison he had been having for several years with a woman married to one of his old friends. In the manner of the enlightened Russian intellectuals of that time, they had settled into a selfless, sensitively organized *ménage à trois* in which the husband, wife, and lover cared deeply for one another and talked of their feelings openly. But the early passion that Judah felt for the woman had grown even deeper and he became impatient with the situation. Before his departure for the United States Judah had a lengthy discussion with husband and wife, arguing that a time had come for the woman to choose between them. He wanted children, but most of all, he wanted a wife who would be free to go with him on his travels. He felt that the present relationship would in the end be unjust to them all, even though it was intelligent and moral. Each of the three tried to see it from the other's point of view, and after a night of talk the woman asked to be given time to make up her mind. In a letter of forty pages that awaited Judah on his arrival from abroad, the woman explained why she had decided to stay with her husband. Buttressed by lengthy passages of poetry and political philosophy, her real reason was stated clearly. Judah's love, she wrote, was a great one. She loved him with equal fervor and would carry his image in her heart forever. But the fact that he had made demands, even though they were motivated by his love, frightened her. Perhaps therefore she was not worthy of him, for if love were not free of demands, it was not the kind she wanted in her life. She loved her husband as much as she loved him. Love had to be equalitarian or it was a mask for the exploitation of one sex by the other.

He protested her decision, humiliated himself by constant and eloquent pleas to have her change her mind, and in the end agreed to go back to the old relationship. It was too late. The wife and husband refused. Deeply moved by Judah's suffering, they left Palestine for a commune of working-class Jews that Baron de Hirsch had set up in Woodbine, New Jersey.

Soon afterward Judah's mother died. The loss of the two women he loved put a seal on his bachelorhood. If he missed having a family of his own, he never admitted it. His bull-like strength seemed to have sufficient release in the single-minded absorption in his work. Here he could make demands; at Atlit he was master. The uncertainties of his early failures made him remote from people; his late success made him impatient with them. Both increased his isolation from the Palestine community.

Entering the port area of Haifa, the lovely hill city that embraced the great bay with the arms of the Carmel, he hurried to the place of meeting, a one-room stone house in the Arab quarter, and arrived exactly at the time set. He was met outside the door by a tall, dour Ukrainian, Shmul Lorchanovsky, a man he had never gotten along with. Lorchanovsky waved him in and locked the door behind them.

There were two other men and a young woman seated behind a wooden table drinking tea. They rose, shook hands, and greeted Judah with respect and guarded goodwill. He had known them before, although not well. They were from the 1905 immigration, ten or fifteen years his junior. One of them was Remenov, whose home this was, a thin man about twenty-five. A silky blond moustache made him look like a Russian princeling or a character of Turgenev's. His girl friend, Mara Schalet, affected the shortened hair of the Russian intellectual. But she was pretty, despite her glasses. And Levine, with a mane of black hair and a round shining forehead, who had been wounded in Father Gapon's march on the czar's St. Petersburg palace ten years before.

"Thank you for making this time for me," Judah said.

"It is all right," Mara said.

"I have not asked to talk with you to revive old arguments," Judah said.

"Very good," Levine said pleasantly. "Agreed. What would you like to propose to us?"

"I have some questions to ask first."

Levine nodded. Lorchanovsky sat down and began to sip his tea noisily. Mara stared at Judah admiringly, blushing as she met his glance, although he seemed unaware of her presence.

"What is the intent of Hashomer in face of the new situation?"

The Ukrainian looked up coldly. "Are you thinking of applying for membership?"

"That question is out of place," Levine said. "Haver Shmul, let us please not have arguments."

"If the haverim wish," Lorchanovsky said sullenly. "Still, I merely want to express my views that if *Mister* Singer doesn't know how a Jew meets a new situation, we who are so used to new situations that even infants who have just been circumcised know the way, why then let him join us and find out."

"Haver Shmul, please!" Mara protested.

"It is true that we could use some new men. After all, he has his station and his coterie. Still, party decisions are not public."

"We have no secrets from a man like Judah Singer," Remenov said.

Levine sucked at a piece of sugar. "Are you pro-German?" he asked Judah.

"A friend has written to me that when Dr. Weizmann was asked that question he replied, 'I am not pro-German. I am not pro-Russian.

30

As far as the war is concerned, I am pro-British.' I agree with that entirely."

Levine said quietly, "Some of us, as you know, consider this war an imperialist war, and we would like to see all the empires sink into the sea forever."

"A black year on them," Lorchanovsky spit out and gulped down some tea with a grimace.

Levine went on. "I don't hide the fact that some of the haverim are indeed for the Germans and some for the French and British. The Zionist organization internationally may opt for neutrality, but as for us here living under the Turkish rule, we have no choice." His heavy black eyebrows were raised sadly. He sighed. "With the death of the Second Internationale, the murder of Jean Jaures, we have absolutely no choice. We must keep alive. Our position is precarious. We will support the sultan and Enver Bey. Absolutely, we have no choice."

"This is a time for willows, not oaks," Remenov said suddenly, as if he were forcing himself. "We must survive at all costs. We did not build our Jewish colonies with so much sweat and suffering to have the Turk destroy them."

Lorchanovsky slapped his hand sharply against the table. "Willows or oaks! Who heard of such prattle? We will defend ourselves! If anybody tries to take away our gains, let them try! The Yishuv can count on the shomrim."

"Against the Turkish and German armies?" Judah asked.

Mara spoke. Her Hebrew was flawless. "We are talking about bedouin and thieves—and protecting our women, children, and the old parents."

"All our people must give up their Russian passports and become Ottoman citizens," Levine added. "We want them to join the army. At worst, it will mean we will be killing Russian soldiers. At best, we will learn how to use guns."

"I have heard that they are searching for arms. Will you give them up or fight?"

This was too much for Lorchanovsky. Singer was a capitalist, a renegade, a snob! He detested the man from the first day he had gone to Atlit and asked him to hire Jewish workers instead of Arabs. Judah had replied then, "When they learn how to graft three hundred vines a day instead of sixty I'll hire them." "Such questions must remain with the haverim," he said angrily. "We have no reason to discuss them with you."

The hot tea in the glass suddenly burned Judah's fingers. He put it down on the table.

Levine broke in. "We will take care of the searches. We have already. Baksheesh is like sunlight that blinds their eyes. We'll give them an old hunting rifle. Other things are well hidden."

"You will need money," Judah said.

Lorchanovsky exploded.

"Money! That's all he thinks of! People we need. People who don't hold their noses high up in the air. People who will hire Jewish workers. People who will understand that private business has no place in Zion redeemed. Don't come to us with your talk of money. You want to help the Yishuv, become one of us. And don't lecture us on your great work. And how long you've lived here. We also suffered, we also died from malaria and bedouin bullets. We also broke our hands on the hard rocks. But from the first, you and your kind fought us! I don't forget you hired Arab labor because you could pay them less!"

Mara started to say something but remained silent.

Judah waited for the others to speak, but they sat quietly like priests who had suddenly heard the devil named. Levine sipped his tea and studied Singer over the rim of the glass. Judah rose from the chair slowly. He was making a great effort not to reply with anger.

"I am not a child and I do not react to bad manners. I came here despite our past conflict of principles because I thought it would be for the good of all to find out if we could work together in these evil times."

"Work together? Whom do you represent? Your old father and that Brandt, a mad poet, and maybe two, three landowners from Romania like yourself? You want to cooperate, then become shomrim. Take up guard duty at the colonies. We'll give you work!"

Judah continued as if there had been no interruption. "Under the circumstances, I don't see how there can be any *rapprochement*."

The French word fallen among the Hebrew words made Lorchanovsky snort. He put his big worker hands on his head as if it suddenly ached.

"I must protest," Mara said. "Mr. Singer deserves more than rudeness."

"Haver, behave," Levine said to Lorchanovsky. "It is not becoming to disrespect a guest. And please, Mr. Singer, sit down. Or I'll have to get up too, and I hurt my bad leg the other day trying to halt a runaway horse."

32

Judah nodded and sat down. Someone from the house next door was cooking. The scent of olive oil was sharp.

Remenov pushed the tea toward him. "Another glass?"

"No, thank you."

"I hear your sister, Rachel, is getting married," Mara said. *"Mazel tov.* From here?"

"Her fiancé is from Constantinople. Nahum Cohn."

Remenov said, "A beautiful girl. And what a horseman. Up and down the hills like a cossack. A remarkable type. The new Jew. How I wished my father had come up to Eretz Yisrael when I was born. To grow up here, not to know the darkness of the Diaspora." His gray eyes shone and he stroked the blond moustache wistfully. "How lucky you are, Mr. Singer. I envy you."

Judah knew they were his equals in devotion and intellect. Their vision of a redeemed land was not different from his own. Was it only the principle of the means that separated them? They spoke for hardworking devoted people who, despite factionalism, sickness, dogmatic errors, failures of impossible projects, raids by thieves, pressures by Turkish authorities who harried them whenever they bought land for their cooperative colonies, had managed to dig footholds from the Galilee to Tel Aviv. And he? With all his labor and skill and achievement? Lorchanovsky was right. He represented no one but himself, his loyal father, the coterie (damnable word!) of a poet, some students, his adoring sister, who would follow him anywhere, and a few important friends in America who supported his station.

Levine thrust his lionlike head forward impatiently. "Nu, Mr. Singer, what can we do together?"

"If you are asking my opinion, Levine, I must first say that you and your comrades are living in an illusion."

Lorchanovsky shouted, "You said that in 1911 when our people established the kibbutz of Degania! You said it——"

"Please let him go on," Mara said.

"The illusion I refer to is your program of separating yourself from the rest of the Yishuv. By that I mean the small private landholders, the businessmen, and even the Old Yishuv of the religious of Jerusalem and Tiberias and Safed who will also suffer if the Turk turns against the Jews."

"Why should the Turk turn against us?" Remenov asked.

"I don't predict that he will. But he is unstable politically. He hates minorities. I needn't remind you what he did to the Armenians in 1907. There is a strong pan-Turanism in Constantinople."

"He has always respected our religion," Mara objected.

"But suspected our Zionism. If the socialists and the Hashomer would organize a united front of all the forces here, we would be in a stronger position vis à vis the government."

Lorchanovsky made a face and clicked his glass with a fingernail.

"Further, we will be able to get better support from the American Jews. They are all we will have, at least as long as their country is neutral. Weizmann in England can't help us. Your German and Russian haverim will soon be cut off from funds."

Levine lit a Russian cigarette, saying between puffs, "A united front is not bad. It all depends on what one unites on."

"A Jewish Palestine."

"It is not so simple, Mr. Singer," Mara said breathily. "We want a socialist Jewish Palestine."

Remenov had taken out of his pocket a large gold watch on a chain and laid it in front of him. "Excuse me, Mr. Singer, but we have another meeting soon. I agree with haver Levine. We invite you to unite with us."

"On what terms?"

"You will have a vote in the executive."

"One vote?"

"Naturally."

"That's not unity."

Levine smiled but without humor. "We value you, Mr. Singer. We wouldn't be taking this time if we didn't. We are willing to combine forces. Our people and you and your contacts in America. You have very rich friends. But"—his voice rasped like a file on metal—"we are not offering you leadership."

Judah fought to control himself. Levine had touched a bruised spot.

"I will accept only on condition that the executive of which I would be a member cannot act without a unanimous vote."

"Ha! I knew it!" Lorchanovsky said. "He wants to take command. A general." The Ukrainian rose to his full six feet. "I am younger than you are, Mr. Singer, but I am no child either. When you came here to talk about the Yishuv's future, were you talking of the Jews or of yourself?"

"That is a libel!" Judah said coldly and stood up. "It is senseless to talk to closed minds! I demand an apology."

"Sha," Remenov said. "Don't get so excited, Mr. Singer. With all respect, don't accuse the comrade of libel. Isn't it the sense of your own proposal? We believe in majority vote. We can't have a one-man veto. And you're not even a socialist."

"I will not consider anything else."

"So—you don't want cooperation?" Remenov said.

"On your terms, it is capitulation."

"What are your plans, Mr. Singer?" Mara asked. "We may have something to say about them too."

He turned back to the young girl. She and Remenov were standing alongside each other. He suspected she was even stronger in her views than he was. Women had resources of commitment that men could not even approach.

"My plans are simple." Judah's Hebrew became charged with prophetic gravity. "When the time comes, I will act in a useful manner for what I consider to be the best interests of the Yishuv."

"What you consider to be 'best interests' may not be 'best interests' at all," Levine said curtly.

"I have confidence in my judgment."

"That is sheer individualism!"

"Only puppets deplore individualism!"

"Mr. Singer . . ." Remenov leaned forward, resting his thin arms and slender fingers on the table. "If you change your mind, get in touch with us. Or with Dr. Bloch in your own village. Also I must say, with all respect, mind you, that if you should ever act in a way that we don't think is to the 'best interests' of our people, we will oppose you with everything we have."

Judah bowed coldly and walked from the room. He heard Lorchanovsky say in Yiddish, "Who has time to waste with little gods?"

Judah was drained by the meeting. It had been a mistake, after all. He should have known better than to expose himself to "committee disease." If once, he told himself, he had cared about finding a modus operandi with these people, it mattered no more. They were the enemies of reason. Politics was insanity. One could waste a life on talk and compromise. There would be other leaders. He had important work to do in agronomy. No matter how much he had achieved, he had only just begun. Wars would come and go; the soil was eternal.

5 ◆◆◆◆◆◆◆◆◆

Rachel decided to confess the truth of her dilemma to her fiancé. It was the first time she was acting completely on her own on a matter of such importance. Papa, frail and worried about the war and his vineyards, which he treated as if they were also his children, would have said simply, "It is immoral for a Jewish girl to marry a man if she loves another." But was that the answer she wanted?

As for Judah, she adored him. But he was fifteen years older, as much father as brother, and she believed that he expected too much from her. If she disguised the question, he would see through her. If she stated it in some generalized form of being uncertain about the future, he would comment sympathetically that she was troubled by the usual anxieties of a bride who fears change. Her adoration of him paralyzed her.

She had no other choice than to pursue her own character, which despised uncertainties and deceit. But had she the courage and the wit? In those two aspects of herself she thought she was lacking.

"I admire Judah," Nahum was saying. They were strolling through the village after supper. "He's a giant. That's clear. But a giant among pygmies wastes himself, no? In Berlin he'd be a professor. Why didn't he stay even in America and become a professor? Honors, fame . . ."

He had not taken her hand, and she was relieved. But how should she begin? Her nerve was failing her; she had so little courage. The growing moon made the path bright. People passed by talking of the war in Europe.

"It is so peaceful here," he went on. "And in the Alsace and Belgium, East Prussia with the cossacks burning good German towns, people are dying. I am a born German, but I am not for the war."

His neat figure in trim, well-cared-for city clothes was a little out of place in the village. He had a black moustache, cut short; his large moist eyes were beautiful, she thought.

They were passing Avram Fishel's house. Avram was sick. She remembered how she used to cut the dandelions under the Fishels' carob trees and suck their juices. Somehow they never grew there anymore. Or had she stopped looking?

"Talk of war," he said, "is a sin on a night like this. One should talk of blessings. Your family is a blessing. I would like a large family like yours." He coughed shyly. "But of course this is no time to talk of such things, either."

Now they had come to the wooden shack of Reb Mottel, the butcher. The moon had roused the chickens in their pens. Once, when she was a child, Judah had taken her there to explain how eggs are laid and made her watch the breaking of the shell by the tiny blind chick within. "They are like grass and stars," he explained. "They grow and move. And not even God in his heaven can stop them." She had almost fainted when she saw the first raw edge of life opening the shell's jagged window. Birth had a cruelty that distressed her. Yet the chick had no choice.

"Nahum," she said suddenly.

He nodded and waited.

Rachel shivered in the warm air.

From the other end of the village Chana Haimowitz was shouting to her husband to bring in the bedding. Nearby, Reb Mottel clucked to his children to come to bed. Some young people were humming a waltz as they walked down the road, and from the little prayer house old men were humming the Psalms. The yellow lamps through the windows, the noises and the voices, the long wailing cry of the Carmel jackals, the scents of orange and grape, were the sinews of her life.

"I don't know how I can ever leave here," she said. It wasn't what she wanted to say.

"Of course you will miss your home," he said, trying to make his deep voice light and gentle. It pleased him that she should say so. It meant that she was making a sacrifice for him. "We will come back as often as we can. And don't overlook the advantages of Constantinople. But still, home is home."

She spoke in a whisper. "I am thinking also of other things."

"Beg your pardon? I didn't hear—"

"You know how flattered I was when you asked me to marry you."

He laughed, a man permitting himself the enjoyment of his own virtue.

"I admire and respect you, Nahum."

"Naturally, or you wouldn't have agreed to be my wife."

"I'm deeply troubled."

"By all means, tell me——"

"Honor demands it. Something you must know before more time passes."

"What is it, Rachel?" He sounded frightened.

She saw herself suddenly as a romantic figure, not quite Anna Karenina or Natalie Bolkonsky, but love was painful, and she was now about to sacrifice some part of herself for it.

"Please understand. . . . I know I'm at fault. But my heart tells me. Nahum—" She held her breath and let it go. "I am in love with another man."

Nahum stopped walking, brushed against her arm inadvertently, then moved away quickly.

"I can only beg your forgiveness for not telling you before. But I don't deserve forgiveness. I don't know what I deserve. But I could not marry—I could not—"

He was motionless and silent, his large eyes on her face.

"Scold me. Anything. Please."

She realized suddenly that she was talking Yiddish. It was easier than Hebrew for such a moment.

"The man—" Nahum said hoarsely. "Who is this man?"

"Does it matter?"

"His name?"

"Do I have to tell you?"

He was coldly insistent. "Under the circumstances, I must ask you to tell me everything."

The night whirlpooled around her. "Naftali Brandt."

"Oh, yes. The poet." There was a touch of contempt in his tone. "Does he love you?"

"No."

"I am confused."

The night turned even faster. She wanted him to yell at her. She could have fought back. But his coldness made her feel like a punished child. "He has always considered me troublesome and immature."

"Troublesome? Immature? You are a grown woman!"

"He has known me since I was a child. He thinks I am interested only in Strauss waltzes and French novels."

"In such things he is not interested?"

38

She had loved him; bitterly, he hadn't loved her. What else was there to explain?

"Now, you have decided to tell me. It is very late."

"I'm sorry. I beg you to forgive——"

"Never mind, there is never a good time for such news."

Around her the velvet night fell still, the whirlpool dissolved. Nahum was silent. His white shirt gleamed between the borders of his black German-style jacket. By the stiffness of his body she sensed that he was struggling to keep himself under control. Once he had told her that his only vice was violence of temper.

"This poet—how long do you *think* you've been in love with him?"

"I don't know."

"Does he know you *think* you love him?"

She disliked his way of speaking of it. "I never told him."

"I admire your good manners. It is, of course, unwise for a woman to pursue a man. And unsocial, so to speak. But if you will forgive me this lapse of good taste myself, I do not understand"—he had switched to German and spoke formally—"how you could take seriously a relationship in which you think you love a man who doesn't know that you think in that way of him. Furthermore, what kind of man is he that you could not with all respect for yourself confess to him the burden of a heart? When you started to talk, I was confused. Then I became angry that you should have kept all this from me until now. But I cannot help think that you are perhaps imagining things. Please, I do not intend to be harsh, but I must examine this situation frankly. You are imagining that you love him."

She followed his words closely, her mind feeling its pain unheroically.

"The sum of my impressions is that you could not have loved him if you could not at the same time confess it to him."

"He did know," she cried out in self-defense.

"But I thought— You told me this very minute that he didn't know, that you never confessed it to him."

"I had forgotten——"

"That's scarcely so unimportant——"

"Nahum, please be patient."

"I think I'm being very patient."

"You are. But— Oh, it is not easy. What I meant was that he didn't respond, he didn't take me seriously. Once— Yes, I think it was

39

when we were climbing the Crusader ruins at Atlit. It was two years ago, when he first came back from Paris. I told him then." She stopped.

"Please go on."

"I said I loved him."

"That's all?"

"He laughed."

"A poet without feelings!"

"He asked me a question. 'Who knows what love is?' "

It had always been like that, Naftali's mocking her, rebuffing her with a laugh, a question.

"He talked about love as luxury for a revolutionist. He had notions about Palestine. More than just practical Zionism, building colonies, agriculture. He wanted us to overthrow the sultan."

"Madman. A blind madman!"

Was it that? How could Naftali not read the torment in her face, feel the trembling of her fingers as he grasped them to help her climb the fallen masonry?

"And that was all, Rachel?" Nahum had to satisfy himself that it had been no more than words.

"Later, before I met you—a week before—he brought up the subject and said that despair was poison to love. And he changed the subject."

"Forgive me, Rachel, but I must take advantage of this frankness between us and ask a question that had never entered my mind before. I hesitate. It's embarrassing. I'm not accustomed."

She understood. "The answer is no, Nahum. If he touched me it was as a brother would touch a sister."

"Thank you." He wiped his face of the sudden perspiration.

Without saying anything, they started to walk again. The clucking chickens were quiet. The scent of the night earth grew sharper.

"I am ten years older than you are, Rachel. Excuse me if I say that I have some experience in judging people, perhaps more than you have. I am no poet. Maybe I should say, 'Thank Him Who is our maker.' Perhaps I am not as interesting a man as——"

"Nahum, you are a good man."

"I will finish what I have to say, if you don't object. I am not angry anymore. But I must speak in my own manner. I am perhaps not a romantic figure out of Turgenev or Schiller. When we first met—the very day after Judah introduced us at Jaffa—you yourself said that you desired someday to marry a man who had his feet on the earth and was not a village fiddler, a *Luftmensch*."

40

She had to protest. "Naftali is not a *Luftmensch.*"

"Permit me to continue. In a manner of speaking, I did not think you would find me suitable. Not only my age but—well, because of what I am. A businessman, a Constantinopler. Still, a man with background, with learning, with a good ancestry, a German born. But not a pioneer like Judah or this Brandt. Yet you found me suitable. You said, in your own words, mind you, that I had some of the qualities—forgive this conceit—of your brother, Judah. Very well. I proposed, and you accepted."

"I did gladly, Nahum. You are worthier than I am."

As they walked, she kept her eyes ahead, not wanting to see Nahum's face. She was glad that there were few passersby. From an Arab village on the crest of a nearby hill she heard the sheep. The moonlight had made them restless.

"So I had reason to believe that you wanted to be my wife."

"Yes."

"Now, Rachel, if you tell me this story about the poet with the thought that our marriage should not take place, let me answer you. I have never believed that love is needed for a good marriage. Respect, yes. Common background, yes. But love? Love is quicksilver. A matter of feeling one thing today, another thing tomorrow. It can come and it can go. It's untidy, if you understand me. And it's unstable. If it is only love that makes a marriage, what happens when the love flies out with the teakettle steam?"

He stopped walking and looked into her eyes. The emotion in his deep voice increased her guilt.

"You say you respect me, Rachel dear. And you I respect with all my heart. And with me you'll know where I am and where you are. So—" He reached for her hand, then thought better of it. "The words are the words that you know so well from hearing your father speak them on Sabbath eve to your mother, may she rest in peace, 'Where is there such a woman, her worth to find?'" He paused again and cleared his throat. "I ask you again formally, Rachel. Will you marry me?"

With the sound of a flute from the Arab shepherd on the hill, Naftali entered her mind more painfully than before. He was everywhere, this very path, the same trees and shadows, the silvered Carmel. She must run away or die.

"Rachel?"

The tiny island of Zion could not contain them both. She would have to find her own island.

Defiantly, she said, "If you still want me, Nahum, my answer is yes!"

He kissed her cheek gently.

"You will never hear me talk of this again," she said with fervor.

"I am gratified. I am honored." A note of self-assurance. "It is all clear now between us?"

"It is clear."

She thought that whatever had been obscure in her life before had at last been clarified, the hieroglyphic deciphered. It would not be a large life; it was obvious that she had neither the strength of will nor the courage to reject compromise and risk loneliness. There had been no joy in love and the time for it was past. Now she would strive to fulfill herself as a loyal wife, a good mother. It was not so inferior a fate.

6 ◆◆◆◆◆◆◆◆◆

The wedding took place late afternoon in the courtyard of the experimental station at Atlit, where there was more room than at Har Nehemia. The day, a dream-foyer to a dream, had moved slowly for Rachel. She did not quite remember how she had gotten to her place under the silken canopy alongside Nahum.

She struggled to listen carefully to the flowing words of the prayers; she wanted to hear each sound, to invest herself with the holiness of the binding; she tried to see clearly the red face of old Rabbi Guttman, with its sparse white beard, to read God in his nearsighted eyes behind the spectacles, to sense Nahum at her side, to mark out the smell of the sun on the canopy roof and on the grass, to press the wine against her palate and taste the sweet grape. But despite the dutiful demand to offer herself consciously to this sacred passage, veiled and obscure were prayer and face, smell and touch. Finally she sensed rather than saw a moving light pass in front of her—the symbolic glass, reminder of the fall of the temple, being passed from Papa to Nahum—and she imagined that it was the sword of God cutting her in two. Wanting to cry out in protest, she was stopped by a loud crash. Nahum had completed the ritual. The glass was broken. The wedding was over. "*Mazel tov! Mazel tov!*" The shouts filled her head. Nahum was kissing her. Now they were all embracing her.

Papa, his long thin arms around her, whispered, "Long years and happiness, my little Rachel!" The feel of his beard, as in the old days. She wanted to laugh. Suddenly she felt relieved, as if she had passed a crisis of illness. Then Judah, his eyes no longer aloof. "Let it be for good." Dr. Bloch, who had brought her into life when her mother had given birth in the fields; Miriam Bloch, weeping and giggling; from Hadera, the cousins Liebermann—dark Dmitri with a poem of joy (after Lermontov) bound up like a Torah scroll with a silver ribbon, and Avram, tall, handsome, fair, a farmer and huntsman, a single rose in his hand. Sheik Faris Ben-Yusif, fat, gouty, royal, blessed her in Arabic and spoke softly of the six sheep he had brought as a gift; Dr. Bloch's stout wife from Vienna dressed in clothes she had brought with her thirty years before; the Fishel family; Reb Mottel, his reddish hair sticking out like porcupine quills from beneath a Galician *streimel;* her cousin, the happy Manfred Gersh, with his violin, who seemed to dance in his clothes as he praised and congratulated her; the Singer coachman, Ibn Djavid, tall and respectful. All, all passing before her like pictures in a child's book.

"I will not congratulate the bride," a voice said close to her ear. "She neither requires it, nor am I in a mood to give it to her."

She knew, of course, that Naftali was there, but until the silver sound of his voice she had somehow pretended in her numbness that he no longer existed.

"I must acknowledge that she is beautiful in her mother's dress. *'Herr, es ist Zeit. . . .' "*

His favorite Rilke; she hated him for quoting it. But she smiled, avoided his restless, defiant black eyes, took his light kiss on her cheeks, and moved away to accept the good wishes of Father Gregory, the bearded Greek priest from Haifa, a friend of Judah's. As she was turned from side to side by the embraces of her friends, she saw Naftali walk away alone, his dark hair combed to one side like a French student's, his graceful and strong shoulders erect, the back of his head vulnerable, like a young boy's.

"Weddings make me uneasy. All ceremonies, all rituals . . . They are based on pretense that one's life will change because of them. We Jews live on rituals. The holidays, the Sabbaths, the three-times-a-day prayers. When life is desperate, ritual is the chief means of keeping it going. We think, 'Ah, next day, better; next season, better. Things will change.' "

Naftali was talking to two friends, Mordecai Anuskevitz and Nissim Vidali. Mordecai smoked Russian cigarettes constantly and thought of himself as a soldier of fortune, although he had been born in Naftali's village and had never left the country. But he was warmhearted, bright, and loyal. Naftali cherished him more than anyone else of his friends. The other, Nissim, was a descendant of Spanish Jews who had come to Palestine five hundred years before. He was slim, darkly handsome, and burdened by a frail mind that had attached itself to Naftali as if in its weakness it convinced itself that the passionate Naftali was its only

44

hope for enough equilibrium to manage to survive the complexities of the world.

They were standing near the tree nursery drinking slivovitz.

Nissim, of course, nodded agreement to anything Naftali said. He loved the sound of his voice, certain that the angels sounded the same way.

"When Rachel told me that Nahum proposed—she hadn't accepted yet—I asked her what her idea of marriage was. She replied, 'A new life.' You see what I am talking about. She thinks her life will be different. Nonsense."

Nissim nodded. Mordecai, shifting from foot to foot, lit a new cigarette from the ashes of the old. He was unusually restless and tense.

Naftali continued: "On the surface it will seem different. But where it matters she will not change. She will be happy and unhappy, looking for answers, not knowing what she wants to know, thinking sometimes that her life has meaning, other times that it is meaningless, wasted." He sipped the burning liquor slowly and peered at Mordecai, who was about to speak. "Don't say it, Mordecai. I know. When we describe something else accurately, we are describing ourselves."

"I wasn't going to say that at all. I was going to say that I have often wondered why she didn't marry you."

Naftali rubbed a drop of the slivovitz on his palm to increase the scent. "Rachel, like all Jewish girls, thinks of love only as the prologue to marriage. We are all bourgeois, even when we try to play at being socialists or bohemians. You watch and see what happens when children are born out of wedlock in the socialist colonies. The parents will drive the rabbis crazy to get themselves married. How could I marry anyone? For marriage you need work, money. No. I am fooling you." He took a deep breath of the late-afternoon air with its smells of the summer grain and peach trees. He saw his mother, gray and beautiful, talking with Papa Singer; the noises of the guests shot through the day like firecrackers. Manfred was tuning his violin. He looked for Rachel. She was hidden by people.

"The truth is, I have never been in love. . . ."

"You have made love?"

"Of course he has made love," Nissim said, angry without cause. "Tell him about Paris, Tali."

"He told us all about Paris. You have forgotten," Mordecai said sharply.

"But I want to hear it."

Naftali put his arm around Nissim's thin shoulders to calm him, but said nothing, for he was increasingly troubled that Rachel was going away. After all, they had been friends; he had read all his early poetry to her; they had fired each other with heated talk of books, of God, of Zion; they had read Herzl and Bialik, and Gordon and the others together; on the shores of Atlit and Tantura, on the Carmel hills and Ephraim's, in the fields and winter wadis looking for bird fledgelings to save; they had shared ineffaceable passages of life.

Mordecai drank deeply and began to cough. His body danced with the effort.

Naftali slapped him on the back. "What is it? You are more nervous than the bride."

Mordecai calmed himself; then, after lighting another cigarette, he said abruptly, "I'm going into the army."

"Keep your jokes," Naftali said.

"It's serious. I am already listed. My father wanted to buy me out but I refused. I'm going away tomorrow or the day after."

Naftali studied his friend's excited eyes and the snub nose that seemed to have a humor of its own.

"You're not serious. You are also out of your mind."

"What's the matter?" Nissim asked, feeling Naftali's rising temper.

"The Turkish Army, mercenaries of the most corrupt——"

"Mercenaries get paid better, Tali. We have to show the young Turks that we are responsible citizens. Everybody is for it. The Zionist executive, the rabbis, the——"

"They are washing the body of a corpse."

"It could be different."

"It will never be different. This is a futile state. Not like Europe." Naftali shook his head. "Why did you wait so long to tell me? Didn't you trust me?"

Mordecai grinned broadly. "I trusted you—to try to talk me out of it."

"Please reconsider, Mordecai. As your friend, I beg you."

"I know your views, Tali. I won't even say I disagree. I even thought of running away and joining the British. But I'm a Turkish citizen, not a Britisher. And I won't fight on the side of the Russian anti-Semites. No matter how bad it was here, it was never as bad as the cossacks and the Black Hundreds of the czar's. Besides——" He paused with the nervous shyness of a man who is about to reveal too much of himself. "Besides, Tali, I don't care about the principle of things anymore. I want

46

once before I die to be part of the—part of it all, not to be separated. To be a Turk, not a Jew. If I were a German, I'd want to be in the army, if I were French or English, the same. I want to be part of it! To share everything with everybody. Can you understand? For once not to be with the minority."

Naftali saw how much this admission cost his friend, for it was a surrender of the notion that one must act on principle, forgetting one's private needs, and that living in Palestine was different for a Jew from living in the exile of Europe. But under the sultan Palestine was also the Diaspora.

He understood, and to reassure Mordecai that he did, he threw his arms around his friend. "Bless you, Mordecai!"

"Bless you, Tali!"

For a moment they tightened their embrace to mark with the feel of their bodies the love they had for each other.

"What is this?" Nissim asked, bewildered. "Tell me, Tali. Where is Mordecai going?"

"To the army."

Nissim's eyes filled with tears. "He'll never come back. They'll make a Christian of him!"

"No, no. You're thinking of the Russian Army in the old days."

"Oh . . ."

Manfred Gersh's violin was starting a slow dance. People were raising toasts to the bride and groom.

"What will you do, Tali?" Mordecai asked quietly.

Naftali closed his eyes momentarily to fix more clearly the image of himself. After the day at the station with Mustafa, he had had an inconclusive talk with Judah Singer, who reported on his meeting with the Hashomer. But Judah had nothing positive to propose other than to wait for developments. If his master and teacher had no program, then what was there for him to do?

"What is there left to do? Starve to death. . . ."

"But that's cynicism. Doing nothing. At least, in the army we'll be helping to overturn the czar, free our people in Russia . . ."

Naftali could not restrain himself. "I want to free our people here! Then they'll be free everywhere."

"Ah, yes." The sigh of frustration.

"But don't worry, Mordecai, my dear, nothing will be done here. The rich will protect themselves with baksheesh, the colonies with their few guns against the bandits. Our friend Judah will be quiet and aloof and worry over his grain. And the pious of Jerusalem will praise God for creating the twilight."

"Mordecai rubbed the side of his cheek, puzzled. "It's all waste then. . . ."

Naftali shrugged. He wanted more slivovitz to burn his throat and stomach. "Perhaps we'll be condemned to enough life to keep from dying altogether. Hasn't that always been our fate?"

"At any rate, I'm going into the army."

"You're a fool, Mordecai, but take care of yourself."

"They're dancing!" Nissim cried. "Come, Tali. Make them do a hora!"

Below the lawn, where the wedding guests stood, the Washington palms fell away gently toward the rocky shore, beyond which the even Mediterranean lay like a glassy moat between them and Europe. Huge tables of food and drink were everywhere, and the guests were beginning to enjoy themselves with the good Rothschild wines, the pear and peach brandies, and the vodka. Manfred's violin was singing wedding dances, the handkerchief, the scissors, and the good morning. Later, when everybody had sufficient to drink, there would be a kazatzke and the hora which was shedding its Romanian identity and becoming Palestinian.

Arches of violet streaks supported the skies. The afternoon sun was leaving the tips of the hills of Ephraim for the shores of Greece.

Naftali glanced across the wedding world from which came the sounds of laughter and the talk in French, Arabic, Hebrew, Turkish, Yiddish. It saddened him.

At the other end of the garden stood Rachel, her gleaming white virginal dress reddened by the last rosy sunlight.

Restlessly he touched the bark of a tree.

"Is it your view, Singer Effendi, that our sultan made a mistake in going to war?" Sheik Faris asked Papa Singer. The sheik had helped raise the first walls of Har Nehemia.

"The mind of the Turk is not always clear. How shall one guess what he hopes for?" Papa replied in Arabic.

"There are many unruly children in his house. Are they not like those who await the weakening of an old father to take what flocks and grain they consider rightly to be their own?"

48

"In that case, Sheik Faris, the war will do harm to the sultan, will it not?"

Papa knew the rebelliousness of some of the Arab villages. Only recently, two of Faris' nephews had been beaten for delaying tax payments. One had died, the other was in prison in Damascus.

"Yes, but is he not our master?" the sheik asked, closing his large, bulging eyes as if he were in pain.

Papa sighed and was silent.

The Liebermann cousins from Naftali's village were arguing with each other about the assassination of Franz Ferdinand and whether that single act had truly caused the war.

"Can a madman overcome all by himself the great forces of nations?" Avram demanded. He had read Marx and Engels and was swayed by their views.

"Princip was no madman," Naftali said, a little drunk. He was on the way across the garden. "But a patriot who loved his country."

"For this, shall millions die?" Dmitri, a Tolstoyan, asked.

"Look at us! We deafen God with our talk. And we are soul strangers here in our own land, beggars to a beggar sultan."

His voice became louder.

"Quiet," Dmitri said with a nod toward Judah, who was talking nearby with a Turkish Army colonel.

"Let him hear," Naftali replied, overcome by a wanton need. "What have I to lose?"

Dr. Bloch, the tall handsome socialist from Vienna, came up quickly. "If you want to make a display," he said, "do it on the middle of a road between villages, not in front of the colonel."

Dmitri calmed him down. "The colonel's Hebrew is not good. He probably thinks we are discussing Bialik."

Colonel Sayek, a tall scholarly man from Izmir, had met Judah when Judah was in Washington.

Glancing at the arbors and field, the colonel said, "It is beautiful here, Singer Effendi. But how difficult it must have been to use this grainy, rocky soil."

"I chose Atlit precisely because it seemed impossible. If I could grow things here, why then everything was possible."

"His Excellency Jemal Pasha shares your passion for agriculture. He admires your work in particular."

Judah bowed an acknowledgment.

Father Gregory and Sheik Faris walked by, talking Arabic. The priest held a large orange in his hand and was biting the skin off, the golden juice dribbling down his gray beard.

Colonel Sayek touched the side of his long, thin nose thoughtfully. "You know I have been studying Hebrew."

"It pleases me, sir."

"The grammar is not difficult, but I gather that there are new words being invented daily. It is difficult keeping up one's vocabulary."

Judah nodded. How could he ever persuade Naftali to choose time and place carefully. He would always plant in the wrong season.

"I had the pleasure earlier of meeting that guest of yours. His name is—"

"He is a poet."

"He speaks loudly."

"Like all poets, he feels deeply and in metaphors."

"Unfortunately we do not live in a world of poets. In time of war, poets are by definition an uncomfortable danger."

"Please don't be concerned. He speaks only for himself."

The Turkish officer smiled.

Someone had opened another champagne bottle with a great noise. Everywhere voices said, "*Mazel . . . Mazel . . .*"

Ebria, six years old, the youngest child of Dr. Bloch, came up, saying shyly, "Uncle Judah, will you dance with me?"

"Yes, darling, I will. But I'm talking with a friend."

Colonel Sayek bowed. "By all means, dance with your charming friend. The rest is unimportant. Nevertheless, do warn the poet. How shall I describe it? Say that my conscience, a necessity in times of peace and the first casualty of war, requires it."

"Papa, you look younger than ever," Rachel said. She had already danced with Nahum and the guests and was sipping a glass of fruit juice with her father.

"When children marry, parents become children," he said and stroked her hand with fingers roughened by work in the vineyards. "Remember the Wedding Psalm: 'My heart overfloweth with good things. . . . Thou art fairer than the children of men, Grace is poured from thy lips.' "

"But that was sung at the wedding of Ahab and Jezebel," she said in mock protest.

50

He smiled. "The Targum of the psalm says it is the marriage of the Messiah with Israel. I am permitted my own interpretation. I see it as sung for the marriage of my daughter to the man of her choice."

She felt a keen pang of love for this now lonely, bereft old man. Not once had he led her to think he was sad remembering his dead wife, her mother. She knew, however, that no one day, particularly one so important to him, could be free of her memory.

"Papa, you know how much I wish that Mama had been here."

He nodded and stroked his thin, trim white beard. "But this is no time for lamenting. She is in peace. And we are commanded not to grieve too long. And at the wrong times."

"You never complain, Papa."

He pressed her hand in his. "To complain would be a sacrilege."

She kissed him suddenly. "I love you, Papa."

He shook his head, suddenly made shy.

She would miss him, this man who had that rare quality of *hitbo'de-dut,* a fearlessness and reverence before God and an innocent joy in the company of life.

The moral use of memory, Naftali thought, is to judge not the past but the future, for in that obscured, clouded, infinite vista lies the proof of action. He tried to push his thoughts ahead. Was Mordecai doing the right thing? Was his own resignation an evil? Would he have to wait until the future became the present before he would dare to obey the clarion of his heart and mind?

Judah came over to warn him about Sayek.

"They have not lifted their sword yet," Naftali replied, "and already they want our tongues cut out. By ourselves."

"You have no sense of the proper moment," the older man said.

"What is the key? How does one know?"

"It can't be learned, Tali. It's like pure musical pitch. For your sake and for the sake of your friends, be circumspect."

It wasn't the first time that Judah had touched that misery within him, the dissonance between passion and time that brought so much frustration. For that reason he had relied on Judah's judgments, the older man who had taken him as a disciple, made him his assistant at the station, taught him the joy of the living earth. Naftali had loved his discipleship; he loved even more Judah's knowledge of himself, his appearance of certainty. Up to now he had followed Judah. But for how long could he continue without losing his own soul?

The moral use of memory is to judge the future.

He watched the dancers, their shadows embracing in the candlelight. Jews were too awkward, too masculine to do the Arab dances well. Only the Arab himself was graceful, female, subtle enough.

He linked arms with his mother, quiet, gray, intent on some far sight, and swayed to the music. "I could show them how to dance, couldn't I, Mama?" He had learned this very one from the Mus'aa Arabs with whom he lived in his fourteenth year.

"Did you give a gift to Rachel?" she asked.

"No. I didn't bring any."

"And why not?"

"I forgot. I didn't think of it."

"Is that nice?"

"I didn't have time to think of what's nice." He had stopped swaying. "Can I bring you some wine, Mama?"

She scolded him with her eyes.

"I'll send her something."

His mother touched a small gold watch pinned to her white shirt-waist. "Do you remember this?"

"I brought it back from Paris for you."

She unpinned it. "Give it to her."

"It was my present to you. I wouldn't think of it."

"Give it!" Her firmness surprised him. She had always been a little in awe of him, whose ambitions and tastes she didn't understand.

Rachel and Nahum were dancing alone, a waltz. They danced well, he thought.

"Mama, I won't do it."

"Then I will give it to her in your name."

"I absolutely refuse," he said angrily.

Raising and lowering her hand, she seemed to weigh the tiny watch. Judah had taken Nahum's place. It was getting late. Soon bride and groom would have to leave to get to the train at Merhavia. He wondered where Mordecai had gone. The damned waltz was too sentimental. Manfred Gersh could weep over a broken chair.

"Why do you want to hurt her?" his mother asked. Her wrinkled face was stern.

"I? I don't want to hurt her. We're good friends. She isn't a small soul. She knows what I think. A gift from me is not proof of anything. Would you hate me if I forgot your birthday?"

"Obey me. Give this watch."

"Take it from you—impossible."

"I have another one. Your father gave it to me."

He was surprised. "I never saw it."

"Why should you? I never wore it. Digging out rocks from the fields, chopping wood, milking cows, washing clothes—are those the occasions for wearing a delicate watch? In the old days—" She waved a hand vaguely in the direction of the dark Carmel hills as if the years of her life were out there somewhere, not in her. "When you were a child, we lived by the sun, the Sabbath, the seasons, and the holidays from one Passover to the next. And all the time between was seeding, cultivating, harvesting, rain, drought, bandit raids, a death of a child here and a death of a husband there. For that, who needed a watch?"

It was rare for her to talk of her life with such openness. Rachel's marriage indeed must be important to her, for usually she was reserved and unemotional. Naftali had often wondered whether having once taken that great wild, reckless, impossible leap of hope thirty-four years before, when she broke with her parents in Moscow to go to Palestine as a worker, she no longer had need of feelings. Or retained the strength for them. She never imposed herself on him, not once suggesting he do this or that or become something other than he was. He too, was a fact of her life, like the floods, the *hamsin*, the drought, the deaths. Although he loved her for it, yet at the same time he could not help being resentful of her reserve. Love, he thought, was concern, and concern was the duty to guide, not to leave adrift to their own devices and needs the children of love. He was grateful and respected her, but thought that love was more than compassion and identity.

"When you brought me this from Paris, we were already settled, you were grown up, we could live a little for the hour, between the sunrise and the night. I didn't tell you I had another watch. It wasn't necessary. But I have another one, and this one you can give to Rachel."

She gave him the watch, moist from her hands. He was troubled by it, for he could not remember her ever pleading with him about anything; already the watch had a charisma.

Rachel was dancing with Dr. Bloch, and he went to them.

"Should I not be given a chance to dance with the bride?" he asked.

Rachel was silent in Dr. Bloch's arms. Was there nothing that could save her from this embrace? "It's late," she said at last.

"Not that late, Rachel."

Dr. Bloch hesitated. He knew from his daughter something of Rachel's torment.

53

"I haven't finished my dance yet," he said.

"From him who has to him who needs," Naftali said. The little watch sweated in his hand.

Dr. Bloch looked at Rachel, who shrugged. He gave her to Naftali.

"Just once around," she said faintly, avoiding his eyes.

"The last time I waltzed was in Paris," he said.

She held her breath. He must not see how difficult it was with his arm around her.

"It went too swiftly," he said.

Nahum was talking to Judah and glancing at his heavy gold watch.

"What I mean to say, Rachel, without being sentimental— You and I grew up so quickly. . . ."

"I think Nahum wants me to get ready," she said, proud of how firm her voice was.

"Perhaps I should've danced with you before."

"It is getting late. . . . We are taking the train. . . ."

They were at the darker edge of the lawn, near a palisade of eucalyptus that fenced the new moon. He stopped dancing.

"I brought a gift." He offered the moist watch. "It was my mother's. I had nothing else. That is, I forgot about a gift. I didn't think it was important, but she did." He smiled warmly and apologetically. "I'm not very gracious."

"That doesn't matter. But—I can't take it." She looked at the golden disc that he had placed in her hand.

"My mother insisted. You'll be hurting her feelings, not mine. Take it, it's a very clever watch. It keeps good time." He tried to smile. Something was wrong, like the miss of a heartbeat or the shying of a horse without sign of anything visible.

"Thank your mother for this gift," she said hurriedly. The watch was ticking louder than it should. He studied it in her hand.

His fingers went around hers. "Rachel . . ."

She heard Nahum's heavy stride on the path.

"Rachel, you understand—we're friends." The words were real but wrong. "Perhaps you're disappointed in me. But then, so am I. But don't be less a friend. Talk to me. Say a word. Tell me you'll be happy. Or something stupid like that. Reassure me, even with sentimentality."

Trapped by his eyes, she was silent.

"We have to start soon, Rachel!" It was Nahum, calling in brusque German.

54

Swiftly, without willing himself, Naftali bent over the hand that held the ticking watch and kissed it. Unexpected pain broke inside him like a bone.

"Thank your mother," Rachel managed to say and moved away into the shadowy path leading to the station. Nahum said something inaudible and disappeared.

Naftali's senses ebbed; he felt a drunken loneliness.

When he was fourteen, his father had taken him to the sheik of the Mus'aa tribe and left him there in the old man's care to be taught what he would teach his own son. When his father mounted the big brown horse, saying once more, "Shalom, Naftali," waved and rode away, he wanted to run after him but didn't dare shame himself. He remained without moving, without weeping, feeling the empty stomach of his first loneliness.

Now he felt it again.

He stood in the shadows of the palisade of trees frowning numbly into the darkness as if he were watching his father on the big brown horse descend the long hill from the camp of the Mus'aa sheik.

He saw the lanterns throw splashes of gold on Rachel's white dress as she approached the station building.

There was a miscalculation here.

Behind him someone with an accordion was starting a fast hora.

"Your quotation was wrong, Naftali Brandt." That was Dr. Bloch standing alongside. " 'From each according to his abilities, to each according to his need.' "

Naftali bowed with a brief, bitter grin. "That's exactly what I need at this moment. Thank you."

"Seriously. Are you joining the army like your friends?"

"Neither the army of aggression of the Turk nor the Jewish Hashomer of defense," Naftali replied. "Organize a Jewish Army for independence and I'll be the first to join."

"That'll come, young man."

"So will the Messiah. But who'll be around to make him a cup of tea?"

At the open door of the station Rachel had stopped when she heard the first beat of the hora.

There was a sexual stirring in the blood. Naftali was beyond her reach, and she was jealous of his freedom. Why had she not been wanton when they were alone on the shores of Atlit or Tantura on the

55

flanks of the Carmel hidden from the world? She could have broken his indifference with her body, overcoming his pride and her cowardice.

With the jealousy she felt its corollary, hatred. He had no right to exist without her.

Miriam was at her side. "We have to hurry, Rachel."

A slight nausea made her weak; she took Miriam's arm and went into the station to dress for the honeymoon trip and her new life in Constantinople.

Naftali ran to the dancers like a man pursued, linking arms with them, stamping the earth in tempo, crying out with all his strength, "Galilee! Galilee!" But he could not shout loudly enough. His own dissonances, the crashing ironic anticlimaxes of his life, clanged even more loudly.

BOOK *Two*

1 ◇◇◇◇◇◇◇◇◇

Jemal Pasha's Fourth Army moved into Palestine as if it were enemy country instead of a province of the empire. Martial law was declared. His men took from the people whatever they wanted—work animals, food, homes; they uprooted orchards for firewood, commandeered building materials, machinery, money, even clothing. All imports of food having already been canceled by the war in Europe, hunger grew swiftly in the bereft villages and cities of the November countryside. Searches for arms were made; two men were hanged for possessing old hunting rifles. The few shomrim, members of Hashomer, were open to attack by Hamid Bey's gendarmes as well as the bedouin and Arab bands who swarmed down on the defenseless farms to steal what may have been overlooked by Turkish soldiers.

Zionism became treason. The military governor of Jaffa expelled Ben-Gurion and Ben-Zvi, the leaders of the Jewish workers' movement; anyone seen with a photograph of Herzl was arrested; signs in Hebrew were outlawed; the possession of Hebrew stamps bought for the purchase of community land was an offense punishable by death.

An insane fear of minorities possessed the headquarters of the police and the Fourth Army. It did not stop with the Jews. Three Syrian Christians were hanged in Damascus; two Arab lawyers from the Lebanon were beaten and executed. Arab leaders who dreamed of independence from the Turk drifted across the Jordan to join the waiting tribes of Emir Feisal.

In December of 1914 nine hundred Russian Jews of Jaffa and Tel

Aviv were arrested, put on an Italian ship built to hold no more than two hundred, and ordered back to Russia. The excuse was that they were foreign nationals. Since most of them had left Russia to avoid pogroms and the army, the return meant death.

They were saved by the German advisers to Jemal Pasha under pressure of appeasing the United States. The ship carried the exiles to Egypt instead.

One rarely heard among the Jews these days the golden phrase of consolation, "And this, too, shall pass. . . ." If the starving pious of Jerusalem, selling their clothes to buy an eighth of a pound of bread or lentils, raised their voices to cry, "God has forgotten us," others replied, "He has forgotten us before in the past. If only He will recall the merit of our fathers and award us our death without torture."

It was the time of the bastinado, of prison and hangings, of women taken in hostage for their men; a time of utter despair in which the only hope of the community was that somehow some of their children would survive.

In the only strategy the nature of the ghetto afforded, it was a time of willows that bent before the wind.

2 ◇◇◇◇◇◇◇◇◇

In January, 1915, Manfred Gersh and Mordecai Anuskevitz, who had been in training with the Fourth Army troops first in Safed and then in Beersheba, were arrested for desertion and condemned to die by hanging. Judah Singer and Remenov of Hashomer appealed without success to Baha ed-Din, the military governor of Jaffa. Next they tried to get an audience with Jemal Pasha. The commander of the Fourth Army, preparing his forces for a major offensive against the Suez, was unreachable. As a last resort, Naftali, who as sole support of his mother did not have to serve in the army, volunteered to go to Jerusalem to see an old friend of his father's, Said Ali Pasha, the cousin of the late vizier and a man of great influence.

Naftali dressed formally for the occasion. He wore a white kaffiyeh with an agal of black goat hair and gold around the crown of his head, flowing aba, and red-leather bedouin boots with blue tassels. He looked more like a slim Arab prince than the descendant of ghetto Jews.

Said Ali was past seventy, tired, almost fleshless. Long ago he had lost his greed for life and was therefore incorruptible, except to old age. A stroke had twisted his mouth to one side. In his small office, darkened by wall and window coverings of rugs with Koranic inscriptions, he welcomed Naftali, complimented him on how handsome and strong he had grown, and then inquired for his father, the esteemed Leib Brandt.

When the old man heard that his friend had died two years before, he raised his thin hands to cover his twisted mouth, closed his red-rimmed, lashless eyes, and remained silent for a long time. When finally he opened them, he seemed half asleep and gazed vaguely at Naftali as if he weren't sure who he was.

"Excellency, I have come to beg a gift of you in the name of my dead father. I have two friends, my age, born here, as I was. Their lives are to be taken from them unjustly. . . ."

"I am a very old man."

"A wise and influential one."

Said Ali smiled with pleasure.

Naftali explained carefully. His friends had chosen to enlist in the army rather than buy themselves out, as was their legal right. Just the week before, they and other Jewish soldiers, along with some Armenians, Druse, and Lebanese Christians, had been stripped of their regular uniforms and rifles and were transferred to a labor battalion, where they were beaten, starved, and treated worse than prisoners of war. His friends had left camp one night to appeal to Jemal Pasha for a chance to return to line duty as regulars. They never reached the general. Instead, they were arrested by the gendarmes, tried for desertion, and sentenced to be hanged.

Naftali spoke quietly and with much eloquence to arouse the old man to justice. He searched the Turk's face for some sign of hope. But the eyes were half closed; thin, clawlike fingers trembled along the edges of his chair.

"If Said Ali Pasha, in his generosity and great humanity, would write an order for a stay of execution, could anyone dare oppose it? You will help the innocent in their distress."

The street sounds came distantly through the heavy drapes. The heated air in the room was still.

"One word from you, Excellency—one word to Jemal Pasha . . ."

A long trembling finger ran slyly down the side of the scythelike nose as if there were a bargain in the offing.

"I shall die soon," the cracked voice said.

"Not so. Is not all in the hands of Allah?"

Said Ali nodded. He reached into his pocket and took out a string of black-walnut-wood prayer beads. He dangled them in front of Naftali. "Did you know that we stole these from the Buddhists?"

"Excellency, my friends are in danger. Time is——"

"Time is always fear."

"One sign from you will save two innocent lives!"

"What?"

"I beg you, Excellency. One word from you——"

The old man smiled without humor. His twisted, toothless mouth opened laxly. "But where is there one word for me? Say, Jew, who will speak on my behalf? Answer me! Force and the fear of force is my reading of the day. I have kissed the Kaaba, said the ninety-nine names, but I am a black ant upon the black stone in a moonless black night. You beg me? I have begged Allah, the compassionate, the merciful, for death. But He waits. What did you say your name is? I am an old man and my memory has left me."

"I am Naftali Brandt, the son of your old friend, Leib Brandt of Alona."

Said Ali pressed his hand against his milky eyes, trying to remember. "Forgive me, young friend, the years have shaken me. I lose knowledge of what I am saying and what is being said. But we must be careful. Enver Bey has spies everywhere." He chuckled. "As I said, fear is greater than death. I am close to death, and I fear Enver Bey. Tell me about your father. Is he well? He had a bad malaria."

"Sir, for the sake of heaven, please try to listen carefully."

"I have listened carefully. Tell me about your father."

"He is dead."

"Ah. Fortunate man . . ."

It was hopeless; he could not pass through the old man's senility. Or was he pretending?

"Have I ever told you the story of the banquet?" the Turk asked, suddenly excited. "A long time ago. There was an English lord there. I don't remember which one. In the Yildiz Kiosk. Perhaps the one of your race, Lord Beaconsfield. Someone asked him, in my presence, how does the Ottoman Empire survive? This lordship—he was the guest of honor as I remember it—he took in his hands a goose that had been prepared for eating and threw it into the garden. In the old days dogs used to wait there for refuse. They started to run for it. The dogs for the goose——" He waved a thin arm at Naftali. "Don't interrupt. It isn't polite. Why am I telling you this? Ah, yes. You have come to ask something of me. Well, the dogs never reached the goose. Instead they fought each other. The goose was untouched. 'That's how the Ottoman Empire survives, my lords,' he said. Yes, it was Beaconsfield. At the top of his power. His queen in love with him." He waited. "Do you see my point? Don't fight with the other dogs."

It was an old story. Naftali lost patience. He rose from the settee.

"Will you do nothing to help?" he demanded.

"You are asking too much of an old man."

"Please, sir. Give me your seal on a paper. I will take it to Jemal."

"You are asking an old man to make such a long trip?"

"No! No! Just your seal. You will not need to go. I will go."

"Where?"

"To Jemal to save my friends."

61

"What have they done?"

"They were falsely accused of desertion."

Showing fright, Said Ali looked around the dark room. He put a finger to his gaping mouth. "That's a serious charge, young man. Spies are everywhere." He waved to Naftali to come closer. "They are dead."

"Who is dead?"

"Your friends."

"It is false!"

The old man put a hand inside his jacket. "I have a paper. Where did I put it? All the papers come to me for courtesy's sake. Was it this morning? No, yesterday. Ah, here!"

He took out a folded sheet. Naftali reached for it, but the old man held it away from him.

"It is treason if I give it to you."

"Excellency——"

"All my life I have been faithful to the shadow of God on earth, my sultan and caliph."

"There is no sultan. He is a puppet of Enver's."

"Quiet! I won't show you this paper then." He waved it in front of Naftali as if he were playing a game with a child.

Naftali moved closer, hoping to tear the paper from the old man's hands, but Said Ali sensed the move and put the paper under his thigh.

Should he take it violently? Naftali asked himself. Kill him perhaps? Was this the deed he had marked off for himself? Scarcely. To know that his friends were dead was no deed; it was curiosity. To save them, that would be a deed.

Said Ali straightened in his chair. His eyes lost their vagueness and he spoke with vigor. "Do you know what courage is, young Jew? Ha, I suppose you will say, 'To do God's will.' What, to risk the bastinado and death out of fear of God or for His reward? That's not courage, that's sacred cowardice. You, come closer. I have thought much on these matters. . . . I am an old man. Yet I have troubled myself with it. What have I seen in my lifetime in the haremliks and salamliks of our world, at the Yildiz Kiosk, in Damascus, in the filthy villages along the route to Mecca! Ah . . . What I have seen! Suppose one acts bravely without thinking? Is that any different than a bitch's bite when her young are threatened? Please don't go yet. Listen to me, young man. I will give you the paper, but you owe me something."

"I will listen, Excellency," Naftali said softly.

The old Turk bowed his head and was silent. "Yes, where was I?" he said after a moment. "Courage. Not out of fear or reward, nor like a dog's anger. When I was your age, it was for the sultan, God's shadow on earth. 'Do with me what you will,' I would say. And I fought well. The old wars in Europe. I have lost all my medals but I remember the battles. First, there was——"

"Excellency, give me the paper."

"Ah . . . Then listen to me. To do an act of courage for a sultan, for a woman, for fear of what others will say, for honor? Bah! Or while a child of hashish or a slave of the jihad? When one is not oneself? Are you listening? You are too nervous. Like an unbroken stallion. Pay me for the paper by listening. All those acts of courage are nothing —fidelity, shame, fear, honor, a woman. They are the least, women."

He took the paper in his trembling hands and raised it as if it had the answer to all he had been saying. "Can't you see, young Jew, that courage is—" He coughed and fell back. "I will do something I have wanted to do—I wanted to do—my whole life. Each day when I saw the terror and the cruelty, the blindness . . . I am a cultured man, young Jew, and I did not like what I saw in the haremliks and salamliks of the world. Did I tell you of Lord Beaconsfield?"

"You told me."

The paper was thrust at him. Quickly Naftali read it, his blood in his eyes. It was not a list of anything; it was the famous Cow sura of the Koran: "God! There is no God but He, the living, the Eternal. . . ."

"Are they there, your friends? Did I not betray the sultan to show you the paper?"

Naftali gave the paper back. One has to permit compassion, he thought. "Yes."

"Do you understand? I was saying—the purest courage, don't you see, is infidelity to one's master when he is hateful! As I showed you —treason!"

"You are right, old man! You are right!" Naftali cried wanting to embrace him.

Said Ali wiped his eyes with the backs of his hands. "All my life I lacked—it was my blindness—"

Naftali put his arms around him. "Salaam, friend of my father."

They kissed French style.

"Please give to your father, the honorable Leib Brandt, my blessings," Said Ali said in farewell.

"I will, Excellency. And I am sure he blesses you too," Naftali said softly and left the old man threading the walnut beads through his fingers.

In the building of the Jerusalem Zionist committee in the Old City, Naftali heard the news from Mara Schalet, Remenov's comrade. Manfred had been bastinadoed and sent back into the army; Mordecai had been hanged in Ramleh the night before.

At first the words seemed unreal. But later, as he was riding his horse, Melech, down the Judean hills toward Lydda, there exploded within him the knowledge that he would never see Mordecai again, the warm look, the ready smile, the giver of ideas, the Russian cigarette hanging loosely from his full lips; the loss hit him like a sunstroke. He left the highway and like a madman drove his horse into the wilderness of rocks, shouting curses at the top of his voice until he could hear himself no more. He forgot that he had promised his mother to return directly to Alona to tell her of his visit with Said Ali, he forgot his work with Judah Singer and the station, he forgot his obligation to Mordecai's family to share the mourning with them. He was a senseless husk, blown about the hills, moving without meaning or direction into the sun-scoured deserts across the Jordan and down the bleached ramparts of the Dead Sea up to Penuel, where Jacob had wrested his life from the angel. For a week he shivered in the caves overlooking the valley of Jericho. He did not know why or where he was going; the grief for Mordecai had merged into something vaster and indefinable—a need to be punished, to be burned, to be frozen, to be purged of some great uncleanliness he could neither define nor absolve. "The Lord will not see, neither will the God of Jacob give heed." Those were the only words of the psalmist that made sense.

He lived on fruit and olives and water from bedouin camps that he stole from their wells at night. His clothes, which had been bright and regal for his visit to Said Ali, had become torn from cacti and rock; the beardless face had grown a dark fringe like a mourning band.

When the tears and grief had been burned away and the emptiness of his own waste could no longer be borne, his mind cleared. He was like the sea after a storm, cresting and strong, sure of itself, no longer victim of the wind. He no longer cared about guilt or sin, but only to fill himself with meaning. Anything else was cowardice. Said Ali had given him the definition of his act—treason to an unjust master. There was no hallel like it, no praise of God or man equal to the action he must take. "Not for myself," he thought aloud, "not even in revenge for Mordecai, but for Israel, pure and without blemish."

All the old restless revolutionary hope with which two years before he had returned to his homeland was revived. He would find his way to overthrow the Turk and establish Zion. No matter what Judah might say about the need to find the right time, no matter what the Zionist executive might argue as better strategy and tactic, no matter if he were alone, he would act. So Mattathias and his sons acted, and so Bar Kochba.

He had finished with waste. The dog that had run across the Boulevard Montparnasse would have to find another savior. He had a people to save.

Jemal Pasha and his German advisers ordered the advance against Egypt. Twenty thousand men on camel and on foot crossed the Sinai desert in six days. They had little water and less bread, and after the animals had died of exhaustion, they dragged their huge guns by hand. The attack on the Suez started at dawn; an English warship in the canal was sunk; buildings in Ismailia were set on fire. Jemal sent back a message to the government that he had won a great victory and that in a few days all the English would be driven out of Egypt.

A week later, he was back in Jerusalem explaining that a sandstorm had arisen and that Allah had caused it as a sign to cease the attack and withdraw. He left behind two thousand dead and missing. The English who had dug themselves in at the canal and met the attack with well-sited small-arms crossfire and artillery, if they had known the truth, could have marched into Palestine at will. Instead they remained at the canal and felt themselves fortunate.

Three German captains were shot for insubordination. Five hundred Arabs who had deserted at the first sign of defeat were promised forgiveness if they would return to the ranks. The Arab population blamed the Germans for the defeat, and the Turks suspected the Russian Jews of treason. Jemal swore that he would not attack again until he was better prepared.

3 ❖❖❖❖❖❖❖❖❖

On his way home, tired but exalted, Naftali stopped in the Arab
village of Ein-dor. To the north Mount Tabor rose awkwardly out of
the plains of Jezreel. Sipping the thick sweet coffee in a café, listening
to the talk of some Arabs about Jemal's failure, he felt the serenity
of decision and could have embraced all the humans he saw. Smiling
to himself, he thought of that ancestor, King Saul, who had also come
here before a great battle. But he, Naftali, was no trembling Saul,
bereft of nobility, fallen into the dark irony of soothsayers and witches.

A loud wail of an Arab woman broke his thoughts. In the street in
front of the café a mounted gendarme patrol under the command of a
Syrian lieutenant entered, escorting a dozen or more Arabs tied to one
another by ropes. One of them, a young man with a bandaged hand
from which blood still seeped, cried out that he was too sick to go
into the army.

His mother ran alongside, her loose black gown flaring behind like
dark flames. She pleaded with the lieutenant.

"He is sick, Bimbashi Effendi! Leave him here!"

"It is the law of mobilization, woman."

"In the name of Allah, how shall you use a soldier who cannot fire
a gun?"

"When the sultan calls, it is his duty to obey, even if he were dying."

Older Arab men and women came out of houses to watch. The
bedouin from the café continued to talk quietly. Naftali put down a
metlik to pay for his coffee and left the shade of the café. He stood
against a wall, watching.

The mother tore the bloody bandage from her son's hand. Two fingers were missing, including the trigger finger. Blood trickled to the
dry earth. "Gaze on this, Bimbashi! It is still bleeding." She ran in
front of the officer's horse. The son tried to go after her but a gendarme
yanked him back in line by the rope around his waist.

The lieutenant reined in his horse. "He shot off his fingers when he heard we were coming," he said.

"It was an accident, effendi. I swear by Allah!"

"We will teach him how to shoot with another finger."

"He is a child. It was an accident. Allah curse me if I deceive you."

The officer lost his temper and shouted, "Woman, why do you shame yourself and your son in the sight of the infidel?"

Naftali looked around. He saw three caftaned and bearded Jews in a carriage that had just driven into the village.

"The Jews laugh at your weakness," the officer cried out oratorically.

"Death to the infidel!" the woman wailed and spat at the Jews, thinking it would help her.

The men in the carriage were silent, pretending nothing had happened.

Indignant as much by the silence of the Jews as by the officer, Naftali called out, "How dare you speak of infidels? Are you a Muslim army in a jihad or a Turkish Army?"

The gendarmes and the recruits stopped moving and talking. In the silence only the stamping of the horses and the buzzing of flies were audible. One of the Jews whispered in Russian, "Fool!"

"Your name and village?" the officer shouted, dancing his horse toward Naftali.

"Brandt of Alona."

The officer was surprised; he studied Naftali. "Why does a Jew dress as an Arab?"

"Why does a Turkish officer act like a cossack?"

The Syrian raised his malacca whip to hit Naftali. At the same moment the mutilated Arab lad took advantage of the diversion, slipped through the rope around his waist, and ran toward one of the houses. The gendarmes shouted at him. The officer turned to see what was happening, wheeled his horse to cut off the fugitive, and slashing the lad, drove him back into line. He shouted an order to tie the rope around his neck.

The mother screamed for help, scooping up handfuls of dirt with drops of her son's blood, raising them to the officer as if they were jewels to bribe him. He ignored her, stared at Naftali, then ordered the patrol out of the village. The mother ran alongside her weeping son, holding his bleeding hand in hers until she fell with exhaustion. The patrol disappeared around one of the rounded hills that mark Ephraim.

67

One of the men in the carriage called out to Naftali in Yiddish, "If death is so sweet to you, youngster, we have something for your blood." He waved a paper in the air. "It is not a recipe for tzimmes." Naftali mounted Melech, wheeled around, and picked the paper out of the man's hand. It was an order for a jihad, in Arabic, signed by mullahs from Constantinople and Damascus:

A Holy War against the infidel is a righteous War. Kill them wherever you find them. Kill them with whatever is at hand. If they beg to live, close the door of mercy. The cup of the Faithful is filled to the brim. The time has come to end our suffering.

"Where did you get this?" Naftali asked in Hebrew.

The man replied in Yiddish, "They are all over the Arab villages. This was thrown into our yeshiva in Tiberias. To warn us. Like the butcher warning the cow."

"What will you do about it?"

"Rabbi," one of the other men said, "don't answer him."

The rabbi fingered his graying beard thoughtfully and rocked back and forth in his carriage seat. Finally he spoke in a singsong scholar's chant. "So, when the shadow of the Angel of Death flies over the children of the land, what is there to do? First we will say the Confession Before Death. Then we will remember what Yohanan Ben-Zakkai did. When the Romans, a cholera on them, took our city and burned our temple, Yohanan went before the Emperor Vespasian"—he spat wrathfully over the side of the carriage—"and begged him for a very small thing, to a Roman, a nothing. Not to touch the school of scholars at Yavneh. The Name entered Vespasian's mind and he agreed. So with those scholars Israel lived for two thousand years. And where are the Romans? In the earth! You, beardless goy, you ask me in your ignorance what we will do? Like our forefathers we will do. Obey the laws of Torah. Study, teach, read the Psalms. . . . The Holy One, blessed be He, will watch over us. What else is there?"

Serenely he touched the edges of his beard as if the golden letters of the holy tongue were hanging from it and added, gazing up at Naftali with compassion, "And you, you want to be with the Romans, dead? Is that how Israel will live, with atheists like you, Zionists, secularists, using our holy language to speak the dirt of life instead of praising the Holy One? Because of such ignorance you want to throw yourself on the enemy? Don't you know there are only two reasons to fight the government—to avoid idol worship and to defend the unity of the One. Don't be a dead hero. Jews are commanded to live."

"Jews are commanded to be menschen," Naftali replied hotly.

"It is to live by Torah that makes menschen!"

Naftali knew from experience the futility of discussion with the pious and he did not intend to continue. Further, the old man had a truth that could not be avoided. The pious had indeed kept Israel alive for the last two thousand years. Their persistence in the commandments and the narrowness of their dogma had been a shield against the dissolution of the Jewish people. But that was the past. The future, he believed, would not be in their hands, but in those of Jews like himself, whose God lived in the redemption of their homeless nation.

"He has a fanatic's face, that one," the rabbi said to his friends as Naftali rode off. "The shadow of the angel of death follows his horse like the dust rising behind it."

"Rabbi, did not our Rabbi Akiba fight on the side of Bar Kochba?" ventured a younger man with a pocked skin and thin, restless face. "And when he, may peace be his, was captured and died from the torture, did not his soul sit on the right side of the Holiness?"

"That much of a wise man I am not," the rabbi muttered. "But *this* much of a wise man I am. When Akiba, peace be his, died, did not the darkness in Israel's long night of exile deepen? For another thousand years; not until the Rambam appeared was there a morning light."

The younger man nodded. "Is it your meaning, rabbi, that Rabbi Akiba, may his rest be in peace, sinned?"

"That much of a judge I am not."

"Then what is the Almighty's meaning?"

The rabbi swept a hand under his beard to stroke it upward. Angrily he said, "One must not ask the Almighty questions like a police-court judge to a criminal."

"Still . . ." The word was spoken with the faintest protest.

"Sha!" It was a command.

The younger man fell silent.

"Oy, oy," the third man keened. "Death is like a bone in that Zionist's throat. Impatient like a colt, will he wait until the Messiah comes to free us? No. He will sin by wanting to do it by himself. So the bone will stick and oy, oy, will it choke him!"

The rabbi gave a signal to the driver to move on and began to recite a passage from the Talmud concerning the leasing of a house in the rainy season. The discussion was finished.

69

•   •   •

On the way back to his own village Naftali saw the signs of Jemal
Pasha's defeated army—the dying camels, the broken lorries, army
scavengers looting villages for food and killing anyone who resisted
them. He thought: If only the British at the Suez could see what he
was seeing. The corrupted Turkish Army in Palestine was defenseless,
hungry, disorganized, even mutinous.

4 ◇◇◇◇◇◇◇◇◇

Toward evening Naftali returned to his settlement of Alona on the plain of Sharon, southeast of Har Nehemia. Like that other village, it had been founded by independent farmers, Russians instead of Romanians, however, and although it too had received help from the Zionist baron, it never became prosperous. It still had the impoverished smell of a Russian Jewish townlet. The Brandt family was among the poorest in the village.

His mother welcomed him quietly and brought him tea and bread. As usual she asked no questions about where he had been or why his clothes were torn.

"Gendarmes came into the village four days ago, a day after you left," she told him. "Hamid Bek himself was in command. He ordered Yanowitz, the *muhktar*, and the village committee to turn over the arms. It was a bad hour. We were all there in front of Yanowitz's house. Avram and Dmitri Liebermann and their parents. The whole village. Yanowitz said they had no arms. Hamid Bek ordered Avram and Dmitri and the young sons of Yanowitz and Yovalsky to be bound up in front of us and they were given the bastinado. We had to look on. They wouldn't let the mothers hide. Or the young children."

Naftali began to tremble. His mother's calmness was more terrible than hysteria.

"Still, no one said anything about the arms. If we had any hidden, I didn't know. But the boys and the men said nothing, even as the blood spurted from the soles of their feet. Not even the mothers cried. Only the little children."

A brief sigh forced its way past her dry lips. The candle on the table at which they sat flickered gently. Outside the common night noises of the village seemed unreal.

"When Hamid Bek saw he was not getting anything from his victims—half of them had fainted before the twentieth stroke—he took out his pistol and held it at Yanowitz's heart. He ordered him to give up the arms or he would kill him."

She rubbed her hands together as if they were cold.

"You know, Tali, that Yanowitz already has had a heart disease, and we thought he would die without being shot. His wife screamed. 'Talk, Yanowitz! Talk! Tell them!' She was the first grown-up to break the silence. Who could blame her? But Yanowitz said nothing. Then his wife took her gold wedding ring off and gave it to Hamid Bek to save the life of Yanowitz. Hamid Bek tossed it to one of the Arabs who were watching. There were many of them who came down to watch. We had trouble with them over the stolen cows, remember?"

Naftali made no reply. He was Yanowitz with the pistol at his heart; the two were one; he was counting the minutes of life. That would not have been a bad way to die.

"Yanowitz said nothing to Hamid Bek but to us he recited the *Shema*. The women began to weep. What was bad was the crying of the children. They wanted to attack Hamid Bek, but the mothers and sisters held them back."

She stopped rubbing her hands together and touched her broad forehead beneath the graying hair as if there was something to wipe away. He suddenly became aware of the knots of flesh at the joints of her fingers. She has rheumatism, he thought, and she has never complained.

"You know how Yanowitz also suffers from overweight. And he puffs all the time. But like a King David he looked. Noble. After five minutes Hamid Bek put the revolver away and said that Yanowitz wasn't worth killing. But he wanted our arms. If he didn't get them in an hour, he would take with him all unmarried young women. That was too much for the men. Yanowitz walked to Shlomo's blacksmith shop. Shlomo said, 'Where are you going, Yanowitz?' But Yanowitz went to the door of the hut without answering. Shlomo called out again, 'What are you doing, Yanowitz?' And Yanowitz turned to Shlomo and said, 'Not for the desecration of the Holy Name would I do this.' You know how Yanowitz sometimes thinks he is still an actor in Kiev, and his voice was deep and loud. 'Not for the desecration of the Holy Name would I do this, Shlomo, but to save the virgins of Israel. Come, help me dig up the arms.'"

She told how no one moved at first, but then the fathers of the girls went into the hut and soon it was all over. Hamid Bek's men kept some of the arms but others they gave to the Arabs of Sierja. Naftali's own revolver too. The Smith and Wesson he had been given as a gift by a British friend.

"When Hamid Bek left the village, Yanowitz went to his wife. Everybody was watching. And there in front of our eyes he slapped her face and said, 'That is for your advice. Next time don't advise me to betray my friends.' Then he kissed her. 'And that,' he said, 'is for the wedding ring.' "

Naftali was angry suddenly. Why didn't his mother weep?

As if to punish her, he said without introduction, "Mordecai Anuskevitz is dead. They hanged him for desertion."

She unlocked her fingers and lowered them to the table. The candle-light throwing tufts of shadows accented the fleshy joints. He hated age; he hated the rasp of time.

He had never known her to weep, not when she buried his brother, his father, nor even when she was in great pain at the time she had torn part of her arm as an ax she was wielding slipped. The infrequent sighs passing her mouth were the involuntary speech of her body. But now he wanted her to be as angry as he was. Her reserve, her control, seemed sinful; worse, they seemed unreal. They deprived him of his connections with the living and the dead.

"Tomorrow I will have to leave again," he said abruptly.

"Yes?"

"We can't go on like this. They eat us up."

She ran her fingers across the wooden table as if smoothing out its grain. They sat like this a long time. The bitter, sugarless tea in front of them became cold.

"I heard that Miriam Bloch received a letter from Rachel," she said.

He had been watching her hands; now his eyes darted to hers.

"Dmitri Liebermann stopped by this afternoon on his way to Haifa to ask if I needed anything. He told me."

He leaned his head to one side and shrugged. A large fly descended to the rim of his cup.

"Dmitri said the letter was filled with questions about what our life here has become."

The fly, much too large for so early in the year, continued its rounds.

"She asked Miriam to tell her the truth."

Impatiently he rose from the table; the fly left the cup at his movement.

"I may be gone for another week, Mama. Do you have enough food?"

"Enough. The Yanowitz family and the Liebermanns are good to me. They help with the garden and give me a quarter of the produce. The cabbages will come in early. Our eggs I give to their children. When Passover comes—" She leaned her head to one side the way her son did. "We will see. . . . The American consul told Avram that some food will be sent from abroad. Mr. Morgenthau, the ambassador to the sultan, being a Jew will help. . . ."

He went to the window. A faint silver smear of moon behind the clouds. Alona lay unarmed and vulnerable. The sound of the chickens, the field mice, the wisp of a breeze through the tops of the eucalyptus, held menace. There was a light in the Liebermann house. Dmitri probably writing in his diary like some backwoods Tolstoy. Avram's little house, next to it, was dark. A child cried—the Yanowitz infant. The silver from the sky fell on the rock-strewn street. They had taken the rocks from the fields in the old days. Later there would be time to take them out of the street. His father had founded this village twenty-five years ago.

"Why should Rachel be burdened by the truth?" he said. "If things are easy in Constantinople, let her live there in peace."

Awakening to the sounds of a barking dog and a distant knocking, a dream receded—a dream about Paris, the Café Flore—he had felt joy of some kind and tried to hold the vanishing images: Café Flore . . . the girls . . . Rachel . . .

The knocking was louder; the sound of horses. A man's voice calling out in Arabic, "Where is his house?"

At the window, he saw a light in Avram's house as well as in Dmitri's. How long had he slept? There were many lights and people's voices. Someone, not a friend, said, "The one near the Jew trees, that is the house." By the time he dressed they were knocking on his door, and he saw the Syrian officer.

5 ◇◇◇◇◇◇◇◇◇

Rachel remembered that Naftali had once said, perhaps quoting one of his French friends, "Marriage is a contract between devils who were angels while single. . . ." It was a bad joke, ungallant and antiromantic, a pose in order to discourage her from thinking too seriously about themselves. But now in Constantinople several months after her marriage, she was willing to concede some truth to the jest. During their honeymoon trip Nahum behaved as she had anticipated, with consideration, gentleness, and an ordered way of doing things that she found rather pleasantly reminiscent of Judah. It was a relief to be with a man who planned things well. Even their first night together, her timidity at the sacred event of love, was helped by his behavior. He left her alone until she was ready and joined her in bed with the calmness of a man who either had vast experience (which she did not believe) or had studied the act of love with such care and thoroughness that no gesture was unplanned, no contingency unprepared for. His attitude was reassuring. The confusion of an inexperienced woman's first act of love did not seem strange to her. Sexual pleasure as a thing in itself was a remote notion talked about by the French novelists or the Russian anarchists. Her romantic impulse went beyond it, as if the body's life, unperceived by the rational mind, followed its own laws; the mind could satisfy itself by concepts of duty and the sacrament of marriage. Yet she was too filled with Jewish spirit to consider the body as degrading. With natural womanliness she tried to overcome its inhibitions, although Nahum's deliberate behavior in bed did not help her. She could not suppress her excitement—she was not at all passive—and she did not blame either of them for the absence of pleasure.

Her first disappointment came when she saw the house Nahum lived in. It was on a narrow, dark, furtive, ghetto street near the Bosporus, smelling of fish markets and noisy with the noises of a thousand people living on each other. The contrast with the open fields and skies of

Har Nehemia was painful. The defensive, inbred suspiciousness of her neighbors was far different from the independent spirit of her family and the Jews she knew at home. In Palestine she had been one of a people; here she was soon to learn that she was part of a cult.

The inside of Nahum's home was filled with tasteless German furniture that he had bought secondhand. Here and there a dark wood Turkish chair or table from the bazaar did not lighten the atmosphere. Nor did his requesting her, on their arrival, not to open the curtains or shutters; he said it was not seemly that the interior of a home be seen by passersby. When, the day after they arrived, he found her on the balcony, he reminded her that it wasn't the custom for a woman to show herself and he begged her not to do it again.

Nahum demanded that each meal be served exactly on time, the *karvalto* at eleven and the *yemek* at sunset; that three afternoons a week at four she receive his relations and the other two afternoons call on his mother at precisely three-thirty. She accepted these mandates. But it wasn't until she added up certain small decisions of her husband's that she discovered with dismay the one thing she could not have foreseen, had not indeed even imagined—Nahum was a miser!

Dutifully she listened to his protests that she was buying too much food. "To spoil food is a greater sin than avarice," he told her. Or, "I do not like guests. There is no end of going back and forth. They invite us, we invite them. It is a costly and questionable pleasure. Besides, it means we have to stay up late, and I cannot work well the next day unless I have my full sleep." Or, "There is no need to go to the theater. Haven't we enough books to amuse you?" He refused to use the money that had been given them as a wedding gift to buy one of the new talking machines. "It is a fashion that will destroy real conversation and music. A waste of the gift, that will be better used in my business." The player piano he had in the house was broken, but he kept putting off getting it repaired, until she stopped asking. She knew he had enough money; it was simply that he wanted to avoid spending any.

Saddened by the revelation of her husband's weakness, nevertheless she fulfilled all the conditions he put forth except one. She would not polish his shoes every night before going to bed to save him the few metliks it would cost in the street.

After a while she discovered that even worse than his niggardliness was his jealousy. He was even annoyed at her if she went out for a walk during his absence.

76

"It is the custom for a wife to ask permission of her husband before leaving the house," he explained patiently.

"But we are not Muslims!" she protested.

They were together in a small cold salon where she served him coffee in the evening. A tiny brazier did not give enough heat.

"We live among them," he replied stubbornly. "We must not be different. If you are seen alone in the streets by people I do business with, it casts doubt on my position as well as yours."

"I do not wear a yashmak. Or do you expect me to hide my face too?"

"On that score, the Young Turks have created a more liberal atmosphere, my dear. Besides, the yashmak is more religious than national. Enver Bey is opposed to it, you know."

She stared at the burning coals in the brazier, where, it seemed to her, life itself was being consumed. "I hate to oppose you," she said after a long silence. "But I will not ask your permission every time I go out for a walk."

He brushed his beard irritably. "I do not have a slave to guard the harem, so I must be content with your decision. But I ask you to think of my position."

"I will never endanger it."

"Yet two days ago you were seen walking with a young man across from the Yildiz Kiosk."

"I told you about him. Abba Nierman from Zichron Yaacov."

"So you told me."

"What more is there?"

"Why did you have to go to the school where he studies to meet him?"

"I received a letter from home saying that Abba would be there. I longed to see a friend's face. To talk about what's happening. Besides, he is only sixteen."

A defensiveness entered her voice, and it troubled her.

"Did you ask him about Naftali?"

She had yearned to talk with the young man about Naftali, but had not even mentioned him. "I did not. I told you that I would never say his name again. What more do you want?"

Nahum saw that he had gone too far and apologized. Next day he brought her a gift, tickets for a performance of a Viennese opera at the Jardin de Petit Champs. They even took a carriage to the theater. The silvered shafts of the sultan's mosque against the moonlit, clouded sky reminded her again of how beautiful Constantine's fortress city could be. She loved the slow-moving ferries that crossed the Bosporus carrying chains of yellow lights from one shore to the other, and wherever one looked were ships from the outer reaches of the world. She loved the ships and didn't mind when their sad whistles interrupted the arias.

When they returned home—a fog had come up and they were delayed—Nahum prepared himself for love by taking out his special blue-silk bathrobe when they entered the bedroom. It was his way of giving her notice of what was to come. She lay in the bed wondering about the duties of a wife, hoping that she would not become pregnant. He entered from the washing room, the blue robe tightly belted against his stocky body. A faint musk smell of the perfume he had just put on his hair reached her. From the Bosporus the ships warned each other in the fog. Slowly he made the rounds of the windows to check the inner locks. He hummed something from the opera. Then he lit a small candle and brought it to the marble-topped commode near the bed. He smiled at Rachel and turned off the single electric light. As she expected, he paused at the large walnut closet to see that his pants were hung correctly, took a key from under a box, locked the closet, put the key carefully inside an old painted seashell. She thought: Now he will open with another key the bottom drawer of the commode, take out the small bottle of prune brandy and two tiny glasses, pour out a little for me and a little more for himself.

He did as she expected, lifted his glass and said, *"Le chaï'yim."*

She tried to smile.

He drank the liquor, waited for her to sip hers.

He took both their glasses, lifted them high to catch the last drops on his tongue. Carefully he walked into the bathroom and washed the glasses.

Rachel thought: He will bring them back and say, "Am I not a good housekeeper?"

After a moment he reentered and held the tiny glistening glasses in front of him. "Eh, Rachel, am I not a good housekeeper?"

He put the glasses and bottle away, locked the drawer, hid the keys beneath his pillow, blew out the candle, stood at her side of the bed, and took off his blue silk robe.

She accepted him dutifully (was there any more to it?) and felt sadly her own inadequacy. Then, suddenly, without her willing it, Naftali's face bloomed in her mind and breached her resistance to memory. She surrendered and clamped a hand over her mouth to keep

78

from saying his name out loud. She felt anger and longing, guilt and the presence of sin at this irrepressible adultery.

A ship's whistle, hopeless and lonely, broke the room's silence.

For a moment she had a wild, irrational impulse to leave the bed and tell Nahum that she had betrayed him. There had to be some ideal of purity a human being could live by, some ineradicable and unwavering honesty.

"*Le chaï'yim*, my dear," he said. It was his signal that he was going to leave the bed. She was released from his heavy body. (Oh, Naftali . . . Naftali . . .) Then she began to laugh at the absurdity of Nahum's signals. And she could not stop laughing.

"What is it?" he asked.

She shivered and laughed.

"Are you well?" he asked, and that seemed even funnier. She tried to say something, but she laughed.

He had his slippers and robe on. "Shall I get you a blanket?"

"Yes, yes." Anything to get him away from her. The laughter rippled up and down her body in cold waves. She was laughing at Nahum, at herself, at Naftali and the sacraments of marriage. God must have a sense of humor, she thought. She yearned for Har Nehemia; she saw Naftali on the balcony of the station waving to her, behind him the lucid Palestine sky; she saw him climbing the ruins of the tower of Atlit, fiery in the morning sun; working the grain, the young palms.

The laughter ended. There was nothing in life, she was thinking, as important as love. Nothing. Nothing.

Nahum brought her a blanket, said his night prayers, and went into the bed on his side. Before she fell asleep she tried to relive her last talk with Nahum before the wedding, when she might have changed their lives. If only she had had the will, the courage; if she had had any character at all!

The winter in Constantinople was a bad one. Snow fell daily and the smoke of the ships lay like a low fog on the gray Bosporus, the white cups of the mosques and the minarets nearby. The streets were crusted with ice and dirt, and Rachel stayed at home. But even the smallest room of her house wasn't warm enough. She tried to keep her mind on sewing and reading but she missed more painfully than ever the clean, swift rains of the Palestine winter and the ever-present promise of its spring.

She had managed to find a way of living with Nahum, unmarked by argument but scarcely satisfactory. She did what her husband demanded without opposition, and he, in his turn, was more considerate. Because of the bad weather he did not insist that she pay as many calls on his mother and aunts.

In January she received a letter in Hebrew from her father, brought by a traveler:

> My dearly beloved daughter, I have not written you for some time and I beg your forgiveness. If the commandment to honor one's father and mother is worthy of obedience, then it is also necessary for parents to honor their children. But you must ask yourself why I have not written for so long a time and then suddenly write? The truth is that I turned my thoughts away from writing you because neither could I tell you the truth of what is happening among us nor could I deceive you. I know that your brother, Judah, does not write the truth for fear of distressing you. Yet I, at last, write because I honor you.
>
> How shall I begin? Things are bad for all mankind, as always in war, but the Jews, who are also part of mankind, feel the evil the worst. We share their hunger and uncertainties, but we know that we will not be permitted to be like all the others! "Because the Holy One loved Israel He multiplied sufferings for him." And in the Mishnah it says, "Three precious gifts did the Holy One, blessed be He, bestow upon Israel, and all of them He gave only through the medium of suffering: they are Torah, the land of Israel, and the World to Come."
>
> Many of our people have been sent into the wilderness. All organizations are prohibited. Our few rifles and ammunition have been taken from us by the kaimakam of Jaffa and his cohort in evil, Hamid Bek. Jemal Pasha knows what they do and he must share their sins, for without these defenses our fields and our village have been open to thieves. Dr. Bloch was shot at, but thank God escaped injury. So far nothing has come to harm our family, and we hold ourselves up with dignity.
>
> But the worst news of all—and this part I tremble to write but I am not one of those who fear to carry bad news. I am not an old woman who is superstitious and I trust you, my daughter, to hear what I say with courage. Our family has always faced our days that God has given us. Our friend Mordecai Anuskevitz is dead from hanging by the hands of the wicked one. And our friend Naftali Brandt has been arrested, but we do not know where he is. Your brother, Judah, and other friends are trying to find him. . . .

Naftali! Sudden tears burned her eyes. Her breath strained as if she had a noose around her neck. Poor Mordecai! Naftali!

A wild grief overcame her. She must go home. Constantinople was betrayal. They needed her at home. That was the motive behind Papa's letter, no matter how he avoided saying so, no matter what excuses he made for breaking the news.

She read the rest of the letter. But Papa's energy seemed to have faded after the bad news. There was little more than the priestly blessings.

She must not wait another day. She ran into her bedroom to pack a small valise. A dress, underclothes, scarves, handkerchiefs, one pair of shoes, her small jewel case with Naftali's watch, a small pearl brooch that had been her mother's.

"What is happening? Where are you going?"

Nahum had entered. She had forgotten him.

"I've received terrible news from home. They need me."

"Is Papa sick?"

"No, thank God. The family is well. But there is hunger there. They are in great danger. Some of our people have been hanged and imprisoned. Papa himself wrote me."

"I have heard nothing here about such things."

"Who would dare print it in the Turkish newspapers? But you know what travelers have reported."

"Jews have a tendency to hysteria, my dear." He stood near the open valise. "Why are you packing?"

"I must go home, Nahum."

"This is your home."

"To Har Nehemia. To be with Papa."

He saw the open letter on the bed, where she had dropped it, but said nothing. "I couldn't think of permitting you to go. If they need food and money at Har Nehemia, I'll send some immediately."

"Come with me."

"You know that I am doing work for the government. I cannot get up and take my leave. Perhaps when summer comes, although—"

"Nahum, even without you I must go."

"To cross the Taurus in wartime and during the winter would be suicide. You must wait."

Recklessly she said, "I will not wait. I will leave tomorrow!"

"If that is the letter that has raised you to such a madness, may I read it?"

Without waiting for her reply he took it from the bed. She watched his face, certain that he would have to agree when he read Papa's description of the evil times.

"Naftali, eh?" It was an accusation.

She was surprised. "No!"

"Your father does not ask your return. But he does mention that Naftali is in prison. That's why you want to leave."

"I want only to help my family," she said stubbornly.

"I need you too." He fought against his rising temper. "You're my wife and I do not want you to leave."

"I swear to you I'll come back. You have no reason to be jealous. I know how to behave as your wife."

"Rachel, don't drive me——"

"Please, Nahum, I am very unhappy. Let me go for a month. Just a month."

"Unhappy! How dare you? You hear that your beloved is in danger and suddenly you are unhappy. How dare you? And what is worse, you use your old father's complaints to hide behind. Unforgivable!"

"It is not true!"

"God in heaven, I'm no fool!"

"I will die if I'm not there," she pleaded.

"If you leave for Palestine without my permission I will divorce you."

He crumpled the letter in his hand and threw it on the bed. Then he walked to the door, drunken with anger, bumping against a chair, shouldering the open mirrored door of a commode. In the swinging mirror his reflection advanced and receded and disappeared. She sat at the edge of the bed, running her hand senselessly over the woolen coverlet. Nahum was right. The cry to return was for Naftali. She sat silently for hours, then slowly unpacked the valise and put away the jewel box.

For the next several days, shivering in her cold room, she fought against the image of Naftali drowning in the hangman's rope. The gray snow strands outside silently wove his burial sheet. On the third day Nahum, who had gone on a business trip to Smyrna, returned and knocked on the door of her sitting room.

He had a cold and was pale and uneasy. He asked if she had heard any further news of Har Nehemia. There had been none.

"I did not see your mother while you were away," she said.

He nodded, as if he had known it. "I have also heard reports that the days are heavy on the Jews in Palestine. The people around Jemal and the police are fearful of a Zionist uprising." He stopped to blow his nose. "No amount of promises the Zionists make reassures them. Our government doesn't even know itself. Here we Jews are trusted. In Palestine they are distrusted. It is not anti-Semitism, but—you know how things are—" He raised his hands in a gesture of helplessness. He was silent, then began again. "So, Rachel, I admit I was unjust. . . . accusing you— I withdraw what I said. I apologize. I am ashamed of threatening you. Your family may need you—" He stopped himself and lifted a warning finger. "I am still fearful of such a trip in wartime and in the winter, but—Rachel, you decide. If you want to go, I will help you as much as I can to make your travel easier."

He wanted to talk more, to fill up the emptiness he was feeling, but his sense of the appropriate—the basis of the conservative character—forced him to stop.

It had been painful for him; he was suffering; she could see that in his face.

"Nahum . . . I thank you—"

He shrugged. "Excuse me," he said and wiped his nose with a handkerchief.

"I must also say—" It was difficult but she had his example before her. "You were not entirely wrong."

"So?"

"You understand?"

"So—how could you help yourself? You thought of your family and you thought of your friends. You are no monster, without feelings."

She smiled, her blue eyes suddenly lively. She almost loved him at that moment. "You are also not without feelings, Nahum. And you will not have cause to wonder about me."

He sneezed into his handkerchief, excused himself, sighed, and said, "There is a train tomorrow. An army train, but I can get you a place. It goes as far as Angora, and there you will have to take a diligence across the mountains to Konya. From there it should be not difficult to get to Aleppo. . . . I will give you enough money. . . ."

She left the back of the chair where she had been standing and went to kiss him.

But he pushed her away roughly. "You will catch my cold," he said. "This is no time for that."

6 ◇◇◇◇◇◇◇◇◇

The gendarmerie nearest to Alona was at Caesarea, an hour away. The Arab fishing village had lost all signs of Roman greatness, its harbor fallen into the sea or masked by the greedy sands. A few solitary stone columns, bereft of grandeur, kept a now innocent vigil. Several houses had been built over the ruins, using part of the walls. There were two Turkish-style mansions erected more recently by a businessman from Tyre, but for what purpose no one knew, since he was never seen there.

They put Naftali in a stone dungeon, one wall of which was part of a half-forgotten Roman ruin. He was kept there for twenty-four hours without food or water. Outside it rained, and inside it was wet and cold. He knew that they had isolated him to prevent anyone from knowing where he had been taken. At home his people would be making inquiries at the different gendarme stations—that alone would take days—and only a huge amount of baksheesh would buy news. He hoped that his mother would go to Judah Singer first.

During the first day he felt a recurrent anger at himself. It didn't matter that he might die soon; it was the irony that the revolution that was to be his would be lost before it had begun. His light would vanish before it was lit. A waste . . . Why had he not killed the Syrian officer instead of permitting himself to be taken prisoner? An Isaac passively being taken to slaughter.

On the evening of the second day he was taken from his cell and marched under heavy police guard to an adjoining house. He was led to a large room lit by two crystal chandeliers and furnished richly in Turkish style. Coal stoves gave good heat. Thick rugs curtained the windows. No one was there except his guards. At one end of the room stood a black-walnut desk, and in front of it was a small table with a chessboard and pieces set up to play. He started to sit down, but one of the gendarmes prodded him with a rifle.

A door opened and the Syrian lieutenant entered. He stood aside ceremoniously and saluted Colonel Hamid Bek, who followed. The commandant was dressed in a brand-new tan army uniform with medals from the Balkan wars gleaming across his chest. He held a fez in his hand and placed it carefully on the desk. Naftali thought that Hamid Bek did not look the role. He was thin, with an ascetic pallor that his baldness and his dark, deep-set eyes accented. His nose had been broken and badly set; he breathed through his mouth and made little noises like sighs. Unlike most Turkish police and army officers, he made the effort to imitate the Germans by standing erectly and moving stiffly. But despite this, his movements were graceful and manly. Rumors to the contrary, Naftali thought, he was not a homosexual.

Hamid Bek dismissed the Syrian officer and the guards; then, with a gesture to a chair near the desk, he said in Turkish, "Please, Brandt Effendi."

Naftali didn't move.

"You speak Turkish, do you not?"

"Does the colonel speak Hebrew?" Naftali asked in Hebrew.

A quick smile like the shutter of a camera. "Not as well as you speak my language."

Naftali thought: I must take my time. Make this last as long as possible. And I must not lose my temper.

"The colonel flatters me," he said and sat down.

There was a knock at the door and an Ethiopian servant brought in two tiny cups of coffee. He placed one on the desk and the other on a side table near Naftali, and left. Hamid Bek read some papers in front of him. His breathing was heavy.

Naftali waited until the colonel sipped the coffee, then he tasted his own. It was thick and sweet, exactly the way he liked it. . . . They had not searched his house, Naftali remembered. There would be no evidence that he had Hebrew books or Zionist pamphlets. Herzl's photograph had been taken down by his mother. If this was to be a charge that he had interfered with the Syrian officer, it should not be difficult to argue that it was not to the best interests of the police to create enmity among the Arab villagers.

"You have lived in France, I see."

"Yes."

"I envy you. My military duties took me to Germany. I do not prefer that country to France. Were you ever in America? No? Too bad. A very wealthy nation. So rich it can afford to be neutral. I have seen photographs of New York and Chicago. Myself, I dislike traveling. It modifies the imagination. To know less is to be more daring."

Naftali thought: He builds a forest so I shall not see the trees he has marked to cut down. Carefully he listened for a clue in the half-tones and stresses. Suddenly he sensed danger as one feels rather than sees from a boat the sweep of a fish beneath the water.

"Your friend Judah Singer—he was in America last year, was he not?"

"Yes." Carefully.

"It is a great matter for us that he is so famous an agronomist that the President of the United States should invite him for a visit."

"Scarcely the President this time, colonel. He was invited by the federal Department of Agriculture and several universities."

"And he talked with many rich Jews too, eh?"

"He has friends there."

"Who hate the czar?"

"We Jews do not feel kindly to those who treat us badly."

Hamid Bek nodded. "Do you think that Singer Effendi would be inclined to talk to his friends on behalf of the German and Turkish war effort, since we all share a hatred of the Russian?"

"You will have to ask Singer Effendi."

Hamid Bek disliked the brevity of the reply. "You are his friend—"

"He is my teacher. I work with him."

"Yes. But still his friend. Has he not confided his views of the war?"

"I take all confidences seriously."

"You have worked in the experimental station in Atlit. Many important people have stopped there to visit and inspect. The American Ambassador Morgenthau was among them. Certainly you are aware of many things that could help us in our holy war against the Russian."

"Sir, I am not aware of such matters."

Naftali felt a great thirst, which the coffee did not allay.

"Brandt Effendi, you are a poet, I understand. Have you written anything in Turkish or Arabic?" The tone was soft again, the forest being rebuilt. Into the heated, thickish air the smell of a refuse heap on the outside came through the heavy curtains.

"I have written only in French and Hebrew."

"I also dabble." A sigh. "You cannot tell us about Ambassador Morgenthau?"

"Sir, I was arrested forty hours ago, taken from my village in the middle of the night. I have not been told the charge. I have not been given water or food. I am pleased to discuss poetry and politics with you at your convenience, but since I have done nothing I demand to be released forthwith." Naftali paused, his thirst gone.

Hamid Bek showed nothing on his face, not even that he had heard. Naftali decided to rouse him. "In addition, I expect an apology from the officer who made the arrest."

"Do you play chess?" The contained black eyes, distantly glowing with the electric bulbs from the chandelier, were raised to Naftali's.

"Sir, may I have an answer to my questions?"

Hamid Bek lifted his body from the chair, walked slowly around the end of the table, and stood at the chess set, looking down at the pieces. He opened the collar of his uniform.

"You are charged with violating martial law. You did not turn in your arms."

"I was not in my village when the search was made. Whatever arms I owned—a pistol—were turned over to your men."

"You were in Jerusalem. You should know better than to try to bribe so noble a soul as Said Ali Pasha."

"Said Ali Pasha was my father's friend." Had the old man in his senility made up a story? "I offered no bribe; I asked only his help with Jemal Pasha to save the lives of friends who were unjustly——"

"Unjustly, effendi? It was my General Baha ed-Din who sentenced them. Jemal Pasha approved. It was I who executed his orders. We are not monsters. Innocents we do not hang. You have no business having such friends. Now, I have answered your question. You have not replied to mine. Do you play chess?"

"If one was innocent, so was the other."

"We are the judges."

"Nor did I violate martial law."

"Very well."

"Then I am to be released?"

Hamid Bek picked up a white pawn and rubbed it on his sleeve. "You are further charged with selling wheat to the British. This charge is worse. For the other you would have been imprisoned. This one is treason."

Naftali rose angrily. "You are mocking me, colonel."

"I have no sense of the ridiculous. That's why I got along well with the Germans, yet admired the French." He pointed with the pawn to a chair at the chess table. "Sit there."

"Even if I had wheat to sell, how could I get it to the British? Suez is three hundred kilometers away, and the Fourth Army of Jemal Pasha stands between here and there."

"Logical but not necessarily true. You Jews make a god of logic—and miss everything else. There is no logic in life. I could just as easily accuse you of murder. If I were to rely on logic, would I be Hamid Bek, a colonel? No. I would be Hamid Bek, an underling like your Syrian officer, who, by the way, would be very pleased to execute you. Now sit down. Your life may——"

"My life is not in my hands."

Hamid Bek showed genuine curiosity. "*We* say that, we Muslims. It is all in the hands of Allah. But you, a Jew?"

Hamid Bek moved a hand to brush away a fly, then put his fingers on the king's pawn. As if suddenly uncomfortable, he unbuckled his holster belt, lifted it from around his slim body, and placed it casually on the large desk halfway between himself and Naftali.

"It is impolite, young man, not to answer my question."

Naftali stared at the white hand that held the pawn, then shifted his gaze to the gleaming butt of the revolver, which lay in its holster within arm's length. Naftali did not move; again his throat hurt from thirst. Hamid Bek seemed absorbed in the chess piece.

Slowly Naftali sat down at the table across from Hamid Bek. "I have been told I am a good chess player," he said and wiped his sweating hands against the side of his aba.

"Then think about this pawn, effendi." The Turk raised it closer to his own eyes. "By definition, is it not the weakest piece? Yet if one uses him correctly, guards him, manipulates him, works him, as one says, as you would work a good horse, in the end you can exchange him for an important piece—a queen, a knight. . . ."

Naftali picked up the king's pawn from his side of the board. He understood the colonel. "What, for example, would one get in exchange for this, colonel?"

"A great deal. . . . If well played, of course."

Hamid Bek replaced his piece.

"Are five hundred Turkish pounds—good playing?" Naftali asked.

Hamid Bek moved his king's pawn two squares forward. "White always starts first," he said lightly.

"Six hundred?"

"Why don't you move?"

Naftali played his king's pawn one space. "Seven?"

Hamid Bek studied the board. "I never thought money interested poets."

"Not me. You."

"But I am also a poet."

"A thousand. That's all there is."

"I have told you that I am also a poet of sorts. Money doesn't interest me either. Poets are sensitive to feelings. Money has no feelings. Poets unlock the heart. Money can only feed and clothe people. Their outer selves. Poets experience intensely the inner life . . . joy, beauty, pain. . . ."

He moved his knight.

"So what is the price of a poet, colonel?"

"Your arms. The hiding places of all the arms."

Naftali nodded. "I know of no arms, hidden or otherwise."

"You are not as good a player as I thought. You take too much time to move."

"If Alona has arms, they have already been taken by your men."

"And Atlit? Har Nehemia? Degania? Rishon le Zion? Yavniel? Zichron Yaacov? Hadera? Petach Tikva?"

"You have searched them, colonel."

"We have found little—and not because there was little."

Naftali played his knight. "Why do you suspect the Jews?"

Hamid Bek smiled with evident pleasure. "Who has not had trouble with them? All the nations of the world. Yet we have been good to you, have we not?"

"Your move, sir."

Hamid Bek touched his queen's pawn without moving it.

"You understand, effendi, that Germany is winning the war and that means we are winning the war. Jemal Pasha will drive the British from Egypt at will. If you Jews do not cooperate with us now, how will we remember you on the day of our victory?"

Naftali refrained from mentioning Jemal's first debacle.

"We know that there is a Zionist conspiracy. No matter what you tell us, you hope for a Jewish Palestine. You are worse than the Armenians."

"Sir, as loyal Turkish subjects, many Zionists offered their services to the Sublime Porte and to Jemal Pasha. Why were they turned away?"

"Who would trust them?"

Naftali studied the board.

89

"Young man, help your people by helping us. If your friends had no arms, they would not be tempted to use them. How can we fail to retaliate? Yes, even against your women. Forgive me if I seem to threaten. But as the sun has no choice but to create great heat, we have no choice. I am placing the fate of your Zionists in your hands. I don't even ask you to name the leaders. Only the hiding places of the arms. In the Rothschild wine cellars of Zichron Yaacov and Rishon perhaps? Underneath your outhouses? Behind your holy arks where the Torah is kept? We cherish your religion and would not profane the holy places. If all of you were like the pious Jews of Jerusalem and Hebron, you and I would not be talking of arms. So speak to me, young poet. There will be no uprising, no lives lost. And you will have done it all."

Silence, except for Hamid Bek's sighs.

There is always the morality of evil, Naftali thought, always the seduction to save some by betraying others. Shouldn't a man save a loaf by cutting off a slice? How reassuring the thought. And how revolting. He had no doubt that Hamid Bek meant what he was offering. The Turkish people were not racists against the Jews; they were not anti-Semites, as were the anti-Dreyfusards, the Black Hundreds of Russia, the peasantry of Hungary and Romania, the hysteric intellectuals of Germany. The Turks hated Jews only because of the dream of Zion redeemed.

"Why have you chosen me for this *noble* task?" Naftali asked to gain time, although he knew that the bastinado that could destroy a man's nervous system would be the end game to this chess match.

Hamid Bek still held his finger on the queen's pawn. Now he moved it forward and looked at Naftali with surprise, as if the question was so obvious it needed no answer.

"Because you are a poet. And poets possess a profound power of imagining the future and experiencing it. We feel, if I may include myself, the pain of others more deeply than common people can. I can see on your face, in your eyes, that even now you are still sharing the death of your friend. That is why I have chosen you."

"Poets, then, are weak men?"

"No. You misunderstand. Poets are strong men with sensitive feelings, like flowers that curl up when the sun departs."

"But they can be persuaded to betray others. Is that your meaning?" His hand was at the underedge of the chessboard. He felt himself tremble.

90

"Again you misunderstand. They are bigger than common men. They do not consider saving lives as betrayal."

"Then, on behalf of all the poets of the world"—casually Naftali lifted the chessboard; the black and white ivory pieces slid to the floor—"I protest!" He spoke calmly. Time was no longer an ally, but an enemy.

Hamid Bek arose. He took several noisy breaths as if he were in pain.

Naftali felt his hands and they were wet. Again he dried them in a fold of his aba.

"Jew!" Hamid Bek said sharply.

A great release of tension. Naftali was not thinking of what would come but only of what he had done. A sudden clarity came to him. He had been wasted, because no matter what he said, one way or the other he had chosen to be wasted; now he had chosen another course. His decision made at the Dead Sea, at Penuel, on the ruins of Ephron, in the caves of Jericho, was confirmed and deepened. If he lived he would find the meaning of pain and death. He felt himself enclosed in a mystery like those preached by the wonder-working Hassidic rabbis. Now there were no boundaries on this earth beyond which he could not pass. God was in heaven, but he, Naftali, was here. He sensed the completion of his destiny as part of his people. They had been put on this earth, by accident or design it didn't matter, to die in order to survive. In that way they could live forever. They were the leaven of the world; without them there would be no soul's bread. His fate was theirs—to live in order to die in order to live. This was the holiness of the Jewish fate, in which God was a silent but concerned partner.

If he died now, he thought, it would not be for trying to save a dog or to avenge himself for a humiliation or even to defend himself; it would be an act of survival. Through his death the people would live. That was the mystery, that was why the Jews, unlike other nations, did not disappear and would never disappear.

Without really listening, he heard Hamid Bek say, "You are stones on our souls. When I see a Jew, I see a traitor." He replaced the pistol and belt around his waist and tapped a small bell.

The Syrian officer and two guards entered.

"Bastinado," Hamid Bek said, suppressing his anger. "Fifty strokes. When he is conscious again, call me."

Naftali could not resist an urge to boast as they took him out. "I could have beaten you at chess, colonel. Are you sure you aren't avoiding a defeat?"

Hamid Bek ignored him. He felt no admiration for the Jew, for he could not consider the act of defiance as an act of will. If it were the Jew's allotted fate to be beaten, to suffer, to die, where was the courage in that? In Allah's hands all men are serfs to the Greater Will. Genuine courage is resignation, not defiance.

A small light bulb from the ceiling made a faint stain of yellow on the long wooden table on which they laid Naftali face down. One of the guards, a stout man with expressionless eyes, took off Naftali's bedouin shoes. The other bound his arms behind him with a short, heavy rope. The Syrian officer circled the table slashing the air with short, sharp strokes of a thin, tough, wooden cane.

A little compass that Naftali wore around his neck fell over the edge of the table and hung a few inches below the level of his eyes. When Judah had brought it to him as a gift from the United States, Naftali had said with a wry laugh, "You must think I lose myself easily." His friend smiled and changed the subject.

Now he glanced down on it swinging slowly on the silver chain. On it was inscribed "Chicago, Ill." The needle trembled between north and east.

With the sound of scythe against grain, the Syrian's cane sliced the empty air. Naftali began to hum a hora. The Syrian paused in front of him, picked up the compass, then let it drop.

"We are ready, Excellency," the stout policeman said.

The first lash of the cane cut into the naked soles of Naftali's feet. It seemed to him that there was no pain, only that he had diminished suddenly into a vanishing point, then just as quickly grew large and burst apart. With the second blow he felt the first. With the third, the second; then he lost count. It was as if a flaming torch were burning from his body where his legs should have been.

The compass spun wildly. Naftali tried to keep his eyes on it, but it dissolved in his pain. He fought to disconnect mind and body and yearned to visualize Akiba, who had been flayed alive by the Romans while singing the praise of God. He chanted his favorite prayer, BLESSED ART THOU O LORD . . . WHO PERMITTEST US TO LIVE UNTIL THIS MOMENT. . . . And then when he lost

92

track of the words, he cried out the Hebrew for "mercy," but instead of *"Rachem!"* the sound that split his mouth was *"Rachel!"*

At the eighteenth stroke the Syrian saw that the prisoner was unconscious. He motioned to the guard to add one more, then went in to report to Hamid Bek. But the colonel had already left, and Naftali **was** carried to his cell, where he lay for six hours and awoke finally because the bleeding soles of his feet were being bitten by rats.

7 ◇◇◇◇◇◇◇◇◇

In his thorough way, Judah Singer had organized Naftali's friends and the Liebermann brothers. He gave them money and credentials and ordered them to inquire at all the gendarme stations in Palestine and across the Jordan as far as Damascus. Despite martial law, curfew, and army patrols picking up stragglers and deserters, the friends managed to cover the ground. Nowhere was there word of Naftali.

For himself, Judah roused some of the members of the Zionist committee in Jaffa. They sent him to Diamondstein, a rich merchant and landowner who had established tenuous channels to Jemal Pasha. He tried to arrange a meeting with the general, but no matter how much baksheesh was paid, Jemal was seeing no one.

With only reports of failure, the station was an oppressive place. Judah tried to work, and Nissim tried not to weep all the time.

One day, about a week after Naftali's arrest, footsteps were heard on the outer stairway, which led to the balcony, and a young man of twenty-five entered, a stranger, dressed half like an Arab, half like a Polish peddler, with visored hat on thick black hair. He moved into the room with nervous grace. When he spoke it was in Warsaw Yiddish, singing, colorful, sarcastic.

"Judah Singer, the agronomist?"

"Who are you?" Judah asked.

"My name is Saul Wilner. I live sometimes in Beersheba, sometimes in Tiberias, and any other place in Zion you think of. By profession I am a living maker. I make a living, eh?"

"Why do you want to see me?"

He talks like a pasha or a Poniatowski, Wilner thought. Such a tone doesn't comb dandruff off the cheek of a beardless boy.

He took his time answering and grinned at Nissim. A nervous face, he thought, like a frightened foal, a Sephardi, an inbred Spaniard.

"I was informed, Singer, that you are a friend of Naftali Brandt."

"I am. Where is he?"

"He was in Caesarea. Now he is in Nazareth prison, charged with treason."

"What have they done to him?"

"His feet hurt but he's alive—for a while."

"How do you know all this?"

"I would be glad to tell you. After all, if camels knew Yiddish, they would also like to talk about themselves. But there isn't that much time. Try to save your friend. The angel of death is dancing on his nose. The papers for the hanging are on their way to Jemal Pasha. Even in heaven someone has to approve death." He grunted and made a face as if the mention of heaven sickened him.

"Is Jemal in Jerusalem?"

"In the Holy City, where else would a devil be?"

Judah Singer quickly swept some papers from the desk into a metal box and locked it. "Nissim, stay here until I come back. Don't leave for a minute. Give this man something to eat if he wants it."

He put on a lightweight jacket hanging near the door. "Have you any idea when the order for execution was sent to Jemal?"

"This morning. It will get there tonight. Hamid Bek has good horses. I myself sold his men two."

"Why did you come to me?"

"Mrs. Brandt said you were a *macher*."

Judah turned to Nissim. "If anyone comes to ask for me, tell them where I am. Shalom."

"Shalom, Mr. Judah," Nissim said.

"And me, you don't give a shalom? I also know that much the holy tongue," Wilner said.

"Why do you sell horses to gendarmes?" Judah said coldly, and without thanking Wilner ran down the wooden stairs.

"He moves fast for a heavy man," Wilner said, looking out the window to watch Judah hurry to an American touring car, fix the gas lever, and begin cranking it. "When you are rich enough to have an automobile, you don't have to sell horses."

Nissim had come up to watch. "He's not a rich man. The car was bought for the station by the Americans. It is for his work."

The motor started. Judah got in the car and drove off quickly. A ghostly wake of yellow dust followed him.

"I forgot to tell him about the locusts," Wilner said. "Clouds like

95

smoke from burning villages. That's all we need." He ran a finger along his cheek in front of the ear as if he were curling invisible locks. "How long has this Jew been in prison?"

"I don't know. We looked everywhere. At Nazareth I myself paid baksheesh, and they swore to me he wasn't there. Is he sad? Does he cry much? He never cries, of course. That is for girls."

Wilner didn't like the tone of the young man's voice. A heaven's fool, a dangerous man.

"Nu, where's the wine?"

"We have no wine. I'll make tea."

"What, so close to Zichron—the Rothschild cellars?"

Nissim went to the pump to fill a kettle. "If you don't believe me, look around."

"The high and famous Mr. Singer maybe doesn't enjoy wine either."

"Don't talk about him that way."

"Oh! And why not?"

"Because he is Judah Singer."

"And you are maybe a levite to the high priest?" Wilner moved restlessly around the tables, picked up books, briefly glanced at them, as if they were further annoyances. "Who is this Naftali Brandt?"

"Naftali—" The name hung in the heated air like a small sun. "You never heard of him either?"

"Listen, Spaniard, don't show off to me."

Nissim blushed and lost the thread of his thoughts. "I am a sabra. And so also was my great grandfather and his great grandfather. My family, Vidali, has been here for over five hundred years. When did you come here?"

"Fifteen minutes ago!"

Nissim smiled despite himself.

"You, I make smile. How fast can that automobile of his go? At forty kilometers an hour, it will take him maybe five hours to get to— Ach! Not even a 'thank you.' A 'shalom.' Answer me, Spaniard, why did I go out of my way to help his friend?" He riffled the papers on Judah's desk.

"Don't touch those papers. Mr. Judah becomes angry if they are moved."

"So answer me."

"I don't know you. I can't answer."

"Your water takes a long time to boil. You have sugar or jam?"

"Just the tea. Some biscuits."

96

"The hills going up to Jerusalem will slow him down."

"With God's help, he'll get there on time," Nissim said reverently and poured the hot water from the kettle into a cup with tea leaves.

"Why didn't God act before your friend got into trouble? Or maybe He was too busy making matzoth for Passover."

"Here's your tea."

"Nu, so why is God always too late?"

Nissim went to the other side of the room with his own tea. As usual, he said a prayer before drinking.

"You don't want to talk with me?"

Nissim nodded.

"I am a dirty man with smells?"

The lad blinked his eyes, suddenly confused. It was bad without Naftali. He had a feeling that pins were being stuck in his own legs. If anything happened to his friend, he would die. He had taken such a vow, although he never confessed it to Naftali. This man with his talk, his atheism, disturbed him.

"It troubles you that I talk about God like that? I am not exactly an atheist, so don't get chilblains. It is not the question of whether I believe in Him. The question is, Does He believe in me?"

Wilner finished the tea, stretched his arms, and yawned. "My nobility has tired me, chicken. I'm going to sleep." He lay down on the couch. "You have objections, maybe?"

"No . . ." Satan had many masks. Even a man who came to save his friend. What if he had not come to save him? What if the whole story was a lie to get Judah in trouble?

"So your family has been here for five hundred years. So what does that make you?"

Nissim murmured a psalm.

"Who is this Brandt?"

"He— He is my friend. . . ." Nissim wanted to say more, but he was afraid that he would weep and the stranger would laugh at him. He turned his mind to the wonder-working Master of the Good Name and offered a prayer for his intercession.

Wilner fell asleep quickly. But soon he was dreaming of a distant burning village with smoke rising from it like a flight of locusts. It was a recurring dream, and he moaned in his sleep.

8 ⟡⟡⟡⟡⟡⟡⟡⟡

Judah Singer drove his Oldsmobile touring car as fast as he could to get to Jerusalem before dark. Halfway there he saw a dark cloud hanging over the eastern horizon. It looked like a conclave of birds; for a moment he thought he saw the fluttering of wings. He fixed a point at the top of one of the Judean hills and noted that the cloud was moving southward. He watched as he drove. The mass had no trailing coveys, no outriders. With a sudden shock he realized it was a swarm of locusts. If the wind shifted enough it would fall on Palestine, ravaging the spring wheat and the flowering fruit trees. Hunger would be added to hunger.

With such news, he could force Jemal Pasha to see him.

Swiftly he ascended the valley of Ayalon toward the white-limestone crest of the hills, passing Arab villages and silver-gray olive orchards that circled Judea like forgotten forts. At Ein Karem, the muezzin whined the call for evening prayer. The faithful saw the speeding car and thought it was driven by a German or a Jew, and before kneeling toward Mecca they spit into the dust in contempt.

He had to stop now and then as troop and artillery detachments moved down toward the coast. In the courtyard of a mosque he saw soldiers unloading great stores of shells. By the time he reached the Jaffa Gate and David's Tower, it was evening.

The restless twilight streets of Jerusalem were filled with Turkish soldiers and German officers. From doorways and dark coffeehouses Arabs seemed to be watching everybody else. Few Jews were visible, and he wondered if there had been a curfew set for them. From the direction of the Damascus Gate he heard the Byzantine blare of a janissary band, a sound which he found distasteful. As if in protest, there floated on the air the pure notes of the evening bugle from the army encampment on Mount Scopus. Nearer the upper vanes of Montefiore's windmill caught a final streak of sun.

The city, holy and fateful as it was, always depressed him. Not the smells of garbage and human feces or the dirt in thousand-year-old layers. What grated his teeth was the resigned poverty of the Arabs, the beggars, and the old Jews who used piety as an excuse to live on the charity of the world. He hated this waste of human energy.

Even more degrading were the civil wars of the Christian sects, Orthodox and Catholic, Maronite and Syrian. Seeing them fight each other for a pittance of honors and beggary, he felt he was a witness to outrageous obscenities. Who would dare someday cleanse this city of its scumbling dogmas? Revive the grandeur of its memory? Yet he could not say that he did not love Jerusalem. But for what it had been. And that was not really love, it was ancestor worship. "The tombs of my fathers are besieged forever. . . ."

He drove his car to an alley alongside the American School of Archeology, on Abyssinia Street, told the concierge, whom he knew, to keep an eye on the car, brushed the dust from his clothes, and hurried around the corner to what had once been the palace of the French ambassador and was now headquarters of Jemal Pasha.

The large main foyer was filled with soldiers and petitioners. Judah went directly to the Turkish sergeant who sat at a desk receiving the visitors and addressed him in Turkish. "Get this to his Excellency's aide, Colonel Sayek, at once." He handed him his calling card, on which he had written one word: "Locusts!"

"Effendi, you have been here before," the sergeant said. "I know his Excellency will not see you."

"He will see me this time."

Judah put a gold piece under his card, which the sergeant had dropped on the desk. "There will be another *after* I see him."

"I tried before, too. . . ."

"Try again."

The old man rose and slipped the coin into a pocket. He called over another sergeant, who was dozing in a corner, to take his place.

The glass on the photograph of Kaiser Wilhelm dressed in sheik's clothes reflected the cluster of lights from the wall brackets and the figure of Jemal Pasha behind the desk, his short powerful body straining at the combat uniform of a Turkish field commander.

He was reading a report and did not acknowledge Judah as he was ushered in. His face was petulant behind black eyes, black square beard and Kaiser-like moustache. A German staff officer stood at the window looking out at the garden.

Jemal continued to read, coughing slightly, then looked up and stared with open curiosity at Judah. What sort of a man was this agronomist Singer? Was he ambitious? Did he have a following? How could he be used?

"They tell me you have been trying to see me for a week," he said in a low-pitched voice. "You will forgive me. Time is one of the first casualties of war. Colonel Sayek, who claims your friendship, thought I must see you. Under ordinary circumstances I still could not have given you an audience, but I was captured by the word you wrote. Is it true?"

"I saw them on my way here, your Excellency. From the direction of Damascus. With a shift in the wind, they can swoop down on us in a few days, a week. I know, of course, of your great concern in such matters."

"They have not visited us for forty years. Have you any explanation?"

"None, your Excellency. But I needn't remind you that if they come they will destroy what remains of our crops."

"You hear this, count?"

The German officer turned from the window. He was a willowy man in his forties, with a blank expression.

"Sir, I have heard it."

"We are already in short supply of food," Jemal said, complaining. "Your government has promised us bread and meat. What has come? Nothing. And with these locusts, we will have less than now. My army will become skeletons."

"Five shiploads of wheat and cattle were unloaded in Smyrna months ago, sir. They have been on their way here for two months at least. We cannot be responsible for the breakdown in rail transport."

The German officer spoke with a trace of contempt.

It did not escape Jemal, who closed and opened his eyes, making an effort to control his anger. He turned back to Judah. "Your reputation is well known to me. I share your passion for a fertile Palestine. It was once a great vineyard and granary. Someday it will be again. The locusts are a grave threat to me. I want them destroyed."

An irritable man, Judah thought, who is uneasy with power and therefore deals with it in excesses, demanding too much or too little.

"Does your Excellency command me to this task?"

"Why else have I given you audience?"

Judah felt a moment's triumph. The first step to Naftali was taken. "I will need many of your men to help."

"I cannot spare one. Use the fellahin."

"The fellahin are useless. As they see it, to fight locusts is to oppose the will of Allah. They will not raise a hand."

Jemal Pasha showed displeasure. "I did not give you leave to discuss theology. Our Koran does not preach hunger. No more than your theology continues to demand animal sacrifice."

Judah tested his position with silence.

Jemal gave a slight cough, the black eyes closing as if against too bright a light. Then he placed his hand over his heart in a simple dramatic gesture. "As you have heard from my lips, my soldiers are badly fed even now. They don't receive their legal oka of bread and half oka of meat a day. Yet trainloads of bread and meat are spoiling at railroad junctions because someone has been bribed—or has not been bribed. Do you think, effendi, that I am not aware of the corruption and inefficiency of Constantinople? All these tragedies are heavy on my head, and I do not blame Allah for them either. But I need my soldiers." He raised his hand. "I need them! You will not have one!"

"Sir, I can't do it alone."

"Get your Jews to help you."

It was for this command Judah had hoped. Now he had bargaining power for Naftali's life. He forced himself to bait the hook with silence.

"Come, Singer Effendi, you have a position among the Jews, have you not?"

Judah shrugged.

"You are one of their famous ones. Even the old sultan knew about your finding the wild wheat at Mount Hermon."

Now was the time; he could feel the pieces of his mission fall into place.

"Sir, in lieu of your men, I will need at least two things from your Excellency. I must not be hampered by martial law. I want a pass permitting me and my co-workers to go anywhere they want to."

"Why?" Suspiciously.

"To rouse the Jews of the Galilee and in the south to help me. To follow the locusts wherever they go. To fight them when they land. Arab villages will have to be persuaded to board and feed my men."

"I will give you a *laissez-passer,* but in your name only. What else?"

"I will need my chief assistant."

"Get him."

"He's in Nazareth prison."

"What for?"

"He is being held on a fictitious charge of treason."

"What is his name?"

"Naftali Brandt of Alona."

Jemal Pasha frowned and moved papers on his desk until he found what he was looking for.

"I am disappointed in you, Singer," he said, his voice suddenly sly. "Did you come here to see me about fighting the locusts or to use them to get your friend's neck out of the noose?"

"Sir——"

"I don't care for interruptions." Petulantly he lifted the paper to show Judah. "This is Colonel Bek's order for the execution. It only requires my signature."

His hand reached for a gold pen and dipped it into the ink. The sound of the nib on the heavy paper shredded the silence.

Judah spoke loudly. "Brandt is as innocent of treason as I am!"

"You know the specific charge?"

"It couldn't matter."

"It matters." Jemal coughed. "He is charged with selling wheat to the English."

"Absurd. He has no wheat to sell. And how could he reach the English through your pickets and across the Sinai even if he had wheat and wanted to help the enemy?"

"This is beyond arguing."

"Then, sir, I say you will have to fight the locusts yourself."

Jemal Pasha stared straight ahead at Judah. The German gave Jemal an inquiring and contemptuous look. Finally Jemal coughed, then spoke in an icy voice, "And what will you say if I have you hanged too?"

Judah rose. He thought of all his work left undone. He thought, not sorrowfully, but with a strength he had always known he had, that he must win this battle, even with his life.

"I could say very little, your Excellency. But I am a heavy man. My body would break the limb of the tree and the noise of it falling would reach America. It might be loud enough to affect its opinion."

The German showed more interest.

Jemal Pasha placed his two hands on the desk, leaning on them as if feeling faint.

"You think more of your man than you do of Palestine or your life?"

"First you start with a man, your Excellency—the rest follows."

Jemal picked up the execution order and shifted it back and forth from one hand to the other.

"We cannot have our flanks open to disaffection, sir, nor to locusts," the German officer said in a low voice to Jemal.

The Turkish general brooded over the execution order. If there were only someone else available to fight the locusts. But did anyone care as much as the Jews? He had seen how they revived a dead land with their colonies, their groves, their plantations.

"Selling wheat to the British, eh?" Jemal said as if he had just discovered what the charge was. "How stupid this man Hamid Bek is. As if anybody could get through my lines alive. Policemen make a profession of stupidity." To the German officer: "Write up an order to draft the gendarmerie into the army. I want it when the need arises."

He dropped the execution order to the desk, sat down, and spoke into the telephone.

"Captain, bring in a *laissez-passer* in the name of Judah Singer, of Har Nehemia. And a release from the Nazareth prison in the name of"—he glanced at the order—"Naftali Brandt, of Alona."

He hung up and pointed a thick finger at Judah.

"You will be responsible for this friend of yours. In any case, I will keep the execution order convenient."

"Yes, your Excellency."

"You know, it might just as easily have happened the other way."

"I know."

"You were prepared to die?"

"I'm not ready to die until I'm a hundred and twenty, as the saying goes. But then, neither am I ready to live under all circumstances."

"The death of your friend being one of those—those circumstances?"

"No, sir. The death of an innocent man."

Jemal tightened his mouth angrily. "You Jews want special bargains in justice. As if you were the only innocent ones."

A staff captain entered, saluted Jemal Pasha, put the papers on his desk, saluted, and left.

Jemal Pasha signed the papers sullenly and shoved them across the desk to Judah, who took them, bowed to the two men, and started out.

"Singer—"

Judah stopped and faced Jemal Pasha, who was looking at him coldly.

"That body of yours isn't quite as heavy as you think."

"Sir, I will do my best to keep it—the way it is," Judah said without smiling. At a gesture of Jemal's hand, he left.

"That Jew has learned to talk back," Jemal Pasha said to the count.

"There are always one or two. Once they leave the ghettos and make a little money they smell of insolence. But I like them. They have good minds."

Jemal Pasha coughed and wiped his mouth with a handkerchief. "Call in my brigade commanders."

The count left and Jemal Pasha sat back in his chair. War is a carousel, he thought; the faster it turns, the harder it is to get the brass ring. But it must always go faster, until all the people on it fall off.

9 ◇◇◇◇◇◇◇◇◇

The military train in which Nahum had managed to get a place for Rachel moved slowly south and east toward the Taurus range. The compartment was filled with Turkish and German officers who were eating, drinking, smoking, arguing. She tried to concentrate on the scenes outside the car window or on the German translation of *Anna Karenina* she was rereading. She had felt a little like Anna and wanted to know again what had gone on in the mind of that passion-ridden woman. It was cold in the car, and she covered her lap with a fur coat. On the lapel of her cloth traveling jacket she had pinned Naftali's watch.

She noticed a German captain who kept his eyes directed to her. He was blond and plump and unpleasant in his manner. After they had been traveling for several hours he leaned across the aisle and said loudly, "If madame will forgive this question, I am curious who madame is."

The other officers stopped to listen.

"I am a Palestinian."

"Madame's name and home?"

She told him.

"I am Captain von Fricke."

She nodded an acknowledgment.

"May I inquire as to the purpose of your travel?"

"I am going home. And if the captain will forgive me, I am tired." She closed the book and closed her eyes, leaning her head against the swaying wall of the car. They were running parallel to a broad river. Beyond was one of the nameless peaks of the Taurus.

It seemed to her that hours had passed.

"Madame!"

She opened her eyes. The river was still there. The German captain was addressing her.

"My questions are not to be taken lightly," he said aggressively.

"What else do you want to know?" She strained to keep her voice calm.

"To get a seat on this train, one must have given a considerable bribe or have a pass from supreme headquarters. May I know how you managed it?"

She knew that Nahum had paid a large sum of money to get the seat and her traveling papers, but it would have been dangerous to admit it.

A Turkish officer interrupted. "She wouldn't have been permitted to leave Constantinople without the right papers, captain. Why bother her now with it?"

"I am on the intelligence staff of the Fourth Army," Von Fricke said irritably. "I am always interested in civilians in wartime." He turned to Rachel. "Madame?"

She felt herself tense. "If it took a bribe to get this seat," she said, "I would scarcely confess it to you. And if it were an order from supreme headquarters, as you put it, I would think you would be on dangerous grounds to question me further."

Before the captain could reply, several of the other officers broke into applause and bravos. One of them, a Turkish colonel, said, "For such an answer she deserves to remain unmolested, captain."

"Sir——"

"Captain, that will be all!"

"But it is my responsibility."

"The lady told you her name and her town. At the moment she is not yet in the area of the Fourth Army. When that time comes you may question her further. Now, let us be done with the chattering and permit me to nap."

The Germans in the car looked angrily at the Turkish colonel. Von Fricke arose and with a show of displeasure left the compartment.

Rachel smiled her thanks to the colonel and returned to her book. Then she slept restlessly.

The days and nights splintered one into the other. The train stopped frequently, backtracked, ran out of coal, broke down. Three times the soldiers had to portage their horses and artillery across mountain passes from one railroad line to another. Food was scarce, the nights were cold. Rachel had little privacy.

Captain von Fricke tried several times to talk with her, but the Turkish colonel, an Anatolian trained in Germany, asked him again to leave Rachel alone.

One night, thirty miles north of Adana, they came to a bridge that was burning, and the train could go no further. The train's commanding officer gave the orders to disembark. They would have to march crosscountry to Ulukustu, where, if they were lucky, another train would take them to their destination, Lake Van and the Russian front.

"You will have to get to Adana by yourself," the Turkish colonel told Rachel. "I'm sorry, of course, but war is not kind to ladies. However—" He looked out the car window into the dusty plain that ran alongside and saw by the light of the fire from the bridge a wooden shed where rails and ties were kept. "Wait near there. I may be able to get a horse for you."

She thanked him warmly and left the train. Soldiers were everywhere, running about in a great confusion of commands. Cavalry and artillery horses led down from the open cars, were being saddled and hitched to field pieces. One pair, terrified by the shouts and beatings, ran away pulling a heavy gun. They dashed for the shed where she was standing. She heard the shouts and saw the runaways in time. The gun carriage smashed into the shed and destroyed it. Shivering and frightened, she stood near the broken structure, hoping that the colonel had not forgotten her. Many of the men had already marched off. The dawn light was growing. She moved up and down the stalled train looking for her benefactor.

"Madame—"

It was Von Fricke.

"Madame, I am arranging for a carriage to take me to Adana. Will you join me?"

She wanted to go with him, to take any step that would get her away from the chaos and the cold that was numbing her. But she was afraid, and shook her head.

"Perhaps you would rather stay with the train, madame? I understand it will be returned to Constantinople." He waited for her answer. "No? Then you intend to walk to Adana, twenty miles. The terrain is not made for walking on shoes like yours. Why not permit me——"

A rain of dust fell on them as a troop of cavalry sped by. Rachel covered her mouth with her scarf.

"There are not many people living between here and Adana. It is bad country to get lost in."

"The colonel said that I would be taken care of. Thank you, captain."

His hand was on her arm and he dropped it. "Your colonel has already ridden off with his staff."

She did not know whether he was telling the truth and hesitated.

"Madame, my interest in taking you to Adana is impersonal."

She tried to find the truth in his eyes. She was reminded of a steel engraving she had once seen of Philip II of Spain, haughty, mirthless, cruel.

"The colonel is a man of his word. He will help me."

"As you wish, madame. Perhaps we shall see each other again in Jerusalem or Har Nehemia."

Without saluting he left her. She waited for the colonel to find her. But she never saw him again. When morning came, she left, carrying valise and coat, and walked to a farm nearby, hoping to buy a mule or to hire a man to take her to Adana. No one was there except an old woman, who sullenly sold her some goat cheese and dried wheatcakes and pointed vaguely to the south when Rachel asked for directions.

The countryside was open and rocky and uncultivated. In the cool day she walked for several hours. Before noon she thought she saw the smoke of a distant farmhouse and cut across the fields toward it. But the house was empty, although recently lived in, and the smoke seemed to come from another place on the far side of a ridge. Near the house, on a branch of an apple tree, she saw a woman's blue scarf hanging loosely, and below it on the earth an icon of wood. She picked it up and placed it on the limb near the scarf.

Back on the path, she sang Hebrew songs and thought of Naftali, then stopped in the shade of a copse of oak to eat the cheese and wheatcakes. A long train of large black ants moved past to a tiny hillock nearby. She watched for several minutes, and curious as to where they were going, followed them over the hillock across a slight depression, past a rock pile built like a covering of a holy place or grave, then through two trees and on to the road that was a continuation of the one she had been following earlier.

She screamed. Ahead of her was the body of a man, partly covered by a blanket of ants. Fighting terror, she forced herself to move to it until she could see the dead man's face. He was old, sunburned, his blue eyes open. A few ants caught in her coat reached the skin of the back of her hand. With a cry she brushed them away, ran to a rock, and wildly beat the coat against it. When she exhausted her terror, she thought she ought to go back and bury the man, at least cover him with rocks. But she was sure she didn't have the strength to drive the ants away. She walked on, dazed, frightened, ashamed.

At a turn of the path she saw a teakettle, then a torn woolen coverlet, several wooden icons, a bolster with its fleece hanging out, and a broken cart filled with household goods. She heard a child crying and ran toward the sound. In a ditch alongside the road was a dead woman and a dying child, a swarthy, black-haired girl of about four, moaning and gasping for breath, her tiny fingers holding a crucifix. Blood from a knife wound dripped from her side. As Rachel raised the child, its head fell back and the crucifix slipped from its fingers.

Numb with horror, Rachel laid the child down alongside the mother, lying in her own blood. A knife was in the dust a few inches away from the outstretched swarthy arm. Had the mother tried to kill her child, then herself, and died before the child? Who were these people? Who had done this to them?

Rachel tried to walk on, sobs filling her. Images of the dead mother and child grew larger in her mind, and she started to run, losing control of herself. A tree root tripped her; she fell against the trunk and lay there half conscious and weeping until she fainted.

She dreamt that she was a child watching her father work in the vineyards of Har Nehemia. She thought he might cut himself with the shears and that his blood would flow over and drown her. "Papa, Papa, be careful!" He went on working, not hearing her. Crawling, she reached his feet. He didn't look at her. It wasn't Papa but Naftali. Not seeing her, not hearing her. "Naftali! Naftali!" He brushed the hair from his eyes and continued to work. A wind swept over her and she became cold. "Papa! Naftali! Judah!" No one heard, no one helped.

Then she began to choke and tore the covering over her face. She awoke, not knowing at first where she was. It was night and cold. She saw a small fire nearby. In front of it were three men and a boy—Arabs.

Trying to move away quietly, she made a noise. The boy saw her and cried out fearfully in Arabic, "The dead are awakening!" The men jumped up quickly, the bravest of them coming closer. He was tall, his face half hidden by a kaffiyeh. A cartridge bandolier crisscrossed his chest; a knife was in his hand. Rachel started to run, but the man caught her and dragged her toward the fire. There he looked at her face and dropped her arm.

"Don't be afraid," the man said in Arabic. "We are not Turks. We are from the Lebanon."

"Salaam, effendim," she said in a whisper. Her lips trembled with fear.

"Who are you?"

"I am from Palestine."

"Why are you here?"

"I was on a train but now I am walking to Adana."

"You are alone?"

"Yes."

The man was incredulous. "Are you a Turkish woman?"

"I am a Jewess."

One of the men muttered to let her go, but the leader, the man with the courage, said, "Between here and Adana and all around unto the sea itself are Turkish soldiers. It is not good for a Jew or a Christian to be alone. We are Christians."

"What is happening here?"

"There is a killing. Villages and villages, a great blood feud between the Turk and the Armenian people. They are called enemies of the sultan and spies for the Russians. We ourselves have seen near a thousand dead. Not soldiers, but people."

She could no longer control her body and crouched to her knees.

There was a long silence; the burning twigs in the fire broke like gunshots.

One of the men kicked some earth over it. The flames fell away. An animal screeched nearby.

"Stay here," the leader said and with the other men walked off to one side and talked quietly. The boy guarded her.

She thought: I will give them all that I have if they will let me go.

The leader returned. "My name is Ahmed. You will come with us to our village. It is not far from Chaqre, two days' march from Metullah where there are Jews."

"I thank you, Ahmed Effendi. I will go alone."

He became angry. "It is decided."

"I will pay you for a horse and go alone."

"Woman! It is decided."

The fire flared up in a current of air. Ahmed stood sternly with hands on his hips, insulted by her unwillingness. He was dark skinned; a scar cut his forehead below the kaffiyeh.

"Perhaps the woman Jew hates Christians too?" he asked.

"No! No!"

"Then why do you refuse? You are more afraid of us than of the Turks?"

She was silent.

Slowly, he took a small silver pistol from the broad leather band around his waist. "Here."

The pistol shone in the yellow light.

"If you do not trust us, then take this weapon and go on alone, God willing it."

She looked at the pistol and at Ahmed's angry face. The night beyond the campfire was moonless and menacing. She did not trust him, but neither did she trust her courage to go on by herself.

Reckless in the face of no alternative, she said, "Keep the pistol. I accept your hospitality."

He nodded gravely. "Do you have anything with you?"

"A valise, a coat . . ."

"Get them," he ordered, "and bring them to us by the fire. We will stay here until we eat."

"She has no horse," a man said. "She will have to walk and keep us slow."

"My horse will carry two," Ahmed said.

When she went to the tree to get her valise and coat, she heard one of the men say, "If we bring her safely, the Jews will reward us."

10 ◇◇◇◇◇◇◇◇◇

Brought home to Alona from Nazareth by Judah, Naftali remained in bed for several days while his mother and Nissim, subdued and anxious, took turns medicating his lacerated soles and massaging the muscles of his thighs and abdomen, where neural damage from the bastinadoing could first show itself. Naftali was silent most of the time and never mentioned the pain. When Judah had explained about Jemal Pasha and the locusts, he roused himself enough to thank him and asked that his thanks be conveyed also to Saul Wilner, who was known to him as a horse trader of dubious reputation.

Naftali's silence was not apathy or despair, but rather an incapacity to grasp the chaos within him and force it into the fragile meaning of words. The phrase "I will live" repeated itself over and over in his mind. It carried something archaic, not anything as simple as the conviction that never again would he permit them to beat him. It went beyond the mystery of his ineradicable Jews, beyond his residue of dignity that could bring him to prefer death to humiliation. The splintered notions that filled him had to do vaguely with innocence and death. Something like the shadow of man falling over the face of God.

Within him was an uncontainable and discontinuous clash of ideas; he was like a child faced with too many choices. And then, as always when he was under great stress, his thoughts turned to the Bible story of the *akedah,* the sacrificial binding of Isaac, which of all the sacred stories roused in him the deepest response. From the first time he had heard it as a boy of two or three, he was fascinated by its drama and hidden meanings. Often when playing by himself over the young years he would climb one of the low hills surrounding Alona and pretend that he was ascending a mountain in the land of Moriah with father Abraham. Fearfully or bravely, depending on his mood, he would place himself on a rock, close his eyes, and await the knife thrust of his father and the cry of the angel, "Abraham! Abraham! Lay not thine hand upon the lad."

As child and adult, Naftali distrusted the traditional homage to Abraham for this example of his unquestioning fealty to God. Naftali thought otherwise. After all, didn't it require more courage for Isaac to obey the all-too-human father than for the father to obey the all-powerful Jehovah before whom he had no choice? Abraham's courage was the "sacred cowardice" that Said Ali Pasha had described.

But what continued to puzzle Naftali was Isaac's silence. He had spoken no word before or after the great event. (As silent as I am, Naftali thought bitterly.) What had gone on in the lad's mind?

Naftali felt an identity with Isaac that he had never dared reveal to anyone, least of all Judah, who at best would tolerate the notion as feverish poeticizing.

Judah came often to report on the locusts. They had been swept back east of the Hauran because of the high winds coming in from the sea, but this might turn out to be temporary. In the meantime, he had instructed the villagers to send him word the minute they were seen again. He had also taught them how to look for the eggs and how to destroy them.

"I haven't received much cooperation. The Arabs distrust me for affronting Allah by trying to blunt His will. The Jews distrust me because I am an agent of Jemal Pasha. I am utterly at a loss," he confessed. "I fail to communicate, to persuade. If grain were as difficult to cultivate as men, we'd be living on stones instead of bread."

The two men were sitting outside Naftali's house under a carob tree. From the schoolroom nearby the children chanted their lessons. A few old men stood at the approaches of the village to warn of gendarme patrols.

"Is Rachel home yet?" Naftali asked suddenly. "My mother told me she had left Constantinople."

"We are worried. It's been two weeks since we heard from Nahum."

Naftali marked out a line in the earth with a cane he had used since his whipping. "Tell me, are the British still at Suez?"

"Yes. Nothing is happening there. They send out a plane now and then to drop leaflets. There is talk of an Arab rising in Syria. Some of the Arab regiments, I have heard, are ready to join it. The British are definitely behind this."

Naftali's sunken dark eyes followed a hummingbird toward the branch of the tree.

"The English think the Arabs are worth saving, but not the Jews," he said.

"There are millions of them and a few thousand of us. The English will use strength, not weakness."

The bird stood off from the branch, flickering in the quiet air.

"The Jews are weak because they choose not to be strong."

Judah felt the accusation and was silent, then said, "We are in the midst of the whole Turkish Army. Shall we gather our women and children to the top of Massada and kill ourselves in a demonstration of useless courage?"

The hummingbird had made a decision and was now perched on the limb, but the tiny wings were not quiet. Such a creature, Naftali thought, is worthy of love.

"I am not the commander of the English," Judah added. "I can't tell them what to do about Palestine or the Jews. If the war ends soon——"

"Then the Arabs will own us instead of the Turks. We will become true Levantines. Baksheesh Jews. The end of Zion."

The children finished chanting and were about to leave the school.

"Help me inside," Naftali said harshly.

Later Mrs. Brandt took Judah to his carriage.

"I have never seen him like this," Judah said.

"Mr. Singer, my son is disappointed."

"The bastinado is a great humiliation. It gets inside a man's soul."

"My son has a greater soul than that. And his disappointment is not physical. May I be truthful with you?"

"Please."

"You are his star, Mr. Judah. He is a poet, you are a scientist, but you are his star. But now the skies are clouded and he can no longer see the star."

Judah untied his horse's reins from a wooden rail. "Mrs. Brandt, a star may not be a star at all. But someone's idea of a star. What does he want of me?"

"I don't know. He says sometimes that Jews must die in order to live. Other times—that we must live in order to be sacrificed. He talks of Isaac's binding and Abraham. I do not understand any of that. If a man dies, he dies." She gazed past Judah to her home and said simply, "My husband built that house. But he is dead, and that house does not keep him alive. It is not easy for me to understand my son!"

114

"I do not understand him, either," Judah said.

Mrs. Brandt did not reply, her face concealing the thought that Judah somehow was not worthy of her son.

A few days later Naftali felt well enough to mount Melech and ride to Atlit. When he arrived there, Judah had just received word that the locusts had been seen near Der'a and that Rachel was at Har Nehemia. Together they rode as fast as they could to meet her. The locusts could wait another day.

11 ◇◇◇◇◇◇◇◇◇

When Naftali first saw Rachel after the year's separation, he felt a curious confusion of place and time. It was as if she had never gone away and that somehow he was the one who had left and was now returning, departed a child to come back a man. Or was it that this new growth of his own was a reflection of hers?

"Shalom, Rachel. Blessed be your coming."

Hesitantly she offered her hand and said, "Shalom, Naftali."

The ancient Hebrew greeting made him tremble. He could not keep from staring at her. She was thin. Her blond hair had just been washed and was still damp and drawn tightly in back of her head. Her wide blue eyes had a sadness he had not seen before in them.

"Shalom," he said again. He wanted to obliterate the place and the Singers, who were watching, and take her into his arms. He wanted to cry out, "Rachel, we have lost so much time. I was blind. Rachel, the day of the heart has come. I love you."

Rachel felt her own nervousness rise to her throat. As before, his presence possessed her. For her, nothing had changed.

"Your beard," she said, trying to find something to say.

"I let it grow in prison. Do you like it?"

"It makes you seem a little older." She lowered her voice. "Was it terrible for you?"

He shrugged. "Well, shall I keep it or shave it off?"

She tried to smile. "It's too important a question to answer quickly."

Later, after supper, she could talk of her trip from Constantinople. It had taken eighteen days instead of the usual five. She touched lightly on her adventures on the train and moved quickly to the terrible scenes of the Armenian villages.

"At first I didn't know what I was seeing. There were the families, women and children, killed or left to die. With my own eyes I saw the evidence that one mother killed her child and herself. I kept thinking of our own people and how our mothers and fathers killed their children and then themselves . . . at Massada . . . at York Cathedral. . . ."

She wept. The family, Naftali, Dr. Bloch, and Miriam sat silently like mourners.

"What I saw myself was enough. Ahmed told me more. The soldiers came to the Armenian villages and ordered the people to leave in twenty-four hours. If the commander was merciful, he gave them two days. In some of the towns, the kaimakam was not cruel, and in some places, like Diabekir, the governor put the priests to death by burning. Many women, Ahmed told me, became Muslims to avoid being raped. There is a mountain facing the Mediterranean, Jebel Musa. Several hundred Armenians tried to defend themselves there, but Ahmed did not know what happened to them."

Naftali wanted her to stop; the suffering in her face, the half gasps in her voice, choked him. Judah's eyes were steady on his sister's. Papa leaned his head on his arm and swayed back and forth as if in prayer. Miriam tore at a handkerchief to keep herself from weeping out loud.

"Once, as we crossed the outskirts of Adana, I saw a camp. Barbed wire and guards. They were only women and children there. And later I saw an open grave with the bodies of a hundred people at least, women and children as well as men."

She will not go on, Naftali thought. She will tear her clothes and scream.

"Germans were in charge along with the Turkish officers. I saw them. It must be told to the world. But who is there who will believe me?"

She licked her lips as if she had a thirst.

The handkerchief in Miriam's teeth tore with a loud sound, but no one looked at her.

Naftali saw Judah wipe the sweat from his face. He is like Rachel, he thought, but without the capacity to weep.

Papa murmured something inaudible. He wanted to take his daughter into his arms and beg her to forgive the world—and himself.

"Rachel—"

"Naftali?"

"Rachel, was there any word, except at Jebel Musa, of resistance?"

"No."

Again silence.

"No news of the massacre reached here," Judah said, speaking for the first time. "Not even the American consul knew. He would have told me."

Dr. Bloch stood up. "It is not believable."

"I swear . . ."

"Rachel, I don't mean that I don't believe you." He went to the door, his shoes creaking loudly, then walked back to the table. "But the Germans wouldn't permit such a wholesale murder of a people as a matter of policy. This—what you saw—was the madness of an army. Soldiers. There are always such things in wartime. But a whole people . . . as a matter of policy. Never."

"The Jews have often been the victims of such a policy," Naftali said sharply.

"This is something different," the doctor said, annoyed. "The Armenians are Christians, and so are the Germans. I can expect anything from the Turks. Or the Arabs with their holy war. But the Germans. They are civilized. It is impossible."

"Rachel is tired," Papa said.

Dr. Bloch put a small paper envelope on the table. "This is for you, Rachel. It will help you sleep tonight."

Naftali's cane fell to the floor loudly. "What next?" he demanded accusingly. "Are we next? What's the lesson? There is a momentous algebra in Rachel's report. What are the answers?"

Judah said, "We'll talk about this later."

"How much later, Judah? And where? From one end of a mass grave to the other? When, Judah?"

"The locusts have been seen at Der'a. We must begin our fight against them."

Naftali laughed harshly. "Locusts!"

Judah ignored the outburst. "Tomorrow we must gather all our friends to plan the campaign."

Naftali picked up his cane and limped to the door.

"Where are you going?" Judah demanded.

"To find a Jew who will fight Turks instead of locusts."

Judah reddened.

Naftali was at the door.

"Tali!" Judah said. "I want to talk to you. Stay." There was a spine of command in Judah's voice. Naftali could not disobey.

12 ✧✧✧✧✧✧✧✧

Judah's apartment was in a wing separated from his father's house by a small flower garden and a large cedar tree. By his choice it was furnished Turkish style—dark furniture, shell-inlaid taborets, a brass coffee table, heavy rugs, and glass-mosaic lamps. On the walls hung hunting trophies, a Turkish sword, painted photographs of his mother, and one of Herzl that had not been removed despite the risk of arrest for possessing it. High glass-covered bookcases held part of his library. Together with what he had in Atlit, it was the largest collection of agricultural books, manuscripts, and pamphlets in the Middle East.

Judah lit one lamp and put it on a small table in the center of the room. He brought over two chairs, closed the windows, locked the doors, and motioned Naftali to sit next to him. The shadows of the two men stained the high white ceiling.

Judah began by admitting that Naftali had some reason to feel disappointed in him and his inactivity. It was true that he had taken a passive role during the first six months of the war, but that was because he had confidence that whatever might be the fate of the Palestinian Jews under Jemal, it would never result in mass destruction of their villages and the massacre of the people. Now, since Rachel had brought the tragic news of the Armenians, he was forced to conclude that if the sultan, with the acquiescence of the Germans, could do this to a Christian people, there was no reason for him to withhold his hand from the Palestinian Jews.

"We share," he said, "with the Armenians a dream of nationhood. The Young Turks, Talaat, Jemal, and Enver, who are ambitious for a revival of the old Turkish Empire, cannot permit the dream to survive. It explains why Hamid Bek has been sent in, why the Hebrew language has been prohibited, the Zionist leaders exiled, the organizations dissolved. I expected hunger, Tali. Hunger and disruption. Even the expulsion of the Russian Jews. Even the closing down of our secular Zionist schools and papers. But I had not remotely understood that Jemal would consider the murder of a whole people." He smiled wryly with his broad mouth. "And I am no ghetto Jew."

As Naftali raised his head and began to speak, Judah stopped him.

"As you know, Tali, in the past I have thought about methods of struggle. Once I had the romantic notion of an invading army of Jews. But of course that is hopeless." He smiled with self-deprecation, like a man admitting a youthful indiscretion. "There is, however, another approach."

"There is only one way, Judah. One way!" Naftali interrupted loudly.

"Speak softer."

"Oh, Judah, I have wanted to speak for so long. I am weary of two thousand years of being a victim. We have been the world's children to be beaten at whim. My soul is tired of being a child. I am also sick of defending ourselves. I want to attack. I want to overthrow the government. But as Jews. Not as Russian Jewish socialists, or French Jewish republicans, or Italian Jewish revolutionaries. But as Jewish Jews. In our own homeland. In the cause of our own freedom and independence. For that enterprise death might not be so bitter. I have thought of how to do this thing. More than thought—I know. The idea of it is like the sound of the sea. Wherever I turn, there it is. But I have never dared speak until now. What we must do, Judah—" He forced himself to quiet down. "We must kill Jemal, Talaat, and Enver."

He locked his gaze into Judah's. The shadows of their heads on the ceiling were one. Naftali distrusted Judah's frown.

"Don't tell me that is un-Jewish, Judah. Don't say that it is a violation of our moral principles. Don't say that we must have scruples. With an *attentat* of this kind, we will shake London and Paris. They don't even know we are here. The world thinks of Palestine as old ruins, romantic bedouin, dirty streets, picture-card mosques, and the glory-colored backdrops of the places where Jesus was born, preached, and died. The world knows of Gethsemane, the Mount of Olives, Capernaum, the street that was crooked, the manger at Bethlehem, the Jordan and Tiberias. But of Jews here they know nothing. If they ever think of us, they have a picture of pious beggars. The Palestinian Jew does not exist for the world; we, you and I, the pioneers, your parents and mine, who farm this land—we don't exist except in the hothouses of Zionist committees. Let us do this thing, this deed, and the chancelleries of Europe will awake to us, our needs, and our ambitions. They will know Jews are men alive!"

Judah's face was rocklike and grave. He brushed a moth away from the edge of the candle.

"Assassination is drama, not politics," he said at last.

"Who cares for politics, other than politicians? And we've had enough of them. Jewish as well as Christian. Politics changes nothing but the fortunes of politicians."

"What is your object, Tali?"

"To save our people here from being destroyed."

"The same motive of the young Serbian who killed the Austrian archduke. Yet what happens to Serbia will depend not on Princip's shot but on the political needs of the nations that win the war."

"Good. But when the victorious powers turn to look at us they'll see only an Arab country, a rock of Allah, with sprinklings of Christian and Jewish holy places. Palestine will become a Muslim colony of whatever side wins, and we Jews will be swept under the carpet. But —" The thought of taking action thickened his voice. "The death, by our hand, of those unspeakable men who tyrannize this land——"

"Will define us as assassins, anarchists, and men incapable of running their own affairs."

"Considering our situation, there is no other way, Judah!"

"There is a much better way. You speak of your feeling of waste. Of how you yearn to fulfill yourself. You admit to a mystique of destiny. I also have a yearning not to be wasted. It is stronger than ever my desire to make Palestine the milk and honey of the Middle East as it once was. Since the war started I have been thinking of a way for us. A formula for action. I waited for the right moment. Now it has come. I have a plan as practical as irrigation. I have a plan, Tali, that will put the politics of the future of Palestine in our hands."

He straightened up in his chair and looked around at the windows and door.

"If the victors are Germany and Turkey, we are lost," Judah went on quietly. "Then certainly we will be forgotten. A tiny Levantine fragment. . . . But if the English and French are the victors, and I am certain they will be, then we have our chance. I mean, as Jews, for ourselves, you and I and our friends as the trustees of the whole Jewish people. We who pioneered have won a moral position for ourselves. We are not socialists, we have no commitments to an ideology except a Jewish homeland. We are neither for labor nor for business, neither for socialism nor for capitalism. We are for a self-sustained, independent country of independent farmers. Exactly what we are. For the first time in history there is a peasantry consisting of educated men. We are the first generation of Palestine-born Jews with a mission to redeem Zion. We are our own messiahs."

Judah's low, harsh Hebrew filled Naftali like a drug. His eyes were locked into Judah's.

"First, we cannot count on the Jewish leadership," Judah said without pausing. "I have talked with them. They will defend themselves against unwarranted attack, but they will not move one inch to overthrow the government. We can count only on ourselves and a few friends. What does this mean? It means a conspiracy. It means that we must create a small brotherhood willing to risk all to gain all. But this band of willing men will never be large enough to lead an armed rebellion. We would be destroyed in a day. My plan is to do otherwise. To do two things at the same time. To win two victories. To save our people and at the same time force the victors to recognize our leadership. As I said, it is my conviction that the Allies must win. Sooner or later the United States will have to join them. The odds will be overwhelming against Germany, Austria, and Turkey. Then what? Palestine will fall into the British sphere, since it already has Egypt under its dominion. That's the long perspective. . . . Now, if the British Army would move into Palestine from the Suez quickly, our people can be saved from massacre or starvation. But the British have not moved yet. Why? Because they are not strong enough? No. Rather it is because the generals don't know how weak the Turk is. What would happen if we, you and I and our friends, make it possible for the British to move in quickly and without great loss of men? Would they not look to us as leaders of our people? When they come to setting up local government here they will call on us, the very men who made their victory possible. With one stroke we keep our people alive, a guarantee that they will not be swept under the carpet of history. Palestine will become Jewish, perhaps at first a Jewish colony of England's, but Jewish! And we—you and I and our comrades—will be the first council of its ministers."

Naftali remained silent but profoundly moved. He had never heard his teacher talk with such passion.

Judah went to the window to look out, then walked softly to the door, opened it, saw that no one was there, and closed and locked it again. "The nature of my plan is such that I do not want to include my family," he said, returning to the table. "The risks are too great. If you go with me in this, you must also keep it from your mother." He sat down and moved the lamp to one side. "You and I already know from simple observation the disposition in Palestine of the Turkish and German troops, their stores of arms, airplane fields, and artillery sites. We've seen them every time we travel from one place to another. We will have to know more, of course. I propose that we use the campaign against the locusts to record every piece of information available in the countryside, then find a way to get it to the British at Suez. With this information they will understand that they can invade Palestine immediately, with victory assured. They will get a quick success, thanks to us. My plan is to organize a small espionage group——"

"No," Naftali said softly, with pain.

"You object?"

"Spies, Judah?"

"Spies, Tali."

"Compared to political assassination, spying is filth."

"If we are at war against the Turk, what is clean?"

"No! Spying is personally repugnant. It's beneath——"

"The dignity of an oppressed people? Is that in your mind?"

"It is shallow, slimy. One can't be oneself. There is——"

"Nothing heroic. Nothing noble. All undercover and underground. But when we unmask ourselves with proof that we have saved the Yishuv and brought us freedom——"

"Informers——"

"Whom will we be informing on? Our own people? No. On our enemies! Moses did not have qualms about sending the spies into Canaan. We will become the advance guard of the Allies. Their eyes and ears. We will save them casualties!"

"But, Judah, for six months the English have been sitting at the Suez doing nothing! How do we know they'll take advantage of our information, that they'll attack?"

"We don't know. We don't know anything until we try. It is our only chance, our people's only chance. Otherwise the Turks will do to us what they did to the Armenians. It is our only chance to win a place in the sun for ourselves when peace comes."

"Spies . . ."

"Soldiers in different uniforms. Soldiers without guns but with memories and a knowledge of the terrain that no one else has. Once the British enter, they will give us arms. Then we will become soldiers like the others."

"How will we get our information to the British?"

Judah stopped for the first time to wipe the sweat from his face. "We will go and tell them. You and I."

Naftali laughed softly. "Through the Turkish Army, across the Sinai, four hundred kilometers . . ."

"Or by neutral ship from Jaffa or Haifa or Beirut."

Naftali thought it was as if a poet had created an impossible combination of words—the forgiving wood, the laughing iron, the loving paper. Judah's idea was something of that kind, a joining of new connectives. Yet in the final meaning of poetry, as well as of life, that was precisely what made greatness. To see behind the obvious, to do the contradictory, to act the illogical. Judah's plan was more feasible than his own.

Yet he was not satisfied. "We will not accept one penny from the English," Naftali said firmly.

"Naturally not. We are not their agents but our own."

"We will tell them why we are doing this for ourselves as well as for them."

"That will depend on the circumstances of our meeting."

"No. Under any conditions, we must tell them."

"I will determine whether we do or not."

Naftali was stopped by the peremptory tone.

"I will lead this group," Judah said quietly. "There will be discussions, of course, but in the end the decision as well as the responsibility will be mine. And who will not have it so should not join me."

"Still, the democratic principle must not be destroyed."

"It is the absolute goal. In that you are right, Tali. But we are entering a conspiracy, and the history of conspiracies teaches that without a single will to which all are obedient, failure is inevitable. We will have no debating after the decision has been made. Nor any sullen anarchy either. Are you with me?"

Naftali could not surrender easily. "It is politics. . . ."

"Yes."

"It is demeaning to hide from the world, to sneak. . . ."

"Is it less demeaning to assassinate a general?"

Naftali was silent. There seemed a difference that he could neither confirm nor communicate. It had to do with the meaning of the deed, indeed the purpose that one had or did not have for one's life. To assassinate the oppressor gave one a clear identity—with the act, with the victim, with the cause for which it was done. It was not, finally, surreptitious. It was there for all to see and to learn from. But with espionage, the secretive life, the mask and deceit of action, there could never be a clear thing to be learned from and emulated. It was a kind of baksheesh. No one would know what had been done or not been done. The British would be the owners of their spirit as well as their information, and when it was all over, what would the victors say? It would be easy for them to say that nothing had been done. And as for the Jewish community in Palestine, since it would not be part of this conspiracy its life would be risked without its knowledge or consent. In the end it might disavow Judah and his comrades. Where then the meaning of the act? Where, then, the blow for a people's freedom if the people did not know or share the blow—or approve what was done on their behalf?

"I would risk myself, Judah," Naftali said at last. "But if we fail— I mean, if the Turks should find us out, will they not take their revenge on every breathing Jew from the Bosporus to the Dead Sea? It's a grievous responsibility."

"I have thought of that," Judah said calmly. "But no matter what we do or what any group of Jews does, the risk is the same. Even the shomrim of the colonies take that risk every time they shoot at an Arab cattle thief. But because we will be a very small group, the chance of being detected will be small. I admit, the risk is there. But there is also a risk, a greater one, that if we don't act there'll be no Jews left in Palestine to put in jeopardy."

How strange and contradictory, Naftali thought, that a method of deceit should be conceived by a scientist, while the poet insisted on clarity and openness. Was this the scientific mind's need to compensate for the remorseless precision and frankness of the laboratory whenever it left it to deal with the more amorphous stuff of human life? As for himself, he knew the frustrating ambiguities in his own work; the poet at the end is always defeated by the failure of words to match his feelings. Perhaps he also compensated; perhaps that is why the poet in politics is always a revolutionist where principles are clear and simple.

Naftali, however, sensed from the first that he would have to follow Judah, no matter what path he would take, as long as it was a path of action. Practically, Judah was the only one with a reputation beyond Palestine. The British would have to listen to him. Further, he had the moral presence of leadership, the psychic distance, the grandeur of certainty, the suggestion that beneath his words was an intuition and knowledge that others, lesser men, did not possess.

To be in the shadow of such certainty was like being in the sun. Naftali had rarely known it in himself. It was a good feeling; it was a better feeling than impulse, than the self-doubting calculations that in the past had caused him so much anxiety. If he, Naftali, had always suffered from a dissonance of action, a life that had rarely been lived synchronously, Judah's life, it seemed to him, was lived on time. What Judah offered was certainty and hard action. Not exactly the kind Naftali wanted or needed, but hard enough. He would live, then, on Judah's time, not his own.

He rubbed his right eye. Something had irritated it. "All right, Judah," he said quietly.

"Let us draw up a list in our minds," Judah said evenly, as if he had known Naftali's agreement would come. "I want men whom we can trust. A handful. Say six or seven. Preferably young and unmarried. You and I will ask them to meet with me at the station. Say that we meet to plan the fight against the locusts. We will start the first thing in the morning."

Gravely Judah offered his hand and Naftali shook it, surprised at the formality of his friend.

" 'There is a time for love and a time for hate. A time of war and a time of peace'," Judah said, speaking each word slowly, as if to savor history. "Now is our time, Tali."

Naftali kept rubbing his eyes until the irritation was gone.

When Judah left Naftali to go back into the main part of the house, he found Rachel alone and asked her about Nahum. Soon there would be even less time to talk of personal matters.

"Rachel, I know you are very tired, but tomorrow I will have to leave early and you and I might not have the opportunity. Tell me how things were with you."

"They went well."

She had known these questions would come and had worked out answers based on pride.

"Your letters told us very little. You understand, I want you to be happy." He waited. "Were you happy?"

"I was homesick."

"Naturally."

"Did Nahum disappoint you in any way?"

She tried to smile reassuringly. "You could also ask Nahum that question about me. After all, what couple really knows each other before marriage?"

Judah lost patience. The decision made with Naftali was burning him.

"You are avoiding answering me. Is anything so terrible or so secret that you can't speak of it to a brother?"

"Don't shout, Judah."

"I'm sorry. But can't you say simply, one way or the other, whether you have been happy? Relatively happy or relatively not? You've been married a year. I'm interested. I love you. You know I would help you in anything."

"I know."

"Then?"

Her pride and reserve were not that strong. Sooner or later she would have to tell the truth. Yet she hesitated. She wanted Judah to respect her and not to be disillusioned. To confess failure might make him think that she was an impulsive, thoughtless child without the substance he could admire.

"Every first year of marriage has problems," she said falteringly.

"They are not what I'm talking about!"

"Please, don't get angry. You are not so experienced in these matters either."

She saw that she had hurt him and went on quickly. "My dear Judah, I am here and not in Constantinople. Doesn't that say something to you?"

"Was it because Nahum treated you badly?"

She retreated. "No! No! It was because I was worried about you and Papa."

"You are being mysterious. You say, 'Doesn't my being here and not in Constantinople mean anything?' You are suggesting it means more than your normal anxiety. I must assume that there were problems between you——"

"Yes, there were problems."

"You don't love him anymore?"

"It is not that simple."

He felt her reproach and was annoyed with himself.

"If you will not confide in me, Rachel, I can't force it, of course. I will have to let the facts speak for themselves. You understand that I would prefer you not to be here, where there may be greater dangers for us than there would be in Constantinople, but I won't insist. However, I want you to answer two simple questions. Will Nahum join you here?"

"I don't think so."

"Do you intend to stay here, then, until the war is over?"

He had trapped her.

"Perhaps."

"Even if it lasts years?"

"Yes," she whispered.

He went to her and kissed her awkwardly. "I'm sorry, Rachel. I'm sorry. . . ."

Tears came into her eyes, and she embraced him.

"I should have been closer to you, Rachel. Forgive me for thinking so much of myself and my work."

It was intolerable to her that Judah, the commander of the family, should ask for forgiveness.

"There is nothing to forgive, Judah," she said.

"It was my fault, Rachel. I wasn't brother enough to you."

"I will not have you say that! I married Nahum because I wanted to. Nothing could have changed that. And you are not responsible!"

He saw her pale, weary face and felt something of the depth of her suffering. "We won't talk any more about it, darling. And whatever you want shall be done."

Before they separated she asked him not to say anything to Papa about this talk. "He will want to know too. But I will tell him that Nahum agreed to let me stay here until the war is over."

She could not resist asking if he were disappointed in her.

He was aghast. "As if anything you do could disappoint me," he said with complete sincerity.

She felt satisfied.

13 ◇◇◇◇◇◇◇◇◇

Naftali couldn't sleep. Images of conspiracy clashed with images of Rachel. When he first saw her that day he had tried to teach her with a look that he was not the Naftali she had left. Nor was she the Rachel whom he had known. The markings of love covered him, he thought; did she see them? Or had she succumbed entirely to her marriage? Had time damned them? Thinking of her, he cursed himself and blessed her.

Since he couldn't sleep, he left the cot Judah had made up for him, washed, and went into the garden. Dawn was his favorite time; the succumbing night meant more to him than twilight, for although both held a mystery of passage, it was the triumph of light that brought him closest to reverence. It must have been dawn when Abraham saw Jehovah, when Moses received the Torah at Sinai; it was the light over the ark of the world.

He limped up and down alongside the stone garden wall, breathing in the scents of jasmine and the cool night earth. There was no moon and the stars had their own way with the sky. Stillness. Even Reb Mottel's chickens were asleep. In the Jew trees there was yet no sound of the sparrows. The dovecotes above the house were as silent as the sky. What could he say to Rachel? When should he say it? Should he say anything? He damned himself again. The sudden cry of a jackal in the wild, dark foothills of the Carmel mocked him.

Nor could Rachel sleep, for like Naftali, two images fought for her mind—the tragedy of the Armenian dead and Naftali. Now that she had seen his vulnerable face, made beautiful by the thin, black, student's beard, she knew again that she loved him. But if it had been hopeless before, as a married woman it was doubly hopeless. She lay awake, impatient with herself and her life.

• • •

At breakfast, over the tomatoes and cucumbers, tea and bread, Naftali said nothing. But when the time came to leave with Judah, he went into the kitchen, where Rachel was washing the dishes. "Did I tell you how happy I am that you are back?" he said. "It is selfish of me. Here it is more dangerous than in Constantinople to be a Jew. But will you stay?"

"Yes."

"You know that I missed you, Rachel."

She was silent and went to a closet to get a towel.

"Was the watch as clever as I said it would be," he asked, limping after her.

She smiled. "It was an obedient watch. When I wound it, it kept time."

"I didn't write you as I had promised. But I couldn't."

"I understand."

"I didn't dare to."

From outside Judah called to him to come.

"Rachel—"

"Judah is waiting."

"Rachel, I don't know when I'll come back to Har Nehemia." He paused. "I've been stupid and blind. . . ."

"Judah is waiting for you." She had to say something to keep from throwing herself into his arms.

He saw the desire in her eyes, and he thought of Nahum. For the first time sexual jealousy invaded him, sharp and painful, all the more because he knew that it was his own fault. She had loved him and he had been a chaotic child with visions of a life that had not included love.

He heard her breathing; he saw the strain of her full body against the kitchen table.

"It is always the one who pretends to see the most who sees only himself," he said. "Poets are like that. We wear a Greek mask. We live in symbols. We look into the mirror and see the mask, not the face. It is a kind of madness."

"Go now, please."

"At least let me tell you, Rachel, that since you left here, since I saw you last on your wedding day, leaving with Nahum . . ." Again the blow of jealousy in the stomach. ". . . I have not written one poem,

130

nor one line of a poem. There is no mask anymore. Can you see my face?"

She walked past him to the door, holding a plate in her hand as if it were a chalice. She couldn't listen. She knew he loved her.

"Look in my eyes, Rachel. Do you see what is in them?"

The shock of fear and mortality that the massacre had imprinted on her made her yearn for life. But the wall of Nahum stood between them. It was too high, too strong; her vows . . . How could she warn him?

Judah called again noisily. "It's time, Tali!"

Naftali did not move.

Rachel turned away slowly, like the tearing of a leaf from a branch, and he left.

14 ◇◇◇◇◇◇◇◇◇

It was early morning, the sky outside the station a pure white and yellow.

The friends had gathered in the upper story of the station, the men who were not already committed to the party or Hashomer, sons of independent farmers or young men who had worked with Judah and Naftali and had formed a circle around them. There was Manfred Gersh, freed from the army after payment of considerable money; Dmitri Liebermann, the Tolstoyan, with aristocratic manner; his cousin Avram, tall, dependable and reserved; Reuven Schechter from Har Nehemia, a quiet man, talented in mathematics, a distant relative of the Singers.

Naftali and Judah had discussed Saul Wilner at great length. Neither liked him but they thought he could be useful. Ever since he brought the news of Naftali he had adopted the station, living and working there without asking anyone's permission.

"He has chutzpa," Naftali said. "And we need such."

They were also unsure of Nissim Vidali. Naftali thought he ought to be taken in. "He follows me wherever I go. It will be impossible to keep him from knowing. And I believe he can help if orders are given to him clearly, with no area for misunderstanding."

Naftali stationed himself at the window to warn Judah of gendarme patrols or strangers. Judah moved a blackboard to the center of the group of men, drew the outlines of a locust, and listed some of its characteristics. None had been seen in Palestine in forty years and the insect was not well known.

Then Judah put the chalk in his pocket and said slowly, "Before talking about my plans for fighting the locust invasion, there are a few other matters I want to discuss. All of you may not know that my sister, Rachel, has just come back from Constantinople. She has brought terrible news."

He described the massacre of the Armenians as Rachel had seen it. He pointed out that this was the result of the Turkish policy of elimination of minorities. So far this policy as it affected the Jews was political and not military, but there was no reason to think that Enver Bey and Jemal Pasha might not do to the Yishuv what had been done so bloodily to the Christian Armenians. He referred to the search for arms in the villages, the expulsion of the Jews from Jaffa, the exiling of Zionist leaders, the transferring of Jewish soldiers from combat units to labor battalions, the execution of Mordecai Anuskevitz and the bastinadoing of Naftali.

"Even more dangerous signs are visible," he went on. "There have been arrests without cause of some of the leaders of the settlements. In the Jewish quarters of Jerusalem and Hebron and Safed thousands are starving. In my judgment, we are losing one percent of our people each week, either to prisons or by disease and malnutrition. If something isn't done quickly, the Yishuv will be destroyed. And I have called you together not only to fight the locusts but also to fight the greater enemy."

The men felt a growing excitement. Saul Wilner, who had been paring his nails with insolent indifference, put his hands in his pockets and listened with half-closed eyes. Manfred's fingers tapped on the table without his willing them. It was a violinist's tic that possessed him when he became nervous. Nissim strained to understand all Judah was saying, but his eyes went to Naftali's face.

Seeing these men in their silence, Naftali felt himself grow a second body enclosing the others. Intuitively he jumped ahead in time, projecting the synthesis of a group, a unity, an intermingling of desires and actions and fate.

Judah described briefly the political situation in the Yishuv. As a result of the expulsion of thousands of Jews, the economy of the settlements was greatly disrupted. If not for the fact that one of the leaders of the Palestine Zionists was a German subject, all financial aid would have been stopped. The leaders were in conflict. Some were pro-Turkish; some, secretly pro-Allies, encouraged the young men to get out of the country and join the British Army in Egypt. All were forced to use their energies to keep the Jewish community organs from falling completely apart.

"In this manner, we are living through one of the great episodes of man's history," Judah said. "Defensive, our noses just below the level of subsistence. We shall go under if that is all we are willing to do. We shall not be worthy of our destiny. But there is another way. I do not claim perfection for it. Nor do I guarantee its success. But it is the only way I know that may keep the Yishuv alive and at the same time promise great strength for its future. I have a plan."

He paused. In the silence, Wilner cracked his knuckles with a loud sound. Dmitri said, "Sha!"

"It will require chutzpa. At stake are our lives. Naftali and I will go ahead by ourselves if necessary."

"Nu, tell us already," Wilner said.

"Do I have your pledges that if you decide not to join us you will keep this meeting a secret?"

"On my honor!" Dmitri said quickly. "Speak!"

Others murmured assent.

"Like buying a horse without looking into his mouth," Wilner protested.

"In this case, you'll have to trust the seller," Judah said.

"Nu, boychik," Avram said to Wilner. "It's Israel that's being offered. Your horse should have such a long life."

Wilner bent his head to one side with a half smile of contempt. "I am also a gambler. I'll hear. And I'll pledge to be deaf and dumb if I don't like it."

Judah breathed in deeply, took the chalk out of his pocket, then replaced it. "Our only chance of surviving is to bring the war in Palestine quickly to an end. Only the British can do this. Therefore I propose that we help the British. If we do our task well, the British will be able to pluck this land from the sultan like an overripe orange. She will then recognize our contribution. We, you and I together, will welcome them to the Holy City. We will be their allies. Trusted allies. It will be the beginning. From that time on the Jews will have to be reckoned with. . . . And how will we help the British? We will deliver to them information about the Turkish Army."

He had put it to them simply and compactly. It was his way. . . . The men moved a little in their chairs or on their feet. Manfred scratched a match to light a Russian cigarette Mordecai had bequeathed to him.

"Ah," Avram Liebermann sighed. Judah's plan was a surprise. But it was a good one. He trusted the British.

"Spies!" Dmitri said in a shocked voice.

"Patriots!" Avram replied quickly.

Dmitri was flustered and uneasy. "No! No! I don't want to be misunderstood. I am not afraid of a word. But there are moral questions."

"The Bible is filled with spies," Avram said, annoyed at his cousin's tendency to philosophize. To him life was a simple fact obscured and made complex by ideas.

Dmitri stood up to confront the taller man. "The Bible is filled with angels, but that doesn't mean we can fly. I can see the political ends of such a plan. But is there no more to it than that? What of the spiritual goals? I don't mean religious, I mean spiritual. You understand, don't you, Judah?"

"Finish what you want to say, Dmitri," Judah replied.

"Forgive me for lecturing. But these matters must be taken seriously. We are all part of the life force, are we not? The state and power are only particles of the life force. We have to be consistent to its demands."

Avram interrupted. "I don't understand a thing you're saying, cousin."

"You never understand anything but hunting and fishing."

"Let him continue, Avram," Judah said.

"The question can be put like this, Judah. Within the life force we must ask, 'What is the meaning of this act? Will it be for good or evil for mankind?' "

"Oy, now it's mankind. Let's first see if it's good for the Jews," Avram said.

Reuven broke in. "Dmitri asks the right question. The particular is proven by the universal."

"Who is he?" Saul Wilner asked Nissim, who was next to him.

"Reuven Schechter."

"That's his name. What's he do?"

"I work in the vineyards," Reuven said. "I am also a mathematician."

Dmitri marched to the blackboard. "I must complete my thought, Judah. My thought is this. I'm not opposed to your plan, mind you. I refuse to call it 'spying.' But if every man duplicates what we would do, will it be good for mankind and—yes, Avram, for the Jews too? Although I'm not orthodox, I believe that out of Zion must come forth Torah. By Torah I mean wisdom, understanding, compassion. Not deceit, not expedience, not shortsighted politics. What kind of freedom will we have if the first steps we take toward it are contrary to Torah?"

"Does he always talk such nonsense?" Saul Wilner asked.

"It is not nonsense!" Dmitri said angrily.

"Quiet!" Naftali said at the window. "Patrol."

Four mounted gendarmes moved along the Caesarea road in the direction of Haifa.

"Remember we are learning about locust killing," Judah said.

"How will we move around the country?" Avram asked softly.

"I have Jemal's *laissez-passer*. I will sign orders for each of you in his name."

"And getting the good news to our tea-drinking friends?"

"That will be discussed when there is something to give them. Tali, the patrol?"

"They are passing the crossroad. It's clear."

Dmitri wiped his glasses and stared around the room nearsightedly. "I have nothing more to say for the present."

"You have asked questions, Dmitri," Naftali said. "They are good questions. I asked the same kind when Judah first talked to me. But what is morality, Dmitri? Is it not action taken for moral ends? Is the good of man a moral end? We are Jews. How have we lived? In the exile we are a silent people, defensive, apologetic, fearful. At best we imitate others. We are ashamed of murders we didn't commit, heresies we never heard of. We condemn our children even before they are born to the life of crippled souls. Here we of the second generation of pioneers are beginning to feel what it is to be men. Yet we cannot fulfill ourselves as long as we remain serfs of a corrupt society. Is it moral to act to make humans fully human again? Wait, Dmitri, you have had your chance. I think I know what is in your mind. You are wondering, as I wondered, can we risk other lives, innocent lives, men, women, and children who are not being asked to approve our acts? What can we answer Mottel, the butcher, if we are caught and he, innocent of our so-called treason, is beaten and hanged? What of Dr. Bloch and Miriam, Rachel, and your mother and father, Dmitri? Dare we act without their approval?"

Dmitri nodded. The others, even Saul Wilner, listened with great intenseness. Naftali was describing their hearts.

"I also asked that question. I will tell you now how I understand the answer. To decide a course for others is the heaviest responsibility a man can take. Judah said that the Yishuv is in jeopardy of being wiped out, even if we do nothing. Still, that is not enough of an excuse. The truth is—there is no excuse. *None!* Bar Kochba had no excuse to call on his people to die. Moses had no excuse leading his people into the wilderness. Indeed, they revolted against him. No prophet ever has an excuse. God commanded Moses, the rabbis say. But God has been silent a long, long time. We have wet His face with our tears, and He has not uttered a sound. Perhaps He is waiting for us. Perhaps He is tired of spineless people. Perhaps the meaning of being a chosen people is precisely that when we act He will speak."

The word "God" did not come easy to him. The religion of his fathers was not his. Yet Jewish history was inseparable from God's history. That was the mystery binding him to the Adonai he knew and did not know, believed in and doubted, affirmed and at times cursed and denied.

"We will act for the Yishuv without asking its permission. It is a risk we take. But we have no choice. No conspiracy can live by majority votes. We will have to pretend, as Moses pretended, that God will not forget His promise. My conscience is clear. Do we act for money? No. Our first condition with the British will be that we do not accept payment for our information. For applause? I predict that our people will despise us for what we are doing. Jews have a long hatred against spying, despite what the Bible says. We have suffered from informers and we have no experience, modern experience, if you will, with espionage on our own behalf. They will despise us if we fail, for our failure will hurt deeply. They will despise us if we succeed because they did not share our action. Indeed, Dmitri, our action would be opposed by the socialist colonies, for it is far removed from their dogma and program. No, we will be without honor in our own country."

Naftali paused, momentarily confused, feeling that he had not completed his thought. His words, even those he had just spoken, seemed unspoken, a blank.

The men waited and he began again. Slower this time, trying to hear himself.

"It is moral not to be dirt beneath the feet of the nations. It is moral not to die meaninglessly. It is moral, isn't it, Dmitri, not to die as Mordecai died, as the Armenians died, cattle in the abbatoir? If all men duplicated our action—the question you asked—then there would be fewer tyrants. I tell you, it is moral to act to fulfill the promise of what we are as human beings, Jews or non-Jews. It is moral to act on behalf of freedom. Now, yesterday, tomorrow. For all peoples, anywhere. Anything, *anything,* we do to overthrow the Turk is moral, Dmitri. We share the pain of our people. This is Torah, this is wisdom, this is compassion!" He caught his breath. "We have a special duty, Dmitri. The survival of the Jews is a commandment laid upon every Jew!"

No one moved.

"Ah, Tali," Nissim whispered adoringly. He understood exactly what his friend was saying. If one beats even sheep too much they will fight back.

One by one the men turned their faces from Naftali to Judah, waiting for him to speak. Dmitri suddenly felt a devouring regret that Naftali, not he, had spoken that way. Why was it his lot always to obscure, to oppose? Had he really been anxious about the morality of spying or were his questions a method of masking his own fear of action?

Judah broke the spell. "Dmitri, are you with us?"

Dmitri took his time answering. "I am, God help us!"

"Reuven?"

The young mathematician opened his mouth to speak, changed his mind and nodded.

"Nissim?"

The young Spaniard looked surprised.

"Nissim, do you understand?"

"If you beat sheep long enough, they will fight back."

"Bravo!" Avram said.

"I will do anything Tali asks," Nissim said.

Naftali said, "Not for my sake. You must understand that it is your decision."

"Are you not my friend, my teacher?"

"That's not enough."

Nissim frowned. It was becoming cloudy in the room. As if the heavens had descended. It was difficult to keep track of one's thoughts. Tali shouldn't say such things.

"I do it for your sake, Tali." He paused, troubled, pleading with his eyes. Then he grinned happily. "I do it then for my own sake too. Eh? Isn't that right?"

Naftali waved assent.

"Avram?"

"Absolutely."

"Wilner?"

Wilner pulled at his finger, cracking the bones loudly. "All this dreck about hurting people. If they're hurt, they're hurt. Does anyone know what's good for others? Dumb and blind, that's what people are. Men are not sheep. They are dogs. A bone, a little sleep, a little spasm with a bitch."

"I protest!" Dmitri cried. "That's monstrous. A libel!"

"People aren't beasts, Wilner," Naftali added, shocked by the brutality of the comment.

"Quiet, please," Judah interrupted. "We are not debating morality anymore. I asked a simple question, Wilner."

"Personally, I spit on the British."

"No jokes!"

"It is not a joke, Mr. Singer. I spit on them. I don't trust them. Am I a historian? So don't ask me to prove it. But then, I spit on the Turks and Germans too. And as for the Russians, ten feet of earth on top of them all would be too little. I would drown them all with spit. Personally, I don't like your plan. It is like a chicken scratching at the feet of a camel. But—" He shrugged and pushed his Polish student's hat to the back of his head. "I personally sometimes put myself in the soul of a chicken. Will there be any feed for me? Idealist, I am not."

"No money, if that's what you mean," Judah said. "But the station funds will be used to supply food and other necessities. You can live here."

"That's better than nothing."

Judah was relieved. The group could use a tough-minded man.

"Manfred?"

Manfred stopped tapping against his knee. "Once," he said, "the great Leopold Auer and the great Eugène Ysaye told me that I couldn't ever become a first-class fiddler. No one ever said I couldn't become a first-class spy."

The tension broke; the men laughed and moved around, talking among themselves. The morning sun was high; the room was hot but no one noticed.

Dmitri had picked a Bible out of the bookcase and in deep concentration was turning pages.

"For the first time since Bar Kochba, almost nineteen hundred years," Naftali said quietly to Manfred, "we're organizing to overthrow our oppressors."

Dmitri stopped at a passage, murmured a Hebrew phrase, "*Netzach Isra'el lo ishaker'. . . .*" He repeated it loudly.

The others stopped to listen.

"What is it?" Wilner asked. His Hebrew was not as good as the others'.

"Judah!" Dmitri cried. "Why not a name for our group? *Netzach Isra'el lo ishaker'!* We can use the initials NILI."

Judah repeated the Hebrew to himself.

Dmitri didn't wait for Judah's approval but shouted, "Our name, our password, our destiny! NILI!"

The men repeated the phrase, "NILI!" They liked it.

Businesslike, Judah broke in to give a brief outline of the plan. They were to leave at dawn the next morning from the station for Der'a, where the locusts had been seen. The men were to observe every Turkish encampment, troop movement, supply depot, and airfield. Each night they would pass on to him or Naftali what they had learned. The material would be coded, and when enough of it was put together, a way would be found to get it to the British.

"We are amateurs at this," he said. "Amateurs expose themselves by their eagerness or by what they think is bravery. We will not take any chances. No one is to write down a word. Memorize what you see. Our task is to remain undetected. If anyone is caught, I will naturally claim I knew nothing about it. This is the manner of international espionage. It may even come to pass that I will have to jeopardize the safety of one or more in order to protect the others for the greater mission. Is that all understood?"

The men nodded solemnly. The exaltation of a few minutes before was being tempered.

"I will give all the orders. Or Naftali, whom I commission as my aide. Order number one. You will not reveal to your families our mission or the existence of—" He paused, then nodded. "Of NILI. If anyone is found disobeying this order or any other, the penalty will be expulsion." His tone grew cold. "We are not bandits, but it may be necessary to rid ourselves permanently of the incapable. Any comments?"

Dmitri coughed as if in protest but said nothing.

"If there are no questions, leave here two at a time. The Liebermanns first. If anyone asks in your village where you are going tomorrow, answer, 'Under orders from Jemal Pasha to fight locusts.' If gendarmes stop you, be respectful. If there is trouble, refer them to me. And no one is to carry arms."

"I have a pass for my rifle," Wilner said.

"Then keep it."

Before the men departed as they were ordered, each one came up to Judah to shake his hand, to make the bond physical. When it was Dmitri's turn, he whispered fervently, "NILI. *Netzach Isra'el lo ishaker'.*"

"NILI!" Wilner said with irritation. "What does it mean?"

" 'The Eternal One of Israel will not deceive her,' " Judah replied in Yiddish. "From Second Samuel."

"A name for a child's game," Wilner said and sauntered out of the room without a word of farewell.

When Naftali and Judah were alone, they worked out a code, based on the Psalms, using the text of the eighteenth, which both men knew by heart. In Hebrew the numerals added up to the word that meant "life." An acrostic, working forward from the last verse, was the code's alphabet. A set of keys was established to shift the alphabet back and forth from any one verse.

Toward evening Judah went home to Har Nehemia, but Naftali remained at the station, needing to be by himself. The future had to be tasted in solitude.

15 ◇◇◇◇◇◇◇◇◇

From Mesopotamia or from the valley of the Euphrates, from the forgotten desert ranges of Syria or from some as yet unnamed place, locusts came for the first time in forty years to the plains of Sharon and the Shefela, the valley of Jezreel and the hill country of Samaria. They came out of a wilderness of rock and sand, the engraved directional tic of their bodies leading them hundreds of miles toward growing things. The drumming of their wings was as loud as the sea breakers off Ashkelon. Their swarms hid the sun from the earth and the earth from the sun. Wherever they went, there was no day, only night, and the track of time was lost.

Like a crawling skin, the locusts covered the faces and bodies of the men, women, and children, filling their nostrils, nesting in the hair, crowding into the open, panting mouths, beating against the closed eyes. In a rage people fought to strike back, to kill, to destroy the destroyers, and ran insanely from one end of the assaulted fields to the other, beating the locusts with flails and stamping on those already dead in order to feel some pitiful triumph. At night, unable to stay awake because of exhaustion, they screamed in their sleep and tore vainly at their own skin to rid it of the obscene memory of the invaders. Men stopped thinking, stopped making decisions, lost all sense that they were human, and became part of a mindless crusade that drove them, like the locusts, into a battle that was hopeless for both.

There were no victories. The earth was stripped of corn and cabbage, of wheat and barley; the orchards of almonds, oranges, and olives were turned into skeletons of trees; even the bark was devoured. The land was a corpse covered with the yellow shroud of dead locusts.

And still they came, flying and humming, borne on the *hamsin* winds, destroying the villages, turning green into yellow.

Judah and his men fought them stubbornly. They were joined by Jewish farmers and Arab fellahin, even by Turkish soldiers from nearby camps who had been farmers and suffered at the sight of the death of crops.

Judah's men followed the locusts from Der'a, Nablus, Rechovot, Petach Tikva, Rishon le Zion; from Degania at the Jordan to the Arab villages of Ephraim, Samaria, and Judea. He commanded the farmers to build ditches and flood them, the children to beat drums and kettles and drive the crawlers into pools to drown. He ordered vats of boiling water poured along the edges of fields and fresh water to moat the base of trees. With kerosene he burned alternate sections of fields and vineyards to make firebreaks. He used sprays with cresols and vinegar. But there were no victories, for he could not reach other places where the locusts were left to mate, bury their eggs, and start the cycle of destruction again.

When the tide of locusts ebbed for a day, the men, as weary as they were, plowed the fields to turn up the eggs and grubs, hopeful that some part of the produce still could be saved. But then a new humming would be heard, again the sky above them clouded, and again the trembling air was filled with a winged fog of insects. And the men would start all over again to destroy the invaders.

Each day Judah assigned a different man to leave the fighting and go into the nearest town or settlement to pick up information. Or he would send them into a Turkish Army camp ostensibly to get help against the locusts. Over the weeks his notebook became filled with the disposition of Turkish troops, schedules of supply trains, the siting of new and old airfields, depots, etc.

The Turkish soldiers talked easily, but they didn't know much. The Germans knew more but were suspicious.

One day Reuven Schechter was arrested in a Nablus café by a German corporal with whom he was having coffee. The corporal thought he was asking too many questions. A German officer interrogated Reuven.

Reuven showed the *laissez-passer* signed by Jemal.

The officer, a knowledgeable young Bavarian who could read Turkish, asked him his name and pointed out that the pass was limited to duty against locusts and there were none in that area.

"They are near Tulkarem," Reuven said.

"Thirty kilometers away."

"I have been fighting them without rest for two weeks. I came here for a change of scene."

"Fighting them alone?"

"With friends."

"They are like yourself, Jews?"

"They are like myself, Jews who are Turkish citizens."

"Tulkarem has cafés. Why have you come here for— How did you put it? A change of scene?"

"Is there a law against entering and leaving Nablus?"

"Now, tell me what was your real reason? To see a woman perhaps?"

"I have no woman here. If you have any charge against me, I refer you to his Excellency Jemal Pasha. I am under his orders."

"A Judah Singer is under his orders, not a Reuven Schechter."

"Mr. Singer asked me to work with him."

"How many are there of you?"

"We come and go. No fixed number. No more than five or six at any time."

"How is it that you speak German so well?"

"I studied mathematics at the University of Berlin."

The Bavarian smiled wryly. "Congratulations. You chose to return here when you might have remained in Germany. How is it possible?"

"Palestine is my home, sir."

"Would you be interested in working for me?"

"No, sir."

"Why not?"

"Because I am working for Jemal Pasha. I have enough to do."

"I pay."

"Thank you. I don't need money."

"That is very doubtful." He rose. "Next time, if I see you in Nablus, I will charge you with espionage."

Reuven stood up, shaken. "Espionage? Absurd! For whom?"

"For whom? For anyone. For Jemal, for Enver Bey, for the French, the Russians, the English. This is the most corrupt country in the world, Schechter. Absolute corruption. I don't trust anyone. Now, to prove my consistency, I will ask you to show me everything you have in your pockets."

Reuven had nothing suspicious in them. He had memorized the information the supply corporal had given him.

Reuven reported the experience to Judah.

Next day an Arab they hadn't seen before came to the village where they were working and offered to sell Avram a rifle. When Avram told him to go away, the Arab hung around and followed the group from village to village. Whether or not he was spying on them was never known, but the men had to be very careful.

One day in early April rumors washed over Palestine that the British were planning a major invasion. Sailors from neutral ships entering Jaffa said they had seen fleets of transports loading men and artillery in Port Said.

Word went from village to village; Jews and dissident Arabs whispered it in the cafés and suqs. The sheiks began to worry that they had given their allegiance to the sultan too lightly. German Jews began to make overtures to their friends whom they knew were pro-British. As the days passed, hopes rose from the secret places of the land.

Naftali talked to Judah about stealing arms from Turkish Army camps and preparing guerrilla action behind their lines. He mentioned caves he knew in the Judean hills, defiles and wadis where they could hide and ambush retreating Turkish columns.

"This is the time to make a raid on Jemal's headquarters. If he were killed, along with his German advisers, the defending army would be headless and demoralized."

Judah refused to approve Naftali's plans. "To take action prematurely would destroy us long before the British could get here."

"Release me from fighting locusts. On my own, Judah. Only my life will be risked."

"I will not permit it, Tali. We must wait for facts, for evidence. If you disobey me, consider yourself expelled from NILI."

By the end of April the evidence was clear. Large English forces had indeed left the ports of Egypt. The goal, however, was not Palestine but the Gallipoli Peninsula of European Turkey.

Although this was a disappointment to Judah and his friends and to others in the Jewish community who were pro-Allies, they could see the strategic wisdom of the move and prayed for a quick British victory. But as the months went on, through the summer and into the fall, the victory seemed more and more distant. Even the British advance under General Townshend against Baghdad did not lessen Judah's and Naftali's anxiety. The war was being taken out of their hands. There was no possibility of a British offensive from Egypt into Palestine as long as all the empire's strength outside the Western Front was spent on Gallipoli and Baghdad.

Judah's men were becoming tired and impatient. Four months fighting locusts, four months playing with the hangman. There were as many locusts now as when they began, and the notebook was still in Judah's pocket and not with the British. The disruption of their homes had grown sharper. The attack on Gallipoli had frightened the provincial governors; martial law was being administered with renewed brutality.

Naftali had spoken to Judah privately and was put off with the sharp reminder that he never had a sense of "the right time." But one night in Judah's tent, where the men gathered after work, Wilner spoke up for the others.

"It's time for an accounting," he said to Judah in his customary sharp tone. "When are we sending the messenger?" He used the code word "angel."

"Keep your voice down," Dmitri said quickly. The tent was on the outskirts of an Arab village in the Galilee.

"He makes a point," Avram Liebermann said.

Judah replied calmly that nothing was going to happen on the Palestine front until the decision was clear at Gallipoli.

"Maybe we can pinch their fat behinds," Wilner insisted.

"The time is not right yet," Judah said.

"It may not be right for an offensive," Manfred said, "but why isn't it a good time to show them who we are?"

"It's our necks we stretch out every day. And I'm sick of locusts!" Wilner shouted.

Judah could not tell them his real reasons for the delay. Who was to go to the British? That question had him in a vise. He wanted to go himself, take all the risks, establish the fact of his leadership with the British from the beginning. But his absence from Palestine could endanger NILI. Jemal might at any time ask to see him; he himself would have to report to Jemal on the situation with the locusts. He trusted no one else, not even Naftali, to do the job well. Arguing with himself back and forth left him where he started from: He could not go and yet he did not want to stay.

"We will not send the 'angel' until I am sure that it is the right time for it," he said slowly, his impassive face even more aloof. "Our friends are totally involved elsewhere right now. They would put us in their files and forget us."

"Sounds like a rabbi nibbling at his beard," Wilner said. "Is there a law against voting? If we decide the 'angel' should go, then we send."

"Wilner!" Judah's voice was clear and icy. "I make all decisions. But you are free to get out of here."

The men waited and looked at Wilner. After a moment he bowed mockingly, shifting his shoulders as if they carried a heavy pack. Then he grinned. "A king talks like that. Not a prime minister."

"I am equally bored with your analysis of character. Do you want to leave us?"

"Saul, sit down and play chess with me," Manfred said, hoping to break the tension.

Wilner swayed above the smoking kerosene lamp, enjoying the attention.

"Well?" Judah pursued.

"Well . . . For the money I'm making, I can't afford to give up this job," he said.

The men began to drink their tea and talk among themselves.

Wilner sat down at the chessboard with Manfred to hear for the twentieth time how Manfred missed the opportunity to debut the Glazunov A-minor concerto because he was absent at a lesson with Leopold Auer when the composer came to ask his advice. Mischa Elman, another student, was there that day, and Glazunov heard him and gave him the concerto.

"Luck," Manfred said. "A career is luck."

The Gallipoli campaign turned into one of England's greatest defeats. Even at Baghdad General Townshend was forced to retreat to Kut-al-Imara. The NILI group renewed its demands on Judah for action.

"We will break apart," Naftali told him, "if we don't get our findings to our friends."

"I am not ready yet," Judah replied coldly.

The same day, word came that locusts were seen at the borders of Judah's fields at Atlit. Every man would be needed to fight them.

16 ✦✦✦✦✦✦✦✦✦

Judah and his group arrived at Atlit just before dawn. Papa, Rachel, Miriam Bloch, and some of the Arab workers had already prepared ditches and kerosene torches. The locusts were at the eastern borders of his land but had not yet crossed over.

Naftali found Rachel alone in one of the fields. It was still dark and he couldn't see her face clearly. They greeted each other quietly. They could hear the demented humming of the locusts.

"You mustn't be afraid," Naftali said. "Make sure your hair is covered. When I hear them coming, I'll light the torches."

He heard her say, "I'll try not to be afraid."

"They don't bite or sting. But keep your mouth closed."

A slight rise of wind came from inland. The leaves of the trees and the wheat sighed.

Papa's voice called out, "Please God, the wind will carry them to sea."

"Amen, Papa!" That was Judah.

From other places in the fields the men repeated, "Amen! Amen!"

Rachel was silent and Naftali said softly, "Do you remember when I left? You were in the kitchen. I asked you to read my eyes. My God, it seems like a hundred years ago. I asked you what you read there."

Jackals barked in the Carmel hills.

"What did you read, Rachel?" He moved and inadvertently brushed against her arm. She moved away.

Rachel could not overcome her dark conviction that to say one single word, yea or nay, would bring catastrophe to them both.

Her silence made him uneasy. "In the old days, Rachel, before I went to Paris, you were a child and I was also a child. Perhaps more stupid than you. When I came back I wanted to rouse the nation, and there seemed nothing to rouse. I became blind with despair, maybe even with a little self-pity. . . . Can I explain it? Never. It's not that simple. In life it is never that simple. . . . Rachel, are you listening? Ever since your marriage I have been filled with longing."

She turned away. He started again. "When you returned I said, 'She has changed. She has grown up. She has suffered a little. She is not the same Rachel.' I said to myself, 'I have changed. My being in prison changed me. My being beaten changed me. My yearning for her changed me.' "

He peered through the darkness to see her.

"No, Rachel, all that's too simple. So—let me put it another way. Say, for example, that in the old days I could see only myself in the mirror and now I see beyond the mirror. What am I trying to say? Describe the ambiguities of heart and flesh according to some standard. Who can put a human being in a measuring cup and say this much he is and this much he isn't? Tilt the cup and say this much and no more has been spilled. No, my dearest Rachel, it's all nonsense. All of us are full of chaos, unmotivated and unclear. We defy analysis. And of all the things we are, the one that absolutely defies us to understand is love. Tear me apart, Rachel, I cannot answer why I did not love you before. But now I love you. I love you!"

He waited hopefully for some sound from her.

"Remember Pushkin's *Eugene Onegin?*" he said. "In the first part of the novel, he didn't see Tatiana either, although she loved him. Onegin learned too late. Tatiana was married too. . . ."

Rachel heard his words and embraced them. She lay under their weight, trembling with joy and a great wantonness. Her flesh tightened in all the forbidden places, mocking her vows. She wanted his hand against her yearning breast, but she didn't move. They remained apart, taut and motionless. She heard her own breathing. She heard his breathing.

"My love," he said.

Her mind exulted with pride, crying wordlessly, "Know me, my beloved! Know me! Know me!"

"My love," she said at last.

In the trembling darkness Naftali reached for her. Desire, new and awkward, to receive as well as to give, invaded them both. Their hands touched. She raised her fingers to her lips. They stood for a long time in silence, separated and indisseverable. Suddenly, from the farthest corner of the field, the darkness was exploded by the red flames of a torch and Nissim's scream. "The locusts! They are all over me!"

Just as suddenly, the humming was everywhere, like a machine the size of the world.

"Light the torches!" Judah yelled from the borders of his land.

Naftali scratched a match and put its tiny flame to his own torch. Rachel's blue eyes and flushed fair skin, alive and loving, bloomed out of the darkness. He held the torch to light Rachel's. He kissed her quickly and said, "God in heaven, bless us!"

As the dark locust swarm detached itself from the dark sky, the ditches of kerosene were set on fire, their flames lighting up and burning the first ranks of the invaders.

"The nursery, Judah!" Miriam Bloch screamed.

Some of the Arab workers beat them off the seedlings and young trees.

"The wheat!"

Judah, his eyes and face streaming with tears and sweat, ran to the wheat, yelling, "Kill them! Kill them!"

The locusts swarmed over the land.

Judah gave orders to wet the forward fields with kerosene.

Dawn opened fast. Huge ribbons of sky were blue and pink on the eastern horizon; the first rays of the still-hidden sun touched the rim of the Carmel.

Papa ran up to Judah. His wide eyes were full of anguish. "Did you tell them to wet the wheat with kerosene?"

"Yes, Papa."

"But the wind, Judah! It is shifting. It can wait! Don't burn the wheat yet."

"I'm doing what I think best." Judah wiped his forehead; he was drunk with fatigue. "I did it with fields belonging to others, vineyards like ours too. Sometimes I was able to save a little that way."

Papa put his hand on Judah's shoulder. "The wheat is everything. The wind changes," he said hopefully.

Judah looked into the sky. The dawn was darkening. It was as if night had risen from the land. The beat of the million wings was heard more clearly.

The locusts covered the first row of trees, which was used as a windbreak. While Judah watched, the life of the trees dissolved leaving behind pale skeletons standing crookedly against the dark clouds. The drumming of the wings filled his head.

"God of Abraham, God of Isaac, God of Jacob," Papa prayed. "Re-

150

member us in their name. . . . Your children die of hunger. . . .
Save this little bread for them. . . ."

A green blizzard of wings fell on the field of wheat.

Judah grabbed a kerosene pail and poured it over the golden stalks.
"Burn it! Start the fires!"

Naftali threw a torch. A huge flame swept to death the first pha-
lanx of locusts. The heated air lifted the onrushing swarm behind the
fire and carried it into the air.

"Keep the fire going!" Judah ordered.

Row after row, foot by foot, yard by yard, wheat and locusts died
together. There was nothing more for the defenders to do.

No one spoke. Judah stared at the flames as if he no longer had a
life beyond them. Papa prayed silently. Naftali and Rachel, side by
side, wept with anger and loss. The Arab workers of the station pitied
neither Judah Singer nor themselves, even though much of their own
livelihood was being burned away. There would be another year, another crop, another breath of Allah before which all men had to
yield.

As more of the wheat caught fire and the tides of hot air grew
stronger, the great dark humming swarm was raised higher. Now the
locusts were at the roofs of the nursery sheds and the shoulder of the
windmill; a moment later they were being swept toward the second
story of the station. But there the cooler thrust of air from the nearby
ocean blunted the heat and drove the swarms back into the fields.

"God of our fathers, let it be for life!" Papa prayed.

The cool air above the furnace of wheat expanded and became
warm. The swarms were raised again toward the nursery, the windmill, the station. Now in a flickering screen of dark and dawn light,
they drifted past the roof of the station, over the lines of palms, over
the wadi; they hovered in the turbulence at the edge of the sea near
the jagged tower of the Crusader ruins. Once beyond the shore, they
fell through the thin contracted air into the open mouths of gulls and
the dissolution of a waiting sea.

"Blessed is the Lord!" Papa exulted.

The others cheered and laughed and sang, filled with wonder and
thanksgiving.

All but Judah. He stared at his wheat fields, the part that was
burned and the part that was not burned. He would have to plow the
field under and plant again in the season.

"We've saved the nursery anyway," he said wearily and moved his body around to face the green oasis where the future lay.

The morning sun reached the Crusader ruins and glazed the high broken tower with bright red. A flock of wild-crying gulls swooping in from the sea feasted on the burned locusts that lay in mounds at the edges of the smoldering wheat.

"Tali—"

"Yes, Judah."

"Take all the information we have gathered and code it." He spoke heavily, with exhaustion.

"It's done already, Judah. The camps, the airfields, the troop movements, the numbers of the regiments."

"Get a good sleep tonight. Tomorrow you will go to Jaffa and get on a neutral ship. The American consul will help you if you need him. But tell him nothing." He hesitated for a moment. "I choose you to go."

"I understand."

"I will have to see that this debris is cleared and report to Jemal. He would be suspicious if I didn't. Leave as early as you can, Tali. We have waited long enough. It is my fault. I thought I would be the one to go."

"I will leave directly from here if you can find me some clean clothes."

Judah nodded. "Don't you want to see your mother?"

"It will be better if she thinks I am still with you."

"And, Tali—" A sigh. "See only their top men. No junior officers. Otherwise you will get nowhere. They won't take us seriously."

"General Murray himself."

"That's hoping for too much. . . . You understand, I would go if it weren't for Jemal."

"You are doing the right thing. If Rachel asks why I have left, tell her it is an errand for you. To the Galilee or Damascus."

The older man stared at his friend for a long time. "I'll tell her," he said at last.

BOOK *Three*

1 ◇◇◇◇◇◇◇◇◇

The office of Colonel Trevelyn-Jones of staff intelligence in Cairo was too small, too noisy, and too hot. From it could be heard people incessantly ringing bells for their orderlies or darting back and forth to consult with one another. A bloody Indian railway station, one of the officers had called it. The colonel had posted a stubborn Scotch sentry outside the door to keep off all junior officers while he collated the reports of his agents for a meeting with General Murray. But the general himself had ordered him to talk over the reports with an insolent junior from the Arab Office who squatted on a divan in aba and kaffiyeh and listened with open contempt as the colonel summed up his views. And before he had half put this chap in his place some sticky lad from the American Embassy had sent a bearded nomad into the sanctum. A Caucasian obviously, but also dressed in an Arab outfit. But what made the day even more hellish was another heart palpitation. It was a damned nuisance, of course, to feel the inside of one's chest beat like a drummer gone mad. He had not said a word to the staff medical officer and he didn't intend to. If he were found out, he'd be shipped home and that would end it all. No war, no promotion, only a half pension, and an unforgiving wife who believed she had married beneath her anyway.

The chap standing in front of him had managed somehow, with beard, aba, and kaffiyeh, to look a little like Jesus, and Trevelyn-Jones permitted himself to reflect a moment on Pontius Pilate.

"Now, just what do you want of me?" he inquired coldly.

Naftali was shocked by the tone; he expected better. For nearly a month he had been looking forward to this interview. Other senior officers whom he had tried to see had been too busy. Those who admitted him were juniors who listened with sympathy but said they could do nothing and would pass his proposals on to their superiors. During the third week he fell sick with malaria and shivered and sweat with a high fever as he went from office to office. At night he struggled home through the crowded bazaars to the hut of a poor candlemaker, a Jew from the Caucasus who had taken him in. Naftali avoided the rich Jews. He was afraid someone of their households would recognize him and send word back to the Turks, for there were spies everywhere. Finally he had approached the American consul, who knew of Judah Singer's experimental station. Without revealing anything, Naftali begged him to arrange for an interview with a responsible intelligence officer. After many delays Colonel Trevelyn-Jones had agreed. Naftali was sure that his mission was at last to be consummated.

"Go on, lad. I don't have all day."

Naftali was further dismayed by the presence in the room of the man squatting on a divan, his face half covered by a kaffiyeh.

"What I have to say, colonel, is for you alone."

"Eh?" The colonel's pale eyes followed Naftali's gesture. "Him? Don't worry. Perfectly reliable. He's not what he seems."

"Still, I would feel better, sir, if he left or I was introduced to him."

"Can't do either. Now, shall we get on with it? Your covering note said you'd just come across from Palestine. How did you get here?"

"I smuggled myself aboard an American ship at Jaffa. The USS *Albany*."

"How did the Americans permit that?"

"They were carrying people with Russian passports to Egypt."

"Are you a Russian?"

"No, sir. A Palestinian. I carried a forged passport."

Trevelyn-Jones's heart pounded hard. He should be in bed, not at this desk trying to figure out what was suspicious about the man.

"You talk English with a French accent. Why?"

"Because I learned it from a Frenchman."

"Well, what have you to say?"

"It can be put briefly, colonel. I represent a group of Palestinians; I myself was born there. We are in a position to help you. That is, we have managed to observe and record the situation of most of the Turkish forces, their guns, airfields, supply depots. We are prepared to give this information to you and to continue to supply more. We are responsible people, sir. The leader of our group is a world-famous scientist."

"I see. What else?"

"Naturally, we want to establish a line of communication with you so that the material can be transmitted quickly."

"I see. What else?"

"We are convinced that the Turk can be overrun by a forceful advance of General Murray's troops. If Palestine had been chosen instead of Gallipoli, the war here would be over by now. There is great disorganization and inefficiency in Jemal's army. Much of the coastline is without defense or even patrols. A landing anywhere between Jaffa and Haifa would cut Jemal's army in two. With enough arms, my group can organize a rebellion behind his lines. Jerusalem and Damascus would fall in a fortnight."

In the corner the man with the Arab dress raised his kaffiyeh to study Naftali's face. A brief smile of sympathy lit his own.

"I see. What else?"

Naftali took from his inside pocket a thin black notebook. "I have here, sir, some precise information about the latest movement of Jemal's Fourth Army."

"Let me see it."

"It's in a Hebrew code."

"Not very helpful, is it?"

The colonel shifted in his chair. Sometimes leaning one way or another made the heartbeats less noticeable.

"I can read you a bit of it, sir."

The colonel nodded halfheartedly.

"Two regiments, one from Smyrna, one from Lake Van, have been transferred to Damascus. We believe a second offensive against Suez is being mounted."

"What are the numbers of these regiments?"

Naftali read off the numbers, the names of the commanders, and the strength of the battalions.

"What else?"

"There is an ammunition dump in the Franciscan church in Nazareth. There is an airfield on the outskirts of Kfar Saba."

Trevelyn-Jones interrupted severely, "There's no such place!"

"Of course there is. North and east of Tel Aviv."

"We have no record of it on our maps."

"It's a new Jewish colony. Founded a year ago."

The colonel had not the slightest intention of believing Naftali. But he would take what he had to offer and check it elsewhere.

"Translate all that and turn it in to my sergeant, will you, like a good fellow? Now, how much money do you want for it?"

"We don't want money."

"How much?"

"I told you, sir. We don't want money. We are patriots!"

"Yes, yes. I understand. How much?"

Naftali locked his hands behind his back. "I thought I was making myself clear. We are offering our services because we believe it is the right thing to do. We want an English victory."

"Who is 'we'?"

"My group and most of the Jews of Palestine."

Trevelyn-Jones tried to recall the reports from his agents in Syria and Palestine. They never mentioned Jews.

"Look here, you're a bright chap. What's the *quid pro quo* for this 'gratis' patriotism?"

"Sir, you are a fool!" Naftali burst out.

The man in the corner smiled broadly.

"I don't have much use for spies," the colonel said, ignoring the insult, for he took it as merely a step in bargaining. "I don't trust you. All this crying nonsense about being patriots. Let me tell you, I don't believe you. I don't at all!"

Naftali was lost; he didn't know how to begin again, how to reach this stupid man. What had Judah said? Talk to the top. Otherwise they won't take you seriously. But this was the deputy chief!

"You're a Turkish citizen, are you?" the colonel said.

"I am. What about it?"

"Where is your loyalty? To Sultan Hamid or to us, your enemy?"

"Damn it, colonel, we're not your enemy."

"Why do you fight us then?"

"The Turkish leaders are fighting you," Naftali said, controlling himself. "But not the people. Why, half the Palestinians, the Jews, Armenians, Circassians, Arabs, would welcome you if they were given a chance. Is it possible that I am clear now, sir?"

"Possible. Then what?"

"Beg your pardon?"

"If you don't want money, you want something else. This group you mention. What does it want for its so-called patriotism?"

There are moments when a man understands the flaw in himself and sees it clearly, yet seeing it cannot resist showing it off to the world even though it kills him.

"We want independence!" Naftali said passionately, knowing the moment he spoke that it was the wrong note. As always, he told himself angrily, his timing was bad.

"Pardon?"

"We want independence for the Jewish people. A Jewish state."

Trevelyn-Jones felt both an immense relief and indignation.

"I've never heard any such policy in the War Office. Or the Foreign Office either. And, mark you, if there were such a policy I'd oppose it with all my strength."

"Then you are a bigger fool than I thought!" Naftali retorted. He had no restraint left.

"You are insulting, but I am not moved. I can jolly well have you arrested. Entering a military zone without permission. Citizen of an enemy country and all that. But it pleases me to let you go."

Suddenly the colonel was aware that his heart had stopped palpitating. Now he felt better and he smiled briefly, as if to himself. "But with a bit of advice. Whoever sent you here is incompetent. Spies must be paid for, understand? And they shouldn't make their *quid pro quos* so absurd that even a fool . . ." He grinned. "Yes, even a fool could see through them. If you are Jews, and I doubt that, for Jews are much too smart, then you are whistling up a whiffletree. A state? I didn't know there were enough Jews in Palestine to fill a clothing store. Ah, yes! Disraeli's novels. Rather liked them myself when I was a youngster. But fiction, you know. All fiction." He waved a hand at Naftali. "You may go now. But I suggest that you get out of Egypt as quickly as possible. In another twenty-four hours I will see to it that you are picked up and sent to one of our prisons. Good day."

With a sudden calm that surprised him, Naftali said, "Somewhere, colonel, there must be an English officer who will have as much confidence in his nation as I have in mine."

He turned and walked with forced jauntiness out of the office.

"Bit nervy, that chap," Trevelyn-Jones said to the man in the corner, who was slowly getting to his feet and moving toward the door. There he paused and studied the colonel with deep-set, mocking blue eyes. "Colonel."

"Yes?"

"You *are* something of a fool, you know."

The man closed the door behind him sharply.

Trevelyn-Jones stood up as if to call him back, then thought better of it. What can one do with one of those Arab Office irregulars with orders from God knows how high who camp out in one's office to see what's going on? Murray's Egyptian Army had become an oasis for misfits. Damn them all! Well, his heart was beating in order, and that was the most important thing.

2 ◇◇◇◇◇◇◇◇◇

Naftali had a notion that Trevelyn-Jones might not be as empty-headed as he appeared. He looked around to see if he were being followed. The day was cool as he walked down the crowded street toward Government House. The street was noisy with military traffic and soldiers on leave—Australian, Indian, British. Here and there were quiet oases of cafés where Egyptians of the middle class were playing cards as if the world ended at their tables.

He paused to look back again and saw the man from the colonel's office. Naftali turned off the Giza into a small side street filled with shops. He waited. The man turned the corner and entered the street. Naftali walked away, keeping to the shady side, looking for an alley. He didn't know Cairo well. Each alley he came to was clearly a dead end. He entered a shop selling old pots and kettles. Over his shoulder he saw the man pause at the doorway.

Naftali told the Greek proprietor that he would come back and asked if there was a rear door.

"Sir, it would take you nowhere."

"Would five shillings lead me somewhere?"

There was a crash of a kettle at the entrance.

"Ah, my friend, Nicolaides, I have damaged one of your wares," the man said, entering. "Forgive me. I will pay you for it." Seeing Naftali, he nodded.

The Greek studied the kettle. "It will cost you fifteen shillings, sir."

"That's quite a bit, isn't it?"

The Greek stepped between the two men and looked at Naftali. "Perhaps this gentleman would like to buy it for that? It is a very good kettle, and the damage is slight."

The Greek looked past him toward the back door. Naftali hesitated. His pursuer was slight, of medium height. He could knock him down and get away with the help of the Greek. For fifteen shillings it might be cheap.

The man smiled a little at the corners of his full wide mouth. The smile did not relieve a profound intensity in his eyes. He seemed to be daring Naftali to leave flaw and weakness to others.

"Gentlemen," the Greek said. "I despise bargaining. But when two customers prefer the same piece, I am helpless. I cannot show prejudice. Therefore, I leave it to you. Whoever shall pay the highest shall get what he wants."

"Nicolaides, you are angelic," the man said. "But this gentleman and I are friends. We wouldn't bid against each other, would we?" He touched his bony cheek to flick away a fly.

Naftali fingered the kettle.

"By the way, my name is Lawrence, and I quite agreed with you. The colonel *is* a bloody fool."

"My name is Brandt."

Naftali looked closely at the man, trying to read what there was behind the intense blue eyes, calm enough, if it weren't for the full, sensuous mouth curved to the edge of a mocking smile. But there was a strength in his long horsy face that appealed to him.

Lawrence indeed did smile, but in a sad, abashed way, with only a trace of mockery, for he was trying to win the Jew's confidence. Not stupid, not insensitive. Capable of pride and anger, as when he met Trevelyn-Jones's rebuff. A strange Jew for a Palestinian, more like a transplanted Englishman.

"Nicolaides," Naftali said, handing back the kettle, "it is against my principles to pay more than five shillings for a damaged kettle."

"Ten shillings, sir?" the Greek persisted.

Lawrence shook his head gravely. "Sorry, old man. Business, you know, is the art of getting more for something less. In this case, neither of us has more or less. Just nothing. Shall we go, Brandt?"

Outside, Naftali stopped and asked, "Why were you following me?"

"Have a drink?"

"Yes, but I'd like to know."

"To do you a good turn. I'm in an eleemosynary mood."

"I like a good wine, do you?"

Lawrence nodded. "Any kind. Just so long as it's French. I know the place."

They talked all afternoon and evening, and by three in the morning they were both sitting in a café pleasantly drunk, watching three stout women accompanied by a flute show off their round bellies. Elsewhere were sleepy Egyptian gentlemen, a French naval lieutenant, two Greek merchants, and an American civilian who insisted that he had seen the same dancing ladies at the World's Fair in Chicago twenty years before.

Lawrence and Naftali had weighed each other's temper. For his part, Lawrence decided to take the Jew seriously; he liked him and he thought he could use him. Naftali responded. He did not know for certain but suspected from some of the Englishman's comments that he was connected with the Arab Office, but despite that he was determined to get Lawrence's help for NILI. At least he was no Trevelyn-Jones. They could talk to each other.

With great passion Lawrence had praised the Arab spirit, erratic and devious as it was, for it seemed to him that there was in it a kind of lost innocence, a racial integrity that the West needed in order not to destroy itself. He was not unfriendly to Naftali's views of what he called pan-Judaism instead of Zionism, but he thought it was a lost cause. He drew a map of the Near East on the table and pointed out how small Palestine was compared to Arabia and how outnumbered the Jews were.

"Numbers are never decisive," Naftali argued. "We have desperation on our side. Homelessness. Our children grow up with Zion in their mother's milk. But whatever, we are now offering to fight against your enemies. Why don't you help us? Put me in touch with a man like you who can understand."

The flute player had left. The three dancers meandered by with their eyes in kohl shadows and their bellies, glistening with oil and sweat, moving in endless oscillations.

"Can't understand that dance. Scarcely sexual, you know," Lawrence said. "Arab sex is most extraordinary. Can't bear the humiliation."

"First things first, Lawrence. Will you help me?"

"First things first, Brother Brandt. What do you think of French poetry?"

Naftali shrugged helplessly. Lawrence could be surprisingly whimsical. An English characteristic? What else could he do but humor him?

The French lieutenant left after arguing about his bill. The American had fallen asleep, head on the table.

"Intellectual. Distillation of words, not feelings."

"Very good." Lawrence waved a hand to a tired waiter. "Another bottle of the same. Come to think of it, Brandt, you, not old T.-J., are the fool. I mean, don't you see it?"

161

"See what?"

"Your only chance is to come in with me. You and your friends. Work together. Both sides of the Jordan. A greater Arabia. Then we'll give you chaps what you want."

"Why should Arabs give up Palestine after they have it? Tell me why——"

"My word of honor! Don't you trust me?"

The waiter brought an open bottle of cheap wine. Naftali filled their glasses.

"I trust you, Lawrence. Ask me anything, I trust you. I trust your taste in poetry, music——"

"You don't really trust me. Have always to fight that flaw of the world. No trust. What about Wordsworth, Keats?"

"English poetry is—is like soap. Gets you clean—only outside. Washes away after a while."

"Bravo!"

"Why not come in with us, Lawrence? Need a military leader. We'd have the Turk out in a month. Jews don't have military experience, you know. Not for two thousand years. Help us."

"Jews have no experience in anything. Absolutely nothing. Except being Jews, that is."

"Don't you like Jews?"

"Absolutely splendid. Met your man Weizmann once. He's splendid. Met your Trumpledor and Jabotinsky once. They're splendid."

"Where did you meet them?"

"They've been round the place—somewhere. They have their own plans. Don't you know?"

"Avoided seeing anyone but British. I'm too recognizable. It's hot in here. . . . Not that these men would betray me! God knows! Might be others, accident. . . . Should be in Egypt fighting locusts. . . . What plans have they?"

"A Jewish Army and all that. But nothin' will come of it. Not only your own people opposed. Think it's double loyalty and all that. But our chaps too. Nothin' a British officer hates more than treatin' an ally as an equal. He keeps all that for the enemy. I put it to you, Brother Brandt. Will you come in with me?"

"No—with regrets."

"Don't trust the British, eh?"

"Arabs I don't trust. Like your great Doughty, I love them. But no sense of use of power, and that's why . . . can't be trusted. Don't know how to use power. Also, time is meaningless to them. The future nonexistent. Doesn't have to be reckoned with. . . . Lawrence, let's stop talking history and start making it. We're not rivals but allies. Help me."

Lawrence decided to be useful to Naftali, a decision that was mostly self-indulgence. He could not resist the green joy of power, the act of dispensing favor to someone weaker and from whom dependence could be won, or admiration, or even, were it not too farfetched a word, love. He was partial to the ruffians, the confused, the innocent. The Arabs were his children, or would be soon. They were the perfect objects of his joy; when he gave them their freedom, he could be their king if he wanted. Besides, it would be useful to have the Palestine Jews on his side when he led Feisal and the princes to their own.

Now that he had made up his mind, he could enjoy the game even more. Lazily he asked Naftali what he thought of Italian poetry.

"Passable. Except Leopardi." He could play as long as Lawrence could.

"What about the Latins?"

"*O rus quando ego te aspiciam.*"

"Vergil?"

"Horace."

"Can't persuade you?"

"Your taste in poetry superb," Lawrence said. "In revolution, dreadful. Yet . . . I feel the old 'mosynary creeping up— See John Miles at Port Said. Good man. Geologist or something. The only intelligent intelligence officer in Egypt. Tell him I said your taste in poetry superb, your taste in——"

"Dreadful." Naftali stood up.

"Where you going, lad?"

"Get rid of some this wine."

"Ah, yes. You're really not, are you?"

"Not what?"

"You're going to leave me for good, aren't you? The other just an excuse."

"Not without saying good-bye."

"Then say it."

"Good-bye and thank you, Lawrence."

"Tell those women not to parade in front of me anymore. Can scarcely keep my wine down as it is." He yawned. "Pardon, not standing farewell, and——"

They shook hands unsteadily.

"Do we meet again?" Naftali asked.

"In Jerusalem, to crown the king of Arabia."

"To install the president of the Jews."

"Go away, you—you perfervid——"

"Zionist."

"Listen—" He pulled Naftali down to him and said with an intensity that was startling in its sudden coldness, "All this is rot, understand. You for the Jews, me for the Arabs. Why do we do it? Bloody Napoleons. Bloody Alexanders. You want to be king of the Jews or president or whatever. You know you're not going to be king of anything. Nor I. People hate their liberators. They really want us to leave 'em alone. Slavery is peace too. You watch, they'll turn against us. They won't let us alone, neither alive nor dead. Ask me, then, why we do it. I mean, the truth. Not bugger words like freedom. I mean the inside truth. The bone of the bone. We are the official sacrificial sheep. All revolutionaries. Our role. We live in a dream of death. God help us."

He stood unsteadily and saluted. "Hail, Herod!"

Naftali recognized a truth in himself that Lawrence had confirmed. The thought of the boy Isaac exploded in his mind. Abraham was the revolutionary. But it was the son that was the sacrifice. What had the lad said when Abraham pulled the knife away from the lad's throat? It had to be more than silence. What had Isaac felt?

"Hail, Alexander!"

"*Salutamus!*" Lawrence said and collapsed in the chair. Naftali gently fixed his head and arms to make him comfortable, then told the proprietor to let his friend sleep there as long as he wanted to and to keep the noise away. It took all the English money he had to pay for the wine.

"Brother," he whispered to the sleeper and left.

164

3 ◇◇◇◇◇◇◇◇◇

After waiting ten days in Port Said for Lieutenant Miles to return from some duty elsewhere, Naftali finally saw him.

There are some Englishmen who possess a boyishness their whole lives. Naftali thought of Lawrence's description of the innocence of the Arab when he saw Lieutenant John Miles in the tiny, book-filled office. He must have been thirty, but he looked eighteen; his blond hair was silky as a babe's, and his round, unmarked face was full and rosy as if with first fat. He spoke in a disingenuous and wistful way like an apology for being where he wasn't supposed to be.

The affinity between the Arab and the English derived from the fact, Naftali mused, that both peoples did not quite take life seriously; they were like children who played at the sacraments of living but in time were bored by them. They lived as if birth, pain, ambition, and death were basically beneath a man's notice. The Arab had a contempt for death and made a colorful game of it; the Englishman did not quite recognize its existence. For him the long sleep was rather like a nap from which his Nanny, who was God, would wake him in time.

"As for the Jews," Naftali thought, "we overdo everything. We take everything too seriously. Including reality."

Miles listened to him with a pained, sympathetic smile and when it was his turn said that he was partial to his ideas and plans. Although he could do nothing with Cairo, at least in Port Said there were a few elements under his direct control and perhaps they could be useful.

"But limited in their use, I'm afraid," he said wistfully. "Don't know quite how to do it." He was silent for a long time, the sun from the window behind him making aureoles around his blond, disheveled head. The port noises of ships and the trucks loading them were loud and intrusive.

Finally Miles brightened. "You must get someone to go to London. Find a way of persuading the War Office. Wars are always fought like games in which no player knows what the other is doing. London and Cairo scarcely talk to each other. It's a miracle that any war is ever won, isn't it? Still, the War Office has some chaps who are decent and influential enough. If they can be won over, they'll pass the word along to Cairo, and perhaps something will come of it. Can't hope for too much, can we? But still—" Miles stared vacantly at his cluttered desk.

"We must find a way of getting in touch with each other," Naftali said. "For you to pick up our information and to tell us what you need."

Miles said apologetically, "Don't suppose you brought anything along?"

"I have a full notebook." Naftali felt relaxed with Miles. Unlike Lawrence, he had an innocence that was serene and not easily corruptible.

"May I read it?" Miles asked.

"It's in a Hebrew code."

"Hebrew! What a dig. Used the Torah, did you?"

"In part. But there are a number of new words."

"Don't tell me you speak the language?"

"Of course."

"The Psalms and Job and Kings and Exodus and all that? The same language?"

"The same."

"Do you use the diacritical marks on the printed page?"

"That's for the beginner."

"I say, that's quite extraordinary—bringing a dead language to life. Say something. Anything."

Naftali spoke several sentences in Hebrew.

Miles was delighted. "It sounds much like Arabic. I caught a word or two. What did you say? Something prophetic, no doubt?"

"I said, 'I promise to teach you Hebrew beginning the day after peace.'"

"How nice. Thank you. Yes."

"Will you arrange something?"

"I have a good man who has a navy gunboat of sorts. A small craft. Captain Clothier. Goes up and down the coast to pick up agents here and there. You know, we do have some in the Lebanon. We'll all work out a bit of a code together. Find the right time and place to drop you and pick you up. I'll go along for the first trip or so."

He offered his hand and Naftali shook it warmly.

166

"You won't regret it, lieutenant."

Miles rose and walked to a small kerosene stove. "Tea?"

"Yes, thank you. When shall we start?"

"In two weeks. There'll be no moon, of course," Miles said as if Naftali should have known it all along.

4 ◇◇◇◇◇◇◇◇◇

Two months and ten days from the time Naftali had left Jaffa on the USS *Albany*, the one-stack, five-hundred-ton tugboat HMS *Loch Ness*, carrying machine guns fore and aft, sailed with him from Port Said. James Clothier, her captain, was a Scot with the Scotch manner of treating everybody as equals and inferiors at the same time.

The sea was fair and calm for the first hour, but as they sailed past Gaza it began to rain. The sea roughened and there was some talk about whether it would be possible to get close enough to Atlit to lower a boat with Naftali.

They had decided on the Crusader ruins as a rendezvous. It was near enough to the experimental station but remote from any village or Turkish Army or gendarme post. And it could be seen from the sea.

Naftali, Miles, and Clothier had worked out a code. A white cloth hanging from the top window of the station would mean that the way was clear and that a messenger would be waiting. On the day before the dark of the moon each month, the ship would sail by close enough to read the signal, then return the next night. It would send a boat in to pick up the reports and whoever wanted to return to Egypt. Miles was enchanted with the code name NILI and the prophetic phrase from which it derived. Clothier didn't even ask what it meant but referred to the group as Nellies, as if it were a women's auxiliary.

The one concern of the captain was a U-boat that he called *Milord Fritz*. It seemed to have the same mission as the *Loch Ness*, coasting up and down, picking up and dropping off agents. Occasionally it harassed small merchant ships, leaving the bigger ones alone. Twice it had attacked the *Loch Ness*, damaging it slightly once.

"It's ma verra private war," Clothier said. "Between *Milord Fritz* and m'self. A proper chap too, I've heard. Sinks 'em and saves the lucky lads from the sea."

Miles and Naftali were in the cold, damp wheelhouse. Miles passed his flask.

"It'll be nippy in the water," Miles said. "You might have to swim the last twenty to a hundred yards, depending on the sea."

"I know every drop of the ocean around here," Naftali said, feeling the good warmth of the whiskey. "I've swallowed half of it in my day and spit out the other half."

Their faces were dimly lit by the tiny lamp over the compass. Naftali thought that Miles looked as if he were out punting on the Thames. Unruffled, calm, assured. He liked the man. He envied his composure.

"What did you do before, lieutenant?" he asked.

"Bit gone on geology and that kind of thing."

"Yes, Lawrence told me."

After a while Miles said offhandedly, "You like him?"

"I found we had much in common."

"It's always easier that way, of course."

"I don't know. . . ." The whiskey had made Naftali freer to say what he thought. "I like you, if you don't mind, and I'm not sure we have much in common."

"But what was it about Lawrence?"

"He seemed modest and arrogant, uncertain and sure, passionate and reserved—all at once."

"Is that what you are?"

Naftali laughed. "I never thought of myself that way. Perhaps I meant a way of looking at the world."

Miles was silent.

"We'll be comin' up on the ruins in half hour or so," Clothier said. "Are ye ready, lad?"

"Yes, sir."

"Doon' forget to use your torch tomurrow night, lad. Find ye a place where they cain't see it from the coast."

"I know exactly where it is, captain."

"What way of life?" Miles asked during a pause.

Naftali thought a moment. "Our wanting to take risks, give ourselves for something bigger than we are. More than this war, I mean. I suppose an Englishman takes it for granted that he has to fight. But with Lawrence it's different. I think both of us have a hatred of wasting our lives. Or our deaths for that matter. We're not following someone's orders. We're marching, so to speak, on our own time, across a terrain we'll make our own, into our own battles. To fill up the gap that is— well, the gap of life, I guess."

"You think that's quite rare, do you?" Miles asked with his wistful smile, which Naftali could see reflected in the dark rain-swept window of the wheelhouse.

There was something so extraordinary in the lieutenant's face, a winning shyness that was almost love. Unlike Lawrence, his questions were untouched by irony. He was like a child asking his older brother about stars or the moon or why blood is red.

"I'm sure it's not rare," Naftali said at last. "I'm sure that you know what it is."

"On the contrary, Naftali." It was the first time he had called him by his first name. "You see, I'd never thought of it before. Quite wonderful too, thinking about how one prefers to die. Of course, none of us has much of a choice. But nevertheless I envy you and Lawrence. You see, don't you, that it takes an extraordinary amount of courage to do what he's doing with the Arabs. And you too. You're going right into the lion's mouth, aren't you? You have no army, no government behind you, no uniform, no acknowledged organization. If they find you out, it's over the hill, isn't it? As I see it, you're in even a nastier spot than Lawrence. I hope you'll forgive all this talk, but I assure you I couldn't begin to do what you chaps are doing."

"I don't accept that at all."

Miles grinned, embarrassed. "We won't argue about it, will we?"

The ship started to make for shore. The wind shifted and the pitching slackened.

Miles was silent.

"I can't see a thing," Naftali said, "but I can sense Palestine out there. Is it like that when you go home?"

"Never went home in such a dark. But I think I'd sense it too."

"Of course, it's not rational. Yet—" Naftali wiped the window of the wheelhouse to clear it of mist. "I suppose if someone whirled me around the globe two or three times and dropped me into Palestine blindfolded, I'd know it. The olive trees, the feel of the earth, the way the breeze falls and rises. Or the feel of the sun. Perhaps even history, its special history can be sensed. There is a line in the Psalms —perhaps you know it—'My soul is continually in my hands.' I think of the line as meaning, 'My land is continually in my hands.' To a Jew they are one and the same. You can't put your finger on the soul and say you have touched it, and you can't put your finger on our love of Zion. It is there; it stayed with us these two millennia. Why, I knew Jews in France whom you would scarcely call Jews if you didn't know them well. Yet their last wish as they lay dying was for

170

some earth from Palestine to be put under their heads in the coffins."

"Extraordinary." Miles hesitated. "I could feel that way about England." He laughed softly. "But I wouldn't dare say so."

"Tell me, lad, when ye see the castle, eh?"

Naftali pressed his face against the window to search for the shoreline. He couldn't even see the white surf around the big rocks and masonry of the ruins.

"When we get to where we want to go, lad, I'll turn to keep the wind off ye and me lads. It's to give them a bit of a free way to get their oars into the lash."

"Thank you, sir."

"An' don't let the wild Turk find ye, hear?"

"I hear, captain."

Suddenly Naftali saw the white line in the dark distance. "I see the shore. But not the Crusader ruins yet."

Miles had a pair of night glasses to his eyes. "I see it. A little to the left. It is darker than the rest." He gave Naftali the glasses.

"Yes. You're right. Keep straight ahead, captain, and you'll come to the south side of it. It's shallower there."

Clothier checked the compass, then rang for half speed.

He gave the wheel to a seaman and peered through his own glasses. "We're better than six hundred yards. Hold the wheel steady, lad."

"You'll have twenty-four hours," Miles said softly. "It may not be enough time to get your information ready for us."

"Whatever there is, I'll have it."

"The important thing, lad," Clothier said, "is to be on time. Exactly midnight. Check your piece with Mr. Miles."

"We have already, sir," Naftali replied.

The door of the wheelhouse was opened with a roar of sea and wind. The boatswain's mate yelled in, "Boat's ready for lowering, cap'n."

"I don't expect any trouble," Naftali said to Miles. "But if I'm not back on the beach tomorrow night, or no one else is there, you mustn't think we've let you down."

Miles nodded. "If no one shows up, we'll try again next month. Or we'll find a way of getting some word from you."

Clothier cut speed down to a quarter. "We're in about three hundred. Bit too rocky with this wind to go in much farther, lads."

"Take the flask with you," Miles said. "It was made in Germany, if anybody cherishes a closer look at it."

"Thank you, Miles." Naftali turned to Clothier, who was anxiously watching the line of surf. "Good-bye, sir. See you tomorrow."

"Get along now, an' good fortune to ye."

Fighting the wind and the shifting deck, Naftali reached the mate and his men standing at the davits of a lifeboat.

The *Loch Ness* was turning into the wind. Naftali tightened the straps of a waterproof bag around his shoulders and climbed into the lifeboat. The men at the davits lowered her into the shifting sea.

"Get for'ard, sir," the mate said, "and guide us in. Sing out. The waves'll kill the sound."

Naftali was dressed lightly to enable him to swim better if he had to. The water shipping over the side chilled him as he hung on the lofted side of the boat and strained to see the ruins.

"Rocks ahead. Keep right!"

The waves lifted the boat. He saw the ruff of the breaking waves and darker line of the shore.

"Straight ahead now!"

The boatswain, at the rudder, had trouble fighting the inrushing tide, which swept him along at an angle.

"Straight ahead!" Naftali yelled.

"Ready to shove off rocks," the boatswain ordered the oarsmen.

The boat scraped a huge block of masonry that once had been part of the castle's breakwater. One of the oars broke against it.

"Back off!" the boatswain ordered.

The four oarsmen, now with three oars left, spun the boat around while the waves splintering on the masonry fell back and poured a foot of water into the boat.

The boatswain called to Naftali, "Can you make it from here, sir?"

It wasn't a question; it was an order.

The shore was fifty yards away at least. In a calm sea he had swum it many times.

"Going over the side," he yelled.

"As you say, sir!" The boatswain couldn't keep the relief out of his voice.

Naftali waited until the waves dropped the boat into a trough, then slid over the side and began swimming. He would have to find the opening between the broken chunks of the old breakwater. The waves lifted and dropped him. He struggled to keep his direction. Again the waves lifted him. He saw the opening, two great stone blocks standing about ten feet apart. He knew them well. He had often swum out to them to study the marine growth on their sides. He let the tide carry him toward the rock on his left. If he calculated correctly, he could turn back into the tide and buck it long enough to get through.

The sea carried him along swiftly. When he made the turn toward the opening, the tide was too strong and smashed him against the masonry. He gasped in pain; water filled his mouth; his left arm lost its strength. With his right hand he held onto a broken place on the masonry near the waterline and straddled its edge with his legs. The waves pounded him and he tried to raise himself to the top of the block, but the sides were too slippery. If he let go he would be broken against the stone blocks. That death was as wasteful as any he had envisaged. His anger roused him; he would not let go; he would not die.

Fighting to remain conscious, he lifted his left arm. There was some strength in it. Inch by inch he raised it toward the edge of the block through the smash and tear of waves. Now both hands held him and he released his legs from their straddle and started the climb. For a moment he hung halfway up, swaying back and forth with each splintering rush of water. A massive thrust of tide carried him to the top. He slid down the other side into calmer water.

On the shore road a patrol from Caesarea led by Mustafa ibn Musa rode by. Orders had come from Colonel Hamid Bek to put out surveillance parties. Signals had been seen along the coast.

Ibn Musa was tired and angry, as usual. He hated night and darkness. Besides, this duty took him from his usual rounds of the Jewish and Arab villages where he could pick up a chicken here, a sack of vegetables there, even a few lire. These night rides were dangerous. People caught in some serious illegal activity would fight. And if, Allah forbid, there should be a landing of the English, which nobody believed possible except the crazy Germans, he would get no baksheesh, but a dirty infidel bullet in his belly.

The night was dark, life was dark, the future was dark. If, on the other hand, he should come upon one unarmed violator of martial law, someone who was both weak and rich—that didn't sound right, for how could one be both?—why then life would be bright, the night would be day, and the future would be as juicy as heaven to the hajis.

Was it this hope or did he actually hear a man's steps crossing the bridge ahead of him? Not a troop, not five men, but one solitary pair of footsteps.

He checked his horse and whispered a halt to his four troopers.

"What do you hear?"

The troopers listened and said they heard nothing but the sea.

Mustafa unslung his newly issued rifle. It was an English make stolen from a British Army warehouse near Alexandria and smuggled by Arabs into Palestine.

"Halt!" he yelled.

Naftali had heard the horses as he was crossing the wooden bridge over the mouth of the wadi. Swiftly, he slid under it and stood in five feet of water.

The horses clattered overhead and stopped. One left the bridge. Naftali heard it move down the bank and come toward him. He lowered himself up to his shoulders into the water. Insects flew around. Bats screeched.

"Ali!" Mustafa's voice called from the bridge.

"I see nothing."

"Did you look under the bridge?"

"There is water there from the sea."

"You won't drown."

Naftali made his body taut. If the man saw him, he would ram him and try to get on his horse.

Ali was a Sunni Arab peasant from a poor village north of Acre. He would not get off his horse to save his life, for it was a new mount, the first he had ever been responsible for, and he did not trust it to stand still for him. He looked around for a tree to tie it to.

"Ali!"

"Yes?"

"Have you looked?"

Ali rode through the water to the edge of the bridge, then bent over to peer beneath it.

Naftali stopped breathing.

A water rat swam by.

Naftali saw Ali's head hanging upside down from the side of his horse. The head withdrew.

"Ali?"

"I see nothing."

"If so, why have you taken so long?"

"To make certain that no one was there."

"Then come at once and let us return."

Naftali waited through an hour of silence, then worked his way up the wadi toward the white experimental station, behind the rows of young palms.

5 ◇◇◇◇◇◇◇◇◇

In the station Saul Wilner was cleaning a German pistol and enjoying the memory of a Greek girl he had slept with five days before. She was the mistress of a high German officer and had been beaten by him. To get revenge, she stole some papers and his revolver, then ran away to an uncle who owned a small café. Saul was there, listening to gossip. They had known each other well, and she told him the story. He asked to see the papers and found that one had great importance.

"The papers are worthless," he told her. "But the pistol is valuable."

"Will he get in trouble if he doesn't have it?"

"Yes."

"Then I'll keep it. And if he comes to get it back, I'll shoot him with it."

"That will not be revenge. It will be suicide. The best way is to get rid of the papers and the pistol. You will be proven innocent if they come and search you, and you will still have the joy of seeing him suffer."

She did not agree right away, but after they drank a bottle of arak she took him to a room in back of the café and made love to him with the passion of a woman who finds that the best revenge is to betray her lover. When Saul left she gave him the weapon and the papers to keep for her, vowing she would never tell he had them if he never told on her.

Wilner had a vertical imagination and memory; beyond the limits of himself was a terra incognita. He was enjoying the memory of the girl and projecting the possibilities of the next time when he heard a knocking downstairs. He put the pistol in a jar of pebbles, where he had already hidden the papers, and ran down the stairs to find Naftali, shivering and wet.

"Heh, boychik, welcome."

"Quick! There's a patrol somewhere around."

Wilner closed the door and helped Naftali climb the stairs. "They see you?"

"I don't think so."

"We never expected you before the end of the war. You were away over two months. What's with the British?"

Naftali wiped his face and looked around. Nothing was changed. "It's all arranged. They got me here on a gunboat and they'll be back tomorrow at midnight. Do we have much to give them?"

Saul gave him a torn towel and lit the kerosene stove to heat up water for tea. "Enough. Everybody's been dancing here and there, picking up pieces with one hand, fighting locusts with the other. We need more help. It's good you came back. Hamid Bek's been asking for you. He doesn't like you."

Naftali stopped drying himself. "My mother?"

"She's all right. He threatened her, wanting to know where you were. She said with Judah. Then he found Judah and the others in Ashkelon, where the Seventh Division was headquartered. It was lucky for them there was a report of locusts nearby. Judah thought maybe someone had seen you boarding the American ship or maybe in Egypt. The Turk has his own thieves there, so he told Hamid Bek that you were at Metullah. We haven't heard since."

Naftali sipped the tea Wilner brought him.

"The bedouin raid the villages once a week. But there's little enough to steal. Can stones lay eggs? But they think they are pashas now, with their guns and with our empty hands. Nobody but thieves and Germans have enough to eat."

"I brought back some quinine, also some new antiseptic." Naftali motioned to the waterproof bag he had carried in with him. "Here's some schnapps, if you want a drink. Save some for Judah. Where is he?"

Wilner had taken the officer's papers from the jar of pebbles. "Give a look, boychik! The German plan for the defense of Gaza. What do you say? I myself got it."

"Congratulations, Saul."

Wilner took a drink of the whiskey. "From the Greek girl friend of a German high officer," he boasted.

"Congratulations."

"No, no, you mean something else?"

"Nothing. Just congratulations again. Lieutenant Miles will be delighted."

"There was something else in your voice."

Naftali put the papers back in the jar and looked into a closet for dry clothing. He found an old shirt and trousers. "Don't be so sensitive." Wilner was right. He had felt annoyed.

"Maybe I shouldn't mix patriotism and pleasure? Is that it? You maybe didn't have a woman or two in Cairo?"

"You're a bit of a scoundrel, aren't you, Saul?"

"Yes," Wilner said flatly. "Or do you think that only angels fight on the side of the angels?"

He looks more like a ghetto peddler than ever, Naftali thought, hating Wilner's Yiddish, hating the shrug and the broad hand gestures, the Polish cap, the smell of the dark, passive past.

Wearily he sat down to undo his packages. "Get all the women you want, but don't keep preaching about it. If that's what you're in this business for, you're more of a fool than I thought."

"What am I in this business for?" Wilner said maliciously. "I don't give such a damn about Jews. Believe me, if I could have been born anything else, even a rabbit, I'd have been happier. But what does a baby do when he finds out the sad news? He cries. Honor? Morality? Freedom? Zionism? I could hardly keep myself from wetting when I heard those speeches. Nobody, believe me, nobody opens wide a nostril for such ideas. Ideals are for gentiles."

Naftali's ears were still filled with water and were beginning to hurt. They were always the weakest part of him. He wondered why Wilner was attacking him. Should he have praised him more for getting the Gaza plans?

"Where is Judah? I asked before. Where is he?"

Wilner grinned suddenly with the malice of a winning cardplayer who is about to enjoy his victory. "Judah is not in Palestine. He is somewhere between Constantinople and Berlin by now, if he is lucky."

Naftali shivered, even in the warm room. "When did he leave? Why?"

"A long time you were away. He figured you had trouble and couldn't get back. Maybe not until the war was over. Two weeks ago he talked to Jemal and told him he had done all he could with the locusts. But he had a scheme for maybe getting oil from the castor plant or from sesame. The Germans were working on it in Berlin. It would help the war if he could go to Berlin and learn the latest results. Jemal fell for it like a heated virgin on her bridal night. . . . Go explain a man. With one hand he kills Jews, with the other he bakes puddings for them. So Mr. Judah told me and Dmitri his plan. He didn't discuss, he told. He was going to Berlin, then maybe slip over into a neutral country like Denmark, then a boat to America. All of this would be kosher. But once in America he would see the British people and make arrangements for us. So exactly where he is now, I don't know. Somewhere between Constantinople and the Woolworth Building."

Naftali felt like laughing. Judah, who had so often accused him of being too impulsive, thoughtless, a chicken without a head running around the barnyard until he died—he was the one who had been too impatient.

Wilner watched him closely.

Then Naftali felt sick in his stomach. With Judah gone, could NILI survive? He was the only one whose presence was a guarantee that the group would hold together.

"Did he leave any message for me?"

Wilner nodded and took another drink from the flask. "I was to be in charge. But if you come back—" He rubbed his nose irritably. "Then, Mr. Naftali Brandt, you are the high priest."

"He shouldn't have left."

"Is that what the high priest gives as his first order? To turn back the calendar?"

Naftali had never wanted leadership. It was why he had waited so long for Judah to decide on action and the course of action. It was Judah who had the certainty of the future, the surety of himself, the skill of choice. Ironically, even this premature departure was a wise step. Hadn't Miles urged that someone go to England to plead the case there? Judah would have had to leave Palestine sooner or later.

He paced up and back from the night-dark window to Judah's desk. He stopped to drink his tea; it was cold and bitter. Wilner watched him with the wariness of a hunter.

"Do the others know what you've told me?" Naftali asked.

"Dmitri, Avram, yes. They in turn told Manfred, Reuven, and Nissim. No one liked the idea. Most of all, they didn't like the idea of me being in charge. Personally, I understand that. I am a peasant." Wilner smiled broadly. He leaned his dark, sunburned face to one side in the old student gesture and talked in a singsong voice. "A lout, a peddler, a rascal of the old style. Ha, but with me he was safe. If it was Dmitri or Avram, respected men, who knows? A new Moses would arise. So Judah was content with me. Even with you, Mr. Naftali."

"You are a fool!"

Wilner put down the flask. "So what's new?"

Naftali was silent. He rejected Wilner's reasoning. Judah had taken Saul because he was good for the work.

"Do you want me in the group?" Saul Wilner asked mockingly.

"Absolutely! And even more help."

"Our Judah-Moses already thought of that. We have three new comrades. Miriam Bloch, a friend of Rachel's. Yoshua Camiel, from Jerusalem, a cousin of the Singers. He's working for the Turkish Army as a supply officer. A good man. And Anuskevitz's brother, Shlomo. He runs a café in Tiberias where the Germans drink and talk a lot."

Naftali tried to sound casual. "And Rachel?"

"He didn't say anything about her."

Naftali's weariness was gone. He looked at his watch. It was three in the morning. He had twenty-one hours before the *Loch Ness* would be back.

"Is all the material coded?"

Wilner nodded.

"It will have to be decoded."

"Why?"

"Because there is no one to do it in Egypt. I had thought I might go back with the boat. I can't now."

Wilner pushed the flask away and leaned back in his chair. "I could go."

"I want you here. I want you to go with me to meet the boat. If Lieutenant Miles is there, he will see who you are in case I am not around next month."

"With the material in plain language, if we are caught——"

"I will ask Miles to find a Jew in Egypt whom we can trust to be our man. I will give him a copy of the code. But this time we must take the chance."

The two men sat down at the table again and began the tedious task of translating from the code into Hebrew and then into English.

"This lieutenant of yours is asking a lot," Wilner said after a while.

"He's risking his own neck. No one else would help me."

Wilner shrugged and went to the stove to heat up water.

"Do the Singers know that Judah may not be back?" Naftali asked.

"He told them only about Berlin. They don't know more."

"Rachel should know."

Wilner opened his eyes wide. "You mean, tell her about NILI?"

Naftali hadn't thought that far ahead. He had merely felt an impulse to inform Rachel of the real purpose of Judah's plans in the event she was questioned. Even though Judah's visit to neutral America could not by itself be called treasonable, Jemal Pasha might consider it a breach of trust if he found out. It would then seem strange and suspicious if Judah's own family didn't know.

"Why not? Rachel should know and she should have a choice about coming in with us."

"You will use your influence on her, naturally?"

Naftali answered truthfully, "Yes."

"To strengthen us, no doubt, my leader Mr. Naftali."

"I'm going to ask you a special favor, Saul. Don't joke anymore with the 'Mr. Naftali' garbage."

"I don't promise. Consider me the stubborn and rebellious son. 'He doth not hearken to our voice. He is a glutton and a drunkard.' And as for your Rachel, you are not thinking of yourself, maybe?"

There will be a reckoning between us someday, Naftali thought.

"Eh, heir apparent, don't you think maybe the others have a right to decide who'll be asked?"

"Did Judah consult them when he brought in Miriam and Yoshua and Shlomo?"

"Bringing Rachel in could mix up a little patriotism and pleasure for you, no?"

Naftali slammed the book closed. "Get out, Saul!"

Wilner looked at him with surprise. "Me, you're talking to?"

"Get out!"

"But you said you want me to work with you."

"I'll find a way to do without you."

"Don't jump into boiling water. I'm like a ruble in an empty cup. Shake me and I rattle to your tune." He smiled sheepishly. "I don't want to fight with you. My bowels run easy. I got a weak stomach and a weaker character."

Naftali was confused; the about-face disarmed him.

"What do you want of me, Saul? One minute you're a——"

"A loud-tongued bastard. And the next minute, I want to be friends. Listen, I'm not a coward." He laughed softly, with clear joy. "The truth is, I don't like to fight with Jews. It's an affliction like boils. Not that I love them, as I say. But I get a softening of the muscle when I have to stand up and hit another child of Israel."

180

The smile that was the residue of the earlier laugh turned inward in a crooked way and vanished.

Naftali couldn't tell whether Wilner was still mocking him. The moist, dark eyes of the ghetto Jew were hard to read. Perhaps beneath the testiness, the rude probing, and the deliberate insolence was the disappointment at not being the head of NILI. He was a man who despised others because he despised himself. To such a man power, even limited power, was a kind of salvation.

"I don't want to fight either, Saul."

"Nu, we're friends again?"

"Let's get to work."

"Friends we're not, then?"

"Saul, you helped save my life, and I am grateful. You are a good worker. And I am grateful for that too. Let's start out by being comrades. Maybe later we'll become friends. Agreed?"

"A scoundrel, but your scoundrel, eh?"

Naftali laughed. "Our scoundrel, Saul."

Wilner nodded briskly and sat down. "There isn't much left of the schnapps. I'll finish it."

"Finish it."

They had worked on the code for about an hour when Wilner looked up suddenly. "You're sure about Rachel, eh?"

Naftali answered angrily, "I've made up my mind. There will be no more discussion!"

"Ha! Already you sound like Mr. Judah."

"Saul!"

Again the crooked, vanishing smile. "All right, forget it, don't get angry, don't listen to me. Can I chop out my tongue?"

They worked until noon and then hung the sheet out of the window. It was a hot day. They lay on the floor and tried to sleep but were too exhausted. Naftali thought about Rachel. He yearned to see her, to embrace her. Had Wilner been right? Was his bringing her into the group a device to keep her close, to share with her danger and daring that would leave her open psychologically to his demands? She would succumb to the seductiveness of tomorrow's death.

"Saul . . ."

"Yes?"

"That Greek woman— You understand, I'm not judging you. It is not my business."

"She was a girl, not a woman."

Naftali laughed. "Just so long as she was pretty."

"They tell me you lived in Paris." Wilner turned over on his side and slapped at a fly with a loud noise. "What about the French girls?"

Naftali closed his eyes. "They have spirit."

"In bed?"

"Yes, that's what I mean."

There was a long silence while each man loitered with desire.

The heat made breathing painful.

"Where are you from?" Naftali asked after a while.

"A little peanut of a village near Zhitomir."

"Why did you decide to come to Palestine? Were you a Lover of Zion?"

"Ha! I came because I am insane. In America, I would be by now a million-dollar man."

"Is your family still at home?"

There was a muffled cry of agony from Wilner.

"What's the matter?"

"Ha! These flies! God can't stand the Jews even when they try to sleep. He sends them punishments."

But his voice sounded like a man who is trying hard not to weep.

6 ◇◇◇◇◇◇◇◇◇

They left at twilight to walk the two miles along the wadi to the shore. Naftali had hidden the information inside a hollowed-out walking stick. The Gaza map was rolled up and sewed into the lining of Wilner's visor. Ahead of them, rimmed red from the setting sun, the great dark north tower of the ruins rose eighty feet above the sea. As they approached the coast road they heard the sound of lorries and hid behind rocks. It was an army convoy going south; it moved slowly in sections and it took a long time to pass. Three lorries had broken down and soldiers were repairing them by the light of small fires. It was too risky to cross there. The two men left the wadi and moved north through fields, hoping to reach the ruins out of sight of the soldiers. A new hazard appeared—a caravan of camels carrying artillery pieces and supplies.

"We have to chance it," Naftali whispered, burrowing down between the tufts of high weedlike grass. "Put your cap under your shirt."

"What are you going to do?"

Naftali made a gesture to hurry and stood up, motioning to Wilner to follow.

Boldly he entered the road and shouted in Arabic to a passing camel driver, "Salaam, brother, we have need of help. My friend is sick and I am hungry."

The man stopped. He was tall and haggard. "What is the sickness of your friend?"

"A witless one. Allah has stirred up his mind into sheep droppings."

"We have no food or work for you."

"Baksheesh," Wilner whined.

"Some dry milk, pitta, anything, O charitable brother," Naftali cried.

The camel driver spat and moved on. Naftali grabbed Wilner and ran after the man.

"Your charity is cold. Have you no mercy? Have you no fear of Allah?"

"We are servants of the Enlightened One, but he has not fed us either."

The two men fell back a few steps on the shore side of the caravan.

"Baksheesh!" Naftali cried.

Some of the drivers threw rocks at them and they ran off into the darkness toward the ocean.

It was twenty minutes after midnight when they climbed to the sea face of the ruins and flashed the torch, one short, two long, one short. There would be no answering signal, for that could be seen by any-one near the shore.

They waited; the only sounds were the waves against the fallen masonry and the faint, high-pitched camel bells from the road.

Miles might have come and gone, Naftali thought anxiously. He would have to smuggle his way to Cairo again and face Miles with an explanation for failing on this first test.

He signaled again.

"The stupid British," Wilner whispered. "They are always on time. How long do we wait? It's one o'clock."

"All night, then tomorrow night," Naftali said. "And every night until the moon makes it too bright. And then we'll try next month."

They were silent a long time. The caravan had long since disappeared.

"So, you're a poet," Wilner said. "A poet. Your friend Nissim told me."

"Once, yes."

"Recite me a poem. Yours. One line even."

" 'In the morning I went into myself to get fresh laid eggs.' "

"That's poetry?" Wilner said, incredulous.

Naftali saw a boat pass the white water flowing through the portal of rocks. He flashed the torch.

"They're here."

He and Wilner ran down along the fallen blocks to the little strand alongside the tower.

Miles was the first to jump from the boat. He looked like a boy at a picnic. The sailors hauled the boat onto the strand and stayed there with pistols ready.

"Thank God, you're here," Naftali said.

"Sorry we're late," Miles said quietly. *"Lord Fritz* is out there some-where."

184

"It's all right. We were late too. This is Saul Wilner. He's in charge when I'm not around."

The men shook hands.

"He brought us the defense plans of Gaza," Naftali said.

"Marvelous. Absolutely marvelous. Won't old T.-Jones suffer." He looked around. "Never seen the old ruins so close up. Wish it were daylight."

"There is other information here too," Naftali said, handing Miles the papers. "Troop movements, airfields. It's all in plain language. But after this we'll code it in Hebrew. I've included the key. You'll have to find someone who knows the language. One thing more. You remember about Judah Singer?"

"Quite. The agronomist. He organized your group."

"He left Palestine before I got back. He is going to try to get to Berlin, then to a neutral country and on to the United States. He plans to talk to your people there. If you can send word along, it'll help. Will you do it?"

"Absolutely! Now I have something for you chaps." He took out three tins of cigarettes. "Prewar Egyptian. No problem, is there? Good. And here's some more quinine and antiseptic stuff. Got 'em out of the ship's stores."

"Next time bring more whiskey," Wilner said.

"Yes, of course. Everything fine with you, Naftali?"

Naftali explained why they had been late and asked Miles to wait if it should happen again.

"Within our power, we will. And the same goes for you if we're late. As a matter of fact, if we don't come at all—storm or change of orders —we'll make it the following month."

"You know how isolated we are," Naftali said, uneasy at the thought that the *Loch Ness* might skip a visit. "If you can't make it, send word to us somehow. You told me you had agents in the Lebanon and in the Hejaz."

"Might be impossible, but I'll try."

One of the sailors called out, "It's time, sir."

"Why impossible?"

"The Arab Bureau is not friendly."

"But it was Lawrence who made this contact with you."

Miles finished putting the papers in his waterproof envelope. "You charmed him, you know. He told me. Absolutely charmed him. But he washes his hands of the whole matter. Will tell Trevelyn-Jones that,

185

too. The Arab Bureau is furious with him. And, I may add, with me. You see, Naftali, as far as they're concerned, there are no Jews in Palestine at all. And if there were, they're not sure they'd like them." He smiled warmly. "But I'll do what I can."

Naftali took Miles's hand and shook it emotionally. "To the end, you can count on me too, John."

"Righto."

Miles said good-bye to Wilner, who reminded him about the whiskey, and moved into the shallow water toward the boat. The sound of the oars could not be distinguished from the wash of waves on the shores and rocks.

Naftali was suddenly emptied of tension; the night that had been filled with risk and enmity fell back harmlessly. He could smell the sea and the scents of wild grass. NILI would succeed, and it was exciting to be living at this time.

When they got back to the station they slept without waking for twelve hours.

7 ◇◇◇◇◇◇◇◇◇

For Rachel the time since the night of the burning of the wheat at Atlit passed in inner confusion. She suffered from Naftali's declaration of love. The hand that had lain fleetingly on her breast was still there in the hard memory of the flesh. At night she yearned for him, teasing her imagination, daring everything, yet his image eluded her, receding as she groped toward it. Her marriage vow barred the way; she could not leap over it, even in the secret cave of her bed.

"Naftali, Naftali," she would whisper. "O wrestler with God . . ."

She was never told, of course, that he had left Palestine, and she thought he was with Judah, either at Atlit or fighting locusts somewhere else. Unsure of herself, she avoided any possibility of seeing him and stayed in Har Nehemia to work with Papa in the vineyards.

Once in a while Judah would come home for a night to get new clothes, and he would report on his labors, mentioning Naftali in passing as being in charge of the work in the Galilee or across the Jordan.

A month or so after the burning of the wheat, Hamid Bek rode into Har Nehemia with a patrol and questioned the villagers, among them Gimmel Cohn, the *muhktar*, an unstable opportunist who had once worked for the Singers and had been discharged for pilfering. Rachel was ordered to appear.

She tried not to show her fear, but when she saw the colonel at the *muhktar's* house, in an airless dark room smelling of old olive oil, images of Armenian dead flared in her mind and she had to fight against running away. Dr. Bloch was present as well as Gimmel Cohn.

Hamid Bek studied her before starting the interrogation. Generally he disliked Jewish women; they were too sure of themselves, too independent and educated. This blue-eyed, full-breasted Jewess pleased him even less. She reminded him of the European women he had known in

Berlin, who seemed to hold him in private contempt. Unlike the passive Muslim women he had bedded but could not excite, the Europeans reassured his virility but at the same time seemed somehow to mock him. How enraged he used to become. He had beaten some of them. But no matter. They still made him feel he was less than they were. And the more he had felt this, the keener his desire to outrage their flesh with his own. The courts of love with such women were like the courts of law—a man was guilty until proven otherwise, but proof seemed never to be sufficient. He exhausted himself in vain.

He was sure that this woman would be like those others, and if he could humiliate her, he would.

"I have been told that you know Naftali Brandt, of Alona."

"I know him."

"He is your friend?"

"Yes."

"Do you know where he is?"

"No."

It was clear that he didn't believe her, and she trembled.

"You would lie to me, wouldn't you?"

"I have no reason to lie, colonel."

"When did you see him last?"

Rachel thought a moment. Was there any harm in telling him? "Several months ago. We fought the locusts at Atlit."

"And after that?"

"Not since then."

"Where is your brother?"

"I don't know exactly. The last I heard he was also fighting locusts, a new wave of them, near Hebron."

"Would this Brandt be with him?"

She felt relief. "Of course."

"He's not. I questioned your brother. He told me that Brandt was in Metullah. I sent word to Metullah. No one had seen him there. Your brother lied."

"That's false!"

"And you are also lying."

Dr. Bloch interrupted. "Excellency, this man Brandt doesn't come from our village. We couldn't know where he was. And, if I may ask, what is the charge against him?"

Hamid Bek's tone softened. He respected scientists, medical men most of all. They shared with him a detached curiosity about pain and death; they had to become detached or they would lose their senses. Admirable men.

"This man committed grave crimes against the government, doctor. He was arrested and sentenced to hang. But he was saved by some Jewish sleight of hand."

"By Jemal Pasha!" Rachel protested. "Does the colonel accuse his Excellency of being bribed?"

Hamid Bek turned to her angrily. She had revealed his true motive. He had never relieved himself of the humiliation of Jemal's releasing Brandt and had joined a secret cabal against him. If Brandt were found to be treasonable, this could badly damage the general. In his anger he lifted his riding crop to hit Rachel, then thought better of it. Such an act would be inappropriate to the situation. Besides, these Singers had Jemal's confidence.

"His Excellency Jemal Pasha," he said to Rachel slowly, biting down on his words with scorn, "is above discussing with you. I forgive your suggesting that I would accuse him of anything ignoble. Being a woman, it would be difficult for you to understand these matters." He turned his back to her. "Dr. Bloch, I am puzzled by Brandt's disappearance. His mother hasn't seen him. His friends don't know where he is or they send me on false leads. Has he grown wings and flown away? Or perhaps he has left the country. I want to know."

Hamid Bek rose, gave an order to a sergeant to bring his horse around. To the *muhktar* he said, "Report to me immediately if you hear anything about this man. If he comes into the village, let me know at Caesarea." He saluted Dr. Bloch, passed Rachel by as if she weren't there, and left.

"What shall I do?" Gimmel Cohn muttered.

"You will do nothing," Dr. Bloch said. "If Brandt visits Har Nehemia, you will stay in your house, close the shutters, and not see him. Agreed?"

Gimmel Cohn nodded unhappily.

Rachel, sick with relief and anxiety, walked back to her house with Dr. Bloch. They talked about the questioning, but they had no theories as to where Naftali was.

Later that week Judah came home for one of his quick visits. When he heard about Hamid Bek, he told Rachel not to worry. Naftali was safe. If Hamid Bek hadn't found him in Metullah, it was probably because rumors of locusts had taken him elsewhere.

Judah had other news for them. Jemal Pasha had given him permission to leave Palestine for Constantinople and then to Berlin to do research. It was a great opportunity, and although he disliked to leave the Yishuv at this trying time in its history, he was convinced that he could help it even more by working among the German Jews.

"They must use their influence on the kaiser to restrain the actions of the Sublime Porte against the Jews."

Rachel did not quite understand her brother's arguments but accepted them wholly. Papa agreed that it was a good thing for Judah to be where there was a strong Jewish community.

"And don't worry about us. We will eat, we will do our work, we will live out the war," he said.

A week or so after Judah's departure for Constantinople, Rachel found an excuse to leave Har Nehemia; she needed a change of place, and when word came that a cousin of her father's who lived in Jaffa was in the hospital, she went to visit her.

One day there was a knock at the door of the cousin's house, on Tarshish Street. Naftali stood there with a wild, elated look.

His presence frightened her. A young David, she thought, and I am his Abigail.

"Your father told me you were here," he said. "Will you go for a walk with me? I want to talk. And it's not for dark little houses."

It seemed to her that the threshold at the door was a dividing line. If she crossed it she would be lost.

He reached for her hand and pulled her to him. "It's a lovely day, Rachel. We'll go to the old city and look down at the world."

She did not pull away but went with him. He said that he knew about Hamid Bek's interrogation and that he had gone to see the colonel yesterday and nothing had happened. "I think he is waiting for me to make a mistake. He will have a long wait."

Franciscans carrying wood and produce walked by them at intervals on their way to St. Peter's Monastery. Arab porters carried the heavier loads. The spring scent of oranges rose from the well-cultivated plantations nearby. In the harbor where the blackened Andromeda's rock stood guard, Turkish and Arab coasters made white scratchings across the blue, polished sea.

"But where were you?" she asked at last.

"Wherever I was, Rachel, I felt 'the hunger of the heart,' as they say."

"Tali—" she protested.

"No! Hear me, my dear. There is more to this. You know, I will never permit you to go back to Constantinople. And if Nahum comes here, I will tell him he must divorce you."

She stopped walking. "You are not kind to me."

"I am! You don't know the kindness I have. Everything is cruel compared to my kindness."

"I will not let you talk about it anymore. I won't listen."

He saw that she meant it. It wasn't his intention to speak of love immediately. First he had wanted to talk about where he had been and NILI.

High overhead a German plane circled the city and harbor like a dark thread stitching the blue skies.

Seeing her raise her head to follow the plane, he was caught by the pure line of her throat. Her shoulders were back and her breasts rounded into the white shirtwaist.

Suddenly aware that her innocent stance revealed too much, she lowered her gaze from the sky, saw his face, and blushed.

"The war doesn't go well, does it?" she said falteringly. "The Germans seem to be winning everywhere." She crossed her arms self-consciously.

The plane left the Jaffa sky and moved south along the coast toward the Suez.

"I was not in Metullah," he said quietly. "I was in Cairo and Port Said. And Judah will not remain in Berlin. He will try to find a way to get to the United States."

She laughed, incredulous. "I will not be taken in by your jokes."

"It is true, what I've said."

"No. You always think I'll believe everything."

He took her arm and moved to one side as a Franciscan carrying a large kerosene tin came toward them.

"Listen to me, Rachel, I wouldn't joke about such things. I came back three nights ago."

She waved to the sky. "On an airplane, no doubt. Dropped from the sky like a bird feather."

"Believe what I am telling you!" he said with sudden fierceness, and she recognized in the tone of his voice the strained impatience she had known. It was not a joke.

"I came back on a British gunboat," he went on more softly. "I was in Egypt for two months."

"Did Judah know?"

"He sent me."

She covered her hand with the other in a gesture of fear. "Is it also true that Judah won't be back?"

"That I don't know. He may or may not, depending on what happens in America."

"But—" She was trying to find a flaw. "Judah left only a week or so ago. How could he have told you what he was going to do?"

"He left a message with Saul Wilner."

"Why is all this going on? What are you doing? It sounds crazy. If Hamid Bek knew— My God, Tali! He would hang you!"

Slowly he told her everything about NILI, the plan to work as an espionage group for the British, his success in Egypt, and Judah's intentions.

"When he decided that I might not be coming back, he moved ahead on his own. It doesn't matter that he left too soon. He would have had to go anyway. The British high command doesn't trust us yet. Judah ordered me to take his place. NILI is the most important action we Jews can carry out. Otherwise we will be lost for another ten generations. Judah believed this. So do I. If the British don't invade quickly, we will go the way of the Armenians. It was your experience that decided Judah."

"The others—the Tel Aviv committee, the Palestine office."

"They know nothing about it. If they knew, they would be our enemies."

She shook her head and closed her eyes.

"Rachel . . ." He wanted to reassure her.

"I wish you hadn't told me."

"I had to. We need more people. We need you."

She opened her eyes with distress and pain. "Not me! Tali, not me!"

"Don't be afraid, Rachel."

"Not me!"

"My love, listen. Remember how we used to talk of a free Jewish people here. How we adored Herzl. How we wished we had been born sooner so that we could have seen him. You remember that July day when he died? It was the week of my *bar mitzvah*. You and I saw each other after I had read my Torah portion, and instead of congratulating me, you wept. And I, proud in all my honors, my new manhood, scolded you. Herzl was dead but there would be other Herzls. I said it was a sin to cry. It meant you had no faith. I wanted to cry but I was ashamed. And later that week we saw each other on the beach of

Atlit. We talked of the *Judenstaat* and I brought you *Daniel Deronda*, which you hadn't read. Oh, Rachel, the dream is alive. More alive than ever before. Closer to coming true. Now is our chance. We need you! I need you!"

"Do you think I am not for you? Do you dare think that I don't want this idea of yours and Judah's to succeed?" She faced him angrily.

"Then come in with us," he said, proud of her indignation.

Twilight had begun to darken the ships in the harbor. In the streets below shadows lengthened like the running of a tide. The scent from the orangeries was sweeter and more pervasive.

Feeling faint, she leaned against the old Roman wall that bordered the sea side of the path. Hysteria tightened her throat. What was there to say in the face of the task that was prepared for her? All the talk, the bravery of the imagination was nothing now that she had to enter such a conspiracy. She thought of the Armenian corpses and the reports of the torture; she thought of Naftali's own agony under the bastinado. She would be too weak. With one blow of the whip she would beg them to listen to her secrets.

"I damn you for telling me," she said.

"Don't be frightened, Rachel."

"I am frightened."

"You were capable of traveling alone from Constantinople in wartime."

"I have always been afraid of pain, Tali. You know that. The slightest toothache. If anyone pulled my hair when I was a child— And how can I keep your secrets? To lie, to deceive— They have only to threaten me a little and I would tell all I know. And—and—" Her eyes were wet. "I would cause such catastrophes, such betrayals. You had no right to tell me this! You burn me with your secret. I don't know what to do. Me, a conspirator? Why, I couldn't even keep from Nahum the truth that I——"

He broke in. "That you loved me?"

"Yes! That I loved you!"

"And you love me now as I love you!"

Suddenly his joy was cut down by the shocking awareness that by asking her to join NILI, he was risking her life. How could he ever order her into danger?

"No! No, Rachel! It was a mistake what I just told you. I mean about our work. Forget it! Please, my darling. I was wrong."

He saw her sadness and dismay; it was too late. And he recalled with bile the old accusations of Judah that he had no sense of timing. It was his curse. Everything had its appointed hour, but in him the clocks jangled, the inimitable propriety and the inner rhythm eternally out of beat. He was an alien in the country of Time.

He begged her again to forget what he had told her.

"How can I forget?" she said angrily. "Your secrets are mine now. I have no choice. I don't blame you, but I blame Judah. How dare he decide this action by himself? If it fails, the whole Yishuv will die with him. He risks innocent people. How dare he?"

He put his arm around her. She shuddered, pushed him away, and covered her face with her hands.

"Rachel," he begged, "let me see your face."

She did not move for a long time, then slowly looked up. Her eyes were dry and lusterless, her cheeks drained of blood. "I am now one of you. And I said that I loved you. But you must promise me in return that you will not tempt me. Please don't touch me again. Stay far away from me." She faltered, assailed by what she was saying. "O my darling, help me. Is it too much to ask? If I am foolish to think that my marriage oaths cannot be voided, then let me be foolish. I'm a God-frightened woman who clings to the old commandments as if she herself heard them at Sinai. Please, my dearest Tali, don't tempt me. Don't even touch me in passing. Even if I am already guilty of adultery in my heart, let the sin lie there. Please, Tali, please!"

He told himself that he must obey her, to force his love into a zero in the larger accounting.

A tiny dinghy had left the harbor for the dark hulk of a camouflaged ship. It seemed not to move, paralyzed between shore and ship. He felt his own paralysis.

"Whatever you ask of me," he said finally, "I will have to do."

Greece swallowed the sun alive, and the Palestinian night fell quickly.

BOOK *Four*

Naftali Brandt came to understand that to keep one's thoughts to oneself is a prerequisite of good leadership. For having become a leader, he quickly saw how dangerous it was to confess his uncertainties and despair to his comrades whose own resolution, great as it was, nevertheless fed itself upon his seemingly undiminished faith. But he needed some confidante, and he chose to keep a diary. He wrote it in code, the key for which he gave his mother, who asked no questions and sewed it into her dead husband's prayer shawl.

His entries were intermittent and they covered the eight months between his return from Egypt and his departure from Palestine to cross the Sinai desert in a last desperate effort to reach the English lines.

February, 1916

I did not believe it possible that there could exist a group like ours under the circumstances of our life and that at the same time life could be so dull. Each of us does his share—what we see we record—although most of it is repetitious since all action except for an occasional airplane or desert patrol skirmish between here and Suez has come to an end. The lions are fighting elsewhere. We read all kinds of wild tales about Europe. The Germans have broken through Verdun and are on their way to Paris. The Austro-Hungarians have retaken Galicia. The U.S., still trembling with anger over the sinking of the *Lusitania*, will not be able to do anything about it because the German population there is so powerful.

But what we do seems in essence to be too easy. No one suspects us. We code the material—Rachel does it well—and once a month, sometimes once every other month, Saul or I deliver it to our friends beneath the shadows of the North Tower. Now and then a gendarme patrol passes, but we are unmolested. Our friends take our notes, thank us politely; give us a *pourboire* of medicine, a little food, something to drink. The ship disappears and we are left on our desert island.

The little food comes in handy. No more U.S. ships come to Jaffa with food and gold from our relief organizations abroad. The German blockade has stopped them. Can it be possible that the German-Americans are as strong as our newspapers say? Inflation has already begun. Turkish money is worth one fourth of what it was five months ago.

Miles says that the Allies threw the Germans back at Verdun. If I did not believe him as a person, I would think it propaganda to keep us going. But why do they want to keep us going? British troops could land without trouble along our coasts any time they want to, but still they sit on their packs at Kantara West or in Alexandria.

I find it increasingly difficult to be with Rachel and not touch her. She is my first love. How could I have not known it earlier? Stendhal says somewhere that a young man's first love is an ambitious love, seldom attracted to gentleness or innocence but to a woman who challenges him to rise in his own self-esteem. Stendhal is wrong. A young man's first love is for a woman he cannot possess—teachers, aunts, cousins, and the wives of others. He must feel both safe and in danger, frustrated for reasons beyond his control, the most exquisite and satisfying kind of pain to the young.

I cannot stand not touching her.

May 5

Word reached us of a great British defeat, second only to the withdrawal from Gallipoli the end of last year. General Townshend, after one hundred forty-three days of siege at Kut-al-Imara, has surrendered to General Khalil Pasha. Thus ends the plan of capturing Baghdad. They say that thirty thousand men have been either taken prisoner or killed during the siege and the two frustrated attempts by other British troops to rescue Townshend's forces. Why don't the British invade Palestine? They could take it with half the losses.

July

I avoided asking Miles about Kut-al-Imara when I saw him. He does not look well, although it is hard to tell too much in the moonless night. We say very little actually, for there is a growing tension during these meetings at the shore. Partly because he cannot give me any news of importance to us, and partly because of the more frequent appearance of Arab sheepherders who use the shore during the summer. We are never sure how close they are to us, and so we make our exchanges brief.

Our routine is the same each month. We leave the station after dark, having turned out all the lights in the upper and lower floors. We move across the courtyard, past the vineyards, over a wire fence and into the wadi. We move slowly, stopping every now and then to listen for sounds of horsemen, voices, or lorries. The riskiest time is when we have to cross the coastal Caesarea-Haifa highway.

Once Rachel and I were held up by a convoy of ammunition-laden camels. When we finally reached the shore, we saw two figures standing near a rock much farther inland than where we were accustomed to meeting Miles or his men. They heard us and without a word started to run toward the sea.

"From the ship," I whispered to Rachel and we both ran after them. Then I thought that if it were a trap I had better drop behind with my pistol to cover Rachel.

The men turned with guns in their hands.

"Don't shoot!" Rachel called out quietly. "I'm from NILI."

One of the sailors said nastily, "Why the blazes weren't you on time?"

When I joined them they recognized me from earlier meetings. Miles hadn't been able to make this trip and they were worried when they had not seen our torch signal and had gone inland to find us.

I ordered them never to do it again. If we were late, let them wait on the rocks near the Crusader ruins. The one who had acted badly to

Rachel apologized. He also had a message from Miles. Judah was in Copenhagen but the British there would have nothing to do with him. He would probably be returning via Berlin in the next month or two.

Rachel and I were angry yet relieved. When I told the other comrades, they were irritated at British obtuseness.

It is incredible that nothing happens. Our people go all over Palestine, even to Damascus and Constantinople and Baghdad, picking up information, talking to people, Arabs and Germans and Turks, then bring their information to the station, where Rachel codes it and prepares it for the boat. We wait each day hopefully for some news of a British move to liberate us. There are, of course, arrests of Jews as well as others on charges of desertion or hiding their work animals and food. But our greatest enemy is hunger and disease. All the cemeteries are growing larger. It is much worse for us now than even in the early days of pioneering, when four out of ten children did not live past the fifth year. Mothers and fathers don't know how to solve the terrible problem of sharing the little food there is, for to weaken themselves too much would mean they would soon be unable to work at all and their young children would be left helpless. To see a woman suffer herself to eat a small portion of bread when she longs to give it all to her children is to know the bitterness and greatness of love.

I saw Hamid Bek in Safed. He looked through me as if I didn't exist. But I don't believe he didn't see me. He is waiting. For what, I don't know. But I have reason to think he has never forgiven me for having eluded his hangman. His broken nose and large black eyes with their implicit cruelty give him an air of strength and yet suggest a hidden weakness. For all I know he may be a pederast, like many other Turkish officers, but only because it is a change from the passivity of his women.

I try—it is my intellectual duty—to understand the cruelty of such men; we both share human life. Could I be cruel? Could I torture a man I believed was my enemy?

I will not judge myself until the time for judgment. On the contrary, I must force myself to say that I am not capable of being Hamid Bek, otherwise I would be Hamid Bek. If this is a myth, then I must live by this myth until shown that I am wrong.

198

・ ・ ・

I sleep badly. I have dreams of terror. I know that they come from the situation of having the lives of comrades in my hands. God, I want no part of Your duties. I never thought of God having duties. But if He exists, why not? And if duties, why not doubts?

I think I grew to love Judah because he is seamless, so to speak, of one piece, without questions. Do I persuade myself that this is so because I need to believe in his strength? Do my comrades think I am stronger than I am because they also need to believe it? No leader dares to confess his doubts, his indecisions. Is that the way the whole world runs, every man attaching himself to someone he thinks is stronger, with God the strongest illusion of us all?

I want Judah to respect me. I sometimes think that that is why I did not want to marry Rachel. Who could be good enough to be the brother-in-law of a prophet? Even now I dare not touch her, although she arouses me sexually as no other woman I have ever known. If King David could arrange an adultery, why can't I?

I have talked with a man who saw the continuous rape of an Armenian girl by a gang of Hamid Bek's gendarmes. I am sure that I could not do this. I am absolutely sure I could not. The myth is not a myth. I am not capable of it. I would not be physically potent under those circumstances.

Nissim hangs around me at the station and I am disturbed by it. He counts on me as if I keep him from breaking apart.

He looks like a Velázquez painting, the Spanish and Moorish blood giving him the sallow elegance of the Castilian. After Judah left, he told me how pleased he was that I was now chief.

"I was never able to speak with Mr. Judah," he said. "People are four elements. The fire people, the earth people, the wind people. Judah is ice people. I am wind and you are fire, Tali." He smiled as if he had made a great discovery. "I can talk with you. You listen, you understand. Wind and fire are brothers. Without wind there would be no fire."

199

"A wind can blow out a fire."

"No! No!" He jumped up and down with excitement. "The harder the wind blows, the stronger the fire."

Nissim is a good lad, loyal and so on, but he is stricken by some mental flaw that may grow progressively worse. His father is no help. I don't know Gershom Vidali well but I suspect that he thinks his son is punishment for some sin. He has never driven him away from his house in Jerusalem, but since there are many other children I suspect he is relieved that Nissim works and lives here. No parent has true patience with a flawed child. He will destroy him sooner or later by too much care or not enough.

In this calm of our work, are we losing our feeling that it is real? Are we beginning to playact conspirators? I notice how Saul swaggers as he brings us material. Dmitri speaks always in whispers, even though no one could possibly overhear. Manfred, I think, exaggerates things he hears. ("The Germans are going to fill their planes with soldiers and drop them behind the English lines.") Avram hasn't changed. He is quiet and efficient. I gave him and Rachel the responsibility of distributing the money arriving via the *Loch Ness,* the money contributed by sympathizers for the support of the Palestine office as well as for the poor. Some goes to the socialists. Part of the money is sent in by Christian groups for their orphanages and other charities. The English have arranged it. And there is still a third part, quite tiny, for our own use in the giving of the damned baksheesh, etc.

It all has to be done, of course, without giving ourselves away. We make up stories to tell. But the socialists and the official Zionist characters who get some of the money suspect what is going on.

Sometimes I feel that I have become the shadow of a movement that has no substance. Judah still has not returned.

One more note about Nissim. When we are alone he asks me again and again to tell him about Paris and the girls I knew there.

"Do you dream of women, Tali?" The question was filled with troubled innocence.

"No," I lied.

"I do. In the Tractate 'Blessings' it says that if a man doesn't dream for seven days he is possessed by evil. But I dream every night. I don't understand it."

"What?"

"I see women in my dreams, but they disappear quickly. I get angry. I get so angry I wake up." His voice faded and he said shyly, "But I have not defiled myself. I have never been defiled. Is that good?"

"How old are you now?"

"I am nineteen."

"Do you know a girl you would like to marry?"

"I have never known one I would marry."

"Why not?"

He was silent.

"You are not married, Tali."

I sensed an identity that troubled me. As lightly as I could I said, "I will when the war is over. Every man ought to marry."

"Do you know who it will be?" he asked quickly.

Before I had a chance to reply, he said, "Would you marry Rachel if her husband died?"

"She is married and her husband will not die."

He said gravely, "When you marry, I will marry. But why can't I finish a dream? Never mind. When you understand it, you will tell me."

I told him to stop the nonsense. He protested, "But if I can't tell you what is in my head, whom shall I tell?"

Rachel has been receiving money from Nahum and giving it to the station to help our work. I have seen the envelopes in her hand. I try not to imagine her returning to her husband or his coming here. I think I would find a way of stopping the reunion, even if I had to force her to tell him again that she loves me. And if she refused, I would tell him.

How can a man go on like this in the presence of a woman he desires so much his spine crackles with it?

Oh, Nissim, I do dream—and the dream is completed!

I try to write poetry:

The winter rains prick the Palestine earth like daggers.

(That is not a very good line.)

The little fists of rain pound childlike against the brown breast of earth.

(I do not like this either.)

I must record the following with absolute fidelity, for the whole point of this diary is to find my own truth.

Although I have avoided being alone with Rachel, one time—it was the moonless phase of June—we were together on the beach awaiting Miles and the boat. While it was still light and warm we went swimming.

Later, as she dressed in a grove of scrub oak, and while I watched the sea (sometimes we could see the smoke from the *Loch Ness* during the daylight), Rachel told me that Dr. Bloch may suspect our activities. They had had a long talk in which he accused her of influencing Miriam against him, Miriam having argued with him and her mother, saying that they did not appreciate what was being done for the Yishuv by people who weren't going around advertising their deeds. (Rachel scolded Miriam for this breach of discipline.) But what was more grievous, according to Dr. Bloch (despite his Marxism he is a bourgeois through and through), Rachel had taken Miriam several times to the Hotel Fast in Jerusalem, where they danced with German officers. Naturally it wasn't a political question with Dr. Bloch, who supports Germany, but the question of his daughter's safety.

Rachel tried to reassure him but had to agree not to take her there anymore. Bloch half apologized by saying that since he was sure she herself was not immoral, she must have other reasons for dancing with drunken German officers. "They must talk freely," he said. "What do you do with that information, send it to the British?"

Rachel replied that she went to the Fast Hotel because she enjoyed the company of Germans, many of whom were quite literate, a few were Jews, and she thought it was her duty as a citizen of a country allied with Germany to be hospitable. She had even taken a Jewish officer home to Har Nehemia for the last holidays.

"He's fishing," I told her. "Don't worry. Even if he were to find out about us he would do nothing. No Jew informs on another."

But while I was reassuring her and myself, I felt a rush of jealousy. I had known about the dancing at the Hotel Fast but hadn't visualized it. The sense of it being a "duty" for NILI had obscured its implications.

"I don't want you to go there anymore."

"But I have picked up very important material. Saul thinks it is the best source."

"I give the assignments, not Saul."

(I record here that I am growing jealous of him too. I've seen how he studies her with the confident insolence, the certainty that he could have her if he really wanted to try.)

Rachel continued to dress and didn't protest.

Between the trunks of the protective trees, the sea hung in dark-blue panels. The distant sound of it was like silk rubbing on silk. In half an hour the sun would become Europe's again. Gulls marked the passage with regretful cries.

I heard the sound of silk rubbing on silk—rustling in her hands and around her body.

"How long can this go on?" I asked angrily.

A quick intake of her breath, the sound of her step on the earth. I turned to face her. She was dressed. Her blond hair, darkened by the sea, fell across her shoulders to her breasts. The white shirtwaist was moist and clung to her.

"There are inner limits as well as outer ones, Rachel."

Her voice was strained. "You promised . . ."

"Did my dreams promise? When I sleep, you are in my arms. Can I stop whatever takes me over when I'm no longer awake? Can I put a meter on my blood and slow it down? Do you want me to tear off my body what makes me a man? There is such a life, such a need for love. I am much lower than the angels."

She stood, unmoving. But I saw the sensual swelling of her mouth and breasts, as if they had already been kissed.

"You promised," she said again in a whisper.

Her bare arms moved uncertainly across her breasts to hide them from me.

"When you are at the Hotel Fast, some of the officers you dance with are drunk, aren't they?"

"Yes."

"Have they ever followed you when you left? In the dark streets?"

"Yes. One man."

Suddenly I couldn't see her. The sun was in my eyes. I moved closer.

"I assume nothing happened."

"Nothing!"

"Suppose you had been overpowered, assaulted?"

"I couldn't have helped myself."

"Did you think of it?"

"Yes."

The simple way she said it made me sick.

"Under the circumstances, you would be an adulteress?"

"No. I could not have helped myself." She spoke slowly, as if the words burned her mouth. Her arms dropped to her side.

"That's insanity!" I cried. "What is taken from you by force is not a sin! What is given freely is! My God, Rachel, that's insanity. That's no law. God Himself is laughing."

I exploded. Raging, I tore her shirt off. I kissed her breasts. I was the German rapist. I would take the sin from her!

She put her hands against my face and lifted it to her mouth. She kissed me passionately—once. Then, still permitting me to hold her, she said in a voice of suffering, "But *you* I love! Don't you understand, my darling? I *love* you."

But *you* I love! I laughed and let her go. It was funny, a Sinai of irony. I laughed and wiped away the taste of her sea-touched mouth on my own.

I don't remember when I stopped laughing, but I know that I left her and ran to the beach, running as fast as I could, to the high Crusader tower, and jumped into the darkening sea. I swam far out, biting the breaking waves, yelling nonsense until my mouth filled with the cold salt water and I thought I would drown.

When it was completely dark, I started back, letting the tides take me, exhausted, ashamed, dissatisfied.

Rachel was not my enemy but I would have raped her as surely as Hamid Bek's men raped that Armenian girl. Or was she my enemy whom I loved? Is that what love is—the coupling of two humans who must devour each other or die?

That night the boat didn't come in. We spoke very little. When we reached the station, Saul was there with news he had heard from a German officer: a secret weapon had been used against the British in the battle of Ypres—poison gas. The war would be over soon.

July 11, 1916

Still no boat. No word from Miles.

• • •

I know it is absurd but it has occurred to me that Dmitri (perhaps I do him an injustice) thinks that Judah has deserted us. Avram, of course, says very little. He is now the organizer of the locust campaign, preparing against their reappearance in the spring.

What a mixture of peoples we are—Manfred with his flat broad nose and slanted eyes (some Mongol warrior raped some Jewish woman); Nissim, Spanish and Moorish in his gracefulness and instability; Miriam Bloch with her Greek face like a rubbing from Delphi; Rachel, more Russian-looking than the czarina. And I— Where do we come from, we Brandts? From the hill villages of the Rhine, driven eastward by the same Crusaders, the blood of Jews still on their English boots, who built Richard's Pilgrim's Castle at Atlit.

Saul, the ghetto peddler, shining black hair and the long nose he keeps rubbing away like a sin, watches us all with a hungry smile of contempt. But he studies Rachel carefully beneath his long womanly lashes. I know he is in love with her too.

What is the infinitive that describes Judah? To lead his people? But there is always something behind the infinitive "to lead."

Is Saul's infinitive to enjoy himself at all costs? If so, why does he bother with us?

My infinitive? I can't find it. Once it was to be Bar Kochba. Once it was to be the greatest poet of our times; once, when I first met Judah—I was twelve and he was twenty-seven—I wanted to be like him because he had even more authority than my father, and besides, not being my father, I could see him as a man. He was rich, being Romanian, and I thought he looked down on the poorer Russians of Alona, but the day he first came into our village and asked me to show him Leib Brandt's house, he won me with his attitude of not descending to children. Nor being superior. And he knew so much more than any man I had ever known. Later I understood that there was a sadness in him at that time, but I took his reserve to be romantic. The fact that he wasn't married added to my feeling. He was the only grown-up man who could do what he wanted.

Infinitives of character accumulate as one grows up. We never lose them. First I wanted "to be Judah." I still do. But I want also to be—I hesitate even to write it down. Whoever reads this will laugh. I want

205

to be a legend of my people. As they would remember the Maccabees, Bar Kochba, so would I also want to be remembered. I lust for this kind of immortality. Is it childish?

But I also want Rachel, as if she were also part of that immortality. And I don't want to die trying to save an unknown dog from being run over.

We had a party at the station celebrating Nissim's birthday. We felt no tension; we sang and drank wine amidst the high stacks of books, specimens of wheat, rocks, and papers and pamphlets—Judah's presence.

The party flawed at the end. Yoshua Camiel, whom Judah had recruited, appeared. He was dressed neatly in the uniform of a Turkish supply officer. He is a cold, slow-spoken man, with thick pince-nez and a cast in his left eye that disturbs me. (To my disgust, I am moved by surface things.) When he talks, he shows his teeth and gums as if it were important to open his mouth wide. Further, he speaks in a pedantic German. His Hebrew is bad. If he were not a cousin of the Singers, distant but still a cousin, I would not trust him. (Is it superstitious of me to feel stupid and depressed in his presence? He is like a raven croaking sorrow.)

"As far as it is possible to determine," he said in harsh Berlin German, "the war goes very badly for the Allies. My dear friends, we must face the truth, bitter as it is. Germany has all of Europe, deep into Russia. England lost the strength of its fleet in the Jutland battle, and workers are striking in London. We must examine the situation without blinders. Soon the Irish will rise and troops will have to be called back from the front. You know the French, they will not last. My friends, we cannot deny that. I am, to speak bluntly, worried."

"What do you want us to do?" Saul Wilner asked with a mocking gesture. "Drop dead?"

Yoshua, openly showing his distaste for Saul, explained at great length that he must do nothing to jeopardize his position, for when the war was won by the Germans and their Turkish ally, his services as a Turkish officer would be remembered and be a help to the Jews.

"What's your complaint?" I asked. There was something else behind his foresight.

"Too many people know that I am in NILI."

"Who?"

The others stopped what they were doing and looked at Yoshua angrily.

"First Avram comes to Damascus to see me. I remind you, my friends, I am in danger."

"Who else?"

"You sent him once." He pointed to Saul. "He drinks and talks with the German nurses as if they were old sweethearts."

"We are," Saul said with a laugh. I noticed that his eyes slid past Rachel to catch her reaction.

"And last month you sent Miriam."

"What's wrong with me?" Miriam asked, flustered.

Yoshua blew his nose daintily and cleared his throat. "I have to be protected. My position is too important. You must be aware of it."

I lost patience. "What did Miriam do?"

"My wife saw her and began to ask questions. Judah warned me not to say anything about all this to my wife, and I didn't." He appealed to Rachel. "You know Deborah. How jealous." He bowed stiffly to the others. "Forgive this indiscretion, but truth is truth."

Miriam was outraged. But Rachel, amused by Yoshua, reassured him. "You tell Deborah in my name that Miriam has no interest in you."

That did not please him at all. After all, why shouldn't so attractive a young girl be interested in him? "Please, from now on, Brandt, send only men. And the same man. My colleague Lieutenant Terunian has already asked questions about my different friends coming to see me."

"Then arrangements must be made for meetings that are less open."

"No! No! That would make it worse. Sometimes I think I am observed. But it is better more innocent, to have a coffee in cafés than to meet at night under a tree or in my home."

"All right, we send only Avram. Agreed?"

Camiel wasn't satisfied. "We have been giving information for six months and nothing happens. Judah said the British would be here by now. I am merely being practical. And where, after all, is Judah? I think we should call the whole thing off!"

"Absurd," I said as coldly as I felt. "But if you want to leave us, you have my permission."

The eyes of the others met on his face and I could see how disturbed he was, this raven with the croak of sad tidings.

"I am being practical," he said weakly. "But I will think it over."

• • •

Fall, 1916

Where is the boat? We wait but it doesn't come!

There are many rumors about the activity of the British agents
(Lawrence?) and Emir Feisal along the Hejaz railroad. The Turks
are besieged in Medina, but of course we are not able to know the
truth of any of this. Nor the truth of what is happening in the war
in Europe. We are told that Romania declared for the Allies and
that Germany overran her and captured Bucharest in a matter of
weeks.

The people who may be close to the truth, however, are certain
members of the Hashomer and Zionist executive. Lorchanovsky, for
example. He has grown even more irritable with the task of finding
food and medicine and money for the Yishuv. He saw me one day in
Tel Aviv on my way to meet Saul in Jaffa and took me into his little
office on Nahlat Benjamin. It was bare of everything but a chair and a
table. No sign of Herzl photos, maps, white-and-blue flags. All these
had been prohibited.

Lorchanovsky has that 1905 pioneer look about him. He wears an
open shirt, he smiles swiftly like melting snow, he chops his hands
through the air in front of him as if it were a rock, he has the malarial
yellow in his skin, he wastes no time, and he acts as if he were a tem-
plate against which every Jew in the world must design himself or else
be thought an assimilated half Christian. He knew my father, of
course, but compared to him my father was a Hamlet.

"Where's Judah Singer?" he asked. "And the truth, if you please. I
have no time for granny tales."

He spoke in Hebrew, rapidly, cutting words off sharply. I think he
has some notion that Joshua, Moses, and King David spoke the way he
does. What I remember about him from my childhood is that he once
refused to help a German Jew who was lost on the road from Hadera
to Zichron Yaacov because the German couldn't or wouldn't ask him
in Hebrew. Those were the days when the fiercest struggle in the
Yishuv was over language. The Germans against the French against
the Yiddishists against the Hebraicists. And all against each other.
Families broke up in civil wars over the question.

I explained that Judah was on a mission for Jemal Pasha. He had heard all about that but wasn't satisfied.

"Dr. Bloch tells me," Lorchanovsky said, "that Rachel and you and Wilner are running the station. What else are you doing?"

"Fighting locusts."

"Nonsense. Then why are you in Tel Aviv?"

"To see the sights."

"Don't make trifles with me, Brandt. What is Judah really doing?"

"Go to Berlin and ask him."

He chopped his hand into the air. "Our people in Berlin haven't seen him in months. That's number one. Number two. Two shomrim from Sejera were riding near Atlit. They saw you and Wilner and one of the Liebermann cousins from your village crossing the road to the ruins. They saw lights being flashed to sea. Number three. Wilner was seen with gold pieces in a café in Beersheba. Where did he get them?" Again the chop of his hand. "Number four. Rachel was at the Hotel Fast talking with German officers. I know she is pro-British. Why suddenly should she, a married woman, become so friendly with Germans? Answer these points one by one, if you please."

"Are you working for Hamid Bek?"

His sallow skin grew red. "The son of Leib Brandt asks such a question?"

"The man who gave up a profession in Kiev to break soil in the Galilee, fighting Arabs with one hand and plowing the earth with the other, shouldn't ask such questions either."

"I have the responsibility of thirty thousand Jews on my head. What have you on yours? A masquerade? It can be very serious. Suppose Hamid Bek, in fact, asked you those questions."

"I respect you, Shmul Lorchanovsky. Respect me equally. I have already had Hamid Bek's treatment. I didn't answer his questions then. I wouldn't now."

"You are sure of yourself. A little bastinado and you are a hero. There are other tortures. What if he took your mother?"

He saw the effect and waited.

"You start by asking me questions about my friends and you end up threatening me with my mother's life. I don't enjoy any part of it."

"I am not your enemy. Or the enemy of your friends."

"Then don't send your guards to snoop around."

"They were there by accident."

His voice was softening, but not the expression on his face. The eyes were opaque and suspicious. I had heard that he was one of those who had organized the 1905 uprising against the czar and had been caught and brutally beaten. Perhaps that is what made him scent conspiracy.

"Why don't you people cooperate with us on our program of work, building new colonies, defense?" he asked.

"Is that all you're doing?"

"Is that all?" Lorchanovsky yelled. "To build and guard new colonies even while the war goes on? To feed people? To teach ghetto students how to become farmers? What more do you want? A revolution? We are the arm of world Jewry. And you and your Singerites—you are the tail of a mule."

"When Judah Singer was breaking rocks and planting his vineyards and wheat, you were cozy in some Kiev restaurant drinking hot tea, eating blini and talking of Plekhanov, not Herzl."

"That's the libel of a reactionary!"

"Don't make overtures for cooperation and don't threaten anymore. They'll help—you'll excuse the Yiddish—like bleeding a corpse with leeches."

Lorchanovsky rose from his chair angrily and slashed his hand in front of him as if he were hitting a hateful image. "Then don't come crying to us if you need help. On the contrary, if you and your friends —that Wilner, for example, whom we threw out of Hashomer because of immorality—get into trouble with Hamid Bek or Jemal, we will oppose you. We will put an end to—to whatever you are doing. Is that clear?"

To my amazement, my voice was calm, even distant, like Judah's. "If you prefer to be spies against your own, it is your dirt that will have to be washed away. Our consciences will be clear. To the end."

I left him without a good-bye. An hour later, sitting with Saul in a café in Jaffa, I remembered what Lorchanovsky had said about him. "You were in Hashomer. Why didn't you tell us?"

"No one asked."

"Why did you leave?"

Saul shrugged. "They kicked me out. Remenov, Lorchanovsky, and Company. I was immoral. I liked women. They said I exploited them. Tsk, tsk. They with their purity. When they relieve themselves in the morning, they don't look. You know what is funny? They didn't yell when I stirred a pot with a comrade. What they couldn't forgive me was the other kind—the bourgeois ladies. Personally, I can't stand idealists with programs. They are the most dangerous people in the world. Not like you or your Judah. You are idealists, but programs you haven't."

I avoided pursuing the subject. We did have a program—the survival of the Jews in Palestine. We did not go beyond that. The official Zionists would call us, if they knew what we were doing, opportunists. I couldn't care less about the charge. If we succeed, we will be the saviors of our people. If we fail, we will be called worse than opportunists, perhaps even the murderers of Jews. (I write these words simply; they do not reflect the horror of the thought.)

The Turks are fighting in Medina against the emir's troops. But it is hard to know what the truth of it is. We are in a tiny box of the war, one of those boxes within boxes. But I am more deeply concerned with the tormenting fact that for four months there has been no contact with the *Loch Ness*. We hang out the sheet from the window and each moonless night we leave the station with our information, descend the wadi, cross the coast road, listen for sounds, and wait. Nothing. We return four nights in sequence. We wait. We give the signal. There is no answer. We wait. In the rain, we wait. Hiding from a patrol of gendarmes, we wait. There is no boat! No sailors. No Miles. We wait. Have we been forgotten?

I tried at first to keep this bad news from the others, who do not go down to the shore with me. But they have to be told.

Dmitri is depressed. Saul says, "The bloody British, a year of a plague on them!" Manfred, with his trembling fingers, accuses me of bad leadership. "We should have been told immediately," he said. "Anything could have happened to us while getting information. And it would have been for nothing!"

He is right, of course.

This year the prayers at Rosh Hashanah ("Inscribe us in the Book of Life") and the prayers of Yom Kippur ("We have sinned—forgive us") are said with greater intensity than ever before. How shall God, if He is, ever change the world without threats of doom? (How the prayers must have tolled in the hearts of the Spanish Jews when King Ferdinand gave the evil decree! Or before him, during the expulsion from England and the Rhineland. Doom is the manure of prayer.)

• • •

We wait at the Crusaders' fort, Dmitri and I, in the cold rain for three nights. Still no boat, still no word from Judah. We are taskless conspirators. I am tempted to go to Lorchanovsky and Remenov and say, "Forgive us. We will become your couriers and help the new settlements. Only take us back into your well-organized Zionist fold."

Rachel stays away from the station. Saul asks about her. He understands something. He is the only one not depressed. His friends among the Germans keep him supplied with cigarettes and schnapps. I sometimes ask myself if he is faithful to us, he is so thorough an opportunist. Yet the thought is degrading, for we remain untouched by Hamid Bek and I am motivated by an envy at Saul's indifference. Contempt and envy are twins.

Shall I leave Palestine and try to get to the British lines across the Sinai? It's the only way. No more neutral ships in our ports. But what shall I take with me? We have nothing of great importance to tell. "An artillery dump hidden in a Carmelite convent at Nazareth . . . A German troop ship with replacements . . ." Yet it would be a matter of pride . . .

Rachel, I can see, is relieved. She, who has never wanted to be part of us, who feared that she would not do her part, now can suggest with honor that we suspend all further work until the boat comes.

The others agree.

I have somehow failed. The despair of the countryside, the starvation everywhere, mock me. Perhaps Miles has also failed. Perhaps Judah has become involved with more important matters. Still, I was the one who made the contact with the British. On my word, we moved forward; now NILI is paralyzed. Our morale is zero.

Still, I break silence now and then. I argue with my comrades. I vow that we are not forgotten. I descend to quoting that venerable oath "If I forget thee, O Jerusalem, may my right hand, etc." Saul grins with that twist of mockery; the others scarcely hear me. Rachel, however, is moved. I dare look at her and say directly, "Keep your eye on the city, Rachel!"

But I fail to win them completely, perhaps because they hear the despair behind my words. Not that we agree to give up entirely, but only to wait until the British find us again. Why risk lives for nothing? "Who needs it?" Saul asks. "To fill up notebooks with troop movements when the worms will eat the notes?"

I have noticed that whenever Miriam Bloch comes to the station she talks alone and quietly with Nissim. Is he responding? I am touched by her concern for him. Maybe NILI will have one success.

When Rachel and I meet, our eyes are like tides sweeping across each other; then we fall back and talk about the few things left to talk about—food, money, clothing, medicines, the rising death rate among the children.

We have no more to give, but I understand that the Tel Aviv executive is working hard smuggling in produce from the Jewish settlements in the Galilee that have been less molested.

A visit from the supply officer with the cast in the eye, Yoshua Camiel. He has a strange tale to tell. His colleague, the Armenian Terunian, whom he once mentioned to us as suspecting something, is acting in a way that puzzles Camiel. It turned out that a week ago Terunian invited him to his house to meet his wife and young child. When the men were alone the Armenian said that he wanted Camiel to know that he hated the sultan and his generals for what they had done to his people. He proposed that Camiel introduce him to any Jews who felt the same way.

I told Camiel that I thought it could be a trap. He agreed and I ordered him to avoid any contact with Terunian.

December
There is a light on the horizon. I had word from Mordecai Anuskevitz's brother, Shlomo, who has a café in Tiberias, that the British were amassing supplies and troops for another offensive against Baghdad. But, before anything happened there, another piece of news even more

significant came just before Chanukah. Troops from Australia and New Zealand had made a forced march of twenty miles during the night from their bases at the Suez Canal to the Turkish-held stronghold of El 'Arish on the Mediterranean and had taken it without a fight. Apparently the Turkish defenders had known they would be outnumbered and withdrew south-southwest to the oasis of Magdhaba. Does this mean the beginning of the offensive against Palestine? We are cheered by the news, but we still have to wait.

It is eighty kilometers from El 'Arish to Gaza, and from Gaza it is only sixty kilometers to Jaffa and sixty-five to Jerusalem!

Oh, if only Miles had not deserted us!

Saul thinks we ought to blow up the railroad from Jaffa to Beersheba, on which Turkish and German reinforcements are pouring south. I veto the suggestion. British planes reconnoiter the railroad almost every day and drop bombs on it once a week. If the British want to destroy the supply line they could. I suspect they want to draw the enemy away from the Baghdad and Russian fronts, particularly the latter, for things, I hear, are not going well with the Russian troops. There is talk of mutinies among them. Remenov, whom I saw in the Meah Shearim quarter in Jerusalem, said in passing that the Russian Socialist party is preparing to overthrow the czar.

All of us are bitter at our inaction. The great dream of striking a blow in order to take our place as an ally of the British seems to have vanished.

Damn Judah!

1917

It is the new year. I tear the skin off my heart with my teeth. We are still doing nothing. But then, the British are also staying behind their new ramparts at El 'Arish. What if this was, as I suspected, only a feint?

Rachel's father is ill with malaria and I went to his friend the Greek priest to get medicine. He treats me kindly and gives me a little of his store of quinine. My own malaria has invaded me twice this last three months but I have somehow lived through the attacks with no help. Then, I am only twenty-six and Papa Singer is seventy.

214

• • •

My old sense of being wasted has possessed me again. No Rachel. No NILI. No action. All around me hunger and disruption, and I can do nothing about them. The ending of my life without issue haunts me during the day, and in my sleep I dream of leading charges of Gideon's lancers across the plain of Megiddo to overcome the Midianites. . . . I dream of all my wars, Bar Kochba's and King Saul's and Josiah's. I am at the fall of Jerusalem to Titus. I die a thousand times, and I awake to another day of doing nothing.

Did Isaac feel the waste of himself when the angel called to Abraham to withhold the knife from the lad's throat? Abraham, the father, had proved himself a man. But what had the son to show? Nothing. The lad knew well enough what his father intended. Had he been frightened? Or exalted with the thought that he was the instrument of God's test? And what happened? Relief or exaltation thwarted? The saving of his life an anticlimax? Was it because of this bruise on his soul that he grew up to cheat his brother out of his rightful heritage? I suppose that part of my admiration for him comes from my feeling that there was a profoundly tragic flaw in Isaac, given to him as the Greek heroes were given theirs, by God.

March 12

Our mysterious Lieutenant Terunian persists. He confided to Yoshua Camiel that he had gotten hold of something that could help the British if only he knew a way to get it to them. When Camiel asked, "Why come to me?" the Armenian replied, "Because you are a Jew."

It doesn't make sense and I am troubled. However, Camiel is half convinced of the man's trustworthiness and he wants me to meet him and judge for myself. I am willing.

I warned Camiel, "If he turns out to be a spy of the police, I may be able to get away, but you will be in serious danger."

"I'm in danger already," he said resentfully, "because I didn't turn him in the first time he spoke to me."

I proposed the following plan. Terunian is to go to a certain crossroads Arab café near Har Nehemia, and Saul is to see if the man is followed. If not, he is to lead him to a cellar of a deserted winery, where I will await him. If, en route, Saul becomes suspicious, he is to start a loud fight with Terunian that I can overhear. I am to run out and shoot the man. If everything goes well, Saul is to stand guard outside the cellar until I relieve him.

I ordered Camiel to make the date a week from today.

March 19

It was a cold day, yet not cold enough to freeze the mud from the last rain or to sharpen the air into something pleasurable. But moist, chilly, uncomfortable.

I arrived at the winery early and hid behind some large casks. I had a bottle of brandy and sucked at it now and then. Saul's German pistol was in my belt.

The celler, smelling of sour wine, was dark except for faint gray light coming through two small barred windows near the top of one wall.

I listened for Saul's warning, but the only sounds were gusts of wind on the roof and the scratching of field mice, then steps.

The door opened and closed. A man stumbled against a wooden shovel near the door. It fell with a loud noise. I put the brandy bottle down and took the pistol out of my belt.

"Is there someone here?" the man asked in Turkish.

"There is a candle and a match on a table in the center of the room," I said.

There were more steps; the match flared and suddenly I could see through an opening between the two casks that hid me the flickering reflections of the light on rows of empty bottles racked on the opposite wall. But the man was out of my sight.

"Where are you?" the man asked. His voice was high pitched and nervous. All I could see was his shadow. Steps moved in my direction.

"Don't move any closer. I have a pistol on you. Stand in back of the candle."

The steps moved back. Now I could see the man. According to Camiel's description, he was Terunian. Swarthy and hook-nosed, wearing glasses. The reflection of the candle on them hid his eyes. I regretted that.

"You said you had something of importance. What is it?"

"I must know who you are."

"You can't know."

"Then you don't trust me. Is it because I am an Armenian?"

It was a fair question. If he had been a Jew, would I have gone to these lengths? In truth, I doubt it.

"I cannot do anything else, lieutenant. You are free to go now if you want to. But I remind you that it was you who asked for this talk."

His words came back at me passionately. "Hear me. For almost two years I have lived with the sadness of my people. And I have done nothing. Could I bring back the massacred from their common grave at Lake Van? I am not an angel of the resurrection. Could I, I asked myself, strike down the murderers of my people by myself? I am not your Samson. I would simply be adding myself to the dead. I could live with my soul using this argument and that argument to appease it, but in the end I can no longer love my soul or my family. Do you understand me, sir?"

"Go on."

"It is not a life for a man. I had to do something. My mind went to thoughts of poisoning my commander, assassinating Jemal, going to Constantinople to blow up the headquarters of the Yilderim and the Yildiz Kiosk. Or should I shoot Hamid Bek or Baha ed-Din, who were there in the bloodshedding of my people at Lake Van? Then I concluded that there was a way to do even more—to destroy the whole of the Turkish oppressors by opening the gates to their enemy. That is why, sir, I talked with your friend. I thought a Jew is like an Armenian. But he didn't trust me. Now, neither do you. . . . Let us talk man to man. Do I not put myself, my own life, in your care?"

I remained silent.

"What I mean, sir, is that if you should be caught, do you not have my name in your head and are there not means that the gendarmes have of emptying a prisoner's head?"

"That is exactly why it is better that you don't see me or know my name."

A long sigh. The candle wavered and the thousand lights in the bottles wavered with it.

"I have brought you something, sir." He sounded sad.

"What is it?"

"For two months, each day—each day a little—I copied the general staff code book."

I almost left my place to run to him to see it. A treasure, if it were the real thing.

"Will you leave it with me?"

"That is why I brought it."

"If you will leave it, I will try to get it to those it will help."

"But you don't trust me."

"After a while we will be in touch with you."

"My soul, sir, is tired of waiting."

"But you have already done something of great value."

"Can you understand me, sir, if I say that I will not consider anything of great value until I see the results? And I am alone. Without brothers. Do you know what it is to be alone with a fire in one's heart?"

"I know. . . ."

"To be alone, sir, is a great waste. One demands to hear his voice come back to him through the throat of another. Have I told you that not even my wife knows my feelings? Women are not the most reliable people in these matters." A pause, as if he were pondering still another confession; then: "How will you get this document to your friends?"

I felt a sharp warning. I wavered like a vane between trust and suspicion.

"I am not able to tell you any more."

"Will it be soon?" I remained quiet. "I see, sir. There's nothing more to say."

"Nothing more at this time."

"Where shall I leave the document?"

"There is a wooden box filled with straw in the corner. Put the papers there and cover them with the straw."

I watched his shadow as he moved. Then he returned to the place beside the candle. "Sir, I beg you to trust me."

"We shall see, lieutenant."

"And again I remind you, I am tired of waiting and tired of being alone. My hunger to avenge myself and my people grows each hour. Don't wait until it is too late, sir."

Suddenly he blew out the candle. I tensed and held up the pistol. I heard the door close softly, then the spatter of rain, the whiskings of the field mice.

I left my hiding place and went to the box. Carefully I lifted the straw and saw a thick manuscript. It was a code; at least, it said that it was the "Secret Army Code," with German and Turkish signatures traced on the first pages. But was it genuine? Or was it a trap, not for us but for the British?

· · ·

I study the code, but mostly I study myself. Shall I risk crossing the Turkish lines, then the Sinai in winter to get it to the British, even though it might be a fake? What hangs over me is my pattern of miscalculation of time. I am caught in my own wariness. What if I go to the British and they confirm that it is a fake code; my standing with them would be nil. For myself, in all honesty, I am prepared to be ridiculed. But I am not ready to turn our drama into a farce.

I consult Rachel, the quiet and solid Avram Liebermann, and the poetic Dmitri. They are against my going. The British have already advanced to Rafa. Avram thinks their objective is Damascus and Aleppo, but they have to take Jerusalem first. In a little while we might be able to reach their lines easily. If the code is legitimate, it can be used just as effectively later. The risk is too great to go now.

Nissim, as if nothing had ever been mentioned between us, tells me that he is falling in love with Miriam Bloch. They have talked of getting married after the war. I am pleased. When I saw her I told her so. "Nissim is a very good lad," I said. "He will be a good husband."

She nodded. "It is his strangeness that I love. He needs me. I understand him even when he doesn't talk. Or when he talks without logic, I love him more. He tries too hard to understand the world."

"If you love him, all the rest is easy."

She was wearing a gray wool dress and her dark hair was combed into a tight bun. To make her eighteen years seem more, I suppose. She has grown up in these two years.

She clasped her hands together on her lap and bent forward a little and wept.

"Why, Miriam?"

"Because—because I am grateful to you for Nissim."

"I? What had I to do with him?"

"He told me that you have kept him alive."

"He is making up a story. I've done nothing."

"He told me that when he felt bad—there were times he didn't want to live—just being with you, seeing you, hearing your voice, kept him alive."

She wiped her eyes with the back of her hands like a child.
I said, "Now you will be all those things for him."

Rumors: The British will attack Gaza or Beersheba within the
month.
Rumors: The czar has abdicated.

I have my tragic evidence about Terunian and I am heartbroken. I
was in Metullah when I heard the news. Two days before, Terunian
had attempted to assassinate Jemal Pasha as he was leaving a staff car
to enter his headquarters in Jerusalem. Terunian was killed in the attempt. Jemal scarcely knew that anything had taken place. Now I
am certain the code is correct, and I have to get it at once to the British. And at what a cost. The lonely man couldn't wait any longer. I
must arrange for Yoshua Camiel to help Terunian's wife and child.
What an irony that our first casualty, indirect though it is, should be a
righteous gentile. It is my guilt and I can't evade the burden of it. If I
had trusted him, if I had acted quicker, if I had found a way of bringing him into NILI . . .
Now there is no jeopardy great enough to keep me from going to the
British.

From Metullah to Har Nehemia to say good-bye to Rachel. There I
heard the first news of Jemal Pasha's expulsion of the Jews, all Ottoman citizens, from Jaffa.
"Rachel is in Jaffa," Papa Singer told me. His gray beard has lost its
neatness; his eyes behind the glasses are fierce and glowing, as if with
a constant fever. His voice has suddenly aged. "Jemal Pasha ordered the
expulsion of all the Jews from there and Tel Aviv. He says it is because the British have advanced to El 'Arish and he wants to protect
the population from naval bombardment. Ha! He lies, of course, that
monster, that Haman!" He spat on the ground and clapped his thin
hands together in a curse. "Why doesn't he clean out Haifa or Beirut?
They are also on the coast! I tell you, Naftali, every day and every
night I pray to the Almighty in heaven, 'Finish us up already. Erase
us from the face of the earth. Give up your promise to Moses our
teacher. I relieve you of our immortality. We won't be Jews anymore.

Put us all in a common grave and say your own kaddish over the dead.
. . .' I asked Rachel to take me with her. But I was too old. I couldn't
carry the children or the sick. Nissim and Manfred Gersh went. Now
you will go, eh? Quickly?"

Despite my anger I asked myself what was more important—to help
Jaffa Jews or get the code to the British?

"Over ten thousand men, women, and children are now already in
the desert sand outside of Tel Aviv."

I nodded and took the feed bag off Melech.

"To save one man's life," Papa Singer said, quoting the Talmud, "is
like saving a whole world."

"And what if one tries to save the whole world first?" I asked.

Irritated at my question, he pulled at the ragged corners of his beard.
"Only the Messiah can do that. Only a crazy man tries."

Melech was tired but I had to go on.

"Tell Rachel that I will be away for a little while."

"You're not going to Jaffa to help?"

"Papa, I'm no Messiah and I'm not crazy either. But maybe if not a
whole world can be saved, a remnant can. Don't be angry at me."

I embraced him, but he was angry and didn't give me his blessings.

I found a message from Nissim at the deserted station. Everyone had
gone to Jaffa to help the refugees. Except Saul. He hadn't been near
the station in a week. Someone had seen him in Acre.

I knew he had a girl there and I went to find him.

The wild spring flowers are growing everywhere. The meadowlands
glisten with buttercups as if the gold of the earth had been washed to
the surface by the winter rains. Elsewhere aroused wild seedlings
thrust up clumps of blue and yellow iris. The freshness of the season
excites the air. Even the occasional war plane overhead remains aloof.
Swatches of anemones, scarlet, crimson, purple, pink and lilac, lie on
the land like a Persian shawl.

There is something apt about this time of my decision to cross the
Sinai to the British. The crest of the year is breaking and perhaps the
turn of our fortunes has come.

Haifa port is filled with German freighters unloading supplies. Second only to Jerusalem, I love Haifa, its green hills and deep-blue cup
of bay. I recall each time I'm in Haifa the great Elijah preaching on
that high Carmel. He is one of my favorites, for his times were like

mine—the storm of kings and betrayals. Elijah, restless, impatient, always seeking out an act by which to make men live. He moved with a suddenness, appearing, disappearing, marching here and there as if there were some slipup in the cues from God.

". . . Behold there appeared a chariot of fire and horses of fire . . . and Elijah went up by a whirlwind into heaven.

"And Elisha saw it and he cried, 'My father! My father! The chariot of Israel and the horses thereof.' And he saw him no more, and he took hold of his own clothes and rent them in two pieces."

When I die I would like to be able to see the chariots of Israel and the horses thereof.

I found Saul in an Acre café outside the khan of Jezzar Pasha, with its high-arched galleries of red-and-gray granite.

An Arab boy guarded my horse for a few piasters. Camels, donkeys, and army lorries filled the square. At the café were German officers and nurses and a few Turkish civilians wearing European clothes.

Saul's voice: "To Kaiser Wilhelm!" He was raising a toast to two nurses and two officers. He seemed drunk.

"Prosit!" they replied happily.

"To our all-powerful caliph and sultan!"

"Son of Allah!" one of the nurses shouted.

Saul saw me but made no sign of recognition. After a few minutes he rose unsteadily from the table and said something that the others laughed at. In the meantime, I moved to the entrance of a narrow alley out of sight of the café. Saul appeared, grunted something, and relieved himself against the wall. I said:

"The Armenian is dead. He tried to kill Jemal and they shot him down."

Saul rubbed his nose briskly and replied in Yiddish, "So at least he knows whether after death there is a life."

"It means the code is genuine."

"Why do you bother me?"

He started toward the opening of the alley.

"Jemal has expelled all the Jews from Jaffa and Tel Aviv."

He shrugged and buttoned himself.

"If we don't get our friends to move quickly, we'll be wiped out. All of us. The code may be all they need."

222

"Across the Sinai? How will you go? Maybe steal a Fokker? Can you fly?"

"Quiet!"

"Write your poetry on the sand and leave me alone."

"We wouldn't have to go all the way, Saul."

"One step out of Beersheba is too much. Go home and dream. I'm busy."

A German captain entered the alley, bowed as he saw us, and said, "Your good health, gentlemen."

Saul and I walked away.

"Two men stand a better chance, Saul."

"To hang. I'm not interested. Look, boychik, I resigned. I am a man of leisure. A bourgeois. A materialist. I am my own Zion. You understand?"

I tried once more. "Saul, think it over. I'll be leaving from the station tomorrow at dawn."

"I won't be there."

A German nurse left the café and called over, "You take a long time, beautiful."

Saul waved to her, then looked at me defiantly and said, "At dawn tomorrow I'll be riding a different kind of mare."

The German captain staggered past, buttoning his pants. "Your good health, gentlemen. Your very good health."

I returned to Atlit. Saul's refusal could have no effect on my plan. My only worry was that if anything happened to me the code would be found and its usefulness ended. But there was no way to help that.

As for Saul—I confess I do not understand him. It isn't enough to think of him as contemptible or summarize his life with the infinitive "to please himself." I hate the role of judge, and I suppose I have my own Saul within—the inerasable impulse to reach for a nirvana of nonresponsibility, to be able to say *"J'emmerde tout le monde."*

But if it isn't meaningful to condemn him, then what is there left? I think of the hassidic tradition. Perhaps with a wink and a shoulder shrug it would say of Saul: "Nu, just so long as he lives out his life, fulfills his feelings, commits with joy—God forbid—even bad things, sooner or later something he does, something of his livingness, will pour over and will please God. Just as long as his heart *feels.*"

• • •

It is early in the morning.

I am writing this final entry at my mother's house. She looks older since I saw her last. New lines engrave her face near the calm eyes and the firm mouth. I knew her in her youth and I didn't see her; now I am seeing her.

"I'm on my way to the station for tonight, then I'll be gone for a few weeks," I told her.

"I have never asked you where you go. I will not ask this time." Suddenly her lips opened and trembled; she pressed her fingers against them.

"What's the matter, Mama?"

"You never came to say good-bye to me before."

She kissed me. As far back as I can remember, this was the first kiss. I wish I had said nothing. I had indulged myself at her expense.

"Mama, you will be given these pages to be put away with the others. This will be my last entry until I return with our victorious ally."

"God bless you."

"He hath made everything beautiful within His time."

BOOK *Five*

1 ◇◇◇◇◇◇◇◇◇

During the night of March 28, the day before Passover, orders had been posted on the walls of Jaffa and the Jewish suburb of Tel Aviv announcing the evacuation of all civilians immediately. When morning came, mounted patrols moved through the streets firing rifles and driving people from their homes to the desert outside the borders of the two towns. The schools were closed. Parents separated from their children were prevented from looking for them. The sick and homeless were hurried out of hospitals and orphanages by Hamid Bek's horsemen. When word swept back along the lines of refugees that the Arabs had been permitted to camp on the outskirts of the cities, whereas the Jews had to get out of the province, the Jews, prodded by lances and swords, became stricken with the certainty that what had happened to the Armenians would happen to them.

The nearest Jewish settlements, Rishon le Zion, Petach Tikva, Kfar Saba, and Rechovot, opened their homes to the refugees but soon ran out of food and water. Couriers were sped to the Sharon and Galilee, although no help could be gotten from those distant Jewish settlements in less than a week. With no place else to go, the bulk of the Jews, already weakened by the war's two years of malnutrition and disease, fled into the sand dunes north of Tel Aviv.

The rabbis and community leaders protested to Jemal Pasha, who said that the expulsion was a military necessity. Their arguments he rejected angrily as tainted with treason.

Lorchanovsky and Remenov of the Zionist executive bribed a Turkish railroad engineer to take a train of three cars of refugees to Rosh Pina, in the Galilee. But when it came to choose five hundred out of the thousands who were pleading to be helped, Lorchanovsky became paralyzed with indecision. Remenov and Mara Schalet had to complete the task, than ran from the cries of those left behind when the tiny wood-burning train departed from Ras el-Ain.

On the dunes people moved northward, anticipating the worst. One crazed, bearded old man, wearing his phylacteries and prayer shawl, walked into the ocean until the water was over his head and drowned himself. He was convinced that he would be forced to deny the God of Abraham, Isaac, and Jacob.

Everywhere were lost children and lost parents looking for each other.

The first Passover seder was celebrated in the sand. Men recited from memory the ancient Haggada, which told of the exodus from Egypt, and wept loudly for a Moses and a miracle.

The few matzoth that had been brought with them were broken into tiny pieces so that all could eat the bread of affliction. In the presence of such terror, the Armenian example always in the mind, no one needed the symbolic bitter herbs.

The refugees were harassed during the nights by Arab thieves, who attacked isolated groups and tried to kidnap young girls. The men fought them off by throwing rocks and sand. The shomrim did what they could to protect the refugees and move them to safety. But they were no more than a dozen men with arms, and to open a fire fight with Hamid Bek's gendarmerie would have created the massacre they feared so much.

It took a week to reach the settlements of the north, and during that time about three hundred died, the old and the very young.

When Rachel joined the refugees, she had taken on the task of gathering the lost children and reuniting them with their families. During the first days she had as many as forty; she sang to keep up their spirits, huddled with them during the cold nights, fed them with food and goat's milk she got by bartering her earrings and Naftali's wedding gift with Arab villagers. Each day she led her troop through the lines of refugees calling, "Lost children! Lost children!"

By the time she approached the outskirts of Alona, the first Jewish settlement north of Tel Aviv, she had only six children left.

One was a Yemenite boy of four, half blind with trachoma. He couldn't remember his name.

A cart filled with refugees passed going north. Suddenly a Yemenite woman jumped out, screaming, "Dani! Dani!"

The blind boy let go of Rachel's hand and ran stumbling and falling toward the sound of his mother. The woman hid him in her skirts and yelled at Rachel, "Thief! You have stolen my son!" She sped back to the cart with the child and climbed in. Her cries of "Thief! Thief!" lasted until she was out of sight.

People around Rachel looked at her suspiciously.

An eight-year-old girl, Yardena, tried to reassure them. "She is no thief. She helps us." Nothing Rachel could say convinced Yardena that it didn't matter to her.

Rachel turned the children over to the village committee of Alona, except Yardena, whom she took to Naftali's mother's house.

"Naftali was here this morning," Chana Brandt said.

"Is he well?"

The mother's face was troubled. "He came to say good-bye. He said he was going away for a few weeks."

"Did he say where he was going?"

"I didn't ask him, he didn't tell me. I think that tonight he is at the station."

Rachel was worried. This sounded unlike Naftali. Then she remembered the news of Terunian's attempt to kill Jemal, confirming the validity of the code. Naftali was going to try to cross the desert with it. A wild, impossible mission. He must be stopped.

"Don't worry, Mama," Rachel said. She called her "Mama" for the first time.

"What have I to worry for, Rachel?"

Naftali's mother put her hand out to touch Rachel's cheek, then changed her mind.

Rachel kissed Yardena and left.

2 ◇◇◇◇◇◇◇◇◇

When Rachel arrived at the station she saw Melech in the barn, but there was no light in the windows of the second story. Moving quietly, she climbed the inside stairway and entered the room with its warm smell of dried wheat. Naftali, fully dressed, lay asleep on the cot near the window, one hand flung halfway to the floor as if pointing to some discernible center of the earth, the other under his cheek, childlike. With his great black eyes closed, his features seemed to her to be younger, the mouth fuller and more compassionate, the pale skin above the black fringe of beard translucent.

She thought of what he was going out to do—the risk and danger, the fearful consequences if he were caught. She thought also of the love she had withheld from him. The misery of the refugees on the sands north of Tel Aviv had angered her against God as well as man. The fear of heaven was obscured; the law that stood in her way seemed pitifully absurd. As before, when she had seen the Armenian dead, to live never seemed so desirable. She felt a ruthless energy to fulfill herself.

The light blanket with which Naftali had covered himself had fallen to the floor.

She whispered to herself, "I divorce thee, Nahum. I divorce thee, Nahum." Then, moving quietly, she went to the bed and covered her beloved with the blanket.

Quickly the black eyes opened, flickered alertly, then incredulously.

"You are leaving?" she whispered.

He nodded.

"For the British?"

He nodded again.

Slowly, wonderingly, her hands descended to his face, held it, and brought his mouth up to hers.

. . .

Later, when he looked at her, she was asleep, a faint frown on her forehead. Her closed eyes were slightly swollen. The frown and the half-open lips made her face more sensual than ever before. The voluptuous sharing of sin marked pleasure more deeply. He wanted to bless her in an unknown language that had not yet been worn into shreds.

The silent Palestine night, the silent workroom with its smell of grain, sealed the perfection of what they had done.

Her eyes opened and the frown faded at the same instant. She reached for his hand and kissed it. Gently he bent over and touched her mouth. In afterlove there was intense peace.

"Without you . . ." He left the thought unfinished.

"Without you . . ." she said.

They remained silent.

He had a feeling of dawn, and he raised the shade over the window. They watched the first bleaching of the night.

"I bartered your watch away," she said. "For food for the refugees."

The peace was broken and he rose from the cot. "I'll bring you another one from Cairo," he said. "My own gift, not my mother's. It will be soon."

He went downstairs to wash himself and to feed and saddle Melech. The gulls and sparrows, sensing the dawn as he had, were beginning to move about.

Rachel had the tea ready. In the manner of the wedding wine, she took a sip from his glass before giving it to him.

"We are blessed," she said.

He kissed her gently.

"Where will you go first?" she asked.

"To Beersheba. I'll buy a camel there. It won't be difficult getting through the Turkish lines. I left a note for Lieutenant Miles. Give it to him if he comes before I return."

He tore a page out of his notebook, folded it, and gave it to her. She put it in her pocket carefully, and thought: Could she keep him from going?

Naftali said, "When you see Nissim, tell him privately that I would have taken him if there had been time. It is not true, of course, but it will please him. You will be in charge here, Rachel, dear."

"Not Saul?"

"I saw him. He doesn't want to go with me. He considers that he is no longer bound to us."

She forced herself to remain calm and went to fill his canteen.

"Was it terrible for you at Jaffa?" he asked.

Accidentally she broke a drinking glass. Suddenly vulnerable and weak, she turned to him.

"Don't go!"

He was silent.

"I can't stay here without you, Tali!"

"If I didn't think it was absolutely necessary— You know that."

"Tali, darling, I don't care about the code!" she cried, raging. "They haven't thought enough of us to make contact in a year. What do the British care? We are nothing to them. Let them wait for the code. Don't go, Tali! In a week or two they may be in Jaffa. Give it to them then."

Carefully he put the pieces of broken glass in a basket of waste, then wiped his hands free of the splinters.

"Judah wouldn't have wanted you to go," she said.

"Judah gave me the responsibility," he said, feeling rebellious. "I have taken it."

He moved aimlessly in the room, fixing papers, straightening the piles of pamphlets.

"I don't want to be in charge when you're gone!" she said angrily. "This whole business appalls me. I'm sick with it, Tali."

"Rachel, please. This is not the time. It's too late. If you want to give up, ask Avram or Dmitri to take over. They'll do it well. Or Manfred." His tone was sharp and severe.

"I dream of men hanging. Not only you, my beloved. Or our friends. But strangers. They're hanging alongside us, body to body. Because of us! Because we have been found out. Innocent people dying because of us."

Raising her wet eyes, she demanded that he give up and dissolve NILI. How dared they risk the whole Yishuv? How did they know they were right? It was too much to bear, being executioners of their own people.

"Who are we?" she asked fiercely. "What voice did we hear? Who chose us?"

The questions were like the slashes of the bastinado. And equally unanswerable.

"We must act. We must," he said. "We mustn't doubt." He had to rouse her in some way. "Keep your eyes on Jerusalem, my love. Hold the precious city in your mind. Feed your soul with it. Someday it will be free. Whisper 'Jerusalem' hour after hour. 'If I forget thee, Jerusalem . . .' That's the meaning of our deed, Rachel."

He kissed her gently, thinking: Was it truly the meaning of their deed? Or was he a victim of a myth, an idiot prophet repeating the verbs and nouns of the past?

"Don't go, Tali," she pleaded hopelessly.

He thought of his own people. Was the long night of Jewish endurance a meaningless accident of history? Why hadn't they given up long before now? Was it the senseless reflex to survive? Like animals who circle a hunter's fire at night at the risk of their lives, had they been seduced by the promise of the Eternity who indeed had not kept His word?

If he reached down inside himself into the farthest corner of the knotted darkness that was his reality, to his own Naftali's Naftali, would he find nothing there but words, slogans, the mimicry of history, the rationale of accident? Would he find only a belief that men were either animals or hunters who invented wordy ideas for the purpose of fooling themselves?

If this was what he really believed, then Zion was a fraud, and all the rest of it too. The Eternity could deceive. . . . No. Suffering was not a waste, not refuse in the errant seatide of man. How it was used he did not know, but that it was used he was sure.

"Keep your eye on the City," he whispered stubbornly; then in a wild wave of desire he lifted her to him and kissed her mouth and eyes and breasts, plunging himself into her, finding another truth in the far reaches of the flesh.

Later, when they came out of the station together, they saw Saul Wilner, dressed in bedouin style, with a long rifle strapped to his back, riding toward them. Grinning, he halted and studied them. "So, that's how one cooks a noodle. Have you missed me, Racheleh?"

"You almost missed me," Naftali said with a smile of relief.

"Rachel, if you know what he is planning you also know he's an idiot," Saul said.

As if it were a reply, she kissed Naftali without shame; she kissed him with her whole life.

"I will keep my eye on the City," she said quietly. "And I will do what I have to do."

Naftali trembled and tugged nervously at the edge of his kaffiyeh. "Shalom, my love."

He mounted Melech.

"Eh, don't I also deserve a kiss?" Saul protested, and without waiting for an answer rode over to Rachel, bent down, and kissed her.

"Shalom, Saul. Watch over him."

Saul shrugged and gave a slanted smile. "A charity institution, I am not. We'll both look out for each other and we'll be back with rings on our fingers and bells on our toes."

The men circled, filling their eyes with her, the clear morning light on the fair face, a lone figure standing at the door of the station like the biblical Yael before her tent of courage.

Naftali brought his hand down sharply on Melech's flank, and the men rode away through the palm trees toward the coast road. She called out strongly, "Blessed be those who go!"

Rachel watched them pass the line of trees, bright in the pure untroubled air. Beyond, the sea's horizon seemed close enough to reach with her fingertips. The morning had the unabashed clarity of a child.

She ran upstairs to the second story to see them as they crossed the bridge over the wadi, and when they were finally hidden by a row of cedars and a turn in the road, she permitted herself to weep. But there was exaltation in her tears. She would be strong for everything now, including the decision to write Nahum that she wanted a divorce.

Later she read Naftali's letter to Lieutenant Miles. It was in French. How like Naftali to choose that language; it was like a plume in his hat:

My lieutenant:

My decision is taken. I am going into the desert to rejoin forces with you on my own. I do not know if what I am doing is wise, but I must do it. It is a long time since we saw each other. We have been left here isolated and uncertain. For months we have been like blind men not knowing in which direction to take our next step. Yet I cannot believe that we have been truly deserted. There must have been some reason for this, although I cannot begin to guess.

My nature abhors melodrama, although my life seems to lead me there. I mention this by way of apology, for I must add that if I do not reach El Kantara—enemies, storms, accidents, etc., may prevent me—I want you to know that your first Jewish ally remained faithful. I do not ever want it to be said the man you trusted was not willing to risk everything to repay you for that trust. I beg you to bear witness so that if anything happens to me this act of mine will be reckoned to the credit of my comrades.

I also remind you of your promise that my people will never be forgotten for their service to your king, who may someday be ruler of Palestine and Mesopotamia. In that day, will justice be done?

I leave now to face my destiny.

Faithfully,
N.B.

When she finished reading it she hid the letter in the lining of an old book of Psalms, then read from the book, as was the custom of her people in times of anxiety.

3 ✥✥✥✥✥✥✥✥✥

They rode south along the coast highway, and as they approached Caesarea, Herod's tribute to Augustus, they were stopped by Mustafa ibn Musa and a patrol.

"Brandt Effendi, salaam."

"Salaam, Mustafa."

"You and your friend deceive by looking so much like bedouin."

"Is there a law about how we should appear?"

"Our book commands us to be what we are."

"Mustafa," Naftali said, "we are in a great hurry. Have you reason to delay us longer?"

"Are you still fighting the locust, Brandt Effendi?"

"As long as they molest our lands."

"And is Singer Effendi also fighting them?"

"Ask Jemal."

Mustafa thought that there was a new face on top of the old face of this young Jew. It was stronger, clearer, more sure of itself. Had he fallen heir to money?

Mustafa walked his horse around the men. How could they be made to feel his power? There was baksheesh around in the air somewhere.

"You carry much food."

"We are going to Jaffa."

"The Jews are forbidden there."

"To the refugees. They are starving."

"Do we not all starve? Why should the Jews be different?" He pointed to Wilner's rifle. "That is also forbidden."

"His Excellency Jemal Pasha permits us arms," Wilner said.

"His Excellency Hamid Bek has given strict orders——"

"When he is as powerful as Jemal, we will obey them," Naftali interrupted. "Now, let us pass in peace."

Mustafa hesitated. "When will you be back, effendi?"

"In a few days."

"I will be at the station or in your village in three days with orders from Hamid Bek to——"

Naftali moved his horse close to Mustafa's and whispered, "Come in six days and there will be a gift for you." He slapped Melech, yelled "Salaam," and rode swiftly with Wilner past the patrol.

Mustafa signaled his men not to follow. He would wait, and this time the gift would be greater, perhaps even as much as a hundred liras.

All day they passed the lines of refugees going the other way, hearing the children cry, seeing the confused faces, sometimes resigned, sometimes angry. Naftali kept recalling Bialik's elegy "The City of Slaughter," which he had memorized as a child. That night as he lay in the sand with Wilner he began to recite it in a low voice, hearing the elegiac words anew, as if someone else were saying them. The sea, dyed crimson by the evening sky, sounded its infinite accompaniment.

> "Arise and go now to the city of slaughter;
>   Into its courtyard, wind thy way;
> There with thine own hands touch, and
>   with the eyes of thine head,
> Behold on tree, on stone, on fence, on
>   the wall's clay,
> The spattered blood and dried brains
>   of the dead.
> Proceed thence——"

"For God's sake, Tali, shut up!" Wilner yelled suddenly, standing and kicking the sand away. " 'Arise and go now to the city of slaughter!' " he mocked. "Where is that city? Jaffa? Ha. How many people in Jaffa had their brains knocked out? A dozen? Two dozen? Maybe some of the old ones died a little before their time——"

"I was also thinking of Kishinev and the other places. But if you don't like Bialik, I'll keep him to myself."

Wilner rocked back and forth on his heels, his eyes half closed like a man praying and was silent for a long time.

When the day ended suddenly and the night became cold, the men rolled themselves in blankets and lay on the sand. The nearby surf broke mournfully in low, broken drumbeats.

235

In the darkness Wilner laughed harshly. "I'm an idiot, like you, Tali. For this I gave up a girl. A warm, soft——"

"Bravo."

"I did. As God is my judge."

"I believe you."

"So why did I come with you?"

"Because you like the smell of danger, as you said, more than the smell of a whore's perfume."

"Ha!" Wilner brushed sand mites from his face. "Don't you poets ever enjoy a little carrots and potatoes? Or do you only write about love?"

"I'm tired, Saul. I want to go to sleep."

"About slaughter you'll talk, but about love you suddenly feel the marrow run out of your bones. Maybe you were reading poetry all last night and not *schtuping* a little?"

Naftali rose to his feet in one movement. "You filthy-mouthed——"

"So I'm filthy-mouthed. I insulted your sweetheart. Be brave. You want maybe to fight with me because I took her name in vain?"

"What do you want of me, Saul? Ever since we met, it's the same. Tell me what you want?"

Inland the sound of a convoy of lorries broke the night. Rifle shots were being fired somewhere.

"Just tell me what you want of me, Saul."

"You couldn't give it to me."

"Tell me."

Wilner was quiet, then he said, "I've never been in love. For me a woman is a something in the night. I'm thirty. How many women have I had? Who counts? It's all too easy. When it's over, the only feeling I have is— Ha! All I get is tired. I'm tired, that's all. I can't wait to get the bag of nothing from under me." He stared harshly at Naftali. "It's different with you, maybe?"

"Yes, it's different."

"But of course with a woman like Rachel . . . Maybe it would make a man feel he'd won a big victory, no?"

"Forget it. Get her out of your mind!"

"It was like that with her, eh?"

"Shut up, Saul!"

"You can tell me. We're alone. I keep secrets. She's a good one, eh?"

Naftali reached out for Wilner and smashed the edge of a hand against his jaw. Wilner fell back with a grunt. Naftali bent over to hit him again. Wilner caught Naftali's legs and pulled him down, then grabbed his forearm and twisted it back. Naftali swung his other hand around to find Wilner's eyes. Both men at the same time scooped up sand and threw it into each other's faces.

They were blinded temporarily and broke their holds. The sound of their panting was like the sound of the sea.

"Some other time . . ." Wilner grunted.

"Not a word about Rachel."

Wilner was silent and moved away.

They did not find it easy to sleep. The ocean, the roar of lorries moving south along the coast road, the occasional cry of a child from some hidden clump of refugees, kept them awake.

Sometime during the night Wilner called out softly, "Tali . . ."

"Yes."

"Tali, you know with me, my village. . . . It wasn't so different from Kishinev."

Naftali waited.

"My village . . ." Wilner sighed and turned over in the sand to stare at the night sky.

"I was in the woods with a woman . . . a Christian . . . married to a drunkard, a beater, old enough to be her— Ha!" The cry mocked himself. "So, figure it out. If I wasn't in the woods committing adultery, death would've caught me by the throat. Figure that out, poet! Could I help myself? Could I tear my penis off my body? From the time I was thirteen, I was a man. But a crazy man. And the girls and the women liked it. Ha, how they liked it!"

He kneeled with his hands between his legs as if he were trying to push his sex back into his body. The moon slashed his face in silver-and-black stripes.

"But what am I telling you? That I am great with women? No. I'm telling you that while I was *schtuping* another man's wife my village died in a pogrom and I escaped the slaughter. So don't give me Bialik's poem. It sticks in my brain like a rusty nail."

The night sky was the same sky that Saul Wilner remembered. The salt smell of the sea was like the smell of the blood. The roaring break of waves was like the roaring fires in the village houses. When he had seen the red in the sky, he left the woman who kissed him and made him promise to meet again the next night. In the village the people didn't look dead, for the fire cast moving shadows on their bodies and they seemed to be moving. He ran to his house. At the door, shrouded in the reddish smoke, were his father and mother, lying across each other, their blood still dripping along their arms and faces onto the wooden sill. He yelled for his sister. The crackling fire was the only sound. There was no way to enter the house—the walls were solid flame. He circled it, yelling, "Doraleh! Doraleh! It's Saul. I've come to save you. Where are you? You don't have to hide from me. I am here. Saul, your brother. Where are you? Come out, come out, come out!"

He found her later in an alley, looked once, and turned away as if suddenly she were no longer his sister but some strange composite of twigs and mud remotely resembling the shape of a human body.

He walked away or ran away; the only other memory of that night was that in or near the village he had seen something white and twisted on the summer earth. He thought at first that it was a stream of water, but when he came closer he saw it was a Torah scroll that had been taken from the little synagogue and stamped on by horses. The black rows of words, each letter of which he knew, each letter written by the hand of some lover of the word, roused him to a pitch of anger, for there were the laws that described his deed of that night as a grave sin and there were the promises of life that God had made to such blameless ones as his parents and his sister.

How could he have lived and they died? There was no Torah; there was no Moses; there was no Adonai. He yelled insanely the forbidden name of God and defiled with his urine the already defiled scroll. He felt the final satisfaction of the root that knows what it bears.

The smell of blood was in the sea scents; the rushing sound of the flames was in the giant waves slashing the shore; Bialik's "City of Slaughter" could only make him weep or laugh. To do either was insanity.

He stood up and urinated in the place where he had been lying.

"Saul," Naftali said softly, "talk about it. . . . It helps."

"So who cares about these Jaffa Jews? Bedbugs. Like you and me. You feel a bedbug crawl on you, what do you do? You squash it. If you live your life worrying about bedbugs and whether they hurt or not when you squash them and who their fathers and mothers and sisters are, a man can go crazy. No?"

"There's pity . . ."

"Ha! I'm a poor man. Only the rich can afford pity. Good night, poet."

238

He kicked sand over the wet place, took his pack, and moved away to the other side of the horses. Animals comforted him.

Naftali decided to give half the code book to Wilner. "We double our chances of getting it through," he explained in the morning as they were getting ready to leave. "If I'm taken, there's enough in your section to make the code intelligible. And the other way around."

"Ha! Very smart. It also doubles our chances of getting caught." Wilner rubbed his nose violently—the itch seemed both insupportable and ineradicable.

"Do you object?"

"Naturally. But I'll do it anyway."

"And if anything happens to me, don't forget that Lieutenant John Miles was my contact."

"Miles . . . Miles . . . Not kilometers but Miles . . ."

4 ◇◇◇◇◇◇◇◇

"My friend and I want to sell two horses and buy two camels," Wilner said. They were on the outskirts of Beersheba bargaining with a bedouin, Suleiman of the Beni Sobkir tribe, who had the dark look of a hashish addict. The statement had come only after an extended and polite discussion of other matters.

Suleiman was thinking: If these Yehudim seated with him in front of his tent accepting his hospitality wanted camels, it was only to go south, and not to Asluj, which the dark one with the oily eyes had mentioned as their destination. He lies, and he knows I know it. . . . The other one, with the twist of black beard around the cheeks and chin, distrusts me, and he cannot hide it.

"Camels are more valuable than before," Suleiman said.

"We are aware of that," Naftali said. He did not have the joy in trading that Wilner and this Suleiman had.

"The Turk pays more than last year. The English pay even more. I have heard they bought ten thousand camels from the tribes on both sides of the Nile."

"It is too bad, O friend, that you are not able to sell to the British," Wilner said.

A tiny fly crawled over Suleiman's pocked cheeks. He permitted it to go its way, for to him the insect was more important than the Yehudim.

"There are no camels for sale," he said with a show of regret. "Besides, the British are at Reheiba, not Asluj."

Naftali was pleased. Reheiba could be their crossing-over place. "I have heard that the British will come here soon," he said. "No disrespect meant for the strength of Jemal Pasha and his German, Von Kressenstein. But the British are growing stronger each day."

"You are friends with them?" Suleiman asked.

"We are friends of our friends. Is that not the saying of your people, Suleiman?"

Suleiman nodded, and then, turning away, he said, "Horses used to be valuable, but are no more."

Back and forth they traded, with time taken for general observations on the destiny of man, the change of climate that the war may have brought, and the difficulties of knowing the truth of the present situation. After three hours camels were exchanged for their horses plus two gold pieces.

Naftali was finally faced with the giving up of Melech. His affection for the stallion was like a friendship one takes casually until it ends. He covered his eyes with his kaffiyeh and stood alongside Melech to stroke a farewell on his warm, graceful neck.

Suleiman knew better than to inquire again where the Yehudim were going. It didn't matter, he had gotten the better of them. The camels had been stolen three nights before from a Turkish camp. If they were found, the punishment would not be on him. The enemy of my enemy, he thought, is also my enemy.

Farther south, in the open desert, the heat enclosed the men in an airless vise. The distant Edomite hills were dark beasts lying in wait.

Wilner was uneasy. Open space violated the learning of his life, whose patterns were walls and alleys. He had never learned to look up or over, but only down and sideways. The world was a fugitive's warren, a maze one entered only after making sure he knew the site of the exit. Wilner's years in Palestine had not yet broken the psychic shell of the ghetto.

Naftali, on the other hand, felt at home in the desert. Despite the dangers, he enjoyed its openness; it gave him a sense of freedom, of the irrepressible and limitless resources of life. It revived the identity with those ancestors who had lived on this very same plain of sand and basalt. He could see through their eyes the seamless avenues without borders, without perspective, and without a vanishing point. No wonder they had found a God who was infinite and imageless and indivisible. No wonder that when they confronted Him at Sinai to accept reluctantly the bounds of law a high place had been chosen, for only by tearing their eyes away from the plain of the desert and looking upward could they break the desert's seductive illusion that there each man was alone and his own law.

We Jews, Naftali thought, were formed here, not in exile. Before we were marked by the walls of the ghetto, we had learned how to endure in the hard, unwalled country of freedom.

Isaac had lived at Gerar, not too far away from where he was riding. Isaac, his favorite among the ancestors, the young Isaac, the lad of the sacrifice.

" 'Behold the fire and the wood, but where is the lamb for the burnt offering?' " the boy had asked his father on the way up to Moriah.

But there was no lamb, and Isaac saw his father build the altar, lay the wood, then finally bind him and lay him on the stone.

The terror, the uncomprehending terror that must have ravaged the boy's mind. Where is the lamb? There was no lamb, only Isaac, only himself.

Naftali remembered the midrash that spoke of Abraham's weeping, his tears falling into his son's eyes. Was this the cause of Isaac's blindness in later years? Or, rather, was it the explosive wounding of the mind of a boy who saw his father take out the long sharp knife to plunge into his throat?

What had the lad felt? Was it only terror, or was there a primordial pride that his father, who had talked with God—the God Who had changed their lives and made the world their own—should choose him to be the object of such love that only death could mark its boundaries? Could it have been pride, not terror, in Isaac?

In the afternoon they were within twenty kilometers of the Turkish Army. They moved slowly and carefully, moving behind protective dunes and tels. At dusk they came to Halsa, once a strong Byzantine city, now ruins inhabited by lizards and flies. It was a good place for the night.

The huge red round sun balanced itself at the edge of the white line of desert, then slipped slowly into the slot of Europe.

Next day, after several hours of travel, while pausing to watch a fight between a German and an English plane, they were suddenly surprised by the sight several hundred yards away of a Turkish Army camel patrol.

They couldn't tell whether or not they had been seen and kept their course.

Two of the troopers left the others and sped toward them.

"I'll talk to them," Naftali said.

The troopers came up with rifles ready.

"Who are you?" one asked in Turkish.

"Salaam," Naftali said.

"Speak Turkish?"

Naftali shook his head.

The troopers talked between themselves. One said they had been ordered only to find out who the bedouin were. The other said that since they couldn't speak the language the strangers should be taken back to camp.

The first man tried the few words of Arabic he knew. "Where are you from?"

"Har Ezuz."

That seemed to satisfy him but not the second man.

"They are smugglers," he said. "Maybe they have money."

Naftali saw that the main part of the patrol had moved on. A mile separated them.

"You have guns to sell?" Naftali asked in Arabic, pointing at one of the rifles.

"What does he want?" the second man asked. He was a fat man with a sick gray face.

"I don't know. Something about rifles."

"Maybe they were with the band that stole our camels."

"There were fifteen stolen. Not two."

"Tewfik, you are a fool. Maybe these are two of the fifteen. Let us take them back."

"Our orders were to find out who they are."

"If we take them, we will be rewarded."

"Our captain wants to be friends with the bedu. We will be in trouble. I am tired of being punished. Three men were shot; you know that."

"By the Alemanni officer, not our captain."

"Our captain is the toe-kisser of the Alemanni."

The first man straightened himself to look for the rest of the patrol. They were out of sight.

"We will take their rifles," he said. "That will be enough."

Naftali made a sign to Wilner and yelled, "Ha!" He slapped his camel's neck sharply with his stick and sped away. Saul took the cue and followed.

The troopers tried to head off Naftali's lead camel and did not see Wilner unsling his rifle. The fat soldier fell with a bullet in his heart. The other veered away and tried to swing his rifle into firing position.

243

In Turkish, Naftali ordered him to surrender. "We are two to your one!"

"Scum!" the Turk raged. "You are not bedouin!"

"Drop your rifle or you'll be killed."

The man hesitated. Wilner moved his camel swiftly behind him and knocked him to the ground.

"Who are you?" the Turk asked, picking himself up.

"Deserters from the Twentieth Regiment, Seventh Division," Naftali said quickly in Turkish.

"What are we going to do with him?" Wilner asked in Yiddish.

"Take his rifle and camel and leave him here."

"So he can go and bring that patrol back to look for us?"

"He'll need two days to get anywhere on foot. We'll be through the lines by then."

"The only way to make sure you have a chicken in a stew is to kill it."

"In a fight, yes. Not this. It's murder."

"It's better than suicide, which is what we'll be committing if we let him go."

Naftali took the Turk's rifle and camel, tying it to his own.

The man trembled. "What are you going to do with me?"

"Take your boots off. You're going to walk home."

"I'll go with you, brothers!" the Turk cried. "The war is a curse. It is for the Alemanni, not for me. Don't leave me. I'll go with you. After all, are we not brothers? You know what they'll do to me if I go back without my camel and gun! The captain will kill me."

"We are not deserters," Wilner said in broken Turkish. "We are Jews."

The soldier spat into Wilner's face.

"That's what I thought," Wilner said with satisfaction and drew a Circassian dagger from his belt.

"Saul, don't!" Naftali called.

The Turk threw himself at Wilner, who held him at arm's length and thrust the dagger into the soldier's heart. He fell across Wilner's legs and slid to the sand. Blood streamed in spurts from the rent in his uniform. Wilner bent over, pulled his dagger out, and wiped it on the dead man's sleeve.

"Now, let's bury them both," he said. "So they'll never find them."

"I gave an order," Naftali said.

"Idiot. To take a chance and leave him. Two days to reach his patrol was what you said. Suppose his patrol came back to reach him? Not only NILI would be kaput. But you and me. You'd risk all that? Not me. Such a gambler I'm not. Besides, he spat in my face."

Naftali was rigid with anger. "That was murder."

"Nu, general, when we get home, court-martial me," Wilner said, and turning his back to Naftali, began digging a grave for the dead men in the loose sand.

Later, as they rode deeper into the Sinai, the sun grew hotter, thinning and exhausting the air. The men avoided villages and bedouin encampments and had no chance of filling their waterbags and canteens. Now the supply was low. They had used up the provisions taken from the Turkish soldiers.

They came to a slight rise in the desert and paused to see what lay before them.

During the last few hours Naftali had wrestled with himself over the killing of the Turkish soldier. Finally the sense of Wilner's act overcame his sensibility.

"Saul, you were right. It wasn't murder. It was an act of war."

Wilner stared at Naftali through sand-rimmed weary eyes. He took a tiny swallow from his canteen and wiped the sand from his mouth.

"So what am I supposed to do? Kiss your feet for telling me?" he croaked.

"Let it go. I thought . . ."

"You 'thought,'" Wilner jeered. "I'm the fool, listening to Judah, going with you. Prophets! They should be burned alive, one each day. It would be a good thing. They never leave a man alone."

Naftali felt the accusation deeply. "I take the responsibility for your act. . . ."

"Bravo! You ever kill a man?"

Naftali licked his dry lips. "No."

"So you take the responsibility. Applause! Try to drown the world with your morning urine. That's how your words help."

Naftali was thinking. What do we know of each other? Saul had killed the soldiers as if it meant nothing, yet he was suffering.

Wilner shrugged wearily. "Why should I expect different? A prophet is a man who makes a murderer out of another man."

Naftali did not protest. That was also part of being responsible.

His brooding silence was broken by an awareness of a shift in the atmosphere. Shards of cottony clouds with dark flecks hung over the east. The desert was changing color. A stillness in the air.

"Those clouds," he said. "I think they mean sandstorms."

Wilner wasn't listening. "Murderers . . . with words . . . Prophets!"

He won't let me go, Naftali thought. He won't let me go until I kill a man.

Toward evening, they reached a high granite ridge overlooking the Turkish camp north of Reheiba. The flecks in the sky had grown into thick masses of yellow-and-purple wind clouds. Naftali and Wilner lay in a crevasse studying the camp below.

The tents were spread out for several kilometers. Rows of breastworks and trenches guarded the camp on the south. Mounted men circled the area in all directions, on the lookout for British patrols.

"Can you think of anything more dangerous than to try to get through?" Wilner said angrily. "Not even a space for a dog to crawl. Look, they've even got wire up. There, by the lorries and field guns."

"What about the wadi on the east? There's nothing on the other side of it. If we could get into the wadi in the dark and——"

"You think they don't have it mined? Are they out of their heads? Not even the Turks. And certainly not the Germans."

Although the camp was two kilometers away, Naftali and Wilner could hear men's voices calling, the sounds of lorry motors and generators.

"So, what do we do, general?"

Naftali took the compass off his neck. "We take a fix on that wadi. Tonight we'll try it. In the dark it won't be too bad."

"To a mine, dark or day, it makes no difference."

The sun, low in the west, made great shadows. The wind was beginning to rise, but gently, as at twilight.

Wilner lay on his back with his eyes closed. "Are you in love with death, Tali? Don't smile. You didn't want to kill the Turk, but yourself you could risk. This much I understand about you. You burn for the glory of Zion. But once they put dirt on your face, what's left to enjoy? You don't even believe in a life after death like a Muslim. Paradise, women, and all that nonsense. So can't you wait a little? What's the hurry?"

"There are fifteen tents near the edge of the wadi," Naftali said. "It begins about a hundred meters this side of the camp."

"Death can wait a little," Wilner said, turning around.

They watched intently as three large trucks slowly left the camp in their direction. At the head of the wadi they stopped. Soldiers jumped out and began to carry boxes into the deep ravine.

246

"Garbage," Wilner said, relieved. "It must be German garbage, they're so clean."

"That's good. If we make any noise, they'll think it's jackals or hares come to eat. Do you want to go back? I can't force you to go with me."

"I've been thinking about it."

"Go, while it is still light."

Wilner picked up a decayed rock and broke it in two. "You know why I went with you? Not because I like the smell of danger. I went with you—" he paused and stared at the broken rock. "I went with you because of Rachel. Yes, Rachel, your girl friend." He spoke defiantly, as if ashamed. "I wanted her to like me. To think I was a *mensch*. Ah . . . That's not noble, eh?"

"It's good enough," Naftali said without jealousy, at that moment admiring Wilner.

"Still, it doesn't turn a bullet in the belly into a beauty patch. You can't smell flowers from a grave. Dead is dead. . . ."

The night fell suddenly, as always in a flat country. Campfires marked the desert as far as the men could see. Except for the wadi. There it was dark.

Now, for a few minutes, neither Wilner nor Naftali could see the other's face.

"Tali——"

Night birds sounded nearby.

"The name of my village, my Papa's village, is Turopetz, in the Vilna province. Baruch and Scheindel Wilner. And my sister, Doraleh Wilner. The virgin . . . To this day I refuse to say kaddish for them. . . ."

Wilner scratched his unshaven cheek and nodded to himself. "This Turk, for example. You know, I think I killed him because of Turopetz."

Their camels made no sound as they led them warily across the open desert toward the wadi. A weak moon gave enough light without revealing too much. Jackals cried in the distance. As they approached the head of the wadi, they heard men's voices from the camp and the chattering of hares in the garbage, from which rose a sickish smell. Suddenly a man sneezed in the darkness; someone else laughed. The sneezing went on without stopping.

"Shut him up!" a voice cried out in Turkish.

A sound of choking.

"Put your finger up your nose," a voice called.

Naftali and Wilner started down the side of the wadi into the stinking piles of garbage. One of the camels slipped and fell; limestone gravel and refuse fell noisily to the bottom.

"Sentry, what is it?" It was the same voice that had ordered the sneezing to stop.

Naftali and Wilner halted. They were below the rim of the wadi.

"Engleysi!"

"Where?" the voice yelled.

A machine gun split the darkness with a quick burst. As if that were the signal, rifles and machine guns roared from the southern perimeter. Outside of the line of fire, Naftali and Wilner led their camels forward through the garbage. The great noise of the firing masked whatever sounds they made.

A flare went up, exploding brilliant purple light into the night. Naftali and Wilner stopped. A line of barbed wire stretched in front of them from one wall of the ravine to the other.

Naftali ran ahead to look at it closely. The wire was attached to an iron stake that had been hammered into the limestone. While the firing lasted, he and Wilner might be able to dig the stake out of the limestone with their knives. Wilner brought up the camels, and the two men began to dig at the base of the iron.

The flare died away. Men shouted to continue firing; others ordered it to cease.

The limestone became harder to pierce below the surface. Another flare made a yellowish-purple umbrella of light.

"We'll never get this out!" Wilner grunted. He had his arms around the stake, trying to loosen it with the weight of his body. The barbs cut through his aba and into his skin. The iron stake didn't move. In a frenzy, Naftali dug into the limestone with knife and fingers. There seemed no end to the shaft. The rifles and machine guns raged on, then fell off one by one. The flare died. The silence forced the two men to stop digging. The hares resumed their nibbling and scurrying.

At the head of the wadi, two soldiers appeared with electric torches and lit up the piles of garbage. The hares, terrorized, ran down the wadi floor toward Naftali and Wilner. The torches followed them like giant white fingers. Then one of the soldiers snapped off his torch and joked that the English were hares who ate garbage and ran away from electric torches. The other light went off. The hares hurried back to the garbage.

The noises of the camp fell away slowly. Wilner wiped the blood from his aba, and the two men looked at each other helplessly. After an hour they tried to use the camels to pull the stake out of the ground, but they made too much noise and the work had to be stopped.

In their concentration, they didn't hear three Handley-Pages coming in from the south until the planes were over the Turkish lines and dropping bombs. Again rifles and machine guns exploded the night around them and they were free to work. Before the raid was over the iron shaft had been pulled out of the wadi wall and the barbed wire hauled aside to make room for the men and their camels.

The winding wadi took them ten kilometers past the camp and they left it, euphoric with success.

5 ◊◊◊◊◊◊◊◊◊

Early morning. The air beneath the heavy clouds sighed deeply and shivered, then seemed to breathe in, filling its white lungs with surface grit and sand. For a bleak second there were no sounds, no stirrings. Suddenly, with a throaty rumble, the white lungs expelled their great burden. The desert was curtained with a pebbled darkness. The wind blew from all directions, screaming through the interstices of itself, abrading the skin, enraging the camels. They yawed and bucked, fell to their knees, and refused to move. Naftali and Wilner lay alongside the tormented beasts. Waves of sand broke over them with typhoon force.

For five hours the wind whipped them, then fell away leaving a thick fog of dust hanging listlessly from the invisible sky. The two men dug themselves and their camels out of the drifts that covered them. Every breath of the granitic air was painful. They coughed violently, unable to stop, and fell to the earth exhausted. Later, when they could breathe easier, they looked about them. The fog had thinned enough to see a dozen yards ahead. Naftali studied his compass; the tiny needle moved erratically. It was possible that they were lost.

"I hear something," Naftali whispered. "It sounds like a dog. . . ."

Wilner, wiping his eyes and mouth, nodded and blew the sand out of the barrel of his rifle.

The cry came again. It was a man.

Through the muck in the air that surrounded them they could see nothing.

"Allah . . . Allah . . . Ul-illah . . ."

A shadow in the air. A slight stirring in the mist.

"Allah . . ."

The shadow moved, grew darker, came closer. It was a bedouin, unarmed, his eyes wide and fixed. A blood clot on his face was crusted with sand. He stared at them wildly.

"Don't move," Naftali said in Arabic. He went up to the man, ready to shoot him.

"Are you my brother?" the man asked, his voice breaking. He moved closer. "Ah, you are not my brothers, thanks to Allah. Reach forth thy hand and help me. The Lord be praised. I called upon Him and He answered." He began to chant. "There is one God and his apostle, Muhammad. And I, Hamid. I am His second apostle."

"Hamid, where are you from?" Naftali asked.

"Sent from my tent. To find Allah."

"Lunatic," Wilner said.

"Hamid, what are you?"

"Be praised, ye are not my brothers."

Naftali put his arm around Hamid and shook him gently. "Friend, do you know where the Engleysi are?"

The bedouin nodded eagerly. "Three angels visited the patriarch, Abraham, and three angels visited the father, Joseph, and three angels instructed Muhammad. But I am worthy only of two."

"Where are the Engleysi?"

Hamid flung his arms out and raised his thin, knifelike face upward. "The accusation against me was false. I did not touch my brother's wife. But I have been tested, have I not? The desert and the wind tested me. I am not dead. The angels have found me. There is only Allah!"

"Where are the Engleysi, friend Hamid?"

Hamid lowered his head and gazed at Naftali. "You are Engleysi?"

"Angels . . . To help you. If you are an honest man you will lead us to the Engleysi."

He nodded. Some leap of logic convinced him. The straining wildness in his eyes softened. "Where is the sun?"

The three men looked into the yellow, murky air. They could see a blotch of steaming gold.

Hamid pointed to the southwest.

"How far?"

"How shall you go? On wings?"

"Camels."

"Six hours."

Naftali said, "You can come with us."

Hamid kissed Naftali's hand, then raised his head proudly.

"Am I not proven innocent? Into the desert they drove me. Without beast or water or bread. I swore I didn't touch my brother's wife. They did not believe. But I was tested, O angels, O friends, O true brothers; I am innocent!"

"So the *mishuganer* is innocent," Wilner said wryly, bringing up the camels. *"Avanti!"*

6 ◊◊◊◊◊◊◊◊◊

By noon the next day the air had thinned, but the clouds still hung over the desert like black sacks ready to burst again. The men had not seen signs either of the Turkish or of the British. Once a plane flew by, but it was too high to tell anything.

They were winding their way through the Magnara mounds, which ranged above them to the height of two thousand feet. The heat was thick and there was no more to drink.

Hamid spoke little but smiled constantly, as if he were in some green inner forest of running water and houris. Naftali, slightly fuddled by the daze of heat, daydreamed of the meeting with the British.

As they entered a deep defile of rock, four bedouin mounted on camels suddenly appeared a short distance ahead and stopped. Seeing them, Wilner and Naftali unslung their rifles.

"Salaam!" one of the bedouin called.

"Salaam!" Naftali replied.

Hamid, who was riding with Wilner, screamed, "My brothers!"

"Turn him back to us," the bedouin called.

"They will kill me," Hamid whimpered. "And ye are my angels. Save me!"

The bedouin waited, watching the rifles of the strangers and calculating the worth of their camels and baggage.

"Turn him over, Tali," Wilner said. He was frightened.

"Who are you?" Naftali called out.

"Brothers of the evil one. He has taken one of our women. Give him to us."

Naftali waited before answering. Could he save the demented man? Was it worth risking themselves? The brothers would certainly kill the seducer.

"Tali, for God's sake. This is our chance to get out quickly."

In the meantime, the four men nudged their camels apart. One of the men, his rifle hung loosely across his arms, drifted to the wall closest to Wilmer.

Suddenly Hamid slipped from his camel and ran toward his brothers, yelling, "They are rich Yehudim! Kill them! They have gold. It will be my offering. Kill them quickly! Allah will bless you!"

Wilner, seeing the man at the opposite wall raising his rifle, fired at him and wounded him; then, yelling to Naftali to run, he sped back toward the entrance of the defile. The brothers followed, yelling and firing.

Naftali fired back. The movement of his camel made it difficult to aim. He missed twice. The third time he was sure he had his man, but the camel swung out to avoid a rock and the bullet hit Hamid, who screamed, ran to the wall of the defile as if to escape, and fell over dead.

With a feeling of contempt for himself, Naftali thought of the stupid irony of killing Hamid! If he hadn't delayed turning him back to his brothers!

"Their camels are faster!" Wilner yelled. "Get up to the rocks!"

Wilner caught a bedouin in his sights and wounded him badly. The man's foot was caught by a camel rein as he fell and was dragged head down by the frightened beast through the sand until he died.

Wilner felt a pinch on his own thigh and knew he was hit. He jumped off his camel, rolled over to a rock, and began to climb toward the ridge, where large boulders could be used as a barricade. He kept up a covering fire until Naftali joined him.

"Hit bad?"

Wilner's teeth suddenly began to chatter. "You bastard! Why didn't you give them the *mishuganer* without waiting?"

Naftali knelt behind the rock and fired at the men below until they were out of range.

The wind was rising again; sand drifted upward in wavelets from the desert floor.

"How's the wound?"

"A scratch. It's stopped bleeding."

"If the British are close, they'll hear the firing and come to investigate," Naftali said, looking at Wilner's wound.

"That lucky we're not."

The bedouin, still out of range, left their camels and began to climb the high, rocky bank.

254

"They're going above us," Naftali said. "I'll cover while you climb the ridge to the top."

Naftali waited until Wilner started. Then, leaving the safety of the rocks, he ran toward the bedouin, shooting as he went. Contempt for himself seemed lessened with each shot, as if he had to kill in order to find something he had lost.

He wounded one of the men and knelt to take careful aim at another. He did not see the third man sighting him with his rifle. Wilner yelled to watch out. It was too late. The bullet entered Naftali's abdomen, and he fell over.

Wilner skittered down the hill on his hands and knees and pulled Naftali behind a limestone ledge. The bedouin were taking their time now and shooting slowly.

Naftali opened his eyes. The world was very clear. He smiled sheepishly and said, "They hit me."

"Christopher Columbus!"

Wilner gave Naftali his kaffiyeh to stop the bleeding. The wind sharpened. A gray wave of sand and gravel filled the defile.

"The storm is a blessing for us," Wilner said. "One of us has merit in heaven. Feeling all right?"

Naftali nodded.

Wilner saw the blood seeping out of the stomach, and covered Naftali's body with his own to protect the wound from the flying grit.

"Where are they?" Naftali asked.

"Somewhere . . . I can't see them." Wilner raised himself. There were no shots.

Naftali closed his mouth against the pain. His fingers were growing numb.

"We have to go. . . . Saul, we have to go. . . ."

The swirl and rasp of wind filled Naftali as if he were an empty cave. I am becoming hollow, he thought. He could hear echoes, and he tried to listen for the words.

"Saul!"

"What is it, boychik?"

"In my pocket, Saul. The half . . . code . . . Jemal's pass . . ."

"What about them?"

"Take—"

"What for?"

"If they're found on me . . ."

"They won't be found on you," Wilner said angrily. "Listen, hero. I'm going to carry you down to the camels."

"The enemy?"

"If I can't see them, they can't see us. Just be quiet."

Wilner put his arms around Naftali, raised him up slowly, then balancing himself carefully, began the descent.

Naftali felt Wilner's warm breath on his forehead. What a trick to play on himself—to die so senselessly in the desert at the hand of a greedy nomad. For what? To get the code book to the British? Really, for what? Because he had hesitated to turn over the demented Hamid? For what?

My God, my God!

In a break of pain he heard himself say, "I was killed chasing an unknown dog across—"

He fainted.

Step by step, the sound of the rising wind masking the falling pebbles, Wilner brought Naftali to the bottom of the hill undetected. He saw that Naftali had fainted. The bloody hands that had held the wound were at his side. The open flesh breathed in and out like a heart. He put him down on the lee side of some large rocks.

"Tali?"

After a while Naftali opened his eyes. He saw his friend's anxious face expand and contract. He remembered and said, "The code . . . the pass . . ."

The face disappeared. Suddenly with great clarity Naftali saw that he was on a high place. He tried to move his legs and arms. He couldn't. They were bound.

Bound?

"Boychik. Boychik."

Wilner pushed away the hair from Naftali's face.

Bound? His hands and legs were tied together. Like a lamb brought home from market.

"Tali."

Like a lamb. Then he saw an old man's face hover above him. The sky behind the head was clear and blue. Tears fell from the old man's eyes upon his own. "My son, my son."

Now he understood; he was the bound son, Isaac, to this old Abraham with the knife in his outstretched hand.

He felt a great terror. All the way up Mount Moriah he had wondered what his father would use for the sacrifice. "God will provide a

256

lamb," his father said. But there was no lamb; he was the one who was bound. The knife shone in his father's hand.

"I don't want to die!" he cried.

"Tali, we'll get out of here. . . ."

His father loved him; then how could he kill him?

There would never be again the time for playing, the racing with the other lads, the festivals, the shearing of the sheep in the spring. Where was his mother?

"Mama!"

"Yes, Tali . . . Yes . . ."

Wilner pressed his own hand against the wound.

Where was this God of his father who was said to be merciful and just?

The knife trembled a little. His father's tears burned when they fell on his face.

"Papa! I'm afraid! I don't want to die!"

"My son, my son . . ."

The gaunt, bearded face seemed to split open with the struggle going on behind it.

"Papa, you told me that God promised your seed everlasting life through me? Why should I die?"

The deep anguished voice replied, "I don't understand it, my son. The Lord called me and I said, 'Here I am.' And this woeful thing that He asks me I must do, though I love you with all my heart."

He knew his father's love. It was there, all around him, warm and enduring. And suddenly he was no longer afraid. If his father needed his life, he would give it to him without protest. Oh, father, was there ever a greatness such as this? One could live forever in it and with all the suffering. Was that what God had covenanted?

The thought expanded in him and he rose in his mind high above Moriah and saw the Judean hills beneath reaching up and applauding him. There would never be a day or another deed like it again; with it Eden would be returned and the world's pain redeemed.

"Papa!"

With pride he gazed up at the gaunt old man.

"Papa, I am ready. But do it now! Do it quickly! Please!"

The knife came closer, the hand trembling.

Naftali yearned, exalted.

The father raised his head to listen.

Then the knife faltered; the hand doubted.

"Now, Papa!"

Slowly the knife was lowered and sheathed.

His father's arms, shaking with relief and old age, fumbled at the leather thongs.

"What happened, Papa? I was ready. Did I fail you? Forgive me."

The arms lifted him gently off the stone altar.

"God called to me. He told me not to lay a hand upon you."

"No! No!"

Wilner had lifted him off the ground and was cradling him in his arms. "Sha, Tali. Quiet. They'll hear where we are."

The father and the altar disappeared.

Naftali groaned. The deed that might have redeemed the world was thwarted.

He began to weep. He saw that generations of men to come would have to repeat that incomplete drama. Each in its time would be led to the altar, threatened with extinction, and then by the transient exhaustion of the world's evil be let go impaired and full of its unworthiness.

No sacrifice would ever be enough. There would be no end of it. No end to Kishinev and Turopetz, no end to the suffering of Jews, the Isaacs of humanity.

"Tali. Speak to me. I'm here." He bent close to his friend's mouth to catch the words in the moaning of the wind.

Naftali wanted to say, "You are right, Saul. Nothing recompenses death. There's no memory to keep you warm. Dead is dead."

How could he ever have thought otherwise?

"I'm here, boychik," Wilner said again, his hands slippery with Naftali's blood. He rocked him back and forth in his arms.

Was that how it would end? With the bitter taste of waste in his mouth? Then he would not die! There must still be time to find a meaning, to face down this doom, to demand an accounting from his father and his father's God. He saw clearly what he had never seen before, that Isaac had betrayed his trust. He should have rebelled, torn off the ropes that bound him, raised himself upright before father and God to cry out, "No! I will not die this way!" Instead he had lain there passively, had submitted, had offered himself as martyr for the world's salvation. No wonder he mattered least of all the fathers.

Well, he was not Isaac! That had been a dream. And if he died now, even by the senseless accident of a bedouin's bullet that his faltering compassion had brought him, at least he had not submitted. His life, at least, was not accident. It was the only thing that made death manageable. He had not run after the unknown dog.

And he would not die!

Run down the mount and cry to the bondsmen waiting for the return, "I am alive! And I will never die. There will never be an end to me. Rouse the people!"

He sat up. The wind hummed in his ears.

"Take it slow, boychik. Rest a little more. Then we'll leave."

The arm was warm around his shoulder, and the storm swept past him. He wanted to feel the stinging grit on his face and arms. He was alive. He breathed in deeply and tried to get to his feet.

Wilner held him tightly. "Easy . . ."

The wind screamed and pinched him and he shivered with a passion to live. Now more than ever!

He made a great effort to reassure Saul, to tell him he loved him, that he was a *mensch*, and that he also loved Rachel. Instead, he heard himself cry out, *"Merde!"* And he died.

After a while Wilner wiped the sand from his own mouth and kissed the mouth of his friend. Then he covered the body with rocks to protect it from the vultures and jackals. Although the storm was at its height, he left the place, turning back only once to see the grave he had made, but it could not be distinguished from the other piles of rocks, and he knew it would be lost forever.

BOOK Six

1 ◇◇◇◇◇◇◇◇◇

Judah Singer, thinner than before but still suggesting bulk and energy in his middle-class English clothes, waited in Colonel John West's outer office in the headquarters of the Egyptian Expeditionary Forces, Cairo. It seemed to him that the world of the twenty months since he had left Palestine was one huge outer office in which the mortal wounds of delay and frustration had bled him of patience, confidence, and hope.

This man West, he had been told, was a newly arrived intelligence officer, but there had been other newly arrived or newly posted men to whom he had turned with no results.

His mind was heavy with foreboding. The time in London and Cairo had been wasted. He should never have left Palestine; it had been an act of impulse and against his character. Why had he gone? Was it because he had been troubled by Naftali's absence in Cairo? Or had he really thought that only he, Judah Singer, who had assumed leadership, could be the broker to marry England and Judea?

Colonel West's aide, Lieutenant Stuart, sat at his desk reading reports. A young man with cheeks like wine-stained linen. Like all the others Judah had talked to since arriving in Cairo, he had no knowledge of Naftali Brandt.

Outside the window of the headquarters building cars came and went, important-looking staff officers hurried in and out, urchins begged baksheesh, and old men wearing fezzes walked by with broken dignity.

Since leaving Palestine Judah had been compromised in ways he had never thought possible; he, the aloof scientist, disdainful of petty politics, had become a salesman of a dream turned into a cheap nostrum by the indifference and contempt of others.

How he had toadied to the German ambassador in Constantinople to get permission to enter Germany. He despised Fabricius, yet he had to pretend that the Germans were the chosen people and the kaiser their Moses. He suffered falsehood as truth and knew a self-anger the like of which had not been his since his youth in Metullah and Syria and with Baron de Rothschild. The old failures, he thought, are never forgotten, and the new ones become more intolerable because of them.

And to be with Nahum, Rachel's husband, meant more lies. He had to agree to his complaints about Rachel's leaving, about the confusing letters in which she would say one time she wanted to return and the next time that she might never see him again. He could not tell Nahum that he was unworthy of Rachel, for he needed his brother-in-law to help with the Germans.

Berlin. An endless chain of outer rooms. Waiting for permission to go to Copenhagen, where he hoped he could get passage to the United States.

The Berlin Jews appalled him. They truly believed what he pretended to believe, that Germany was God's own messenger sent by heaven to announce the inevitable victory of the kaiser's civilization. The native Zionists were also firmly convinced of Germany's victory, and he could not trust them and ask their help for his mission.

Day after day, week upon week, he waited for permission to leave. His friend and teacher Professor Warburg, whom with aching heart he had deceived into supporting his intention to study agricultural methods abroad, finally helped him win permission to leave Germany. The Foreign Office made one condition: Judah would have to propagandize in Copenhagen and the United States on behalf of Germany and Turkey.

Although he had no intentions of keeping his word, these accumulated deceits distressed him profoundly. He had no taste for guile; unlike actors, politicians, and writers, he was incapable of transmuting his personality into that of another man's. His imagination had a blind spot; his inventiveness, rich in the world of things, was incredibly sparse in the context of people.

The split in him deepened; his questioning of himself intruded on

262

his health. For the first time in his life he had difficulty sleeping; he had begun to stutter a little; he had even begun to doubt whether his whole NILI project was worthy.

In Copenhagen, one did not only wait, one lived in a shifting morass of espionage. The once-lively city lay dour with mistrust. Judah dared not go to the British Embassy, even under an assumed name. He avoided Zionist headquarters in order not to jeopardize its neutrality. The Jewish community was divided in its sympathies, and there was only one man he could trust, old Jacoby, who earned a small living by grinding eyeglasses, a trade he had taken after becoming a Spinozist. His family came from Holland, had been Danes for several generations, but had intermarried and assimilated until he did not even know the names of the others of his grandfather's descendants. But Jacoby himself, although half Christian, had an inextinguishable devotion to Zion. "Otherwise," he said, "there will come a time when no Jews are left in the world. Who will remember the exodus? Who will eat the unleavened bread? Who will be alive to permit God to keep His promises?"

It was Jacoby who arranged a secret interview between Judah and the second secretary of the British Embassy, Francis Morrison, an elderly bureaucrat with a distaste for Jews ever since his father had been insulted by Disraeli.

"But my dear man," Morrison said after Judah, with great enthusiasm, had presented all the arguments and had offered himself and his group to England's cause, "you are talking of spying. And that isn't within the competence of our mission. There is nothing we can do for you."

Morrison, however, reported his meeting with Judah to the intelligence section of the embassy in order to clear his own position. He suggested that the Israelite was a double agent who might eventually find his way to the United States or England. He should be listed and put under surveillance.

In Colonel West's anteroom, where he now waited, pacing up and down, glancing through the window, studying an old map of Egypt and Palestine on the wall, looking inquiringly at Lieutenant Stuart, he thought back to Morrison, who had been the first as far as he knew to hear the NILI dream. But the impenetrable, self-assured face of Britain had turned away. Judah had believed that it was an incident—history tripping on a man's stupidity. Other Englishmen, he was sure, would be quick to grasp the significance of his proposal. But he had learned otherwise. Would West be another Morrison?

With the help of an American rabbi who was in Denmark to organize relief for the Jews made homeless by the war, Judah left Copenhagen on a Swedish ship bound for Baltimore and New York.

In the middle world of the sea he began to lose some of the burden of his deceit and disappointment. His spirits were raised on reading the essays of the French entomologist Fabre that he found in the ship's library. How brilliantly he had stated the case. "History celebrates the battlefields whereon we meet our death but ignores the plowed fields whereby we live; it records the names of the king's bastards but cannot tell us the origin of wheat. That is the way of human folly."

He permitted himself to dream without guilt that perhaps he might someday be celebrated for both the wheat and his leadership of his people.

His spirits were improved even more by a decisive change that was made in his plans. Off the Orkney islands, his ship was stopped by a British destroyer and searched for contraband. The crew and passenger lists were checked and he was called to the captain's cabin for questioning.

The officer was young, tough and unapologetic. "Why are you traveling to America?"

"I am an agronomist. I plan to do scientific research."

"On whose behalf?"

"On my own."

The officer frowned at what he thought was a naïve effort to hide duplicity.

"Where is your home?"

"Palestine."

"Then you are a Turkish citizen. You will obviously be doing scientific work, to call it by your own words, on behalf of your government, with which we are at war."

"I am a Jew. And I am opposed to Turkish policy."

The officer stared blankly at him. "I don't see that it has anything to do with it. You are in British waters and you are under arrest."

Later Judah understood that Morrison had informed London of his departure from Copenhagen. The Swedish ship had been stopped partly on his account.

He didn't object; on the contrary, he was pleased, for England was his goal and the fact that he had been arrested by the British would serve as protection to his family and friends if word got back to the Turkish authorities.

But they put him in the hot August barracks for internees at Folkestone, where he was kept for seven weeks, a suspension of action that was corrupting. He began to wonder if he were not going to be forgotten; his mind and body became slack, and he longed for Har Nehemia, for Atlit, for the crown of hills above the Kinnereth. He assailed himself for his decision to leave, for his impatience, so unlike him. Why had he violated his character?

Finally he was brought to London to be questioned over a period of a week by Sir Basil Thomson, of Scotland Yard. Immobile and flinty as rock, Sir Basil listened to Judah's entire personal history, his description of Zionism as the spiritual politics of a people, an analysis of the economic and military situation in the Turkish Empire, the reasons for the formation of the espionage group, and an account of Naftali's trip to Cairo and the fact that he had not returned in two and a half months.

At the third interview, the rock felt the rod. Sir Basil had been won over by Judah's seriousness and depth of personality. Equally important, Scotland Yard had received bona fides for Judah as a distinguished scientist and a responsible man from eminent Americans, although none of them seemed to know about the espionage proposals.

"I am your partisan, Mr. Singer," Sir Basil said, "and I will recommend you to the War Office. You understand, sir, that notwithstanding my sympathies for you as a person, you have not made a Zionist out of me. In all candor, I see too many dangers to England in it. Therefore there will have to be appropriate caveats that I will give to my colleagues who will work with you. In sum, Mr. Singer, you are trusted completely as an individual, not as a politician."

Judah did not try to hide his discomfort, but he saw he had no choice.

Sir Basil asked further that Judah avoid seeing his fellow Jews in London. "No one of them knows of your group, you tell me, and I think it would be ill-advised to inform them of such. I can't, of course, demand that you do not go to prayer services at the synagogues or that you refuse social invitations. But keep in mind that your mission is a secret. The fewer Jews you see, the fewer questions you will have to answer."

Judah agreed, and Sir Basil sent him to see General MacDonough, chief of intelligence of the War Office. Judah won the general's confidence swiftly by pointing to a number of errors on the most recent war map of Palestine. His views on other matters, particularly water supply, were eagerly sought. Judah suggested that the coastal plain below Caesarea that now looked like a desert must have much hidden water. He quoted as evidence the apologia of Flavius Josephus, the renegade Jewish Roman general who had described that area as a rich complex of gardens.

General MacDonough promised that within a month Judah would be back in Cairo, attached to the staff of the Egyptian Expeditionary Force, which would have the responsibility of establishing connections with the NILI group.

He felt his first success. But during the weeks of waiting for the final orders, he understood that at least one part of his mission would remained unfulfilled. There would never be a political *quid pro quo*. No matter how eloquently he presented his views to the people at the Foreign Office or how sympathetic they seemed—he actually persuaded some to a Zionist position—his position as a leader of the Palestine community remained vague. They thought of him as a loyal friend of Great Britain, a spy who wasn't being paid. In matters of policy they invariably turned to the English Jews and the man in whom they had the greatest confidence—Chaim Weizmann, the Russian-born world Zionist leader and chemist who was, Judah learned later, working secretly on acetone for naval high explosives under the direction of First Lord of the Admiralty Winston Churchill.

Judah saw that he would remain without the credentials he so ardently needed. Other leaders, not he, would be welcoming the British conquerors the day they passed through the gates of Jerusalem. His only chance was Weizmann himself, a man he had never met but whose speeches at Zionist congresses he had read from afar and found generally sympathetic. He tried to see Weizmann and wrote him several letters, but the chemist was rarely in London. Not until Judah was about to leave for Cairo did an invitation come from the house on Addison Street. Sir Basil had no objection to Judah's accepting but asked him to keep the NILI project a secret from the Zionist leader.

Weizmann welcomed him warmly. He knew about Judah's work with the wild wheat and the experimental station at Atlit, and he questioned him closely about his views on the use of Jordan River water for electrification, the future of farm cooperatives, the temper of the Arab fellahin, and the possibilities of growing cotton in the Sharon.

Judah had never seen a man whose physical presence held such unaffected dignity. Weizmann's simple gestures, the quiet voice, the trim beard, the unstrained use of biblical metaphor—even the slightly mandarin slant of eyes and cheekbones—evoked a serenity, a balance of the inner and outer worlds of feeling and experience. Watching him move among his guests, men of great influence on English life, and seeing how much they admired him, Judah became convinced that this quiet Russian Jew had the magnitude of character to make the world yield to him.

More than ever he was sure he would need Weizmann. Indeed, he saw himself in the mirror of Weizmann's power. There ought not to be any difficulty in persuading him to throw a corner of his toga over his shoulders. Both men were scientists, both shared the same visceral conviction that a nation could be won in Palestine by the stain of Zion's earth on Jewish hands. Weizmann might even need him, for while the Zionist leader, by the nature of things, had to play out his strategies in Europe and America, he, Judah, knew Palestine far better, his strategies were lived daily in the homeland itself. Weizmann would see this point quickly, Judah thought.

There was a great deal of talk that evening about Russia, for there had been a report in the morning news of an outspoken speech in the Duma against the czar's government. Weizmann knew some of the leaders of the Russian Constitutional Democrats, but he had more to say about Lenin and Trotsky, whom he had fought against while sharing a Swiss exile with them.

To sum up his views, he referred to Sultan Muhammad's siege of Constantinople in 1453, when the Christian world ignored the fate of its second-greatest city, leaving it to fight its battles unaided. He described how the city fell because in the great swirl of battle an inner gate, the Kerkaporta, was left undefended by an oversight and was entered by an overwhelming force of Turkish janissaries. On that day Turkey captured Constantinople and began its siege of Europe.

Weizmann posed the question whether the democratic forces of Russia also had their Kerkaporta, the inner gate of poverty and war weariness through which the new janissaries could enter and capture a continent while the rest of the world went on about its own business.

The reference was an apt one, Judah thought, and he used it afterwards, when the reception ended, and he asked his host if he might see him privately. The two men went into a small kitchen in the back of the house, where Weizmann brewed some fresh tea for his guest.

"The Ottoman Empire also has a Kerkaporta," Judah said in Hebrew. "In Palestine it has left a door unguarded, and some of us, a few friends of mine and myself, know where it is. I cannot tell you more than this, except that when we enter that door it will be for the benefit of the British and most certainly for the Yishuv. This much I can say. I am leaving shortly for Cairo and I may even be back in Palestine soon. With the confidence of the War Office. But I need more than that. I need something from you, Dr. Weizmann. As you may know, I have always remained an unaffiliated Zionist. In that sense, I am isolated. For the good of all of us, I now ask for the confidence of the official Jewish movement."

Weizmann remained silent for several moments as he poured hot water over tea leaves. His deep-set eyes were half closed. "I trust you fully, Mr. Singer," he said with a sudden warm smile. "I know your position too, and I have not agreed with it. Still, you have my blessings, whatever they are worth. However, I venture to say that my blessings would not be enough for your purposes. You would like something more concrete?"

"Credentials from you, Dr. Weizmann."

"Ah, yes." He filled two cups with the tea and gave one to Judah. "To break down the isolation? To normalize your relationship with the leaders of the Palestine executive? Is that it?"

"We have never gotten on, these gentlemen and I. I am not an organization comrade. No deprecation meant, sir. It is simply a question of temperament."

Weizmann nodded. "As I said, I already know your position. I also know my comrades. No credentials of mine would be as useful as you think. Forgive me, but you have overrated my position." He glanced quickly at Judah in a way that eliminated any false modesty in his words. "Perhaps, also, my dear Singer, you have underrated your own. When the Yishuv knows what you have done, it will embrace you, if, as you say, your labors will be to its credit. That embrace is the best credential."

"Dr. Weizmann, I'm afraid that your knowledge of the Yishuv is not as extensive as mine."

"I know that. You are part of its bone and flesh. I, sadly, have to work from afar. But I do know how organizations and political parties work."

268

He shrugged resignedly and sipped his tea loudly, as though the sounds were a protest.

Judah realized that there could be no other way for Weizmann to act. "I will have to be content," he said without emotion.

"Who knows you here in the War Office?"

"General MacDonough."

Weizmann nodded. "You haven't touched your tea," he said.

Judah blew across the steaming surface of the cup. "Maybe a little strawberry jam?" Weizmann said. "An American brought some over as a Chanukah gift."

"No, thank you."

"I will check with General MacDonough now and then."

"That will be good of you."

"If I may say so, Mr. Singer, I look forward to the time when we can work together. Openly, so to speak. Perhaps after the war. As comrades, in or out of a party. A man like you, with your experience in Eretz Yisrael, is very precious to us."

When they finished the tea Weizmann escorted Judah to the door and said the Hebrew farewell. "Blessings on your way, my dear Singer."

Judah left London by destroyer for Cairo. He carried no corner of Weizmann's toga; he had no organization that could defend him; he had only the knowledge that he was the leader of a small cadre of spies working for a British general.

Let it be, he thought. If it was all that the task he had set for himself permitted, he would nevertheless fulfill it to the end.

He watched the rushing waters along the bow and recalled "that the race is not to the swift, nor the battle to the strong . . . but time and chance happeneth to them all."

There was still time and there was still chance.

2 ✧✧✧✧✧✧✧✧

Colonel John West was a tall man who successfully hid a thoughtfulness and sensitivity behind the clubhouse manners of a staff officer with a long army past. He glanced sharply across his neat desk to the brusque, fair-haired Jew who for sufficient reason he had kept waiting and who was giving him a bad quarter hour because of it.

Singer's cold, cutting tone disturbed the usual quiet of the office. "It has been six months since I arrived from London, colonel," Judah was saying. "I have spent most of that time waiting in anterooms like yours, being given compassionate cups of tea by clerks in aide's uniforms. I have talked with your political officers, your combat officers, your intelligence officers, your engineers and supply officers. If I handed them the whole Middle East on a platter with the Caucasus thrown in as parsley, they couldn't have cared less. I have been made to feel that I was a salesman of some dubious product. And all the time, General Mac-Donough's recommendations were in front of them."

He gestured with distaste to a large envelope he had placed on the desk. "There are all my London reports, sir. Names, places, dates, what was said and by whom. I cannot give enough emphasis to the fact that General MacDonough promised that when I arrived in Cairo the Egyptian Expeditionary Forces staff would see to it that contact would be made with my group in Palestine and that I would be opted to work with it. Instead, all I have heard was, 'No. Not yet. Come back next week. It is inopportune. See our other branch. We'll call on you when we're ready. We cannot do anything at this time.' Sir, I am sick of this delay. I am sick of English promises."

West felt a quick admiration for this Jew, for his vigor and authority. He even liked the way he made his points, without the usual diplomatic velvet. There was no doubt that he had been getting the edge from Lawrence's friends in the Arab Office, who could not abide the smell of Jewish hegemony over anything but a greengrocer's shop. But despite that, scientist or no, eminent or not, he could not permit this man to disparage the service.

"I'm an Englishman, Mr. Singer. As far as I am aware, I have never broken a promise," he said icily, putting down the pipe he was smoking. "I urge you not to permit prejudice to overcome your good sense."

Judah wondered about the man's own prejudice against Jews. There was something in the tone that seemed to suggest it.

"My evidence, sir, while not all-inclusive, is sufficient."

Judah was surprised by a sudden friendly smile. It was as if the man had read his thoughts and was going to prove his lack of bias. "You see, Mr. Singer, I have just come here myself. I've not been in the saddle long enough to get my staff bearings or to catch up on the situation. However, I did find a note pertaining to your project." He pointed his pipe to a green envelope marked "Secret." "Is a Lieutenant John Miles known to you?"

"He is not."

West was puzzled. "Our records show that Lieutenant John Miles was stationed in Port Said, where he made contact with a Palestinian named Naftali Brandt."

"Naftali! My friend! Of course!" Judah cried.

"He claimed to represent a group of Jews willing to supply information," West read from the file. "Contact continued intermittently. Some important material reached us through this source. Contact broken off August 11, 1916."

Judah was unable to control his anger. "Almost two years! Who in the name of God broke it off? Was your Lieutenant Miles transferred? And if so, what about others of your intelligence section? Why did they let it lapse? While I was begging them in London and here to start something with my group, it was known all along and permitted to die. Can that file of yours explain it, colonel?"

"Quite simply." West laid his pipe to one side, the gesture like a subdued exclamation point. "Miles was en route by ship to meet your people, but the ship was sunk by a U-boat. Our information is that Miles is in a prisoner-of-war camp somewhere near Smyrna."

"And no one thought it worthwhile to send someone else?"

West had seen a note in his files from Trevelyn-Jones: "Hold up on this until further notice." But he saw no necessity to refer to it. Trevelyn-Jones had been relieved after the recent repulse before Gaza.

"I cannot explain, Mr. Singer, why nothing further was done to renew contact with your friends."

"Will you undertake to reach them now?"

West disliked being pressed. And there were other, more important tasks awaiting him. Yet he was caught by this Jew and believed him. MacDonough's views would have to be verified, of course. But the problem was bigger than that. Even if the Cabinet and the War Office had approved working with Singer and his group, was it because of soft diplomacy with important Jews of London or was it hard politics? If politics, and West surmised it was that, any step he would take to encourage Singer would bring his own office into conflict with the Arab Office, which held most of the political power in the Cairo staff. Was it worthwhile? For a small group of activist Zionist Jews?

He was not unaware of his own bias. It was one of the most troubling aspects of his inner life. He had been brought up in a military family that had had no contact with Jews but was, nevertheless, anti-Semitic. As a youth, West had not been able to avoid feeling that Jews were somehow unpleasant.

His first real experience with Jews was in 1910, when, as a lieutenant on detached duty, he was visiting the British consul in Odessa at the height of a pogrom. Through a window of the consulate he saw a drunken peasant attack a screaming Jewish girl. West forgot diplomatic law and custom and ran out of the consulate door, kicked the peasant into unconsciousness, and saved the child. During the next three days, in which madmen, undeterred by police, sacked the Jewish quarter, he did what he could to protect the innocent. When the dying was over, he hated his family, hated himself, and knew for the first time in his life what it was like to experience guilt.

As the years passed his army life in Africa and the Far East did not bring him into any further relationship with Jews. The guilt became quiescent. He was content merely not to affirm the anti-Semitism of his friends. Yet he could not say that he liked Jews any better. The few he met on his occasional visits to London disturbed him either by their aggressiveness or the bow-from-the-waist tone of their voices.

Judah Singer created a presence of dignity quite unlike any other he had known. It was as if he had no inner need to relate himself to the Christian world. Of course, the real matter at hand was the proposal to create an espionage center behind the Turkish lines.

"I appreciate your apprehension and your continued offer of aid,"

West said. "I will do what I can. If you will leave your address with my aide, Lieutenant Stuart—"

Heavily Judah rose from his chair. "I have left my address with more than a half hundred aides from London to Cairo. I am quite used to it by now."

West made an effort to show no resentment of Judah's obvious sarcasm. "I shall read these reports of yours within the next week or ten days, Mr. Singer. They'll have that much priority."

He wished he could reassure this man, tell him how much he favored the Jews. But he had to be certain of his position. "I cannot promise anything more."

"Sir, you don't really believe that Jews are worth using, do you?"

West had started to smile, rising to see his visitor out, but at the cold, accusing tone he sat back and lifted his pipe to his mouth. "Good day, sir."

Judah nodded, turned, and walked slowly out of the office, his thick, muscular body slack.

3 ◇◇◇◇◇◇◇◇◇

Three days later, in the afternoon, Lieutenant Stuart, looking very important and grave, presented himself to Judah, who was living under an assumed name in the Ismailia district with a Sephardic businessman. The officer informed Judah that Colonel West required him at headquarters immediately. His car was outside.

When West saw Judah, he wasted no time and asked him if he knew a man whose name was Saul Wilner.

"One of my men, sir."

"He was found yesterday southeast of El 'Arîsh by an Australian patrol. He had been wounded, but not badly."

"Where is he? Can I see him?"

"I'll go with you to the hospital. We haven't been able to get anything out of him except that he comes from Palestine, and he keeps asking for Lieutenant Miles. When that was brought to my attention, I recalled that Miles had been the contact with your group."

At the base hospital, on the outskirts of Cairo, they were met by a doctor who told them that Wilner had a gangrenous condition but that it was improving. He was feverish and in a state of depression.

The room had the slight vinegar smell of antiseptic. The window shade was down. Wilner, looking ravaged, seemed to be asleep. The doctor, motioning to the men to remain at the door, went to the side of the bed, and turned on the lamp.

"Saul," Judah called.

"Miles . . . Miles . . ." The feverish eyes were opened.

Judah stepped to the bed. "Saul, it's Judah Singer."

A look of incredulity, then fear, filled Wilner's eyes.

"You're in a British hospital in Cairo. You'll be all right. Can you tell me what happened?"

Wilner turned away from the light.

Judah was concerned at the waxen look on Wilner's face. If the doctor had not reassured him, he would have thought he was dying.

"Can you talk? How is my father, how is Rachel, how is Tali?"

"Where were you?" There was accusation in the tone.

"It's a long tale. Mostly in London, then here."

"Why didn't we hear from you?"

"I tried, Saul. It was difficult to get cooperation."

Wilner twisted back to face Judah; then he saw West. In a half cry, half sob, he shouted, "The bastards! They took my papers!"

"What papers?"

West stepped into the room. "He had part of the Turkish Army code with him when he was found. We are working on it now to see if it's genuine."

"It's genuine!" Wilner shouted. "Why the hell you think we'd cross the desert with it? Bastards!"

He began to cough.

Judah sat down at the edge of the bed and said gently, "Rest awhile, Saul."

"For months we waited," Wilner said angrily. "Not a sign . . . not one word . . . not from the British, not from you—" He glared at Judah. "Tali—"

He stopped; the name scorched his brain.

"Saul, where is Tali?"

"Rachel . . . She is with us now. Tali told her."

He stopped again. His teeth chattered and tears rolled across his cheeks to the pillow.

Judah's voice was stern. "What about Tali?"

Wilner opened his mouth and closed it.

"Tali? What about him?"

In a child's whimpering voice Wilner said, "He wanted to cross to the British with the code. . . . We were attacked. . . . bedouin . . . In my arms . . . In my arms . . ."

Judah stood up erect, his eyes and voice cold. "The truth! What's the truth?"

"We fought against them in a sandstorm. Tali . . . In my arms . . . The bedouin . . ."

"No! Not Tali!"

"He's dead! He's dead!"

Judah began to rage senselessly. "Why did you let it happen? Why didn't you protect him? Not Tali! You let it happen!" Then, moving like a wounded bull, he swung toward West. "He's dead! The best of us! Did you hear that? The inspirer of everything! He was holy. He was holy and you British killed him! You killed him with your clerks, your schoolboy bootlickers, your politics, your—" He stopped and swung back to Wilner, and with a voice like the sound of a breaking tree cried out despairingly, "My God, why couldn't it have been you?"

No one spoke. A faint breeze made the window shade flap a little. Wilner's eyes sought out Judah, who had left the side of the bed and was swaying back and forth in a corner of the room, his hands over his face.

So he is praying, Wilner thought, and I, alive, am less than the dead.

His own grief soured with resentment.

"Nu, Mr. Singer," he said, "so pardon me for living."

Slowly Judah left the corner and went back to the bed to stare at Wilner. After an effort to bring himself up to the surface of the living he said, "I beg you to forgive me, Saul."

Wilner grinned without meaning to. "Forgive?" He sighed. "Listen, boychik, if you were with him and you had lived, I'd have felt the same way. There are many Wilners and, yes, many Judah Singers— Ha! Leave me alone!"

Later, when Judah and West were on their way back to headquarters, West, thinking of Wilner's and Singer's grief and of Odessa and the terrorized Jewish girl, said, "I will do everything I can, Mr. Singer. And I mean to do it immediately. You will find me a faithful friend."

4 ◇◇◇◇◇◇◇◇◇

Three weeks after the abdication of the Russian czar, the United States, economically bound to England and France and roused to action by German submarine warfare, declared war on the Central Powers. Two weeks later, Captain Stiles, of HMS *Morley,* an old destroyer, made his approach to Atlit. It was still light, for he wanted to get his bearings on the Crusader tower, flaming in the setting sun. Satisfied, he turned his ship westward and lay over the horizon until midnight. Then he returned to Atlit, hove to while a boat was lowered with four of his crew, some small cargo, and Saul Wilner, whose knapsack was filled with fifty prewar gold coins given to him by the British to distribute to some of the Jewish and Christian charities of the Yishuv.

Undetected, the oarsmen got the boat to shore, where they helped Wilner bury the packages. They would be back at midnight the following night.

As Wilner entered the bridge crossing the wadi, he saw two dark figures coming toward him and heard Avram's voice asking, "Do you see our sheep anywhere?"

"Avram," Wilner called softly.

Avram and Dmitri Liebermann ran forward and embraced Wilner. "Where's Tali?" Avram asked.

"Later . . . Later . . ."

They uncovered the packages and moved cautiously and uneventfully to the station, where they hid the gold under the earth below the basement. When they moved upstairs, Wilner asked about Rachel.

"She is home, sick," Avram said. "Malaria. Almost over by now."

Wilner was relieved that he wouldn't have to face her immediately, for Judah, afraid that it might demoralize NILI, had given him strict orders not to tell anyone of Naftali's death. He was uncertain whether he could carry off the lie with Rachel. To avoid talking of Naftali, he reported that Judah was in Cairo working for the British, that although he had had a hard time getting there, things were working well. He explained what had happened to Lieutenant Miles. But now time at last was on their side. It was possible that an offensive against the Turk in Palestine might be started before the end of the year.

Avram and Dmitri were excited by the news, forcing him to tell them again all the details of Judah's tribulations. Then, when he least expected it, Dmitri broke in with a demand for news about Naftali.

"Tali? Didn't I tell you already? Judah sent him to England." The cousins were dismayed. "He's going to be an airplane pilot. Think, friends, Tali a flier!"

"The British have enough pilots. We need him here," Avram said irritably.

"I know. I know. Myself, I said to Judah, 'They need him in Palestine.' But you know Judah. An ox. Gets an idea, it's like a rock in his mind. I told him, 'Judah——' "

"Who will be in charge now?" Dmitri asked sharply.

Wilner said, trying to be casual, "Me and Rachel. You are to go to Cairo on the boat to work there."

Dmitri stared at him skeptically. "Judah said that?"

Wilner nodded. "I have a note from him. Here."

Avram read it in silence, then showed it to Dmitri.

"Nu, friends, it's your turn to tell me what's happened," Wilner said, pretending not to notice the open chagrin on Dmitri's face.

The news was not as good. NILI had continued working and there was much information amassed. But everywhere one went these last months, the Germans and Hamid Bek had arrested Jews, although none yet from their group.

"In the last two weeks the pressure was even greater," Dmitri said. "Certain Turkish troop movements have been shelled and bombed from the air. They say that the British knew about them in advance. The code book, no?"

"The code book, yes," Wilner replied proudly, almost arrogantly.

The Liebermanns heard the tone and found it distasteful.

"It is not only the Turks and the Germans who are suspicious. Hashomer sent Lorchanovsky to question Rachel about what's going on at Atlit. He demanded to know where Judah and Tali were. He was nasty, as usual. Rachel told him nothing, but he threatened and there was a big argument."

Wilner reassured them. "Wait. When the war is over, we'll be the

278

friends of the British. They'll tell everybody what we've done. Hashomer will be forgotten."

That night he took over Judah's desk as his own and slept on the cot. He enjoyed the sensation of being a leader. The next day would be time enough to see Rachel.

Papa Singer was not at home when Wilner arrived at Har Nehemia, and Ibn Djavid, the coachman, said that Rachel was in her room. "Ask her if I can see her. Saul Wilner with greetings from some friends."

After a few minutes the old man returned and showed him to her bedroom. Rachel, dressed in a white-linen bathrobe, was sitting up, waiting for him with an eagerness that touched him with its beauty. Behind her, a brass bedstead glistened in the sunlight from the windows.

"Shalom! Shalom, Saul!" She took his hand and held it tightly. "I was so worried about you and Tali. Where is he? Tell me everything. Everything! I can't wait. When did you come back? How?"

"You have been sick."

"It's all over now. Where's Tali? Did he come with you? Why isn't he here?"

"Where's your father?"

"In shul, I suppose."

"What does he know?" Anything to delay the talk.

"I've told him nothing. And he asks no questions. But sometimes I think he knows enough."

"I saw Judah. He's in Cairo."

"Thank God!" She raised her arms above her head with joy.

Wilner gave her a letter from Judah. It would tell her all he thought she should know; it would complete the deception about Naftali.

Watching her as she read, he thought she was more beautiful than he had ever seen her. Her blue eyes were brighter against her pale face; her mouth, alive and womanly, was half open with excitement. On her neck lay thick strands of fair hair, which she had put up in a knot quickly; it tempted him to reach over and fill his hands with it. In a wild moment, feeling no shame, he was glad of Naftali's death.

She put the letter down, frowning and covering her eyes. "I don't understand. I mean to say, I understand that you and I will work together. That's clear enough. And Judah's position . . . But Tali is going to train in England to be an aviator. Why?"

Wilner put his head to one side as if to ask, Who can explain such foolish things?

Carefully she folded Judah's letter. "I don't understand Tali. We need him here more than the British need another aviator. Things are not good. We've been out of touch too long. . . . And I wanted to be relieved of my work. I'm not good at it. . . ."

It was a mistake, he thought, not to give her the truth. Judah was wrong. You can't fool a child or a woman in love. Rachel would hate them both when she found out.

A spring fly buzzed at the window and flew out. There was a scent of young flowers at the borders of the garden. He had not noticed the flowers when he came in. But now, looking away from the bed, he saw them through the window.

She sat up against the pillows and brushed a strand of hair from her forehead. "Didn't Tali give you anything, a letter, a message, for me?"

Neither he nor Judah had thought of that. What should he say? God, he wanted to tell her the truth, to console her in his arms.

"Did he or didn't he?"

What kind of lie would be useful?

"He was very busy the last few days. And I was wounded. I was in the hospital. Did Judah tell you that in the letter?"

If she were sorry for him, he thought, she might not press him about Naftali.

"How were you wounded?"

"Some bedouins. They tried to steal our camels. I got a scratch on the leg. . . . Did I tell you about Lieutenant Miles? His ship was sunk. And the British—a black year to them—they forgot. They didn't even try to send someone else. To them we were plucked chickens but with our heads still hanging on. Cairo is a madhouse. Ha, Rachel, such crowds of soldiers you should see. And this Colonel West, he's a very good man. A righteous gentile. I think they're going to make Judah a major. We'll be a success. In fifty years in Palestine they'll name their children after us. Rachel, Judah, Naftali . . ." He grinned. "Saul, also. But come to think about it, Rachel"—how often could he speak her name without screaming?—"We have such plain names, who'll know they're ours and not someone else's. Now, if my name was—"

She had clasped her hands tightly over her knees, and he saw a bated uncertainty on her face, like a child afraid to look out in the morning to see if it were raining or clear.

"Tell me more about Tali. Where will he train?"

"Oh, he'll train near London. Croydon, I think. . . . He might get medals or titles. How would you like to be Lady Rachel? Me, I'll be a simple Sir Saul Wilner of Kfar Dreck. Excuse my language."

The lie was killing him. He could see that she was reading his heart. But he could not stop now and tell her. He had to go on like some kind of Sholem Aleichem making up tales and jokes, a thousand-and-one-night serial.

"Tali wasn't wounded?" she asked almost distantly.

The damned fly was back in the room buzzing death. He lit on the edge of her bed, a moving black spot; he was crawling toward her knees, where her fingers strained into a weave on the faded blue blanket.

"Viscount Brandt of Alona. You know Tali—he's a hero. A regular Galahad."

"Tali?"

"A sandstorm came up, and——"

"Tali?"

"He was there shooting away. . . ."

She pushed herself back against the bedstead. One of the pillows fell to the floor. Wilner left his chair and went to pick it up. Rachel held on to his arm. "Tell me the truth, Saul!"

Her eyes had lost their blue; they had become black, filling their sockets, filling her face, filling the room, filling him until he could stand the pain no longer. He saw Naftali in his arms and he saw Rachel in his arms and he saw his sister and his father and mother and there was too much of death for him. There was only one truth, tough, sharp, hard. Without such hardness there was no living at all.

Yet when he spoke, his voice was soft and compassionate. "Rachel . . . Rachel . . ."

She made no sound.

"Rachel, forgive me. . . . Tali is—dead. In my arms he died. He wasn't in pain. I kissed him for—for all of us. . . ."

Rachel's mouth opened as if to scream, but there was only silence. Then came a rasping, ripping sound of the sheet being torn. The darkness left her eyes as if it were life; she fell back, turned away, and covered her face with the torn sheet.

Wilner waited for the weeping; he didn't understand why there was none. He touched her shoulder gently. "Rachel . . ."

She didn't move and he withdrew his fingers. "Rachel. Nobody else must know. Nobody. It would end— It would be the end of our group. . . ."

Silence.

The black fly, which had darted off at the movement of her body, returned and was crawling up the mountain of the pillow toward her covered face. Saul scooped it up and roughly squashed it in his fingers, then threw it out the window. Let that be the kaddish for Naftali. Let them join each other in heaven.

"Rachel, you listen," he said. "There is no time for this."

Slowly she lifted the sheet from her face. "I don't care anymore. . . ." she spoke in the harshest Hebrew Wilner had ever heard.

"Tonight the ship is coming back."

"I don't care anymore!"

"Judah needs you."

"I don't care about Judah. I don't care about the group! Or the British!"

"I brought gold to be distributed. You will have to do it. It means food for people, for the children. . . . Dmitri is going back to Cairo tonight in my place. Judah wants it that way. He said for you and me to be in charge."

"I don't care! I don't care! I don't care!"

"I need your help, Rachel. If you're not with me, I'll give it all up. It'll come to an end."

"I can't do it. . . . I can't. . . ."

"Then for Tali's sake."

"I never wanted this work. . . . I never wanted it . . ."

Suddenly he began to shout. "Ha! Your heart is broken, so it's all over with everything. You're a widow. Let the world be full of widows. Jerusalem, a brothel of widows. Run, little Rachel! Find a nice kennel to hide in!"

"Stop it, Saul!"

But he couldn't stop; he had to be brutal enough to satisfy himself as well as her, for he was pleading for both.

"Forget Tali! Forget his work! He lies in an open grave. Spit in it! I'll spit in it with you!"

She half rose from the bed, her face pinched with anger, then fell back and sat, crumpled over, hands listlessly at her side, her eyes blind and tearless.

Now Wilner waited, watching her, immobile in the white bathrobe with sunlight at its hem. He struggled against saying anything more, but the silence was too heavy for him. The world outside the **window** was frozen. He was sorry he had killed the fly. He was unable to hold any longer in his mind the emptiness of her eyes, the almost childish way she held her hands, the tightly pressed lips. He took a step toward her anxiously and said gently, "Tali wanted NILI more than anything else in his life."

Her fingers moved. Bit by bit they opened and closed. She sighed a little. The faint movement of her breasts. Then finally she whispered, "Jerusalem . . ."

Her father's steps were on the garden walk coming to the house. She rose quickly.

"I must tell Tali's mother," she said faintly. "Then I will come to the station."

Wilner felt his viscera churn. He had won and spoke quickly: "Tonight Dmitri leaves. If you want to write something to Judah, I must have it right away."

She nodded. Papa came into the room, calling out heartily, "Shabbat shalom," then scolded her for getting out of bed.

That night Dmitri left with two sealed messages.

Wilner wrote: "I have obeyed all your orders. However, to Rachel our friend can never be an aviator. But then, you know what women are. They can see right through a man." He trusted Judah's ability to read between the lines.

Rachel wrote: "I am happy you are near us. More than ever we need each other."

The next day Rachel broke the sad news to Naftali's mother. The two women stayed with each other for twenty-four hours.

5 ◇◇◇◇◇◇◇◇◇

Wilner called together all the members of NILI and made as full a report of the situation as possible, answered questions, and handled well their obvious dislike for him and his new position. Nissim was unhappy that Naftali hadn't returned, and for several days he hung around brooding.

Once Nissim found Rachel alone and confessed wildly to her that he and Miriam had had a fight. "She believes Tali is in London and I don't. I can't believe it, Rachel! Nobody knows Tali the way I do. Not even you. Why didn't he come back with the ship to say good-bye? It's not like him, I tell you. Something has happened to him. It is a feeling of heaviness in my head. I know it. Why didn't he send a letter? Answer that."

"I can't answer why he didn't send a letter. But you heard Saul."

"I don't believe Saul. I never liked him. He makes fun of everybody."

"If there was anything wrong with Tali, wouldn't Judah let me know?"

"Listen—" He grabbed her arm. Then he let her go and teetered back and forth on his feet. His swarthy face was filled with fear. "On the road near Safed I saw a bird come to the edge of a little pool of water. There's been no rain in months. Why should there still be a pool of water? There was no well nearby. In Tractate Yebamoth it says that evil spirits live in stagnant water. And when the bird drank the water, it didn't even ripple. Don't call me foolish, Rachel. You know I love Tali. I used to know what he was thinking even before he said anything. Something has happened to him!"

She spoke sternly. "Those are superstitions, Nissim. Only children and old women believe in such things. Now, take my hand." She forced herself to look at him without wavering. "I give you my word."

"What word?" he demanded with the stubbornness of the demon-ridden mind.

"I know that Tali is all right."

"You say that because Saul told you."

She felt her hands grow cold on the lad's. "I believe him."

His eyes doubted her. "You like him, that's why."

"Of course I like him. I like you too."

"You liked Tali, but since Saul came back from Cairo—"

"Quiet!"

"You're with him all the time."

He's jealous on Tali's behalf, she thought. Poor, poor Nissim.

She tried to settle it for good. Still holding his hand in hers, she said, "You agree that Judah would not lie. I swear to God that he has told me that Tali is in the British Air Force."

Nissim wasn't satisfied. He did not hear what Rachel said but only his own voices telling him that his friend Tali would not have gone away without a message to him. No one understood that. Not even Miriam, whom he loved. They thought he was wrong to think that way. But he was not wrong. The pool on the road near Safed was not wrong. Why did it not ripple when the bird drank? People laughed at demons and mocked the cabala, yet he knew they were truths. Tali was in trouble and needed him. Tali was trying to get some message to him. Jeremiah knew the same feeling. "There was a burning fire shut up in my bones, and I weary myself to hold it in but cannot!"

A plan came to him. He would cross the desert to the British and find Judah. Face to face, he would hear the truth. When should he start the journey? He would have to calculate the right date according to the cabala. He walked to the window, unaware that Rachel was watching with distress. A flight of birds left a clump of oleanders and rose to the sky in the shape of a scythe. Nissim nodded. Already the signs were propitious.

6 ✧✧✧✧✧✧✧✧

Rachel did her work dutifully. Her first task was to distribute the gold. She sewed some of the pieces in her dress and carried them through Turkish patrols to Father Gregory in his dark, incense-flooded Greek Orthodox Church on top of Mount Carmel. He was standing in the shadows of the candlelight in front of the altar, the purpled smoke rising around his head like a halo.

"Don't ask me where these come from, Father," she said.

"He is blessed who sustains the hungry," the bearded Greek replied in Hebrew. "No matter what his name." As she turned to leave, he begged her to carry his greetings to her father. "I still remember the sweet joy on his face at your wedding."

She took some of the gold to the Franciscan Church of St. John at Ein Karem and left it with a young priest. Her face was covered and he didn't know who she was. Other coins were for Dr. Bloch and the hospital and orphanages of the Sharon and Samaria.

"Where did you get this, Rachel?" the doctor demanded.

"We had it hidden," she lied. "It was time to give some of it away."

He was doubtful but did not press her. Instead, he asked whether she had heard from Judah in Berlin. She told him that Judah was well.

"My daughter is away from home too much," he said. "She tells me she goes with you to help the refugees. I worry about her traveling around."

"I'll keep an eye on her."

"You are a friend of this young man Nissim. Is there something between them?"

"Nissim is a good man," she said.

The doctor sighed. "She is so secretive these days. In the past she would tell me everything. Now she is quiet. She sleeps badly. She looks thin and worried. I thought maybe it was love."

"Maybe it is, doctor," Rachel said.

He held her hand and looked at her solemnly. "Rachel, you are her friend. I trust you to take care of her."

Rachel nodded. What could she say? "Don't trust me—I am leader of a conspiracy that might cost your daughter her life"?

"I would lay down my own life to protect Miriam, doctor," she said. "But she is a grown woman now. She will make her own way as she sees fit."

The most troublesome recipients of the gold were the leaders of the Palestine executive. Rachel had a meeting with Remenov, whose Russian-student presence had somehow remained untouched by the troubles of the last year, and Mara Schalet, his sweetheart, who coughed constantly. Five months in the Turkish prison at Acre for hiding arms for the shomrim had affected her lungs.

"Where does this gold come from?" Remenov asked.

"My brother, Judah, had some hidden in the early days of the war. Now that he is in Berlin, I thought that it ought to be put to use."

"Why do you give it to us?" Mara asked harshly.

"You have an organization. It will do the most good."

"Why now?"

"I decided that now was a good time," Rachel answered. She was weary. Since Wilner's return she had lived without rest of any kind.

"Does your father know this?" Remenov asked.

"It is Judah's money."

"Did Wilner have anything to do with it?"

"I mentioned it to him."

"He has some of the gold too, eh?" Mara said. "I've seen him spend it in the cafés in Jerusalem."

"I don't believe your story, Rachel," Remenov said. "We have reason to think that this gold has been smuggled in from Cairo."

"I haven't time to argue you out of your notions," Rachel said angrily. "Do you want it or not?"

Mara replied with equal anger, "We know that Wilner disappeared. Or let me put it like this. He was away somewhere for a long time. We have our eyes and ears, Rachel. We keep track of the Yishuv. Where was he?"

"In the Galilee, across the Jordan. He wanders around."

"He was not seen. And we know him well. A shomer we kick out is never invisible to us. Where was he?"

Rachel put down the glass of weak tea they had given her and stood up. "I have other errands to do. If you want the gold, take it. If you don't, I will give it to the children's hospital for milk. If you know so much already, answer your own questions."

Remenov replied swiftly, "Rachel, we will take the money and thank you for it. But, understand us, we don't want the food and milk and medicines that this money will buy for the comrades to cost us their lives."

Rachel studied the keen face of the Russian and the anxious, strained face of his sweetheart with the tubercular flush on her cheeks. They are Jews, she thought. They want the same thing. Why couldn't she unburden herself to them? Why must the distant goal always be obscured by the dust of the many roads leading to it?

"We live in a time when the lives of all of us are on the edge," she said, forcing herself to speak calmly. "I risked my own to bring the gold from Har Nehemia to you. I can only pray that it is for good, not evil."

Mara Schalet and Remenov were moved a little and shook hands with her in a comradely way and thanked her.

Rachel worked hard, but in the long sea swells of her grief she lived another life. At first she accepted Naftali's death as one touches a fire to prove one's courage. In the tense, hurried days and sleepless nights, while moving around the country, coding information brought to the station, or waiting furtively on Atlit's shore for the meetings with the British, she mourned her beloved without cease. She was insatiable for the evidence that he had once lived. In place of the pin-watch she had been forced to barter away she wore a simple safety pin to remind her of it. She built shrines with flowers in the corners of her bedroom and in the workroom of the station and recited lines of his favorite poems over and over again. In heart-borne elegiac Hebrew she intoned the great laments of David and Job and the unknown Koheleth. The wound was kept fresh, the graft of time torn away hourly.

Then suddenly one day she became sickened by grief. In a vast, cresting sweep of rejection she put away the favorite books, stopped making shrines of flowers, and sought out Wilner as if he were the only one strong enough to blot out the memory of Naftali. His toughness and amoral indifference to ideals had a morbid attractiveness. She would sit with him working on the codes, drink brandy brought in by the British, and listen to his jokes about their comrades.

Wilner understood her change of mood and looked for a moment to take advantage of it. One night they were alone in the station. The warm spring evening drifted in through the open window. Wilner finished a drink, left the table where they were working, and walked

288

restlessly to the window. The scents of seed and the musk of geological cuttings in the room filled him. Outside the insect young and cicadas trilled away the night.

Turning to where Rachel worked, he saw the back of her head bent forward, the uncovered neck golden in the lamplight. Willing it, and yet without willing it, he moved to her quickly and kissed the top of her head.

She didn't move.

"Rachel . . ."

The pen fell from her fingers.

"From the beginning, when we met, Rachel . . ."

He bent to kiss her again, the soft golden hair dancing to his lips.

When Rachel felt the gentle pressure on her hair, Naftali was brought back to her with such force that she cried out, "Tali!" The cry was so clear and real that Wilner pulled away and involuntarily glanced at the door. Was that his step? Would he enter? Then, chagrined, he went back to the window. It will take time, he thought; it will take time.

Rachel sat stiffly, slowly letting go of the illusion. She knew that Saul had kissed her and she did not want to look at him. After a few minutes of silence she left the station and walked along the pathway leading to the sea. At some other time she would talk to Saul, but now she must understand something about her grief. It was wrong to make of Tali an icon; it was equally wrong to revolt against his memory as she had been doing these last weeks. It was this revolt, she knew, that had encouraged Saul. Tali's death had to be lived with wholly. She must be neither the lost hapless widow nor the careless widow on whom the inner substance of propriety had lost its hold. This would have to be explained to Saul, for he must not be fooled. And as for the rest, she would finish Tali's labor. Despite her doubts and fatigue and the nightmares of what her fate might be, she must not surrender the vision of Jerusalem.

There was much to do.

BOOK *Seven*

1 ◇◇◇◇◇◇◇◇

At the end of June, 1917, General E. H. H. Allenby took command of the Egyptian Expeditionary Force. One month later the character of the force was completely changed.

This is the way Colonel West put it to his own staff, including Judah Singer, at Deir el-Belah on his return from a first visit to the new general's headquarters.

"He's an old bull. Or if you permit, gentlemen, he's like some Rugby-playing Jesus driving the moneychangers out of the temple. You should have heard him when a pompous H.Q. hero brought him a pile of papers from the adjutant general's office for his approval. Old-maid details, rules of dress, petty infractions of discipline, and the rest of the rot. Allenby's pressure rose like a waterspout and he threw the whole mess of it into a corner and said, 'General, I forbid you to waste my time on decisions that an incompetent junior officer could very well manage.' And what's more, gentlemen, within a fortnight he's moving his headquarters out of the posh Savoy and right into these dunes. Fleas, mosquitoes, and sand lice notwithstanding. He's lifting this torpid giant of an army back to life. They say that his private slogan is 'What lieth at your hand to do, do with all thy might!' He'll do it, friends. My flesh crawls with certainty."

West went on, his ruddy face gleaming in the late sun coming in through an open tent flap. "They tell me that the Cabinet said to Allenby, 'Give us Jerusalem for a Christmas present.' And he'll do it. He's the man for it. You wouldn't recognize Cairo and Alexandria. Why, they've even stopped playing tennis at Shepheard's and polo at Gezireh."

Someone who had served under Allenby in the Third Army in France said critically, "He's a stubborn man. But he lacks imagination. At Arras he banged ahead until he was bloody, and he hadn't the sense to try the flanks."

"He can't be altogether bad," another man said. "He loves birds. A first-rate ornithologist, I've heard."

In a short time everyone began to feel the presence of the new commander in chief. He was seen making swift and explosive tours of the *hamsin*-blown camps, skewing up great waves of dust in a weathered Ford driven by a half-naked infantryman. He would jump out before the truck had stopped, greet the officers and men who, more likely than not, were taken by surprise, and snapping questions at them, would move his huge column of a body in long, restless strides from barracks to compounds to depots. His sharp gray eyes above a promontory of a nose seemed to see behind sloth, slack, inefficiency, pretense, and ill favor. He burst forth with fury at such and let no guilty man go untouched, no matter what his rank.

The only time he seemed to pause was when he saw a bird of a family unknown to him perching on some tent pole or signal wire. He would stare at it intently as if he were a bigger bird about to pounce on it. If anyone could tell him what it was, Allenby would strike joy out of the heated air with a quick thank-you smile. If the answer was an obvious error or clearly a deceit to catch attention, he would burn the man with a angry look and stride off again as though fleeing from a leper.

He seemed to be everywhere all at once and where he was least expected, the big nose scenting weaknesses in men and organization. Senior-grade officers, when they failed him, were prime targets for his wrath. But when the ailment was repaired, he seemed to forget that he had even been roused to anger and treated the offender with respect.

The camps were wary of him. The rumor got around (Judah had heard it from West) that some signal officer at Allenby's desert headquarters at Umm el-Kelab, "Mother of Dogs," had been bribed to broadcast a general warning to all brigades and regiments whenever the chief left his quarters. The code was "B.L."—"Bull Loose."

Other things were happening. The supply railroad from Kantara at the Suez to El 'Arîsh was being double tracked. Pipelines carrying Nile water from their filtering stations branched out to the forward lines near Gaza. Ammunition dumps and field hospitals built by hordes of Egyptian and British labor were rising swiftly. Allenby's inexhaustible demands, his willingness to live among his men, his refusal to accept excuses, stirred his troops.

Judah began to hope.

2 ◊◊◊◊◊◊◊◊◊

In his office General Allenby stood dumbly alongside the large heavily curtained window, a cable from his wife in his hand, his dark-gray eyes sightless with grief. His only son, Michael, not yet twenty-one, was dead in France.

"Michael . . ." The sound in his throat failed to make the impossible possible. Perhaps he was dreaming? But he had never suffered dreams.

He stared fiercely at the thin white paper in his hands from whose folds had arisen death to break his heart. "But only twenty," he murmured. He leaned his head into the dark rolls of the curtain as if it were a shroud enclosing him with the body of the lad. Absalom, my son. Absalom . . .

"Poor Mabel . . ." The sound of his wife's name made it seem real, she who was always real.

He stood in dumb silence until finally a great spinal wrench of his body thrust a sob past the clenched mouth. "Michael!"

He tried to see him in his mind. No image came. Just the name, torn out of context. Had he ever wept before? He couldn't remember. He had never lost a son before.

There was suddenly the gray recall of the thousand sons he had lost at Arras but three months before. On his own fifty-sixth birthday. The very day they had given him the first casualty lists, the endless lines of type marching into dust. Then he had damned war and himself and yearned to feel each man's death as his own. And couldn't. He had been taught, or had taught himself, that to do so would destroy his worth as the commander of the still living. That was his duty—not to feel, but to preserve and not violate the command distance. Without it he would become useless, the enemy of his own men and their future. Now he must remember that same duty. Slowly he began to hear the sound of the ceiling fan.

There was in his mind the task of making some decision of strategy, a plan for an offensive. He raised his bowed head and wiped away the tears and the traces of tears. What had he to do first? Of course, send a cable to his wife. He would arrange for her to come out to Cairo. She must not bear this alone in Colchester.

Colchester, the wildflowers, the speckle of birds on the alders and primrose. Michael at the trout stream laughing as he held up a flashing fish into the bright English summer air.

There was something more to be done at eleven that morning, some sharp demand.

What did Michael look like? Dare he risk crossing to the desk to the small photograph? Dare he risk it? His adjutant might enter any minute to find him full of tears.

The big clock in the far corner of the large office began to chime softly. Eleven? If it were eleven, Bols, Chetwode, and Dawney should be there to hear his views on their plan for the offensive. Of course. The plan. He had to announce his approval or disapproval.

What was it? One: Mount a feint against Gaza, the long-established military gateway to southern Palestine. Hope to draw to its defense the main body of the enemy reserves. Two: Strike the real blow under cover of night against Beersheba, twenty miles to the east, capture it, and open the enemy's flank.

It was Chetwode's plan primarily, a good plan. Even beyond its simplicity. To the enemy, who had only light defense forces at Beersheba, it would seem too high a risk for the British, for it lay twenty miles from the nearest railhead across waterless, roadless, rugged terrain, impassible to any kind of motor-driven transport.

He closed his eyes to visualize the battle area, the roads, the hills, the placement of his troops, the supply lines, the terrain on which he could move in broad strokes. . . . In France, with its entrenched warfare, he never had such possibilities of maneuvering.

The chimes stopped at eleven. Where were Bols and the others? He started to his desk to ring the adjutant and paused. Had he covered everything?

Jackson's naval support? Could Salmond's planes clear the skies? Water? The main worry. According to Chetwode, thirty thousand camels would be needed to carry water to the troops attacking Beersheba. Could Davies get them? Water? What if Beersheba couldn't be taken with its wells undamaged? Chetwode had calculated that the troops would need at least four hundred thousand gallons a day. New wells would have to be found. And when the enemy pulled back from Gaza, assuming the success of his flanking movement, what about water in the area of Gaza-Ashkelon-Jaffa? Could his air force delay Von Falkenhayn's Yildirim force now at Aleppo from moving south in time to support Jemal? Could the British and Arab forces east of the Jordan strike north toward Damascus and relieve any counterpressure on his own army?

The folders with the plans lay on the desk. What provisions had been suggested for further deception of the enemy? He'd have to give intelligence clear directives. He reached down to open the folder.

Michael's photograph, taken in Paris, seemed to leap up to his hand.

How pitifully young, brimming with the very pride he used to make fun of, erect in his lieutenant's uniform of the Royal Horse Artillery, pitifully tiny against the white cup of Sacre Coeur behind him. But there were the questing eyes, the firm mouth with the seeking smile that always preceded their few mild arguments. ("But, Father, conscientious objectors, after all, are living proof of Christianity. Socialism itself is Christ's message. You can see that, can't you?")

At first Allenby did not hear the gentle knock at the door. It was repeated. He glanced at the clock. Eleven-five. They were five minutes late. Carefully he put back the photograph on the desk. It would have to do. He said, "Enter."

His adjutant opened the door, ushering in Bols, chief of staff, white face and black eyes like a Latin, looking grave; Dawney, erect, straightening his tunic to hide the slight bulge of flesh behind his belt; Chetwode, a stern, brilliant, poetic man who had been one of his brigade commanders in France. He saw that they knew. Mourning framed their faces like black borders. The moment would have to be cut sharply.

"Take your seats, gentlemen."

He sat down and wrote out a message to Colchester. "My dear Mabel . . ." The message was brief. She would understand that his heart was broken and that he needed her as much as she might need him.

He handed the message to the adjutant, who saluted solemnly and left. The three generals had not moved.

"I've studied your appreciation of the situation," Allenby said crisply. "There are some questions. Please sit down."

"Sir—" It was Bols.

Allenby directed his eyes unwaveringly at his chief of staff.

"We have heard the sad news, general. Perhaps——"

"Thank you, gentlemen," Allenby cut in. "I understand your feelings at this moment. Understand mine, and let us proceed. In principle I accept your plan and I will forward it to the Cabinet for their approval. I put the tentative date for the end of October, hopefully before the rains. The two elements still in doubt, however, are water for our troops and deception of the enemy."

He talked briefly about the general strategy, then began a series of probing questions of tactics. The fan worked overhead and the big clock in the corner ticked loudly. He did not think of Michael or Mabel again until the conference was concluded. He did not go to lunch that day nor to the club that night, but sat alone in his quarters and read the Psalms in Greek.

3 ◇◇◇◇◇◇◇◇◇

Judah was given the rank of major and assigned to work with West's forward intelligence at Deir el-Belah. His tasks were many. He had to decode the messages brought by ship from Atlit and prepare questions for information to be sent back. In addition, West asked him to work on the terrain maps of Palestine. These had been drawn by Lord Kitchener thirty years before, when he was a lieutenant in the Royal Engineers, and were obviously incomplete.

"And I want all the Jewish villages and colonies put in," West said. "I never knew until I met you that there were so many Jews living there. Nobody at headquarters knew either. It can make a difference to us."

Judah fulfilled his tasks devotedly, but as he read Rachel's monthly reports of the increasing terror, the high death rate from disease and starvation, and the demoralization of the Yishuv, he became more and more convinced that his place was in Palestine to work behind the Turkish lines. One day in early October, after Rosh Hashanah and Yom Kippur, which brought to an even higher pitch his feelings of obligation to his people, Judah presented himself to West at his advance headquarters in the desert and made a well-reasoned argument to support his leaving Egypt for Palestine in order to organize effective guerrilla warfare in the rear of the enemy.

West had been made a Zionist by Judah, and he understood his personal situation, his ambition and dedication. He did not wish to thwart them—his respect for the man was too great—but West also knew that the main decision about the Jews would not be made by NILI or Judah Singer, but rather by Allenby's conduct of the war. Further, he had already broached the idea of guerrilla bands to the staff. They were against it. Allenby, himself, preferred to work with mass and did not like to have fragmented units beyond his control.

"Sorry, Judah. Can't let you go," he said.

"But it's my responsibility to be——" Judah began angrily.

West cut him off with an apology. "Forgive me, Judah. But may I be frank with you? You mention 'responsibility,' but are you not really thinking 'guilt'? You're worried about your friends. You're saying to yourself, 'If my friends are killed and I'm not there, how can I forgive myself?' That thought of guilt oppresses you. We all have it. If we live through a battle we feel the guilt for those who didn't. The only chaps who don't feel it are the dead, I suppose. And let me remind you of something else, which perhaps you know better than I do. The chaps who feel guilty are the ones who aren't guilty at all. It's the others, the bucko lads who don't give a damn about the lives of the men they lead—they're the ones who should feel the old lash on their souls, but you never hear them yelling, 'Mea culpa.' Instead, they say, 'Toodleoo, lads, I'm still alive and in the saddle.'"

He lit his pipe, glancing at Judah through the smoke and hoping he had persuaded this upright man, who seemed unmoved.

"I promise that with the first sign of danger to NILI we'll get them all out of the country."

"John, can you understand that it isn't only a question of my sharing dangers with my comrades? I am also their leader."

Judah's point was well taken. His people probably needed him desperately. But West also had need of him.

"You won't see Allenby picking up a rifle and leading charges. Blast you, man, the place of a leader is to be where he can lead best."

"I can lead best in Palestine."

West lost his temper. "So you can rouse your people. Become a Mattathias. Perhaps become the viceroy of the Jews!"

Judah was stung by the accusation, partly because it was true. "There is nothing shameful in leadership."

"My God, man, no! I think you may get it. But that's politics, and we're not politicians now." West put down the pipe and leaned closer to Judah, speaking without reservation or secretiveness. "I want you to stay on because I think you'll be more valuable to us here. But just as you have a complex of motives, so have I. You know that you've made me a Zionist, don't you? Well, friend Judah, I'm not sanguine about the possibilities. What I mean is that Balfour and the Cabinet can say and do what they like—there's some talk of a government statement on behalf of the Jews—but here, not London, is where home-government programs get executed. And by execution is not always meant fulfillment. 'Off with their heads' is another way of executing a policy. There are men here like Bols, even Allenby, who are not too keen on Zionism. Let me tell you something you don't know. Three months ago the Zion Mule Corps that had fought so well at Gallipoli was ordered by London to become the nucleus of a Jewish brigade. Assembled and trained in England. When word reached our headquarters that there was some plan to ship the brigade here as part of the Egyptian force, they informed the War Office, subtly of course, that they wouldn't be welcomed. I suggest to you, Judah, that the men who are sabotaging a Jewish brigade are decent, not at all anti-Semites, but simply uninformed. Your presence among them can be enormously persuasive. It may make all the difference between our dealing with the Palestine Jews as citizens of a conquered power or as citizens of a nation about to be formed. Do I make myself clear?"

Judah listened carefully. He was shocked by the news of the staff's attitude toward the Jewish brigade. But West's argument had the opposite effect on him. He protested that it was more urgent than ever that he prove the valor of Jewish soldiers by organizing them in Palestine.

"It has nothing to do with proving valor. It's simply that the powers here don't want any organized Jews around to confuse the issue with the Arabs, whom we admire so passionately. You are a stiff-necked character, Judah. You want to hole up in some cave in the Galilee like your Maccabeus or at Betar like your Bar Kochba. But not with my approval. If you want to go over my head, go and be damned! But I deny your request. No hard feelings, major."

Judah nodded briefly. West then asked him to prepare a message to NILI. Information was urgently needed on the disposition of the Twentieth, Twenty-first, and Thirteenth Turkish regiments. Also, word on the Yilderim army group. Was it still at Aleppo?

"We're sending carrier pigeons this trip," West added. "We'll need information daily. Agreed?"

"Agreed. And I'll hold you to your promise to send a rescue ship if my people are in trouble."

"It's on the daybook. And do you intend to go over my head?"

"When the occasion arises, yes!" Judah paused. "No hard feelings, colonel."

4 ◇◇◇◇◇◇◇◇◇

The occasion came for Judah soon after this talk, when orders reached him to present himself to General Allenby at Umm el-Kelab, some fifteen miles south of Turkish-held Gaza, a small Arab village overrun by a large number of bell-shaped Cawnpore tents and a host of smaller ones. A shell-torn muezzin's tower on top of a deserted mosque pointed crazily to a cloudless sky. Ranged around the tents were clumps of cacti and hedges covered with fine dust from the traffic. Wire-matted roads sprawled gleamingly like fish skeins over a waterless sea. Latrine funnels, looking like periscopes from a nether world, rose out of the sand at intervals.

When an aide escorted Judah to the command tent, General Allenby, sitting at a small field desk, seemed to occupy the full space of the room. Having seen him only at a distance, Judah had had no notion of how tall he was, how calm the gray eyes, or how large the great Viking nose above the trim moustache.

He must have suffered as a boy with that nose, Judah thought.

Allenby put down the book he was reading—George Adam Smith's *Historical Geography of the Holy Land*. "Colonel West has told me about you and your group, Major Singer." The voice was dry and clear. "I note that you suffered a grievous loss with the death of one of your men who brought us the enemy code. He was a brave young man and his contribution to us was great indeed. I am also aware of the dangers facing the other members of your group and I have confirmed Colonel West's orders that they are to be taken out of Palestine by boat whenever they request it."

"Thank you, sir." Had West also told him about his wanting to go back to Palestine?

Allenby continued briskly, "Do you know the area Khalassa-Beersheba?"

"I do, sir."

"Outside of the towns, is there any water?"

"Not at present. But I believe there were wells once. I have found certain artifacts in that area suggesting that it held a Roman fort and perhaps as many as three commercial centers built by the Philistines. Naturally, they couldn't have existed without water."

"Can you place them on our maps?"

"Not precisely enough. I would have to be on the spot myself."

Allenby exploded suddenly. "Then for the sake of heaven, Singer, why do you insist on leaving us and going home?"

"I put it to you differently, sir," Judah replied calmly, relieved that West had told the general. "I want to fight the war from behind the enemy lines. And I officially ask permission, sir, to be sent there."

"They tell me you're a first-rate agronomist," Allenby said, as if he hadn't heard Judah's request. "To you water is prime. In desert war it is equally prime. You must know that."

"I do, sir."

"Then, when you get your orders from the chief engineer, go out and find those wells. Our whole campaign may depend on them. I am not given to exaggeration."

"Very well, sir. First I will go to Khalassa, and then I will go home."

"My orders are that no one is to be seen at Khalassa until the time is right. There is no possibility of your being able to do both." The tone was curt, on the edge of anger.

Judah held his temper, reflected, then said, "Once Jemal Pasha threatened to hang me if I didn't obey him. You, sir, threaten nothing. But if I may say so, you are much more frightening. I will, of course, follow orders."

A brief smile broke Allenby's stern mouth, and he leaned back. The official part of the conference was over.

"Colonel West told me a little about your wild wheat. I'm not much of a student of the science, though I like to grow things. My wife and I. My son once thought he'd go out to Australia and become a wheat farmer." He continued without pause, "But of course that was when he was quite young. Nothing was more extraordinary to him than the very fact of bread. Used to go to the mill and see the wheat ground. The kitchen to see the flour rise. Sheer wonder."

Judah told him of the day he discovered the wild wheat on the flanks of Mount Hermon. He talked quietly at first, describing his experiments at Atlit and Har Nehemia. His tone deepened with feel-

anything to make a paste of your blood for the king's sake or God's? Judah succumbed to that exquisite despair of Koheleth's in which all was in vain, where no city rose above the plain, where men, God's cruel enterprise, were streams of ants moving instinctively from season to season along the Alpine ridges of leaves.

The fallacy of *sub specie aeternitatis*; it rankled him that so late in his life—he had recently passed his forty-second birthday—he should become seduced by it. But there was something in the climate of a war on this history-drunken land that made the fallacy seem plausible.

As he sat in the ruined mill with the dead Englishman in his arms, abashed that while men died he was wrestling with abstractions, he told himself that it wasn't his nature to succumb to purposelessness. He was a scientist of the soil, the water, the fertilizer, the sun. It *did* matter that the wild wheat had been found! Perhaps the answer was that man lived in two logics—the one of eternity, in which, with or without God, meaning would forever elude him; and the other a restless, short-lived dream in which purpose and meaning were clear. For the sake of life, one had to accept the dream. It was, after all, what gave man his only dignity.

Indeed, Judah thought, that fictitious dream had given this dead lad perhaps all he had known of satisfaction for his death. How he would have mocked if Judah had said to him, "You are the same as a weed burned up, as an ant, as a brief rain shower, no more than a zero in the calculations of empire." He'd have laughed and replied: "G'wan chum. I had me reasons. I had me notions. Them bleedin' Huns'll not git their hooks on bloody England."

What if he had been told lies to persuade him to say that? Would the truth have been less a lie?

He put down the fair-haired corpse and later told a medical corpsman where to find him.

The fighting and the dying went on, and Judah pitied the wounded and the dead because their purposes were even shorter-lived than most. Each day brought him closer to his own goal, limited as it was, *sub specie aeternitatis,* to return to his home place, to reestablish himself, despite all criticism and enmity, among those who would be shaping the Jewish world.

Ashkelon, Ashdod, Jaffa, Hebron, Lachish, Latrun. The great battalions of Allenby were moving closer and closer to Jerusalem.

13 ◇◇◇◇◇◇◇◇◇

For fourteen hours the fierce rain had fallen. One could not see beyond a few feet. From Jaffa, from Ashkelon east to the shrouded hills of Jerusalem, the war had paused.

Allenby sat in his tent on a high ridge near Gezer that three days before had been taken by a charge of yeomanry. Before him on the work table were maps, his Bible, and Smith's *Historical Geography of the Holy Land*. For three weeks, since the capture of Beersheba, his troops had been fighting on half rations against a desperate enemy, marching without rest across rocky soil and loose sand, in extremes of weather, from the humid heat of the coast and the burning blasts of *hamsins* to the wet cold that fell on them as they approached the foothills of Judea.

Ashdod, Ashkelon, Lachish were his. Soon Ramle and Jaffa. He was but twenty miles from the holiest city of them all. Ah, but what a twenty miles.

He watched a small stream of water enter his tent and crawl across the hard earth floor like a knowing worm. How long should he wait before attempting the final assault? Ahead were the Judean hills, in themselves a mighty fortress, a country of entanglements, as George Adam Smith had put it, a country of ambush and surprises, with no room for a large attack force to maneuver and with a thousand barricades for the defender. Uphill all the way, up the valley of Ayalon, through which Saul and Jonathan had marched against the Philistines; where Judas Maccabeus and his band started their courageous revolt against Rome; where, in grave warning to him who followed, the Romans had started and had failed; and where, from this very spot, the Lion-Hearted had gazed longingly but in vain at the City of Peace and had been forced to retreat. Allenby knew that to have conquered the Shefelah where the coastal cities lay was no surety of victory.

His men were tired and hungry, his supply lines overextended.

The thick mud clutched at every moving lorry and cart. His regimental commanders reported their great losses and waited hopefully for word that reinforcements would come to relieve their bloodied troops.

More even than this affected his decision. He had received a cable from the War Office congratulating him on his progress but cautioning him not to commit his troops beyond their strength, for it might become necessary to transfer many of them to France after the turn of the year. He knew they were thinking of Townshend's failure at Baghdad, where troops had moved too far too fast.

Intelligence reports coming through Colonel West and those Palestinian Jews of Singer's spoke of the disorganization of Von Kressenstein's armies and the slowness of the movements of the Yildirim group. Allenby glanced at the latest summaries. Twelve thousand Turkish prisoners and one hundred twenty-two guns had been taken. His own losses were less than half. Von Kressenstein's forces were divided. Twenty miles separated the Turkish Fourth Army on the hills from the Turkish-German Seventh Army in the plains. Could his opponent press his flanks together and squeeze him or could his own tired regiments destroy one enemy flank while harrying the other? One could calculate the weakness of an enemy, but the question that always stood unanswered was whether the enemy equally understood his own weakness?

Still, there were other questions: Could he take the city without destroying it, without fighting on its hallowed streets? Dare he risk this great engagement despite London's warnings and the exhaustion of his troops?

And if he waited until new drafts came in from Egypt in a week or ten days, would not the enemy use the time to reorganize, counterattack, throw off balance the momentum of this advance?

Allenby did not subscribe to the strategy of audacity. It was essentially a Gallic notion and, he suspected, a romantic bid for immortality. He thought of his own war in France, at Arras, where he had started with great success only to be frustrated by lack of space to maneuver. The Judean hills were high and steep, their defiles deep; would they be another Arras? Would he be repeating the disasters of the Roman invaders and the Crusaders?

He was a husband of men, using men not like a miser or like a spendthrift, but with a healthy caution and a healthy risk; he was a man who knew what he wanted because he knew what he was.

Allenby knew himself. He acknowledged the force of his will, his confidence in his estimates of the situation and the personalities of his generals. Most of all, he knew that his decisions were not qualified by a need for power or a yen for immortality—that shallow furrow of history marked with his name. His vanities of leadership were of a different order—the quick flare-up of temper, the schoolmaster's inspections, the show of personal physical energy, the use of his deep voice, his gruffness. He acknowledged in himself a certain purity as a leader and tried successfully to make his decisions cold and clear, the logic of a crystal.

He studied the map once more, the map he could draw by heart in every one of its crevices and ridges and brooks and hills. He jotted down some notes. Take the Nablus-Jerusalem road and prevent reinforcements from coming up. Move along the Bab el Wad. Take Nebi Samwil and overlook the city's defenses. Bring Chetwode up from Hebron on forced marches to cover the south. The Romans and Crusaders had had but one line of force up to Jerusalem. He had three —from the south, the east, and the north.

An aide brought in hot tea and Allenby ordered messages sent to generals Bulfin, Bols, and Dawney to see him immediately. Alone once more, he half closed his eyes and listened to the rain, thinking not of tomorrow but of the battalions of wet, shivering men being punished by the rain. The birds were used to it.

When his chiefs came, he would inform them of his decision to advance on Jerusalem and charge them with the task of playing devil's advocate against him for all their worth.

14 ◇◇◇◇◇◇◇◇◇

The NILI code was a difficult one, consisting of Hebrew, Aramaic, and Ladino. It took six days for the Turkish code officer at Tulkarem to break it down for Hamid Bek. Captain Ali, who had been badgered for action by Hamid Bek, delivered it immediately to the colonel at Caesarea.

"It tells me nothing," Hamid Bek raged. "Everything and nothing."

It listed several Turkish and German regiments being held in reserve at Megiddo and described a plan for a counterattack at Lydda. It said that the Yildirim army group had left Aleppo. There was also what seemed like a private message. "I am at the end of my strength. W. has left me. I don't know how long I can go on." Who was this W.? It would have to be a Jew. They were all Jews or else they wouldn't have used Hebrew in the code. But there were too many whose name began with W.

And to exacerbate his frustration, no pigeons had been found so far. What if the pigeons had been sent from Haifa? Who could search a city that size?

About the same time that Colonel Hamid Bek was reading the decoded message, Mustafa ibn Musa, leading his patrol off the coast road, entered the station grounds of Atlit. The failure of the search this far had settled in Mustafa like a disease of the bones. There had been no compensating pleasure in the tearing up of books and pictures and papers or even in the beatings of three or four men at Bat Shlomo and Hadera, for not once had anyone offered him money. Either the Jews had gone crazy or they had given up baksheesh. Since the latter was incomprehensible to him, he concluded that they had no money left. But this was also not to be believed. Not of Jews. What, then, was there left to think? That the Jews were waiting for the British to come and save them? Perhaps, but then they were fools. He knew his master. Hamid Bek would drown all the Jews in the ocean before he let them run to the British like a panting bride to her groom.

In front of the station he called his men to a halt and told them to take what they wanted of fodder and food. He remembered the last time he climbed the steps when that Jew who talked like a pasha threw in his face the few pounds to buy him off. Brandt. Hadn't seen him in a long time. How he had talked! "This place is American. Get out!" Yalla! America was the enemy now. No one could protect this place from search. And he would stick his finger in everything.

The door was locked and he shot off the lock. There was no one inside and it irritated him. The room seemed emptier than the last time. With his revolver in his hand he walked the length of the room, kicking open closets and emptying drawers of the desk and cupboards. There was nothing of value in them. He saw an empty bottle of brandy and threw it against a wall. It didn't break and that rasped him even more. Then he noticed that the bookcases were half empty. Allah, was there no end to the cunning of the Jews? With a muddy boot he kicked in the glass door of a specimen case. It broke with a hearty noise and he felt a little relieved. How he wished Brandt was there. He could hear him plead. "Don't, Mustafa; we are friends. Remember all the checkers we played at the café. We are friends!"

He flung a heavy book through the window, breaking the glass. One of his men below yelled up to be careful. A fellah. They too can rub the skin off a man. The poor are like Jews, always complaining, always keeping their secrets, always at the edge of a field ready to take it from its rightful owners. He threw another book through the window. There were no pigeons up here, but let these Yehudim birds of death know that he, Mustafa ibn Musa, had been there!

Birds of death. He remembered his father calling the Jews that when they were trying to build their first settlements. But then it was because they died off so quickly with malaria, starvation, and hard work. Now they were birds of death of a different kind.

He wiped his muddy boots with the pages he tore from a large encyclopedia; then, standing in the middle of the room, he fired his pistol at the lamps, the remaining glass cases and the huge splendid desk at which Judah had written up his studies.

Below, his men were yelling. Well, let them yell. They will think he is killing Jews.

The yelling below was louder. He heard men running up the outer

340

stairs. At the door of the balcony he shouted angrily, "What do you want?"

"Pigeons! Pigeons! We have found them."

He ran down the stairs and across the field, where a group of his men were standing around a half-open pit.

"They killed them," one of them said. "And buried them. But jackals opened the grave. Look!"

There were the droppings of jackals and there were the half-devoured pigeons.

"We will be rewarded!" the men shouted.

"Allah be praised. Faithful and Only One!" Mustafa said. "Stand guard here and arrest anyone coming to the station. I will return to the colonel."

The gendarmes knew why they had been ordered to remain. Not for fear of Jews coming. But because Mustafa could take all the credit. Even though the betrayal was inevitable, they were angry and made up for it by gutting the station workroom, making fires on the floor with the books. They stole the mirror and the kerosene stove, the glasses and the dishes, and the cot near the window where once Rachel and Naftali had been.

15 ◇◇◇◇◇◇◇◇◇

Nissim had been captured trying to cross to the British, was beaten almost to death, then brought to Von Fricke, who pretended to be his friend and gave him some wine with hashish dissolved in it. After a while Nissim lost all knowledge of where he was and floated in a free, gravitationless space where he saw a thousand suns without being warmed. He would have been happier than at any other time in his life if it were not for the dog on a leash straining to get loose.

"I am your friend," the voice of heaven said. The sound was color streaming to him.

He pushed aside the streaming light to see the voice's face. It blossomed like a rose, petal by petal, one by one falling into the air. The scent of the roses could be touched. The petals formed the full name of God. He began to weep with joy.

"Nissim, tell me why you wanted to go to the British."

Everything was visible, even the secret behind the name. How splendid! How noble! "To crown David," he said gaily.

"Who is David?"

"Our king. We will give him back his throne."

The laughter in his throat was like wine. Red, light, bubbling. Then it was swallowed, and no more. . . .

"Who sent you to the British?"

The dog on the leash ran in circles silently.

"You must tell me!"

Nissim felt himself being shaken back and forth. The leash was slipping from his fingers.

"Their names!"

He saw the names like scattered jewels. Tali . . . Oh, Tali! The god who wrestled with God. . . . Miriam, the new moon embracing her with silver love . . . Rachel, a fountain of tenderness . . . Judah, a man of bronze, a statue . . . Avram, a cedar . . . Dmitri, the sound of ribbon falling from a spool . . .

"Who are they? What are their names?"

The dog opened his mouth but was silent.

Manfred, a singer with his hands . . . Reuven, an abacus, sliding here and sliding there, counting the little wooden balls . . .

"I am your friend, Nissim Vidali. You can trust me. Why did you want to go to the British?"

He found himself in a green fog. There was a noise like a tree splitting. The dog barked.

"He lied! Wilner lied! He came back from the British and he—"

He caught the dog and muzzled it with his ten fingers.

"More! More! Who is this Wilner? Where does he live? Who sent him? When did he come back from the British?"

The green fog pursued him. He cried to heaven to blow it away.

"Answer me!"

The dog opened its mouth through the fingers, the lean red slippery tongue licking at them. Is it a dog? Nissim asked. Or am I the dog?

"The bread of affliction," he cried.

"What?"

"Wilner . . ."

"Where does he live?"

"The Gate of Shalechet. The Gate of Dung."

"Where?"

"Where the oak of salvation grows."

With a great effort Nissim choked the dog to death. The green fog dissolved. Now there would be only silence from him, and he saw sounds and heard colors. If this were not heaven, then heaven was where he was. All else was forgotten. The dog would never bark again.

Von Fricke did not stop trying, but the prisoner sat in the chair with a drool of delight in his open eyes and mouth. Later, when the hashish wore off, Nissim begged for more. The German bargained with him, hashish for names. But the dog was dead. Nissim tried to explain it, and when Von Fricke persisted in not understanding, he got down on his hands and knees to show him how a dog dies. The hunger for hashish overcame him and he began to bark and whine. Von Fricke saw that the prisoner had become unreachable and he ordered him sent to Damascus to be hanged.

A report of the interrogation and the names of Nissim Vidali and

Wilner were dispatched by special courier to Hamid Bek. Afterward Von Fricke lost interest. He didn't want to see the gendarme officer again. It was all a waste. To deal with individuals seemed to him to be a hopelessly enervating misuse of one's talents. The war had changed the world. For the future the one would have to learn how to handle humans not in the singular but as they were, particles of the mass. That would be, in the event of this defeat, the basis of the next victory.

16 ◇◇◇◇◇◇◇◇◇

It was early afternoon of a Sabbath when several large gendarme patrols surrounded Har Nehemia. No one was permitted to leave; anyone entering was forced to remain. Rachel and Papa Singer were in the house, in Judah's room. Rachel was glancing through the memoirs of Glückel of Hameln and Papa had just finished reading Psalms. The quiet was broken by the sounds of horses, men shouting, and Chana Haimowitz screaming. Papa ran out into the garden while Rachel watched through the window. She saw Colonel Hamid Bek and another officer ride along the street. They stopped to speak to a frightened child running home from the synagogue. The child pointed toward the Singer house. Then she knew. The certainty she had imagined had come true. They were coming for her. Slowly, she lowered the curtain over the window, surprised at how calm she was. The moment was a thing with which she seemed vaguely familiar. All the alternatives were closed off. She was no longer a leader with uneasy choices, but suddenly a foot soldier whose life, terrible as it might become, was clear and simple.

Almost coldly she calculated her chances and thought that a time might come when she could no longer bear the torture. She ran into her bedroom and took out from the bottom drawer of her bureau a small Mauser pistol Avram had given her once when they had gone to the shore to meet the ship. In her bathroom, behind the medicine cabinet, was a secret compartment Judah had made long before NILI. She took the medicine cabinet off the wall, put the pistol away, then replaced the cabinet, made sure that it looked right, and went back into Judah's room.

Papa had just entered, saying, "The gendarmes . . . Hamid Bek . . ."

Nodding, she sat down on Judah's walnut chair and waited, pressing her shoulders hard against its high back, and studied a torn place on one of the wall hangings. It reminded her of the Eiffel Tower.

The outer door of the house leading from the garden opened. Men's booted feet marched across the stone floor of the foyer, some going elsewhere in the large house, some moving along the hallway toward the study.

"Papa, don't forget. . . . You don't know anything."

Her father had the book of Psalms in his hand and seemed engrossed by what he was reading.

The door opened. Hamid Bek and Captain Ali entered with their pistols ready. Papa stepped forward, holding the book, and said in Arabic, "*Salaam Aleikum.*"

Hamid Bek stopped, glanced at the old man coldly, then slapped his face hard. Papa fell to his knees from the blow, the book and eyeglasses dropping to the floor.

"Don't! He's an old man!" Rachel cried, getting up from the chair.

"He's a traitor and a spawner of traitors."

Hamid Bek watched as Rachel lifted up her father, found the glasses and cleaned them before handing them to him. He remembered the last time he had seen this Jewess with the blue eyes and fair hair bound around her head in braids. She had troubled him then as if she had been a lover before whom he could not prove his innocence. To rape her would be a mockery of himself, for there would be a visible contempt in her which he could never erase. One had to start out despising this woman, hating her, rejecting any common humanity, reduce her if possible by mockery and pain until there was nothing left but submission. She must never be permitted to make him feel less than he was.

"You are also a traitor, Rachel." By using her first name, he would begin to deprive her of her dignity.

She stared at him frozenly.

Captain Ali was searching through the desk drawers, throwing papers on the floor.

Papa protested. "Those are my son's studies. Have you no respect for learning?"

Captain Ali stopped, momentarily uncertain.

"Continue," Hamid Bek ordered. "Rachel, do you know Nissim Vidali?"

Rachel felt panic. What did he know? Had Nissim been caught? Had he been tortured and talked?

346

One must stay close to the truth in these matters, Judah had once told her. "I know him."

"Where is he?"

"I haven't seen him in several weeks."

"Does he work at Atlit?"

"Sometimes he was there to help in the fields and with the locusts." She must be careful. "I know nothing more about him."

"He was a good friend of Wilner's, wasn't he?"

There were two parts to the question and each was dangerous. Nissim must have been tortured. Otherwise how would Hamid Bek know about him and Wilner?

"I don't know who his friends are," she said slowly.

"But you know Wilner?"

She thought: Not the whole truth, of course, but enough to protest a misunderstanding if caught. "I've met him once or twice."

Hamid Bek nodded, then strolled to the window and looked out. After a moment he turned back to Rachel and said abruptly, "Your friend Vidali was caught trying to cross over to the enemy. He confessed that Wilner had sent him and that Wilner is a spy."

"That's not true!" she protested without thinking.

"How can you say that, Rachel, if you don't know Wilner well? Save yourself stupid lies. I know everything. Wilner is the man I'm looking for. Tell me where he is and I will release you and your father. It's a matter of saving time."

He talked more but she stopped listening.

"Where's Nissim?" she whispered.

"He was hanged yesterday in Damascus."

She made no sound but put her hands behind her back to lock her trembling fingers together out of sight. Nissim dead. Tali dead. The walls of the temple are falling. Not one word, she commanded herself. Not one word more!

"Rachel, do you want this old man beaten in front of your eyes until his bones dissolve?"

"He is innocent!"

"But you are not, Rachel! Your pigeons were found in Atlit. I have a message you sent. Shall I tell you what it said? 'I am at the end of my strength. W. has left me.' W. is Wilner, isn't he? Now, where is he? Who else worked with you? For how long? When did it start? Who are your contacts? How did you get the pigeons? Where do they go? I want to know if your brother, Judah, is in a prison camp in England or in Cairo working for Allenby. I want to know where Naftali Brandt is. And, most of all, where is Wilner? These are many questions, but they won't take long to answer. You can save your father his reward of pain if you will reply at once. You see, I do not beat you. Answer my questions truthfully. I am sure——"

"Papa——"

The old man was straightening his glasses and yarmulke as if readying himself.

"Yes, Rachel."

"Papa, will you forgive me?"

"For what?"

"They will torture you because of me."

"And what else?" he asked calmly.

"If I could save you from this, Papa, you know I would."

The old man wiped the blood away from his cheek, angrily hitched his thin shoulders high, and said, outraged, "And take away my place among the Righteous!"

Rachel could not help smiling, then turned to Hamid Bek, clasped her hands in front of her, and waited.

Hamid Bek nodded and gave an order to Captain Ali, who called in several gendarmes. They threw Papa on the floor, took off his boots and socks, and laid him on the couch with his legs hanging over the end.

Rachel watched, holding her breath, tightening her muscles, straining against the first blow that would come to him.

A burly gendarme whom they called Mahmud brought in the cane. He moved the table and lamp away to give him room to swing his arms.

"Once more, Rachel. Will you tell me what I want to know?" Hamid Bek said.

"I know nothing."

But she scarcely heard the question; her mind and eyes were on her father. His glasses had fallen off again and his yarmulke, which no one dared touch, had slid to the back of his head. His voice came to her clearly as he murmured, "Shma Yisrael."

Hamid Bek gave the signal and the first blow bit into the old man's bare soles.

Rachel screamed. Her only thought: It's not worth it! Nothing is worth it!

348

. . .

Gimmel Cohn, the *muhktar* of Har Nehemia, and Dr. Bloch were brought to the house after Papa Singer lost consciousness. The doctor revived the old man. When his eyes were open, Papa said, "Don't ask me how I feel. When I see my doctor, I know I'm still alive."

"Excellency," Dr. Bloch said to Hamid Bek, "this man is over seventy. I protest the inhuman treatment of him."

"Let his daughter relieve him of it. She has only to answer—"

Rachel had been tied to a chair. Her blue eyes were frozen, her lips knit together tightly by the bloody bite of her teeth.

"Don't talk to them, Racheleh," Papa cried. "My whole life . . . I prayed . . . for strength to love the Almighty . . . with all my heart . . . and soul. . . . Now I can prove I meant it. . . ."

"Evil daughter!" Gimmel Cohn raged at Rachel.

"He's an old man, Rachel," Dr. Bloch said. "Is it worth it?"

"Rachel, let them do what they want with me," her father said.

Hamid Bek made a gesture. Mahmud raised the cane and slashed Papa's feet.

"I confess!" Rachel cried. "I confess!"

"No, Rachel," Papa groaned.

Hamid Bek gestured to Mahmud to stop. Papa began to weep for the first time.

"Don't cry, Papa. It's all right. They won't hit you anymore." Pleading, she turned to Hamid Bek. "I am guilty. No one else. I am the only one."

Papa Singer was carried into another room.

Hamid Bek refused Dr. Bloch's request to attend the old man. Satisfied with himself, he sat down behind Judah's desk and unbuttoned the collar of his uniform. The pressure of the cloth around his neck bothered him.

"Rachel, you remember," he said, "that we talked before, a year or so ago. At that time I inquired about Naftali Brandt. But you knew nothing. More recently, I asked you again about this man and your brother. Again you said you knew nothing. Now I have enough evidence to hang you and the whole village."

"Me, colonel?" Gimmel Cohn cried. "I'm innocent. I never had anything to do with the Singers."

"The whole village. This espionage could not be carried on without the knowledge and help of you people. Aren't you brothers of each other?"

"We have had nothing to do with any espionage," Dr. Bloch said firmly. He was disgusted with the *muhktar,* but he could not find a way to dissociate himself from him.

Hamid Bek coughed and blew through his nose. "We'll see." He would now gain the real enemy. "Rachel, tell me who helped you."

Rachel leaned against the painful ropes that bound her legs and arms. She knew exactly what she had to do to the end. Avram, Miriam, Reuven, and the others must know by now what was happening. She had only to give them enough time to hide or to try to cross the lines to the British.

"I had no help," she said slowly.

Mocking her, Hamid Bek smiled. A chess game was starting. This was the joy of the profession. "You trained the pigeons yourself?"

"The British brought them to me by boat."

"Who made the arrangements?"

"I did."

"By what method?"

"I crossed the British lines at Beersheba several months ago. And then I came back."

"Very resourceful. Did you kill the pigeons by yourself and bury them?"

"Yes."

Hamid moved Judah's inkwell as if he were taking a queen with a pawn. "Did this man Saul Wilner get the plans for the counterattack at Lydda and the positions of the reserves at Megiddo?"

"I stole them."

"From what officer?"

"Someone in Eighth Army headquarters at Kfar Saba."

"All by yourself."

"By myself."

"How?"

She was silent.

"Perhaps you became his lover?"

The rope burned her flesh. How deeply could this humiliation reach? Would she, as she once visualized in a fit of fear, end up offering herself to this lean beast to avoid the bastinado? The imagined actors of the mind had a way of never leaving their stage.

She looked back at him with disdain.

350

"So, you did not. You did not become his lover. Jewesses have high standards of morality. But you stole this information with no one helping. You are an invisible angel with six hands. Do you believe her, doctor? Cohn?"

Dr. Bloch nodded halfheartedly. Gimmel Cohn snorted with fear and incredulity.

"Rachel, you insist on your lies and you have told me nothing."

"I have told you everything. I am responsible."

"Even your friends don't believe you."

"They have nothing to do with me."

"Dr. Bloch—" Hamid Bek left the desk. "You are well known to me. A good doctor, I have heard. And you travel much. You know many of your people. Do you know anyone connected with this business?"

The doctor thought of his daughter, Miriam, and shook his head.

"Do you know Saul Wilner?"

"I think many people know him."

"And you also?"

"I have seen him."

"Do you know where he is?"

"I do not."

"If you knew, would you tell me?"

Dr. Bloch rubbed his hands together behind his back. They were sweating hard. "The question is pointless, colonel, since I don't know."

"You are also a liar, doctor. Hold out your hands."

"I am innocent of any treason, colonel."

Hamid Bek ordered Mahmud, who had come back into the room, to put the doctor's hands, palms up, on the desk. Then the colonel slashed them with the cane. The blood leaped into the air. Dr. Bloch groaned and was silent.

Hamid Bek said quietly. "If I could find Wilner, I might be satisfied. You understand that no woman would be capable of doing any of this by herself. That's logical on two scores. The work would be too much and women are not that clever. Not even Jewish women."

He did not look at Rachel as he brought the whip down again on the doctor's palms.

"You will kill everybody!" Gimmel Cohn yelled at Rachel. "Tell him where Wilner is."

"I don't know!"

Hamid Bek threw the blood-wet whip to Mahmud and told him to clean it, then said to Gimmel Cohn, "Go out to your people and pass the word that no one will be harmed if they bring us information about Wilner. But you must hurry. We have sent dispatches to every gendarme post in the province. If news comes that Wilner is taken before your Jews talk, their punishment will be severe!"

Gimmel Cohn, sweat dripping from his face, backed out of the room.

"But what shall I do in the meantime?" Hamid Bek said, glancing at Rachel. "The old man would rather die than talk. And from you, doctor, I expect no better. Perhaps a woman will find it easier. I hesitate to put women to the bastinado, but in times of war one's sensibilities become less important than one's duty."

The room had grown dark. The last twilight glazed the windows purple. Hamid Bek ordered Captain Ali to light the lamps. In the yellow glow, the faces in the room became warm and human.

Hamid Bek untied Rachel, asking her once more to tell him what he wanted to know. In the darkness his voice had some of the pathos of seduction in it. He ordered her to take her shoes off. She bent to unbutton them and carefully put them together to one side.

Dr. Bloch, his hands streaming blood, his mind fixed equally on the danger to Miriam, pleaded with Rachel to save herself.

"Tell them about Wilner," he begged.

"How can I, doctor? Shall I invent?" She paused to glance at Hamid Bek, who was watching closely, then stared at Dr. Bloch, hoping that he could read in her eyes that she would never betray Miriam. She had not forgotten what her father taught from the Talmud. "If the enemy says to hand over one of you that they may kill him and if not they will kill all of you, then all must suffer death rather than surrender him."

Rachel then asked Dr. Bloch if there was any news of Allenby.

"I have heard the weather holds up the attack on Jerusalem."

When Mahmud led her toward the couch where her father had been beaten, she trembled, felt faint, and reached out involuntarily. Hamid Bek held her arm to keep her from falling. His touch angered her and made her pull away sharply. With this small physical act of defiance she became calmer and lay on the couch face up, her feet dangling over the end of it. She watched Mahmud tie her legs together and fasten the ends of the rope around the couch. It won't be as bad as I imagined, she thought. She breathed in deeply several times to enjoy the sensation of air in her mouth and lungs. More than anything she desired to be aware of herself, to meet the pain consciously. Nothing must deprive this moment of its meaning; no part of it must be blurred.

She heard Hamid Bek move past her and she counted the steps. Above her on the ceiling was a fine web of tiny cracks she had never noticed before. Following the edges of the web, her eyes moved to the corner of the room, where as a child she had once hidden herself in a game with Naftali.

Her legs snapped back at the first lash of the cane on her soles. She screamed. The screaming didn't stop, but she could no longer hear herself.

Hamid Bek bent over to see her. "It will be worse. Save yourself, Rachel."

When she continued to scream Hamid Bek straightened up, buttoned his jacket, then held up ten fingers to Mahmud.

At Colonel West's field intelligence headquarters at El Mejdel, there was great concern over the breakdown of communications with Atlit. No pigeons had flown in for a week. He ordered a ship sent, but as it sailed past the station there were no signals of all-clear, and the ship returned to Port Said. Finally, from one of the Turkish prisoners in the compound, Judah learned of Rachel's arrest. Everyone, he said, was looking for Judah Singer and Saul Wilner. Harried by the news and feeling his full responsibility, he made one more appeal to West to release him to go back to help.

"It'll be suicide," West said. "You're too well known to the enemy. He'd pick you up the minute you crossed the lines. It'll be a mucky time for you, but you'll have to slog through it, old man."

Word reached Chaim Weizmann in London and he cabled to Judah, "The pain you and your comrades are suffering so heroically gives us the strength to carry forward our sacred mission."

Judah read and reread the message in his tent at El Mejdel and thought bitterly of how late this acknowledgment had come to NILI. Yet if only there were a way to let Rachel know that she was not alone.

The rain beat down heavily on his tent, which had become a prison to him.

17 ◇◇◇◇◇◇◇◇◇

After Rachel's arrest and the beginning of the countrywide search for the spies, hysteria, demonic in its intensity, raged through the Jewish community. From the dark hutches of the charity-supported Jews of Jerusalem, Safed, and Tiberias, and from the enlightened farmers of the Shefelah and Galilee, from Hashomer and the Palestine Zionist office, and from the socialists and plantation owners there rose a hatred of those who had risked the Yishuv for what they called a dangerous and disreputable adventure. The Singer family was at the center of this revulsion, but even more it was Saul Wilner who became the Satanic symbol for the others. All that was being suffered—the beatings and arrests—was attributed to him. Wives and children, seeing their husbands and fathers chained together and marched off to the death-house prisons of Damascus, Acre, and Nazareth, cursed Rachel, her family, and Saul Wilner most of all. Jews eagerly combined forces with the gendarmes to search for him. They vowed, if they found him before the Turks did, to turn him over to them or to kill him first.

Beneath the surface of their fear and frustration was the moral uneasiness of a community pretending against the grain to be more loyal than the Turk and abasing itself before its oppressors. No matter how valid and honorable their intention of saving themselves and their settlements for a future time of action, they suspected their own passivity and found release in the hatred of Wilner. He was their own evil to be cast away, as the religious cast away sins in the sea on the first of the Ten Days of Awe.

In the balance of their guilt against his, Wilner's life had to be sacrificed.

He had malaria and was living in the cellar of an Arab brothel in Nablus run by a Russian woman who fancied that she loved him. It was she who told him about the pigeons being found at Atlit, that Rachel Singer and her father had been exposed as spies, and that the gendarmes were searching everywhere for him. She gave him bread and a bottle of wine and told him to leave immediately. Love was love, but to be hanged for hiding a spy was another thing.

He left Nablus with a high fever, not knowing what to do or where to go. Allenby's army was still far away. To try to cross the lines in the midst of battle seemed hopeless. Hiding by day and walking by night, he moved blindly in the general direction of Har Nehemia. He tried to make plans for the rescue of Rachel, but how? With whom? He was afraid to approach any Jews, for they might be unfriendly and turn him in if they recognized him. To go to Alona, where Avram Liebermann lived, was to commit suicide.

What was he to do? Why not find safety? He had broken with NILI. Had Rachel not sent him away? What kind of fool is a man who offers himself to the slaughterer? Even a pullet knows better. In the old Polish phrase, the world was a sty covered with six inches of dung. Why should he try to clean it? He was also dung; why should he expect more of himself?

At dawn he saw an Arab riding a cart in the direction of Karkur and hailed him. His dress of aba and kaffiyeh was a complete disguise. The Arab told him stories about the spies, saying that Wilner had recently come back from Cairo with much gold, that he had a big house on the Carmel from which he sent messages to British ships and where a thousand rifles were found.

Wilner left the Arab on the outskirts of the colony, and feeling too sick to go on, went to a Jewish farmer he knew to get some food and to find out what was happening.

When Goldstein came out of his barn and saw Wilner approaching, he was frightened. He told him to leave immediately. Wilner pleaded to be hidden until his malaria attack was over. Goldstein had three little children and begged with equal fervor that they not be endangered.

"Is that the way a Jew treats a Jew?" Wilner yelled, shivering.

"If I took you into the *muhktar*, there would be a money reward for me," Goldstein said, looking down at his muddy boots. "A Jew doesn't betray, but he doesn't hang his wife and children with his own hands either."

At that moment his six-year-old daughter came out of the house and saw the two men.

"Go inside, Yardena!" the farmer ordered.

Wilner saw his chance. "Yardena!" He ran to her. "I am a sick Jew. Tell your father to help me."

The little girl, a sudden furrow of confusion on her child's smooth forehead, looked at her father.

Wilner leaned against the barn wall. "Go ahead, Goldstein; tell her why you won't help me."

"Is he sick, Papa? Truly?"

Angrily Goldstein rubbed a hand against his unshaven face. "Go into the barn," he said to Wilner after a moment, then yelled angrily at the child to get back into the house.

The straw on which Wilner lay sick for half the day and the night that followed tossed him back and forth like the sea. As he perspired and shivered, his mind alternated between dismaying darkness and explosively lit images of guilt and confession: In the woods with the Christian woman while his mother was being murdered. (My God, tell me, how shall I pay for that sin?) Judah taunting him in Cairo. (Forgive me for living!) Rachel crying out Tali's name when he touched her. Tali wrestling with him in the desert. (Not that too! You know I couldn't have saved him!)

"How long shall I pay?" he groaned.

"Wilner!"

"I couldn't have saved them—him!"

"Wilner!"

Slowly he became aware that Goldstein and another man and a woman were standing above him. He thought he knew them.

Remenov of the Zionist executive, steam spurting from his mouth in the cold air, bent over. "Wilner? Do you hear me? Do you know who we are?"

Wilner nodded and tried to stand but fell back. He was sicker than he thought. The woman, Mara Schalet, gave him something to drink and wiped the sweat from his face.

"You know they are looking for you?" Remenov asked.

Light-headed from the fever, Wilner grinned. "Why not?"

"They say you were the head of a spy cadre working for the British."

"Is that all?" He would show these damned shomrim. "I did everything. The Turkish code, the counterattack plans, the—" He stopped with a rush of clarity. "Rachel? What is with her?"

"Arrested. She and her father at Har Nehemia."

"Is she alive?"

356

"Nobody knows. The village is locked tight."

"With your guns, why don't you save at least Rachel?"

"Why don't I jump from the roof to the moon? They have hundreds of gendarmes at Har Nehemia. With machine guns. Did you know Nissim Vidali and Manfred Gersh?"

"Yes."

"Were they members of your group?"

Wilner became suspicious. "Why?"

"Because they were hanged yesterday in Damascus."

Wilner covered his eyes with his hands. In the darkness, colors bubbled, all red like the flames in the sky over Turopetz village. He groaned and bit his tongue.

Remenov shouted, "Didn't we warn Rachel and her brother? Didn't I personally tell her that if she got into trouble we would have nothing to do with her? Answer me?"

Wilner lowered his hands. "I wasn't there."

"You have damned us with your tricks. Do you know if you're found here this whole settlement will suffer for it? You and the Singers are already murderers! Ten times over. Beasts!"

"It would be better for you if you were dead," Mara Schalet said.

"So, what shall I do, die?" Again, Judah in the hotel room in Cairo. The water in his mouth tasted like iron. "Is that the way to talk to an old comrade?"

"When we threw you out it was the best thing we did," Remenov said. "You and your foul spy nest."

Wilner laughed.

"What's funny?"

"The straw tickles me. Nu, so what are you going to do, leave me here or throw me into the road to freeze to death?"

Mara Schalet flung down the towel she had used to wipe Wilner's face. "Why do we wait? Every minute he stays here makes it more dangerous. He and his friends threaten everything we've built. Their spying, that we had nothing to do with! Their blasphemous spying. Wrong, wrong! Immoral and wrong!"

The creaking of the straw was the only sound as Wilner rose slowly and painfully to his feet. "Why are you waiting?"

"You don't deserve it," Remenov said, "but we're going to smuggle you into the Galilee. We'll try to save you."

Wilner held on to a barn post and grinned. "Thank you, haverim, my dear comrades."

357

"We are not your haverim!" Mara Schalet said with disgust.

They borrowed a wagon and horse from the Karkur settlement and Goldstein's Austrian passport and set out for Merhavia.

Near Megiddo they were stopped by an army patrol. Their passports were examined carefully and they were asked if they knew Saul Wilner. Remenov explained that they had already given all the information they had to the kaimakam of Nablus and that they were taking their sick friend, Goldstein, who had influenza, to a doctor in Tiberias. The lieutenant in command of the patrol didn't want to expose himself to the plague and let them go.

A cold rain began to fall, flooding the roads. Wilner became delirious. Remenov stopped at a settlement near Nazareth for food and shelter, but when the haverim there found out that Wilner was in the wagon they refused to permit him to get out.

"We were warned of a gendarme raid from Nazareth," the secretary of the settlement said. "It'll be bad for all of us, and him too. They'll burn us to the ground if they find him."

Remenov and Mara had to accede and drove through the rain across the muddy fields to another settlement, which, according to the secretary, had already been raided and wouldn't be molested soon again.

They arrived at dusk and this time they carried Wilner into an empty house without asking permission. They lit the oil stove for heat, then left him alone and walked to the communal room to find the secretary to get food and medicine. They were surprised to find Lorchanovsky there with two other members of Hashomer, Dov Berg, a thin, dark Lithuanian with prematurely gray hair, and Levine, his own thick mane rising from his forehead like a glistening black comb. They had heard about the exposure of the spy ring and were on their way to the Galilee for an emergency meeting to determine what plan should be followed to dissociate their group from the spies. When Remenov told them that Wilner was there they were stunned and outraged.

"You had no right to do this!" Lorchanovsky thundered, pounding his big worker's hand on the table, rattling the tea glasses and the spoons.

"We're here now," Mara replied unhappily. "Wilner is sick. What do we do with him?"

"Kill him, that's what we should do if we were sane men!" Lorchanovsky shouted.

358

"We're not murderers!" Remenov protested.

Levine raised his hand for quiet. When he spoke his voice was so soft the rain could be heard outside. He had strengthened his position as leader in the last years and his moral influence was great. The more leadership he assumed, the softer grew his voice.

He observed to his comrades that before any further discussion two things should be done—one, guards sent out into the fields to warn them if gendarmes or army patrols were seen, and two, food and medicine given to Wilner. Three members of the settlement's secretariat were brought in and asked to undertake the tasks. One of them, Deborah Kaplan, a stout Polish woman with gray hair cut short as a man's, remained to represent the settlement, now endangered by Wilner's presence.

Levine began an extended analysis of the situation in which he begged his comrades to disregard their personal animosity toward Wilner and the Singers and to think about the main problem: how to prove that the socialists and Hashomer were innocent of espionage and treason. With a Marxist's grasp of the realities underlying the social and military surface, he described the position of the Yishuv, threatened by a retreating Turkish Army looking for excuses to explain away its own inefficiency; he pointed out that the Germans could no longer be relied on to temper any reprisal actions of Jemal Pasha and Hamid Bek. The Arabs too might use this opportunity to retake by force the land they had sold to the Jews.

He stressed the role of the party in a time when its supporters in the settlements and cities were roused to a hysterical fear. A mistake vis à vis Wilner could damage it badly.

"What, finally, are our alternatives? To turn him over to the Turks in order to clear ourselves? Will we not be open to severe criticism abroad as a party that betrayed a fellow Jew who, no matter how immoral his actions may be, was nevertheless motivated to help the Yishuv? If we try to hide him, collaboration after the fact, are we not equally liable to a severe blow at our prestige? After all, this man was an agent of a foreign power, and the Zionist movement from the very beginning opposed any such act or any act that could be so interpreted."

Lorchanovsky broke in impatiently, "If we hide him and he is caught, this Wilner is the type who'll confess at the first lash of the bastinado. And whose names would he give? Our names! To protect his own comrades. To get even with us for having expelled him. To buy his own cheap life. And his evidence? That we hid him, that we carried him secretly from Karkur to here and from here to the Galilee! What is there left to decide? Kill him!"

Levine rose from the long wooden table at which they were sitting, crowded together at one end. The rain seemed to be letting up a little and the dripping from the eaves ticked like a clock. He walked to the window and looked out, running his fingers through his hair without stopping, in a kind of a tic.

"Levine?" Lorchanovsky demanded.

"I am thinking. . . ." Anguish made his voice high-pitched. "Such decisions must not be made one-two."

In the empty house where they left Wilner after giving him some quinine, the only sounds came from his heavy breathing, for he was almost asleep. Suddenly he thought he heard horses and Turkish being spoken outside. Certain that he was about to be taken, he threw a blanket over his wet aba, put on his boots, and left by the back window. He peered into the rain and saw nothing. Perhaps he had been dreaming, but he was frightened and ran furtively to the communal room and entered the foyer. At that moment, from the main room beyond, he heard Lorchanovsky say, "Kill him!" Wilner stopped, still unseen by the others. He put fingers in his mouth to silence his chattering teeth.

"I see things in front of me," Lorchanovsky went on. "So do you. But you won't reach out and touch them. To die for what I believe in, all right! But to die for that Wilner bedbug—forgive me, Mara—is a joke for idiots. There is only one answer to our problem, and you all know it. Kill him! Or hand him over and let the Turks kill him. It's all the same to me."

Wilner wanted to run away and at the same time wanted to enter the room and defy Lorchanovsky. He remained, immobile.

In the silence he heard Mara say falteringly, "We are not murderers. True, we risk everything. But how can we, just like that, kill a man?"

Again no one talked. Then Dov Berg: "Let's compromise. We don't kill him. We don't hand him over to Hamid Bek. We just arrange for him to be found by some Arabs."

Someone cleared his throat and then coughed.

360

Wilner pressed his hands to his jaw. His teeth had a life of their own. This must be a game he was hearing. How could Jews be executioners of Jews? In the next room there was a long silence. He heard footsteps. Coming toward him? He stiffened and looked around wildly. Someone had left two rifles under a bench. He would not let them kill him without a fight. The footsteps stopped.

"Why should we also be victims of panic?" Levine said. "I have a counterproposal to make. One, we take him to Hamara. It's isolated, with good chances of not being searched. Two, we tell the haverim to guard him. And if the gendarmes come, then to move him north into the Lebanon."

"No!" Deborah Kaplan said sharply. "As long as he is alive we are in danger."

"We can't be judges of a human life," Remenov said.

"We would judge one of us if he betrayed the others. This man has betrayed us. Whether he meant to or not is apart from the question."

"Talk! All talk!" Lorchanovsky muttered.

"Did we want this problem?" Dov Berg said in a rush of words. "If Mara and Remenov hadn't taken it on themselves to bring him here, then we would have no problem. But they did bring him here. Wrongly, I think. Call it fate. Call it sentimentality. But if he is caught we'll all hang alongside him in the Damascus prison yard. If Wilner had any honor he would kill himself rather than cause the death of innocent lives."

Deborah Kaplan said, "Let's vote. I propose that we get rid of him now."

Wilner knew that he could not wait. He took one of the rifles and quietly left. The rain had begun again and it made loud noises as it fell on the large puddles. The settlement paths were deserted. He went back to the room where he had been, took the end of a loaf of bread and the rest of the quinine, then protecting the rifle from the rain, mounted the horse that had brought them from Karkur. Without thinking, he started off again toward Har Nehemia, as if where Rachel lived and suffered was his safety and salvation.

In the communal house the vote was taken. Lorchanovsky, Deborah Kaplan, and Dov Berg were for Wilner's immediate execution. Remenov and Mara were for Levine's plan.

"Since it is a tie," Levine said, "I will propose a compromise. I do this on moral grounds that one is forbidden to risk the community for a single person, and one is equally forbidden to risk a single person for the good of the community. I propose that we take Wilner to Hamara——"

"What's different?" Dov Berg demanded.

"The difference is this, Dov. I propose that we inform our people at Hamara that at the first sign of a Turkish patrol Wilner is to be killed and his body turned over to the Turks. In this way we have done all we could to save him, and equally we have done all we could to save the Yishuv."

After some further talk it was agreed. Lorchanovsky insisted that he be the one to take Wilner to Hamara and the one to execute him, if necessary. Remenov said he would go along.

"You don't trust me, Remenov?" Lorchanovsky objected.

"I trust you. But if such a deed be done, you must not be the sole victim of those who for political reasons may accuse us of murdering another Jew."

"Morally we are all responsible," Levine said, fingering his black mane as if it were a refuge. "Remenov and Lorchanovsky are delegated to the task."

"Take him out of here as soon as possible," Deborah Kaplan said, shivering with cold.

Remenov left to get Wilner, and the others waited in silence. The rain outside swept noisily along the roof.

"He's gone! And taken the horse!" Remenov shouted, banging open the door.

Lorchanovsky cried, "We hang ourselves with talk. Now the talk is over!"

Without waiting for the others, he picked up his rifle and hurried outside, mounted his own horse, and rode quickly out of the settlement, following a trail in the mud.

The next morning, in the heavy rain, alongside one of the flooded wadis leading into the Plain of Esdraelon, Lorchanovsky saw Wilner a short distance ahead of him, standing alongside his horse, looking at one of the hoofs. Lorchanovsky moved closer without being heard. When he reached a place within rifle range he called out, "Wilner . . ."

Wilner looked up and shouted, "Don't shoot!" and began to run toward the wadi. Lorchanovsky fired twice. Wilner screamed, although he wasn't hit. Lorchanovsky thought he was and rode closer to finish him off. Hidden by trees, Wilner picked up a heavy rock and threw it into the water, then crawled into a cutting on the side of the wadi, covered himself with the wet mud, and lay still.

Lorchanovsky passed close by and paused a long time to stare at the water. He went downstream and waited. Then he looked for Wilner's horse, which had run away at the sound of the rifle shots, and found it.

After an hour he started back for Merhavia.

18 ◊◊◊◊◊◊◊◊◊

At Har Nehemia Gimmel Cohn reported to Hamid Bek that no one knew where Saul Wilner was or had heard anything about the espionage.

"Then you and your village will be punished for it," the colonel said.

Twenty men were taken from their homes, bound in ropes and chains, and ordered to march to Nazareth, fifty miles away.

"If Rachel confesses or if we find Saul Wilner, your men will be released," he told the women who gathered in the streets to protest. "Otherwise they will hang."

Prodded with whips, the men were driven out of the village. Their women ran alongside the slow-moving phalanxes, calling to their husbands and sons, kissing those they could reach, pressing into their hands food and the few coins they had. At the cemetery on the outskirts of Har Nehemia the gendarmes ordered the women back.

In their houses, the children wept, and imitating their mothers, cursed Saul Wilner, Rachel, and the Singer family. Only in Bloch's house was there silence. Miriam had disappeared. Ebria, her little sister, went every day to stand in front of the Singer house. She loved Rachel, Miriam's best friend. Yet everybody said that she was killing Jews. Filled with confusion and fear, she watched for some sign from Rachel.

Rachel had been given the bastinado four times, her screams heard throughout the village. The soles of her feet were raw, and her legs were paralyzed by gross spasms of muscular contractions. When she fainted, Dr. Bloch revived her.

"You'll kill her," he warned Hamid Bek.

"She can save everything if she talks."

On the third morning they left her alone. The pain, even hours after the last beating, was a thrust of iron barbs driven outward from her spine through the flesh. There was no pain worse than this, she thought, and tried to turn her mind to other things—memories of her childhood, books, plays, the Bible. But there was no relief. When Dr. Bloch came to see her, she begged him for a drug to ease her.

"All I have left," he said, "is some ammonia and caffeine in solution." He rubbed her hands and arms to increase circulation.

"Is Papa all right?" she asked after a while.

"Yes. He hasn't been touched again."

"Thank God!"

If only Hamid Bek would let her sleep.

"Where is Miriam?" she asked slowly.

"I don't know. She has gone away."

She tried to smile encouragingly to the doctor. He looked black and sad. "Where is Allenby? Is there a chance he'll reach here before—"

He hesitated, then said, "I heard Hamid Bek say that the English were held up in the Bab 'el Wad. No one expects them to take Jerusalem this year. The Turk had brought in reinforcements."

So there was no hope for rescue. "Thank you for the truth, doctor." She was silent for several minutes while he continued to massage her legs.

"Rachel, you've been beaten four times. Tell them where Wilner is. Tell them. You are punishing others, innocents."

"Shall I also tell them about—about Miriam?"

It was his turn to be silent.

"I despise you for this," he said at last. "The Yishuv despises you. They curse you in the village."

She began to cry. "Has no one tried to help me?"

"I have."

"You despise me."

"I tried to help you. I promised Hamid Bek five hundred Turkish gold pounds to let you go. He slapped my face and said he'd have your confession *and* the money."

"You love your daughter. . . . Then don't hate me. . . ."

"My daughter would be safe if it weren't for you," he said bitterly, than added, "Do you think that your Wilner would be as brave?"

Who was brave? she wanted to ask. This was not courage. This was the suffering of an animal that protects its young.

"No one will thank you, Rachel."

She thought of Job. God didn't matter. It was man who suffered. Not because he was evil but because he was man. Man suffers. That was the only truth. It was part of his nature. To laugh, to love, to weep, to suffer.

"How long can you last? Not long, Rachel. Your blood pressure is low. Your heart can't take another beating."

Tali had always wanted to make death meaningful. But her bones were breaking. Who cares about meaning? Why do we do it? Why do we live as if it counted? Yet, if only there was a sign that someone for whom she was suffering loved her for it. Then she could die. But to be alone, despised, hated, cursed. There were no images to sustain her, no metaphors of redemption to prove her. Blackness.

Hamid Bek had a new thought. He ordered Rachel carried into the garden and tied to the post of the gate. Then he ordered the women, their children, and the men left in the village to witness the bastinado. As they approached the Singer house and saw Rachel bound to the gate, they screamed at her, "Murderer! Assassin! Hangman! Killer of our men."

Chana Haimowitz came up to her and spat in her face. "What, are you still too good for us that you want to kill us?" Even Reuven Schechter's mother, who knew that her son was being helped by Rachel's silence, cursed her, not for her silence but for having involved Reuven. Gimmel Cohn yelled that she was no real Jew and ought to be stoned for heresy. Reb Mottel, the butcher, spoke to her grievingly. "I knew you when you were a child, Rachel. Tell them where Wilner is. You are wasting yourself. And bringing us down with you."

A slight soft rain was falling. She was glad of it, for it hid her tears. Her bleeding feet were too painful and she slumped against the rope, trying not to listen to the curses and shouts or to see the faces of those she had grown up with. Next to Dr. Bloch she saw Ebria, bewildered and frightened, staring at her as if a light hurt her eyes. The child's lips moved silently but Rachel thought she could make out the words, "Aunt Rachel . . ." over and over, like a prayer.

"In a little while," Hamid Bek said, addressing the crowd, "your men will die because of this woman." He turned to Rachel. Seeing his gaze, she straightened up despite the pain and looked into his eyes to read there—what?—some code of man that could explain inhumanity?

He accepted the look of the ravaged blue eyes as if it were a kiss. Pain, he thought, does not destroy a face right away. It brings it to life, it calls up to its surface the things of strength and beauty that are usually hidden. He noticed the fair flesh of her arms glistening with the rain and the sweep of her breasts within the soiled wet shirt-waist. He should have permitted her to change her clothes, if only to make her more elegant, more worthy of him. Theirs was an ancient enmity, more ancient than the enmity of the Semitic cousinhood. He had wondered what it would have been like to rape her. No . . . It would be a mocking of him. Still, if he could close those eyes . . .

"Rachel," he said, trying to tone his voice with contempt, for her courage and strength made her admirable. "Look on your people. They hate you. Will you die for such as they are?"

She turned away, first to the Carmel hills, shrouded in a slight mist, then south toward Jerusalem, beneath the heavy dark clouds, and finally to the white, baffled face of Ebria, who was crying and whispering, "Aunt Rachel, Aunt Rachel." Rachel smiled. "It's nothing, Ebria. Don't be afraid, Ebria. . . ." She thought she had said those words, but no sound came from her mouth.

Hamid Bek gestured to Captain Ali to begin. But this was the first time the captain had been asked to commit the bastinado, and uncomfortably he took the thin wooden cane from Mahmud and stared at Rachel. "Colonel—on her feet? But she's standing. . . ."

Hamid Bek was annoyed. "Her thighs."

Rachel was aware of each soft drop of cool rain on her face.

Captain Ali hesitated. To whip a woman was beneath him. He raised the whip, curving it to test its suppleness. What if his European friends were there? Would they watch with disgust? A faint smile touched his thin mouth. Why should any Christian accuse him of cruelty? What Christian had not been equally cruel? Crusader, English, Russian. Who dare mock him?

"Begin, captain!" Hamid Bek cried.

Ali bent a little and swung his arm back. The swish of the cane sounded true. He cut Rachel above the knee. From the crowd came a loud shout of anger. "Beast!" a woman yelled. Others turned away. Some covered the eyes of the children.

"Talk, Rachel! They won't beat you anymore!" Chana Haimowitz cried.

"Send the children away," a man groaned.

Hamid Bek ordered the gendarmes to hold the crowd in place and to keep the children there.

Saul Wilner entered the village unseen by anyone. He had ridden to Har Nehemia as a man moves in a dream, not knowing why or what he would do or what he wanted there. (Only to escape the burning village near Kishinev, to repent the old sin!)

Everyone's eyes were on Rachel as Captain Ali lashed her again. Wilner, holding his rifle over his arm Arab style, moved to the garden fence near the gate where Hamid Bek studied Rachel. He himself stared at Rachel as if he had never seen her before, then with a crooked shrug of his shoulders, took a step that was both predictable to him and yet a surprise. He turned the rifle around slowly and prodded Hamid Bek with it.

"Don't move, colonel. What you feel at your back is my rifle."

Hamid Bek took a deep breath. His nose was clogged and he breathed noisily.

"I am Saul Wilner. I give myself up. Tell that dog to stop the whip and all my secrets I give you gladly. Have him untie her."

Rachel, waiting for the next lash, did not hear anything. The crowd and gendarmes saw what was happening but didn't understand at first.

"Captain Ali!" Hamid Bek called sharply. The captain turned around, surprised. "Get the ropes off her," the colonel said, his eyes trying to send a message to the captain and to the other gendarmes.

"Rachel!" Wilner called.

She opened her eyes at the nightmare voice. Was she awakening from a dream?

"Saul!" Incredulity, hope, fear.

Now the villagers and gendarmes knew. The name "Wilner" went through the crowd like a breaking wave.

"Rachel, go to my horse."

Rachel took a step, then dropped into the mud, unable to walk with the pain.

"Someone help her," Wilner called to the villagers.

"Not yet," Hamid Bek said.

"The bargain, colonel. If you want to live."

Hamid Bek had already seen one of the gendarmes move behind the house. It would take a minute, no more, for him to be in position to shoot.

"First, what have you to tell me?"

"I, Wilner, am the whole thing."

"I won't accept that. There were others."

"For God's sake, Saul! Be silent!" Rachel begged. "I have thrown myself away if you——"

"Yes, there were others. I'll give you three names and then she is put on my horse. Otherwise, I—" He shoved the barrel deep into Hamid Bek's back.

"Name them."

"Saul, don't!"

"With me were Shmul Lorchanovsky, Levine, and Remenov. Now—" The gendarme had reached the corner of the Singer house and raised his rifle. He took a moment to steady himself, then fired. It was a good shot. Wilner fell forward against Hamid Bek and slid to the earth. The colonel wheeled around and slashed at Wilner as he was falling.

Rachel screamed, "Saul!" and crawled through the mud. "Saul! Saul! Why did you do it?"

His aba was bloody as she lifted his head in her hands. "Saul! Why?"

He felt the pain leaving but the blackness coming very fast. He tried hard to see her and said, "Tell me, *bubbaleh,* did I really have any choice?"

He managed a half grin. His pale, wasted face became blank. Rachel bent over and kissed him. Dr. Bloch knelt alongside and felt Wilner's heart.

"He's dead," he said heavily.

The Jews outside the gate were silent. The few that would have prayed were equally silent. Only Ebria's voice rose in a shout of agony, "Aunt Rachel! Aunt Rachel!"

Hamid Bek ordered his men to drive the villagers back to their houses.

Mustafa ibn Musa had a gendarme with him. "Excellency, this is the man who saved your life. He is my cousin."

Colonel Bek, staring at Rachel, who was holding the hand of the dead Wilner, nodded abstractedly. "Yes. You will be rewarded." Then, as an afterthought, he said to Mustafa, "You and your cousin, take Miss Singer back into her house. Be careful of her."

It was the first time that he did not call her Rachel.

The two men carried the dazed woman into the house and put her down on her bed carefully, for they thought that Saul Wilner had been her lover and they respected her grief. Mustafa ibn Musa looked around the room that he had searched three days earlier. The bookshelves were empty, the pictures from the wall on the floor, the drawers of the bureau empty. On two chairs were piled the woman's clothes. Mustafa ibn Musa counted eight dresses, twelve if you added the jackets and skirts. More than his wife owned in her whole life.

And the shoes. Six pairs. And the shirtwaists and the other things these Jewish women wore beneath their skirts. He marked off a dress he would take—a green one. More a suit than a dress. In the suq in Jaffa he could sell it and use the money to buy an ass. Or maybe a goat. During the first search he had taken a small Persian jar, but it wasn't very valuable.

Rachel tried not to cry anymore. Saul was dead! But he had come foolishly and wonderfully to save her. That must be cherished. How could she have guessed the dimension of his love?

She moved to her side. Anything to relieve the pain of the thigh where the captain had whipped her, but when her bare feet accidentally touched the crumpled blanket at the end of the bed she screamed.

There must be an end to all of this. She could not bear another beating or another death. Tali! Nissim! Manfred! Saul!

Where was Allenby?

If only the bastinado killed instead of wounding. Was it only a month ago that she had imagined she would give herself to Hamid Bek rather than take the pain? How stupid. Her body was useless now. It was all one open wound.

Why had Saul named the shomrim? He knew they were innocent of spying. Why had he shown malice at the very moment of nobility?

"Miss Singer!" That was Hamid Bek's voice from far away. "Dr. Bloch, has she fainted again?"

She moaned as the doctor touched her wrist.

If only she could remain in the darkness, hearing Tali's voice. "O ma jeunesse abandonée . . ."

The pain was too much.

"Miss Singer!"

Suddenly she thought of Nahum. For months he had not existed, as if he had never been known to her. How badly she had treated him, fled him, been unfaithful, effaced his image. How had it all started? One acts as it is expected of him. . . . O ma jeunesse abandonée . . .

"I am married. . . ."

"Madame, was Wilner telling the truth about Lorchanovsky and the others?"

An illusion of oneself; one ends disastrously or nobly by trying to live up to it. Tali used to talk about Isaac. We are all Isaacs, she thought, doing what is expected of us.

"I ask you, was he telling the truth?"

370

The full weight of the question broke upon her; an abyss of no alternatives awaited.

Why did Saul prove that malice and courage could be brothers?

"All I need is your word that he was telling the truth and I will release the men of Har Nehemia from prison. They won't hang. They will be free to go home."

She listened to a distant sound. ("Tell me, *bubbaleh,* did I really have a choice?")

An airplane flew overhead. Rescue? Where were Allenby and Judah?

"If you don't tell me, madame—"

His hand was on her arm. It lay there almost tenderly.

She thought: If they beat me again my tongue will break my teeth. I will tell all I know.

Hamid Bek glanced at Dr. Bloch. "You will keep her alive. Your own life depends on it."

Slowly, as one peers at the sun, she opened her eyes. Hamid Bek was above her, looking down, his fingers on her arm. She hated him. She heard herself calling him the vilest names she knew; she threatened him with the vengeance of her people.

"Mahmud!" Hamid Bek called.

"No!" she screamed. "No more!"

"Then answer my questions!"

She was silent with the silence that draws into itself all the sounds around it—the silence of choosing to destroy oneself.

Could she do it? Others before her, discoverers of a suddenly awaked tenderness for themselves and the world, had withstood the cataract of human savagery flowing around and within them and then had chosen to kill themselves. Others would after her, of which the Jews would not be the least who killed themselves lest the Romans take them and who died before the Inquisition could reach them: Palestine, Spain, England, the Rhineland, Russia. . . . There was a kind of farewell consolation in being bound into the gleaming fascia of history, past and future. But sadly, even as she became aware of its cool embrace, the consolation disappeared, for above all she wanted to live. Life was more precious than honor. Life was all. It was greater than history or the example for the future or the command of God or of her people. Life was everything.

She yearned.

("Tell me, *bubbaleh,* did I really have a choice?")

She yearned.

Tali flooded her mind wantonly, his face in the night on Judah's field before the locusts came, at the station under the window, on the crumpled masonry of the ruins at Atlit, glowing and soft against her own.

Had he been anticipating this moment when he talked with such compassion about the lad Isaac, burdened with the wood and the burning question, who ran breathlessly up to the slope of Mount Moriah to halt his father and ask, "Behold the fire and the wood, but where is the lamb for a burnt offering?"

She had no choice; the fire and the wood were ready. But then, it seemed to her that like Tali and Saul she never had a choice. From the day of her birth. Who can revise one's father or revoke a mother? It was the best consolation she could find that she had been bred to a tenderness for herself and the world.

"I am waiting, madame," Hamid Bek said.

Her plan had always lain beneath the surface of her hope. First she must see her father for the last time.

"I will answer your questions," she said faintly. Her lips were swollen. Talking was like sticking needles into her mouth.

A smile of triumph touched Hamid Bek's mouth, but as the smile faded it became edged with regret. Dr. Bloch, standing near the bed, studied his lacerated hands to avoid having Rachel read the dismay in his face.

"I must see my father."

"Agreed."

"You must promise—"

"Yes?"

"Don't beat him. Bring back the men from Har Nehemia you sent away."

Hamid Bek was not displeased that she made conditions. These matters with Europeans had more substance when they were *quid pro quo*.

Now, the key to her plan.

"I will confess only before a court of law."

"A court is not necessary."

She forced her voice to be strong. "I demand it! I respect the law. A court is absolutely required."

It would be a delay, Hamid Bek thought. Still, it would be better than killing her by the bastinado. Uncomfortable questions might be asked by Jemal Pasha. More than that, this woman's death would leave him questioning himself; the paradox of her strength, which had forced him to respect her, would remain unsolved. Besides, it was not so strange to have Jews want courts of law. How else could they have survived?

"Very well, madame. I do this to please you, although it will make no difference in the end. There is a court in Nazareth. I will drive you there immediately."

"After I see my father."

"Yes."

She touched her muddy skirt. "After I have changed clothes."

Complications seemed to be growing. "Madame," he said, annoyed, "I will agree, but if you have any notions about escaping, I warn you that I will hang your father at once."

"I give you my word of honor."

"Captain Ali, see to it that she is never out of your sight. You have ten minutes to be with your father and change your clothes. Dr. Bloch, you will come with me."

Before Bloch left, he paused at Rachel's bed, trying to read her eyes. Was it possible that she would betray her friends, his own daughter? If only she could give him a sign that Miriam, at least, would be protected.

She knew what he was asking and said carefully, "Doctor, when you see Miri—" A pause as she sat up slowly.

"Yes, Rachel?"

Hamid Bek was listening.

Rachel tried to smile. Her numbed, swollen lips made it difficult. "Kiss her. Tell her . . . I love her. . . ."

Dr. Bloch understood, bent down quickly, and kissed Rachel's forehead; then, with a long, last look at her, he followed Hamid Bek out of the house. A light Sharon rain filled the air.

When they were alone, Captain Ali offered his arm to help Rachel walk into her father's room. "I did not enjoy punishing you," he said. "I was obeying orders."

"I'll walk by myself." She bound her wounded feet in towels and hobbled in great pain through the room, across the hallway and into her father's room. He lay in the huge Russian bed, facing away from her, his yarmulke crumpled on his head. Next to the bed was his wooden lectern with a volume of the Mishnah on it. There was a smell of leather and snuff in the room, although he hadn't used snuff for years.

"Papa . . ."

She sat down on the edge of the bed and he turned to her. The

373

pallor of his face frightened her. His beard had grown wild, as during a time of mourning.

"They let me see you for a few minutes, Papa."

"Thank God . . ." The pale-blue eyes were filled with anger. "You suffered. . . . I heard your screams. . . ."

"It is over now."

He seemed not to hear her. "I begged them to beat me instead."

"Papa—"

"But we are alive, you and I! We will remain alive. They won't kill us, eh, Rachel, God willing!"

She couldn't help herself and burst out defiantly, "Is He willing this? Tell me, Papa, is He testing us or doesn't He care?"

"Sha!"

"Why you, Papa? Why you? Why has God permitted you to suffer? You're innocent! You've loved God and served Him!"

He sat up in the bed and held her hand, smoothing it gently with his fingers. "Darling, sweetheart, you are hurt so much. . . ."

"Papa, I'm asking you! I'm asking!" Her plea was a reflex of a lifetime. "Answer me, Papa!"

Papa sighed at the old, very old question. "Darling . . . we're not the first. . . . We will not be the last. . . . Be patient with God. He is patient with us. If He were not, my sweetheart Rachel, man would long ago have been snuffed out by injustice."

She wasn't listening. In her inner ear she heard what she must have always known. No argument could sustain her. She knew them all, from Job to Maimonides, to this old man whose flesh she was. It didn't matter about God. There was only man. As her father chose to be patient with God, whom he loved, she chose to die for the sake of a few Jews. But even at this extreme moment of her life she did not dare to say to her father what was in her mind. She loved him too much to blaspheme in his presence.

"Has the doctor helped you?" he was saying, more concerned for her body than for her question.

"Yes, Papa."

"I pray for you every minute. . . ."

She wanted to embrace him, to tell him what she was going to do and ask for the absolution of his love.

"Madame—" Captain Ali, at the door, made a gesture of regret.

"Papa, I have to go back now."

He raised his hands in a priestly gesture.

374

" 'May the Lord cause his countenance to shine upon you. . . .' "

She studied the line of his cheek beneath the gray beard, noticed for the first time the way the ends of his lips curved inward, the tiny hairs on the edge of his ears, the vein on his neck, the terrible thinness of his age-blotched farmer's hands; she breathed in deeply the smell of snuff and leather and the scent from the vineyards that had always clung to him. She wondered why she did this; these sights and scents could not go with her into the nothingness. Had she only now learned how to live?

He said, using the strong Hebrew, "Praise God, Rachel, even for this. He is our rock. He will redeem us. The earth is the Lord's!"

He seemed to be begging her for something beyond herself. She nodded, swallowing the crust of grief choking her.

"Papa, yes . . ." She kissed his hands, unable to look at him anymore without breaking down.

"Tomorrow, Papa, maybe they'll let me see you again."

He nodded and she turned away and walked out of the room carefully, each step as if on broken glass, although the pain somehow seemed less acute now.

She asked the captain to get her gray cloth suit that hung awry over one of the chairs. She had worn it on her trip back from Constantinople and again last Rosh Hashanah. As she moved slowly across the room, she saw herself in the long mirror. Once, a thousand years ago, it held her image dressed in her mother's wedding gown while Miriam basted the hem; stitches in her shroud, she had thought then. How wicked to pretend a death before it appears! She looked for the Persian jar that Tali had given her. It wasn't on the shelf. Someone had stolen it. Her shell comb and brush were there, and she asked Ali for them.

"I will bathe and dress," she said.

"Madame, I mustn't let you out of my sight," he said respectfully.

"I am going into my bathroom to bathe and dress. I assume you will behave like a gentleman."

He hesitated, then looked inside the large bathroom. There was no other door. He opened the window to call to one of his men outside to stand guard.

As soon as Ali left her alone in the bedroom, Rachel picked up a pencil and a page torn from a Hebrew grammar. The margins were wide enough to write on. She hid the paper in her clothes.

Captain Ali stepped back and gestured for her to enter the bathroom. "You don't have much time, madame."

"Thank you, captain."

Slowly she limped into the room, dropped the gray suit to the floor, and softly fixed the chain across the door. Then making as much noise as she could, she turned on the water in the tub, crossed the room to the medicine cabinet, and took the pistol out of the hiding place. Now, for the first time, she felt safe and sat down on a stool near the window. The rain had stopped; a pale sun taking its place. Quickly she began to write.

Dearest Judah:

I pray that this will get to you. I am about to do what our ancestors did at Massada. Forgive me as they were forgiven. But I cannot suffer any more pain. I beg you to remember that not one word left my lips. I have been faithful. The Turk will learn how Jews can die.

Perhaps others who may at this same moment be suffering will take heart when they hear of this. Oh, if Tali were alive to hear me say that I have kept my eyes on Jerusalem.

Through the door she heard Captain Ali's voice. "The colonel has sent word that he will be back soon. Please hurry."

"Yes!" she replied and continued writing.

Papa will live through it, I am sure. He has been the strongest of us all. I love him. I love you. I love the world. (Is it terrible that I hate, even at this moment, my torturers?) There is so much I have to say. Give whatever share of the property that would come to me to Miriam, my dearest friend, and to Tali's mother. Give—

"Madame—"
"Yes, in two minutes."

About Saul. No matter what you hear, believe me that he was loyal to the end. He gave up his life for us.

She turned off the water, then went back to the letter. She scribbled the last words swiftly.

Don't be angry with me. Don't be angry with yourself. They are coming now—

"Madam, finish your toilet immediately."

376

Tell Nahum I thought of him and apologize for everything.

Swiftly she folded the page of the Hebrew grammar and put it where it could be seen. Even by Hamid Bek. There were no secrets in it.

"I will be ready in a minute," she called out and dressed quickly in the gray suit. When she was finished she went to the shaded window with the pistol in her hand. From outside came the sounds of an automobile and Hamid Bek's voice. How often she had stood in the same place as a child, watching and listening unobserved. The great cedar of Judah's used to be there, dark and strong. Beyond it the fence of rocks from the fields built by Judah and her father. She heard an airplane again but no longer thought of the vanity of rescue. She opened the curtain a little to see the garden. A yellow veil of sun swept past the muddy earth.

"Madame, we must leave immediately." It was Hamid Bek this time.

Deliberately she made her mind a blank and raised the pistol to her breast. Without meaning to, indeed without even hearing herself, she whispered the final affirmation of the Shma. "Hear O Israel, the Lord our God, the Lord is One." She pressed the trigger.

At the sound of the shot, Hamid Bek and Captain Ali ran to the door and butted against the chain until it broke. Rachel was on the floor, the bright blood pouring from her breast. Hamid Bek cursed her and felt her heart. It was still beating.

"Get the doctor!" he yelled to Ali, who was paralyzed at his own ineptness and its consequences to him.

The whole village had heard the shot. Dr. Bloch was already running from the *muhktar's* house.

Hamid Bek raged. "You will hang if she dies. I ordered you not to —" He stopped as Dr. Bloch entered. "She tried to kill herself! Save her! Save her and I promise I won't punish her!"

Bloch quickly pressed the cloth of her jacket into the wound. The arterial gush faltered. But the pulse and heartbeat were scarcely audible.

From the bedroom Papa's voice was heard, "What happened? Rachel! Rachel, where are you?"

"Don't let him in here," Bloch commanded.

Ali left the bedroom and closed the door behind him.

"Is there any hope?" Hamid Bek asked.

The doctor did not reply. He took from his pocket a small tin case

377

that held a flask of caffeine and a hypodermic. He injected the caffeine into Rachel's arm.

Rachel opened her eyes. The darkness that had folded her within it grayed and lightened. She could see a white spot at the center. Dr. Bloch's face was clear.

"And where is Allenby now, doctor?" she asked precisely as if it were important to be businesslike.

"Good news, Rachel. The attack on Jerusalem has started. It goes very well. They are nearing Lifta."

Hamid Bek was about to speak, but he decided not to. It was the truth. The whole village had heard it a few minutes before from a Turkish officer en route to the front.

A ripple of joy moved lightly across her mind, a hope of love, an expectation, a conviction of being alive. The joy mounted. Where Dr. Bloch's face had been appeared Tali's. They were at the station the day the locusts had been swept up from the fields by the wind and carried into the sea. Everyone was singing exultantly. Wild crying gulls. The glad solitary place, the rejoicing desert. The sun on Tali's face. Behind, the torch of victory, the tower in the golden wheat of sun.

After a moment in which she lay still, Dr. Bloch bent over to touch the pulse again.

"Dead," he said with an animallike groan.

The funeral procession left the Singer house at noon the next day. The wooden coffin, built by the villagers, was laid on a farm wagon and drawn by a lame horse driven by Ibn Djavid, the Singer coachman. Hamid Bek had offered something better, but Papa Singer refused. The old man, his feet bound, limped behind the wagon. With him were Dr. Bloch, Mottel, and Gimmel Cohn, who sobbed and beat his breast. Little Ebria Bloch, her hand in her father's, murmured Rachel's name.

As they moved through the street of the village, all but two of the women defied Hamid Bek's orders to stay in their houses and rushed out heedless of punishment to walk behind Rachel's coffin. With loud cries they vented their grief and shame. The two who remained in their houses could not forgive her even then.

At the cemetery, the procession passed the fresh grave where Saul Wilner had been buried the day before. In the section that had been put aside for the Singer family, a grave had been dug for Rachel opposite her mother's and the four tiny graves of the brothers and sisters.

Papa Singer quietly fulfilled the ritual of being the first to shovel earth on the coffin after it had been lowered. He led the others in the mourner's kaddish to the enduring God, and when it was finished, he watched the men take the shovel, one from the other, to fill the grave. With the whole village at his side, he limped back to the house to begin the week of mourning.

19 ◇◇◇◇◇◇◇◇◇

Ali Fuad never forgave himself for forwarding the English plan for the offensive on Gaza, which the fall of Beersheba had confirmed as a hoax. Yet, he couldn't complain of the way he was treated. Jemal Pasha had promoted him to general and assigned him to command the defense forces of Jerusalem. Now, thirty-eight days later, defeat and surrender were at the door of his city again. His cold was worse than ever; his throat ached as he read the latest dispatch from corps headquarters and handed it to Colonel Hamid Bek, who had come with dire news from the hamlets of Har Nehemia and Alona. His dislike for the gendarme commander was such that he could no longer hide it. To him Hamid Bek was the seed of the Ottomanic doom.

"Jemal and the Germans," Ali Fuad said, preferring not to use the names of their generals, "have ordered me to defend Jerusalem. Yet without informing me, they evacuate Bethlehem. If we lose the heights of Mar Elias, we will have to fall back to the city itself."

"There are traitors in the city, Excellency."

"Are you suggesting that they gave the withdrawal order?"

"I want an order signed by you to round up all Jews, Armenians, and Christians," Hamid Bek said sullenly. The news of Rachel Singer's suicide had preceded him to Ali Fuad's headquarters, and he had been criticized severely.

"To do what?"

"To do what is usually done to traitors. Shall I repeat to you, sir, what we found at Atlit and Har Nehemia? A whole chain of treason."

"In my command you will not force people to commit suicide. You will not execute people without some evidence."

Hamid Bek ran a finger around the shining leather revolver belt on his waist. "My orders are from Constantinople."

"Then why have you taken up my time?"

Hamid Bek breathed heavily through his badly set nose.

"His Excellency the governor requested that I have your approval."

Ali Fuad coughed painfully. Would they never find the right medicine for a cold? "This is a matter of the police and the civilian authorities, colonel. I have no need to sign anything."

There was scarcely any authority left, Hamid Bek thought. But he understood. No one wanted responsibility. It was the curse of the Ottoman Empire.

"Riaz Bey told me that it is a matter for the military," he said.

The telephone buzzed. Ali Fuad picked it up and listened, then replaced the receiver. "We are counterattacking at the Wadi Surar. We still hold them at Deir Yassin."

Hamid Bek tapped his boots with a riding crop. "Do you consider evacuating the city without fighting, general?"

Ali Fuad glanced at the map pinned to his table. "Yes, if Lifta and Beit Jala are taken. If the heights above Wadi Surar are lost. If the Germans can't get reinforcements to us from Nablus." He paused to consider something on the map. "I do not intend to fight within the city. I will not have it destroyed."

"The English wouldn't hesitate, sir."

"The sin be on their heads. My own is not strong enough to bear it." He rose. "I am busy, colonel."

Hamid Bek stood up. He had a trump card. "I have orders from Jemal Pasha to take as hostages the leaders of the non-Muslim communities. I will need transport."

"I have none available."

Hamid Bek didn't care whether the hostages walked or rode, lived or died, but he wanted transport for his own men.

"Many of them are sick and old, sir," he said truthfully.

Ali Fuad stared at him and said with broad sarcasm, "You surprise me. I refer to your concern. It does you honor. Perhaps you will also have to walk, colonel."

The day of the eighth of December was also the twenty-fourth of Kislev by the Jewish calendar. At nightfall began the festival of Chanukah. The Jews of Jerusalem took from hiding places old eight-branched candlesticks, polished them, and went out to buy candles on credit from the candlemakers in the Bokharan quarter. It was usually a joyous holiday marking the great victory of the Jews, led by the Maccabees, over the Syrian Greeks. On that day in 165 B.C. Jerusalem itself had been recaptured and the temple cleansed. The sounds of

British artillery nearing the city brought hope. Would Allenby support another Maccabeus? Would the temple be soon restored? And if Allenby failed, would the Turks finish the destruction they had started? Still, Chanukah was at nightfall, and they had to prepare for it. They left their homes and went out into the streets.

Hamid Bek's failure with Rachel became an obsession. She had taken advantage of his respect for her courage and mocked him with her death. His blood was heavy with anger, and he moved violently against the infidel. By his order, his men ranged through the alleys of the Meah Shearim and the other Jewish sections, arresting rabbis and heads of communities. The leaders of the Armenian and Greek colonies were taken from their houses and chained together. Most of them were old men, undernourished and sickly. Mounted gendarmes flogged them toward St. Stephen's Gate for the march to Jericho.

When the Jews who had left their hiding places in the first flush of hope heard what was happening, they ran to burrow again in the crypts and attics. Those who were already too far from home hid among strangers. Only a handful of patriarchs dared all and continued on their way. Despite Turk and Englishman, despite the gendarmes and the threat of arrest and flogging, despite the crash of guns, the candles had to be found, the menorahs cleaned, and the ritual visit made to the one still-standing wall of the old temple to sing the Psalms and wail the enmity of man.

In the early afternoon, a Turkish transport column galloped wildly toward the gates of the city along the Jaffa road, the soldiers yelling that the British were at Lifta. Some of the Turkish infantry and artillery units defending Jerusalem panicked, and leaving behind their trenches and guns, streamed back into the city and toward the roads leading to Jericho or Ramallah.

People saw them, left their hiding places again, and called out to each other, "The Turks are running! The Turks are running!"

Gendarmes fired on the shouting, exulting crowds, and the streets were cleared again of all but the dead.

That night Jerusalem was dark except for the flashes of the guns from Mar Elias and Bethlehem. But behind walls and beneath tables and blankets the Jews lit their first Chanukah candles, quietly chanting in unison the prayers, "Blessed art Thou, O Lord . . . Who commandest the lighting of the Chanukah light. . . . Blessed art Thou, O Lord . . . Who wrought miracles for our fathers in the days of old. . . . Blessed art Thou, O Lord, Who has kept us alive and enabled us

382

to live until this season." Then louder, despite for fear of being over-heard by looting troopers and freebooter Arab bands, they sang "Ma-oz Tzur," "Fortress Rock."

At midnight the civilian governor of Jerusalem, Riaz Bey, received word from General Ali Fuad that all troops were being withdrawn. Riaz Bey was instructed to surrender the city to the British in the morning. The governor, an obese man who moved gracefully and painted watercolors in his spare time, read the message with relief. During the last days, when the possibility of surrender had begun to occur to him, he considered a number of ideas for a deed that would be appropriate to the occasion and his dignity as the last governor of Turkish Jerusalem. He had toyed with the idea of burning the city in the manner of the Russians when Napoleon entered Moscow, but he thought better of it. He did not fancy the association of his name with the destruction of a holy place of Muhammad. Hamid Bek had proposed that a public execution of some of the Jewish and Christian traitors still in prison would be worthy. But that, Riaz Bey thought, might only impel the enemy to do the same with its prisoners, and who could tell but what in the confusion of battle he himself might be caught by some sudden thrust of British cavalry? He ordered Hamid Bek to leave the city for Jericho. The gendarme commander dared to reply that he understood at last why the Ottoman Empire was no longer worth saving. But Riaz ignored him, and he departed Jerusalem forever.

Riaz Bey pondered his own problem while finishing a large bottle of French brandy a German officer had given him. Then, without any seeming logical sequence of thought, he found the notion he was looking for. He would mark his surrender in a way that would never be forgotten.

First he called his staff together, gave each of them a small gift, and dismissed them to go where they wished. He wrote a letter to the mayor calling on him to be brave and to appear at the Jaffa Gate at dawn with a white flag to surrender the city. He sent the message with one of his remaining servants. Then, dressing against the cold December night, he left his palace with Daoud, a young Arab scribe whom he had befriended some years before, and rode in a requisitioned horse-drawn carriage slowly past the Abbey of the Dormition, King David's tomb, the windmill, and the stinking refuse and garbage over Herod's grave. The night was quieter than any that had preceded it. People were hidden in their houses; only an occasional splatter of machine-gun fire from the direction of Nebi Samwil disrupted the silence.

Riaz Bey was tipsy from the brandy, but he and his friend talked calmly of love. Was it, after all, an emanation of the senses? Or were the senses themselves the creation of desire? Man lies dormant, Riaz Bey remarked, until he is exercised. The sense of taste is meaningless without the sweet and the salt, the smooth and the rough. Vision is defined not by the eyes but by what one sees. The trouble with women is that they do not react to reality but to their own imagination. They pretend to be passive but the truth is that they are always forcing themselves on the world and thus they create much unhappiness. A man and a woman making love is the conjunction of opposites. How could that evoke goodness?

They stopped before the telegraph office on Gaza Road near the Terra Sancta. When they entered, they found three civilian clerks and an elderly Turkish subofficer sending and receiving messages.

"Are there any reports for me?" Riaz Bey demanded.

"No, your Excellency," the subofficer replied. "These are for the armies at Damascus and Amann."

"You are relieved of duty. You may stay in the city or go to Jericho."

"But the telegraph, sir?"

"It is my responsibility."

The civilians and officer were pleased by the order and left at once.

The machine clicked on. The little switches and keys distracted Riaz Bey with their malevolent prattle.

"It is my belief," the governor said to his young friend, who was under the influence of hashish, "that the decline of man derives from his inventions." He fingered the round red key and clicked it several times. "Men speak to each other through these wires. Or through that telephone over there. They are not instruments of civilization despite what the scientists and politicians say. They are proofs of its failure. Did Muhammad need this?" He raised one of the sending keys and tore it from its connecting wires, dropping it to the floor as if it were dirty. "Moses, Jesus, and Muhammad needed only their inspired voices to talk to thousands, millions!"

With a petulant stamp of his foot he smashed the telegraph key. To destroy these instruments of corruption would do more than harass the enemy, who could use them if found intact; it would be revenge against the present and future. If only he could destroy all the airplanes, the dynamite, the gasoline engines, the electric generators, the cotton machines, the automobiles!

With growing excitement he took a hard wooden chair in his fleshy hands and smashed the lamps on the switchboard. Let the angels of hell take them! He ground the broken pieces of glass beneath his heels.

"In the name of Allah!" his young friend yelled.

Riaz Bey kicked in the telephone cabinet, pulled the receiver out of its roots, and threw it through the window.

"Muhammad spoke with his own tongue, and the heavens opened!" he yelled.

"Allah be praised!" the young lad chanted. "I see the angels now. More! More!"

Riaz Bey looked around. There were no more instruments. But he saw a photograph of Kaiser Wilhelm with the sultan and knocked it off the wall with the chair. He jumped on it until the glass and wood and paper were shredded. Then he ran wildly around the room hitting the already broken instruments, tearing up the code books and papers.

"There will be no more of this!" he cried happily, throwing the pieces into the air. "We will be innocent again."

Breathing hard from his exertions, he put his arm around the lad's shoulders. "We have come to the end of the world. We have destroyed it before it destroyed us!"

"Allah is just! Allah is merciful!"

From the direction of Jaffa Gate there was a loud burst of machine-gun fire.

"Come, my lad, let us go now into the wilderness of Shechem."

They drove the carriage toward St. Stephen's Gate, near the Muhammadan cemetery. They saw no one in the streets, nothing but the past, and that was dead. The only sound was from Turkish and English guns firing in brief bursts—and the wails of frightened children hidden in the houses.

When it was light the mayor of Jerusalem, a tall, mustachioed man wearing a fez, was joined by three of his councillors and two gendarmes nervously carrying two white flags. They marched toward Lifta and waited for the conquerors. Behind them the city awoke freed of Turkish rule for the first time in five hundred years. A few straggling soldiers forced money, food, and water from the poor and rich, but there was no massacre. As soon as it became clear that the Turkish

385

and German troops had left, the poor came out from their hiding places to loot back what had been stolen from them. Mobs of Arabs, Jews, bedouin, and Circassians took possession of the streets.

When the mayor saw his first Englishmen, two sergeants from the Nineteenth Londoners, he offered to surrender, but the men refused and waited until two majors arrived. They in turn waited for a lieutenant colonel, who said politely that he couldn't accept Jerusalem without orders from higher authority. The mayor felt rebuffed and humiliated and began to shout curses on the heads of the English. Finally a brigadier turned up, but he too refused the offer of surrender. He sent a message to Major General Shea, who passed it along to Lieutenant General Chetwode, who brought it to Allenby, who was waiting anxiously at his headquarters for some word about the progress of his troops. Allenby immediately passed the word back down the line that the brigadier had his permission to accept Jerusalem.

On the morning of December 11 the city and the Judean hills that it crowned were immersed in the vague lemon light of winter. The western faces of the ruined Citadel and the desolate perch of David's Tower in the city wall were masked by purple morning shadows. Thousands of silent English and Allied troops stood in a thin mist. Nowhere was a flag, neither of empire nor of war. The day was beyond ceremony.

The general's car moved upward along the winding road through glistening olive groves and Arab villages. Sitting erect in the back seat, Allenby saw the turret of the abbey on Mount Zion and the round, whitish cup over Omar's Mosque and, in the distance, the impassive mountains of Moab and Gilead. Closer, the rose-stone houses on the plateaus around the city sparkled with dew. The car stopped a short distance away from the city's wall, where the mayor waited. Some twenty years before, a breach had been made in the wall for Kaiser Wilhelm to enter the city on a white horse. Allenby's entrance would be different. He dismounted from the car and, erect as a centurion, walked solemnly toward the ancient Jaffa Gate, open for the first time in a hundred years.

A few paces behind Allenby was his staff of five generals. Behind them, wearing the borrowed uniform of a colonel, walked T. E. Lawrence. He had hurriedly left Feisal's headquarters beyond the Jordan to be present at what he considered to be the supremest moment of the war. Alongside Lawrence was Sir Mark Sykes of the Cabinet and the neat Monsieur Picot of France, who had not so long before joined their countries together in a secret treaty to divide this vanquished province. In the procession was Colonel West, who wondered whether the chief was seeing the bird nests on the ledges of the Citadel's tower. Near him Judah Singer moved in a troubling daze of exaltation and disappointment. He was on the wrong side of Jerusalem; he should not be entering his people's city, City of David, but rather be waiting in the inner court at the head of those who, in the name of the Yishuv, would soon be welcoming the liberators.

At Allenby's approach the mayor and councillors carrying the letter of surrender and the white flag came forward, doffed their fezzes, bowed, and made the sign of welcome. In broken English the mayor said that he now gave over Jerusalem to the protection of his Lordship Allenby. He pronounced the name Al-Nebi, meaning prophet, for the old Arab prophecy had come true that when the waters of the Nile flowed northward (were not the pipelines from Kantara to Gaza filled with the Nile?), a Nebi from the West would drive the Turk forever from the Holy City.

Allenby accepted the letter and handed it to an aide. He saluted briefly and continued toward the gate. Suddenly from the hillside thundered a great cheer, the voices of England exulting.

As he left the arch and its shadows, Allenby stopped. Beyond, in the narrow street ahead of him, waited the people of Jerusalem. As far as he could see—in the open spaces, at the windows, on the roofs—they waited. Nearest him were Roman and Greek priests carrying Catholic and Byzantine crosses and Armenian bishops holding their jeweled insignia above their heads; beyond, rabbis of the Ashkenazic rite with their fur caps lifted brocaded Torahs in their arms, and the rabbis of the Sephardim raised their own bedecked scrolls of the Law as if David himself had come to accept their gift offering.

There was a hush; no one spoke, no one moved.

Then an Arab girl about five with a dark, frightened face, but with the fair blue eyes of some Crusader forebear, came forward holding a small olive branch.

Allenby, awed by the sight of the silent, prayerful city, stepped toward the child. He took the branch, saying, *"Salaam Aleikum,"* and with a gentle movement of his free hand touched her head.

Instantly there were shouts of joy. People laughed and raised the children in their arms to the Prophet, others wept without shame; men

387

embraced each other, the priests shouted thanksgivings to Christ their Lord; the rabbis chanted, "*Ki mi'tzion,*" "Out of Zion shall come forth the Law!"

From the foot of David's Tower Allenby received the notables and ordered the proclamation for the safety of the city read aloud in seven languages.

Judah moved through the crowd looking for someone he knew to tell him what was happening in the villages of the Sharon and Galilee, for they were still in Turkish hands and were likely to remain so for a long time to come. Allenby's strategy after the capture of Jerusalem, as Judah heard it at headquarters, would be to move up to Megiddo with part of his force and with another part cross the Hejaz railroad toward Amann and Damascus. The army on the coast would remain in the environs of Jaffa until all of Syria was taken. It could be six months or even a year before Har Nehemia would be freed.

Judah found himself moving with crowds of Jews through Barclay's Gate at the southern end of the old temple area to the massive rampart of undressed blocks of huge stones, the Wailing Wall, battered remnant of the ancient temple. In the crevices between the time-pitted stones lay like nesting doves thousands of slips of paper with petitions and prayers. Now as always Jews were weeping for their inconstant fate. Even at this time of liberation they were weeping, for there never was a celebration, no matter how joyous, that did not include the anxiety-touched reminder of past sorrows.

Uncertainty of the fate of his family seized him and he wanted to join the tears of the pious with his own, to mourn and to exult over the victory—they seemed to him the same. Tears spoke for both. But he decided not to give in. The day was late and he had to find someone who could tell him of Rachel, his father, and his comrades.

Suddenly he heard his name called. He turned and saw Avram Liebermann running toward him through the crowd of praying men and women.

"Avram!" he shouted.

The two men ran to each other. Avram, grief leaping into his eyes, embraced his friend, saying in a broken voice, "Forgive me, Judah my brother, forgive me. I carry terrible news."

The End and the Beginning

Judah moved slowly to the stone and put his hand on top of it. The simple gesture, tender and loving, brought sobs from the women.

In a voice that he did not recognize as his, he said, "Rachel . . ."

More sobs came like the fluttering of a low fire. Now the men could not control themselves. Their low moans were terrible to hear. The weeping grew loud, uncontrolled, and wild, a cry of regret for life.

With shock Judah felt his own burning tears; his lips were no longer numb. Without shame or self-consciousness he lowered his head over the stone and wept for Rachel, for Tali and Saul, for Nissim and Manfred, and for all the innocent ones cut down like the young trees.

Suddenly his father's angry voice was heard loudly, "Children! What kind of a sin are you committing? The Lord gives. The Lord takes. Blessed be His name. Don't offend heaven!" In a firm voice the old man chanted the words of kaddish in praise of God, "Yisgadal . . ."

One by one the men and women joined him in the prayer, and the weeping stopped.

Then Papa Singer went to the stone and unfurled the banner that hid it. On the four-foot square of rosy Jerusalem stone, one word was inscribed: RACHEL.

When the ceremony was over and Colonel West and the visitors had departed, Judah stayed with his father for a few hours, then mounted his horse and rode over the hills and through the olive terraces to Atlit to see for the first time in three years what the war had done to his cherished fields. In his pocket were two letters that Colonel West had brought to him. One was his honorable discharge from the army with a commendation. The other, requiring an immediate answer, was from Dr. Chaim Weizmann from London.

"Emissaries of Ludendorff and the Allies are meeting in Switzerland. . . ." There would be a conference of the nations to approve and implement the Balfour Declaration and decide which nation should be given supervision over Palestine. A distinguished committee of Herbert Samuel, John Maynard Keynes, Menahem Ussishkin, Lord Rothschild, Nahum Sokolow, and others were already at work preparing the position of the Jews. Would Judah join them in London? He knew the Yishuv, the land of Israel, better than most. "I urge you to come as quickly as possible."

He wanted to see what had befallen Atlit before replying. Did Atlit need him more than Weizmann? Where was his future?

It was late afternoon when he turned inland from the coast road. The sun on the sea side of the Crusader's fort had already reddened its rough wind-scourged edges.

He rode a hundred yards toward the station, then stopped. What he saw stunned him. The Washington palms that he and Tali had planted along the road had been cut down or uprooted. On both sides his fields were covered with weeds and the wildflowers that October had not yet killed. There was no wheat, no barley. The tree nursery had been completely leveled. When he raised his eyes to the white two-story station he shivered. The upper part of it had been burned, the outer stairway torn from its foundation, the walls pitted by gunfire, the windmill on its side, the gardens torn up.

These fallen monuments to old dreams were like a cracked mirror in which he saw his own indecision. He was too tired with the weariness of four years of grief, loneliness, and doubt to assess the damage.

What should he reply to the letter from Weizmann?

He rode a few yards toward the station, paused again, and dismounted. A handful of dead wheat lay in the path where the wind had carried it. He picked it up and rubbed it in his palms. The brittle stalks broke easily; the pebbles of seed were hard. He tilted his hands and watched them fall.

His thoughts went back to the ceremony at the grave. The stone had been unveiled—the one word, "Rachel," spoke for everything he was. He had also been unveiled, for there, after ten months from the time he first heard of it, he had felt for the first time the reality of her death.

What had breached him, his remoteness? What had he been before that moment and was no longer? He did not believe in conversion, the sudden inexplicable shift of temperament. Yet something had happened. Perhaps, unknown to himself, tiny lights, one by one, question by question, discontent by discontent, had been lit during the months in a dark corner of his mind until at last it had become bright enough to see what lay there.

At the cemetery he had broken down and wept, sharing the people's grief. Sharing the grief, he had felt a compulsion to reach out, to touch and embrace Dr. Bloch and Miriam, Mottel, even Gimmel Cohn. At that moment he had been swept by love for them. Was grief a kind of love? And did one have to love in order to surrender to oneself?

God in heaven, had he never loved before then? Did that explain his bachelorhood, his demand to be leader, his need to work alone and with only unquestioning disciples? If this were all true, then how terrible his arrogance, how terrible not to have suffered love.

He watched the gulls coming in from the sea to feast on the insect proprietors of his fields. He watched them circle and descend in a fan of hunger.

If he went to London, would it be the old ironic temptation to be used for high purposes, to sweep fate within his arms, or could he go as a disciple who had learned how to immerse himself in the great sea of Jews that had pounded so vainly and for so long against the unyielding shores of the world?

He knew sadly that no matter how he decided, his name was tainted. Already slanderous things were being said about him and his friends by angry, vindictive politicians. None of the sacrifices made by NILI, even Rachel's death, could allay the charges of men like Remenov and Lorchanovsky that it had endangered the Yishuv and caused the torture of many of their comrades. No recognition by Allenby of NILI's contribution could affect these stubborn critics. For as long as he lived, they would harass him with their hatred and suspicion, until, with charges and countercharges, prejudice and passion, nothing would be left of the truth. Even those Palestinians who, in years to come, might view his deed with sympathy would be forced to distort what he was and believed in either because they were defending him against distortions or because they thought it expedient to use him for their own political ambitions.

There was nothing he could do about the future. The only thing he could be sure of was that the taint would last a long, long time.

He wondered if Weizmann knew what was being said. If he did, obviously he didn't care. Perhaps Weizmann remembered from the book of Numbers the mystery of the ash of the burned red heifer. The priest who carried the ash purged the sins of those to whom he brought it but was himself made impure by the act.

Again Judah looked at his dead fields. Could they wait for him?

He yearned for Tali. He yearned not to be alone anymore, even in the sacred task of reviving his fields. He recognized in this yearning that his choice was made. He would leave Palestine for as long as he was needed by Weizmann and become a comrade-in-arms with the great multitude. There might not be any land at all to work without a victory at the green-cloth table of the nations. This gift of Balfour's would have to be won, over and over again. It would have to be fought for and earned the way Rachel had earned the right to die by her own hand.

The land was exceedingly patient. Men were not.

The sun had gone down to the horizon. Its last rays pierced the arches of the Crusader tower and stained red the broken world of glass in the far-off windows in the white walls of his station.

In the dusk he rode back slowly along the coast road, past the bivouacs of the Seventh Indian Regiment, which a fortnight before had cleared the Sharon of the enemy. The men saluted and he returned the salute gravely. He left the coast to climb homeward along the winding mountain road filled with rocks. Ahead of him was Har Nehemia and behind it the Carmel, still touched with a golden flare of the setting sun. As he passed the cemetery he paused to look at Rachel's grave, then mounted the last hillock to the broad main street. There were many lights in the houses, including his own.

Author's Note

This novel is based in part on a series of events that took place in Palestine and elsewhere during World War I. There were indeed groups called NILI and Hashomer, and although my major characters are fictional, they were inspired by people then living. Since under these circumstances the question of historical accuracy may arise, I feel obliged to say that I used history as Hume defined its use, ". . . to discover the constant and universal principles of human nature." I believe that I have been faithful to the morality of that past time and the spirit of the people who lived through it, even though I have invented scenes and incidents, changed names and places, and added and omitted whatever was required to make my novel true to itself.

There are always difficulties awaiting anyone who writes of other times and places, but in this case they were compounded. By its nature, no conspiracy keeps minutes of its meetings, and there are huge areas of NILI's activities that will remain unknowable. Further, NILI became the subject of violent political partisanship in Israel, only now beginning to subside. Not only has there been in Jewish life a deep-rooted moral objection to spying, but also there are still Israelis in positions of influence and power who have not forgiven NILI, as they see it, for endangering the lives of innocent people. As a result, all the reports of that time, both oral and written, are colored by more than normal bias, pro and con. Private affections and disaffections are almost as alive today as they were in 1918. As I mentioned above, one has to rely ultimately on his own insights and judgments—the truth, not of the historian, but of the creator of fiction.

Now as to the actual history itself: NILI was organized in the early part of the war by Aaron Aaronsohn, a world-renowned agronomist of Zichron Yaacov and Atlit, and Absalom Feinberg, of Hadera, who had already won a reputation as a poet. Their group of Zionist patriots, twenty-five men and women, became the espionage arm in Palestine of the British Army and later worked directly under General Edmund H. H. Allenby's staff. Over the three years of its labors, casualties were extremely high.

The first to go was Absalom Feinberg, twenty-eight, who was killed in 1917 by unknown bedouin while crossing the desert to reach the British. Later that year Sarah Aaronsohn, Aaron's sister, was caught by the Turkish authorities. After many days of extreme torture, she committed suicide and died at twenty-seven, two months to the day before Allenby's forces captured Jerusalem. Soon after her death Yosef Lishansky was caught. He had been with Absalom Feinberg in the desert and later returned to Palestine to share the leadership of NILI with Sarah. He and another comrade, Naaman Belkind, were executed by hanging in the prison courtyard of Damascus. Later others of the group were arrested and tortured and were saved by the arrival of British troops. One man, Reuven Schwartz, followed Sarah's example and killed himself. And, in addition, many shomrim, members of the families of the NILI group and their neighbors, innocent of any conspiracy, were severely bastinadoed, imprisoned, and threatened with hanging.

When peace came Aaron Aaronsohn joined Chaim Weizmann to work at the Versailles Peace Conference. In May, 1919, a British plane taking Aaronsohn from London to Paris in a heavy fog fell into the channel and was never seen again. He had been the oldest member of the group and died at forty-three.

Among the few survivors of NILI living in Israel are Liova Shneerson, who was awarded an O.B.E. for his service to Allenby, and his brother, Mendel, both of Hadera. They gave me valuable diaries and documents, advice, and guidance. Mendel Shneirson led me through the wadi at Atlit and explored the ruin of the experimental station, describing how it used to be. His warm cooperation was highly important. Two other survivors, Rafael Abulafia, of Jerusalem, and Eytan Belkind, brother of Naaman, who was hanged in Damascus, talked with me at great length, contributing many insights into the past.

Miss Rivka Aaronsohn, the last surviving member of the Aaronsohn family was out of Palestine during most of the war years. Her intense devotion to NILI's history impelled her to establish and maintain an Aaronsohn Museum in Zichron Yaacov, which her family helped found in 1882. She has kept the original homestead unchanged and lives in it. There one can see the mementos of Sarah's last days. As a result of her efforts and those of her curator, Yoram Efrati, an ever-growing number of Israelis and foreigners make pilgrimages to the museum, the home, and Sarah's grave, in the cemetery nearby. Now even old enemies of NILI acknowledge Sarah as a true heroine of the early days.

Absalom Feinberg's sister, Mrs. Zilla Shoham, of Haifa, although not a member of NILI, was both generous and encouraging. Through her efforts I was able to read Absalom's early letters and poetry, excerpts from which she has permitted me to use.

I feel it necessary to make absolutely clear that Miss Aaronsohn and Mrs. Shoham and all the other survivors and relatives of the NILI group with whom I talked are not to be held responsible for my fictional version of events and people, for at no time did I consult with them about how I intended to tell my story or portray its characters.

Zvi Nissanov, the late Israel and Manya Shochat, Nahum Hurwitz, and "Eucalyptus" Shneirson, old settlers and shomrim, shared with me their passionate memories of the past. Edna Zamir of the Jabotinsky Museum in Tel Aviv put at my disposal photographs and documents that were enormously valuable. I cannot adequately describe my gratitude for all their assistance.

I have referred by name to historical personages such as Chaim Weizmann, General Allenby, T. E. Lawrence, Sir Basil Thomson, and others, using as source material books written by them and about them to compose their portraits and the incidents that they shared with my invented characters. However, the character of Colonel John West is not to be confused with Colonel Richard Meinertzhagen, an intelligence officer on General Allenby's staff who worked with the Aaronsohn group. Meinertzhagen indeed created the decoy that fooled the defenders of Beersheba and later became a staunch friend of the Zionist movement, but he departed from Palestine long before the capture of Jerusalem. Allenby's words quoted by Colonel West at Rachel's funeral are from the record. Colonel Meinertzhagen himself noted in his book *Middle East Diary*, "My best agent in the 1914-1918 war was a Jew—Aaron Aaronsohn—a man who feared nothing and had an immense intellect."

A personal word: This was a painful book to write, for in addition to all the normal problems, I could not escape the knowledge of how history developed after 1918. Great Britain, on whose goodwill NILI placed the profoundest hope and faith, did not live up to the trust given to it by the League of Nations. The Balfour Declaration almost from the outset was undermined by the proconsuls of the empire. For thirty years the nation that had created the possibilities of a Jewish state worked to thwart it. There is no end to the irony of *realpolitik*.

An even more woeful knowledge hung over me. Palestine, which could have been a sanctuary for the millions of Jews who were to be murdered by the Germans during World War II, a refuge bravely built and sustained by the descendants of Hashomer, NILI, and the other agencies of the Yishuv, was virtually sealed off by the indifference and the same shortsighted politics of all the nations. But in this matter, no one is without guilt. Knowledge of the future has to be put aside in a work of fiction despite the fact that the past is always crying out warnings to us. The real-life question one always asks too late is why we pay no attention.

Of the hundreds of books and documents I used as source material, special mention must be made of a few. The definitive history of the conspiracy is *Nili*, by Eliezer Livneh, Yosef Nedava, and Yoram Efrati. It was published in Israel under the general supervision of Miss Rivka Aaronsohn. An earlier history, published in England, *The Nili Spies*, by Anita Engle, pioneered a revival of interest in the story of the martyrs. I am pleased to acknowledge that it was Miss Engle's study that led me to further explorations of the NILI episode. Other works of great value are *The Story of Nili*, in five volumes, by Yaari-Poleskin; *The Book of the Haganah*; *The Goodly Heritage*, by Avraham Yaari; *The Balfour Declaration*, by Leonard Stein; *The Return to the Soil*, by Alex Bein; *The Realities of American-Palestine Relations*, by Frank E. Manuel; *Army Diary* and *Middle East Diary*, by Richard Meinertzhagen; and *Reliquiae Aaronsohnianae*, Vol. II, edited by Alexander and Rivka Aaronsohn.

My Experience at Scotland Yard, by Sir Basil Thomson; *Trial and Error*, by Chaim Weizmann; *New Judea*, by B. L. Gordon; *Coming Home*, by Rahel Ben-Zvi; *Orientations*, by Sir Ronald Storrs; *Allenby*, by Viscount Wavell; *Allenby of Armageddon*, by Raymond Savage; *Essays on Wheat*, by A. H. Reginald Buller; *The Romance of the Last Crusade*, by Major Vivian Gilbert; *With the Judeans in the Palestine*

Campaign, by Lt. Col. J. H. Patterson; *Seven Pillars of Wisdom*, by T. E. Lawrence; and numerous histories of the Ottoman Empire.

George Adam Smith's *Historical Geography of the Holy Land*, which General Allenby used as a guide for himself, and *A Brief Record of the Advance of the Egyptian Expeditionary Forces, Compiled from Official Sources, with an Introductory Letter by General Sir Edmund H. H. Allenby* made the military situation clear. An equally rare book, *With the Turks in Palestine*, was written by Alexander Aaronsohn, a brother of Aaron's and Sarah's. He helped NILI to win support abroad and lived to enlist his services on behalf of England in World War II.